Harmonies of Hope

BOOK 1
HEALING HEARTS SERIES

ALEXANDRA PALCHAK

Acknowledgements

Writing a book while balancing a career in IT, maintaining an active lifestyle, and raising three wonderful children would have been impossible without an incredible support system. This book exists because countless people believed in the story and the storyteller.

To Joe, my anchor in life's storms and my partner in every adventure, thank you for showing me that genuine love isn't about perfection—it's about choosing each other every day, through every season. Thank you for loving me exactly as I am and helping me find strength I never knew I had.

To my beautiful children, Chantal, Isabella, and Joseph Jr.— you are living proof that the most precious gifts often come wrapped in unexpected packages. Your love has taught me more about resilience and joy than any experience ever could. You make every day an adventure worth writing about.

To my Taekwondo family—thank you for showing me that strength comes in many forms, and that discipline in body helps discipline in mind. Those tough training sessions helped clear my head for writing.

Finally, to every reader who picks up this book—thank you for letting me share this journey with you. Stories have power when they're shared, and you're now part of this one.

Like Leah in this story, I learned that life's most beautiful chapters are often the ones we never planned. Love has been my constant guide through the daily grind and office stressors, martial arts, writing nights, and every challenge and triumph.

This story, born from personal experience and shaped by imagination, is dedicated to everyone who has found strength in their scars, beauty in their imperfections, and love in unexpected places.

Most of all, it's dedicated to my family—my reason for everything.

With endless love and gratitude,

Alexandra Arias-Palchak

Contents

CHAPTER 1

The Invisible Wound

Lightning crackled outside as Leah Miller sat cross-legged on the living room floor, surrounded by the mess of her AP Biology project. Her fingers trembled against the ruler, creating tiny earthquakes that blurred the measurement marks into a watery haze. Each thunderclap mirrored the chaos mixed with stability in her life—the storm outside was nothing compared to the turmoil brewing within her home's walls.

A sharp voice sliced through the air from the kitchen, making Leah's shoulder blades snap together. The ruler slipped, leaving a nasty black line across her carefully drawn diagram. Her heart stuttered as her father's muffled accusations about credit card bills filtered through, followed by the sound of his fist meeting the counter. The impact seemed to travel through the floorboards and into her bones.

Her mother's response came desperate and raw—a tone that made Leah's stomach twist into familiar knots. She pressed down harder with the eraser, desperate to fix her mistake. The paper tore beneath her trembling hands, and helplessness welled up inside her like

1

rising floodwater. The project was due tomorrow, and anything less than perfect would trigger another lecture about reaching her potential. That expectation for excellence felt like a double-edged sword, simultaneously pushing her achievements and leaving her hollow—a puppet tugged by strings she couldn't control.

"Hey, squirt." Brian's voice carried practiced lightness as he appeared in the doorway, his lanky frame casting long shadows across her careful work. His eyes darted toward the kitchen, where their father's voice rose in crescendo. "Dad's really going for it tonight. Think he missed his calling as an opera singer?" The forced humor in his tone betrayed the familiar weight of being the oldest, the one expected to maintain normalcy amid chaos.

Leah managed a weak smile, grateful for his attempt to lighten the mood. "Maybe he should audition for 'Phantom of the Opera."

"More like 'Les Misérables'," Brian quipped, collapsing onto the couch and pulling out his phone. Despite his casual vibe, she noticed how his jaw clenched with each new eruption from the kitchen.

Grace arrived then, her purple highlights catching the storm-light like bruised lightning—a silent rebellion their father mostly ignored. Earbuds dangled from her neck, their mother's music a bitter backdrop to the chaos.

"Are we practicing for an Oscar or what?" Grace flung herself into an armchair, her sarcasm dripping. "Because I gotta say, this performance is getting old. Same script, different day."

"Grace." Leah's voice carried a weariness beyond her fifteen years as she tried, once again, to keep her family from falling apart. Her fingers traced nervous patterns on the ruler's edge, seeking order in measurement while chaos reigned below. The numbers blurred and doubled before her eyes as another crash echoed from the kitchen.

Grace's response came sharp and immediate, her purple highlights catching the light as she gestured toward the kitchen. "What? You can't tell me you're not tired of this. It's like living in a soap opera, but we can't even change the channel." Beneath her theatrical delivery, raw exhaustion bled through—the kind that comes from watching something precious slowly unravel.

Leah turned back to her project, attempting to focus. The cellular diagram was the only place she could exert some control, yet the mitochondria looked misshapen, almost mocking her efforts, just like the arguments warping her idea of normalcy. Her parents' voices rose and fell like storm waves, each accusation carrying fragments of their crumbling marriage.

Brian's phone buzzed, a welcome distraction. "That's Marcus. I think I'll head over for a bit."

Leah couldn't blame him. The atmosphere pressed against her chest like a physical weight, making each breath a conscious effort. Her hand shook as she tried to steady the ruler again, the lines refusing to stay straight. "Coward," Grace muttered under her breath, but Leah caught the envy flickering in her eyes. Brian was eighteen—able to leave whenever. Grace, at sixteen, felt stuck, while Leah, just fifteen, remained anchored deeper in the chaos.

"Some of us know when to make a strategic retreat," Brian threw back, ruffling Leah's hair as he passed. "Text me if you need anything, squirt." His words hung in the air, both a promise and a farewell, leaving Leah longing for her brother's protective presence.

As the front door clicked shut, Leah stared at the empty space where he had stood, her chest constricting. She appreciated his efforts to lighten the mood, but his exits only amplified the hollow echo of their family's discord. Her vision blurred again as she tried to focus on the diagram, the cellular structures swimming before her eyes like abstract art.

"And there goes Switzerland," Grace commented, turning up her music until the bass thrummed through the floor. "Neutral territory just evacuated."

A sudden silence fell over the kitchen, more terrifying than the shouting. Even Grace's music seemed to fade, her earbuds slipping to her lap. Leah's pencil froze mid-stroke, her pulse hammering in her ears as she waited for the next explosion. Her mother's words, when they came, carried a dangerous quiet that made Leah's skin prickle with goosebumps.

The silence that followed felt like glass about to shatter. Leah's hands trembled so badly she had to set down her pencil, her carefully ordered world threatening to spiral into chaos with each passing second. She gathered her art supplies with unsteady fingers, the simple act of organizing them providing a desperate illusion of control.

Taking the stairs two at a time, Leah had fled past Grace's door where the bass had faded into heavy quiet. Her sanctuary had beckoned—the one space where chaos bent to her will. Each step had carried her further from the storm below, yet her pulse had refused to slow, hammering against her ribs like a trapped bird.

Her room had greeted her with familiar order: books arranged by height and subject, color-coded notes pinned with geometric precision, swim meet trophies lined up like silver soldiers standing guard. Yet even here, that slithering feeling of inadequacy had found her coiling around her achievements like ivy around ruins.

Settling at her desk, Leah had spread out her art supplies with trembling precision. The storm outside had intensified its assault, rain tapping against her window in an arrhythmic pattern that had matched her scattered thoughts. From below, muffled voices had carried fragments of accusation, each word sending fresh tremors through her hands as she had tried to focus on her project.

Her pencil had hovered over the paper, creating phantom lines in the air as she had struggled to steady her grip. The urge to text Kate had risen like a tide—Kate would have understood, wouldn't she? But the words had stuck in her throat: "Hey, my parents are fighting again; it feels like the world's ending." How many times could she send that same message before it lost all meaning?

A soft knock had fractured her spiraling thoughts, making her shoulders jump. "Come in," she had managed, hastily wiping her eyes with the heel of her hand, though she couldn't remember when she'd started crying.

Brian's familiar silhouette had filled the doorframe, and the crinkle of a Pop-Tart package had cut through the tension as it landed on her desk. "Hey, thought you could use these." The simple gesture had unleashed a small smile, genuine despite the weight in her chest.

"I thought you were at Marcus's," she had said, surprise momentarily displacing her anxiety.

"Changed my mind." He had shrugged, leaning against the doorframe with practiced casualness that hadn't quite masked his concern. "Didn't feel right leaving you alone with the dueling dragons." The nickname had pulled a reluctant laugh from her throat, even as worry's shadow had lingered in her eyes.

"But Grace is here," Leah pointed out, her fingers absently straightening her ruler until it aligned perfectly with the desk's edge.

"Grace has always been in her own world," Brian said, glancing toward the closed door where angry punk rock filtered through like distant thunder. "You're the one feeling all this. You know that, right?"

Leah's hands busied themselves with organizing her colored pencils by shade, creating a rainbow that blurred as fresh tears threatened. "I'm fine," she lied, the words bitter as medicine on her tongue.

"Sure you are," Brian replied, his eyes falling to her project. "Yeah, we're all just peachy. We're the Miller kids—we're always fine." Irony threaded through his voice like a dark ribbon, highlighting truths neither of them wanted to face.

As they had worked on her biology project, the storm outside had provided a fitting soundtrack to their quiet companionship. Brian had sprinkled bits of cellular biology trivia into the silence, each fact a small lifeline pulling her back from the edge of panic. His steady presence had anchored her as she had carefully reconstructed her diagram, though her hands had still trembled with each crash from below.

"Dad's pushing for MIT," Brian mentioned, carefully outlining a cell membrane while Leah's heart clenched at the thought of him leaving. "But I'm thinking maybe UCLA. Get as far away as—" He caught himself, meeting her gaze with an expression that blended determination and guilt. "I mean, they've got a solid program."

"It's okay," Leah whispered, understanding flooding her voice even as her chest tightened. "I get it. I'd want to escape too." That truth hung between them like smoke, a shared acknowledgment everyone sought refuge from their family's dysfunction, yet no clear path existed.

"Listen, squirt. Whatever happens with them... it's not your job to fix it." Brian's words struck directly at the weight she carried, yet the storm inside her continued to rage.

A violent thunderclap made them both jump, the lights flickering ominously. The sound of shattering glass sliced through their fragile peace, followed by a sharp intake of breath that might have been a sob. Leah's pencil snapped in her grip, graphite dust spilling across her careful work like ash.

The silence that followed pressed against her eardrums, heavy with possibilities she didn't want to consider. Her heart drummed an erratic rhythm as she turned to the window, watching rain stream down the glass like tears. Each droplet reflected her family's turmoil—endless, relentless, inevitable.

Overwhelmed by reality's weight, Leah's gaze drifted to the beach photo taped to her wall—a snapshot of warmth and light, smiles untouched by the shadows now darkening their home. Her fingertips traced the glass, seeking comfort in that frozen moment of joy, but finding only cold distance instead.

"Leah," Brian's voice cut through her reverie, steady as a heartbeat, "you have to remember—you're stronger than you think. All of this," he gestured toward the door where their parents' battle raged, "it's not your fault. You can't carry that weight."

Her throat was constricted around words she couldn't voice, hands clenching into fists beneath her desk. "But what if I could fix it?" she finally managed, each word falling like broken glass. "What if I could just make them understand each other? What if I could stop the fighting?"

Brian's expression softened with a pain that mirrored her own. "You can't fix them, Leah. No one can. They've got to sort it out themselves." His hand found her shoulder, steady and warm. "Just remember, it's not on you to make them happy. You shouldn't have to shoulder that."

The words resonated like an impossible truth. Leah's gaze fell to her nearly finished diagram, each organelle crucial for the cell's complete function. If only her family operated with such precision—each member playing their role in perfect harmony. Instead, they existed in constant friction, wearing each other down like waves against a shoreline.

Another crash from below jolted through her body like electricity. The silence that followed felt heavier than any shout, pregnant with possibilities she didn't dare contemplate. Her eyes met Brian's, reading the same fear in his expression—the terrifying thought that this time might be different, that some fundamental line had been crossed.

"Maybe we should check on them?" The suggestion escaped her lips before she could stop it, hope and dread tangling in her chest like fighting snakes.

Brian's reluctance showed in the tight line of his jaw, but he nodded. Together they descended the stairs, each step feeling like a countdown to something inevitable. Leah's pulse roared in her ears as they approached the kitchen, the partially open door spilling harsh light across the hallway floor.

The scene that had greeted them had stopped Leah's breath in her throat. Her parents had stood on opposite sides of the kitchen, the space between them charged with electricity that had nothing to do with the storm outside. Shards of what might have been a wine glass had glittered on the floor like fallen stars, creating a barrier neither parent had seemed willing to cross.

Leah's world had narrowed to individual sensations: the catch in her mother's breathing, the white-knuckled grip of her father's hands on the counter, the steady drip of the leaking faucet counting seconds like a metronome. Each detail had etched itself into her memory with cruel precision as she had stood frozen, witnessing the aftermath of another battle in their ongoing war.

The weight of unspoken words had pressed against her chest until breathing had become a conscious effort. Her carefully maintained facade had cracked, reality seeping through like water through limestone. In that moment, standing in the storm both outside and within, Leah had felt an overwhelming sense of helplessness wash over her. She had tried to be the glue holding their family together, but some breaks had run too deep for any adhesive to fix.

"What do I even say?" The words had escaped as barely a whisper, her gaze seeking Brian's for guidance he couldn't provide.

Lightning had illuminated the kitchen in harsh bursts, casting strange shadows across her parents' faces. In those fragmentary glimpses, Leah had seen past their anger to the raw pain beneath—a grief so profound it had threatened to swallow them all. The storm had raged on, each thunderous word a reminder of the fractures running deep within their family, while Leah had stood caught between wanting to heal and knowing some wounds might have been beyond repair.

Brian's presence beside her had offered what little comfort it could, his shoulder barely brushing hers—a silent reminder that she hadn't stood entirely alone in this maelstrom of emotion. The kitchen light had flickered, matching the tremor in her hands as she had watched her parents orbit each other like binary stars locked in mutual destruction.

Fragments of their earlier life had scattered across the kitchen like the broken glass on the floor—the beach photos on the fridge, the height marks penciled on the doorframe, the mismatched coffee mugs they'd collected on family road trips. Each item had held a story of better days, now overshadowed by the storm of present discord.

In the harsh kitchen light, Leah had seen every line of strain on her mother's face, every tension in her father's jaw. Their love had transformed into something unrecognizable, like a familiar painting viewed through warped glass. The silence between thunderclaps had grown heavier with each passing second, weighted with years of accumulated grievances and unspoken regrets.

The dripping faucet had continued its steady count of moments, each drop echoing like a verdict in the charged atmosphere. Leah's fingers had found the hem of her sleeve, twisting the fabric in an unconscious echo of her churning thoughts. The sound of her own heartbeat had seemed to fill the room, keeping time with the storm's fury outside.

As another flash of lightning had painted stark shadows across the scene, Leah had felt something shift inside her—a recognition that some battles couldn't be won through sheer force of will or desperate desire. Her role as family mediator, worn like a second skin for so long, had felt as fragile as the shattered glass beneath their feet.

CHAPTER 2

Brightest in the Shadows

The fluorescent lights in Riverside High's AP Bio room buzzed overhead as Leah had ran through her presentation one last time. The past few months since turning sixteen had brought subtle shifts she couldn't quite name - like watching ripples spread across still water, each circle wider than the last. Her father's expectations pressed heavier against her shoulders, her mother's silences stretched longer between words, and the familiar weight of academic excellence felt more suffocating with each passing day. At 7:15 AM, these empty halls offered a brief sanctuary from the storm brewing at home, though even here she couldn't escape the echoes of change.

"Hey, can you tell your dad the mortgage is due Friday?"

Her mom's message hit her like a ton of bricks, dragging her deeper into family drama. Leah squeezed her eyes shut, trying to will the tension away, telling herself to stay focused. She silenced her phone, but the words floated between her parents like a current pushing them apart. The act of pretending everything was fine felt like holding a breath underwater; the longer she held on, the more desperate the need for air.

"Okay, so the mitochondria's primary job is cellular respiration," she said, rehearsing with a voice steady enough to convince her audience and herself. As she went on, the weight of her need to be perfect felt heavier, like a boulder on her shoulders. "Through this process—"

"Are you talking to yourself again, Miller?"

Kate's voice pulled her from her focus. Leah turned to see her best friend at the door, two coffee cups in hand, that bright yellow sweater glaring against the bare classroom walls. Kate's sweater hung looser than usual on her frame, but her smile remained brilliant as ever, though it didn't quite reach her eyes. This sparked a little warmth in Leah, almost grateful for the distraction, a reminder that normal life still existed.

"You're up early," Leah said, taking the cup. The warmth in her hands pushed back against the cold creeping through her heart.

"Somebody's gotta make sure you don't overdo it," Kate hopped up on a lab table, her energy infectious, her legs swung with a slight hesitation, as if conserving energy. Leah couldn't help but envy how carefree Kate seemed, like the world's weight didn't even phase her. "How many times have you run through it?"

"Not enough," Leah replied, adjusting her already perfect poster for the umpteenth time, a nervous habit. The cellular membrane part still felt shaky; her perfectionism turned minor flaws into major screw-ups in her mind.

"Girl." Kate's tone turned serious, and Leah could feel the concern radiating off her friend. "You could do this in your sleep. I swear I heard you mumbling about phospholipid bilayers yesterday."

Leah thought she was alone in her late-night study grind; Her drive to excel had often pushed her away from her peers. But now Kate seemed to see through her mask, picking up on the unease behind her brave attitude. Just before Leah could reply, her phone lit up again, another message pulling her down.

"Still playing messenger for them?"

"It's whatever," Leah mumbled, shoving her phone away, not wanting to dive into how her parents dropped their adult responsibilities on her. "Mom just needs to remind Dad about some bills."

"Right." Kate's tone dripped with doubt, ruffling Leah's feathers. "Like they can't call or email each other? Or act like grown-ups?"

"Kate—" Leah started, but her friend put her hands up in surrender.

"I get it, I get it," Kate continued. "Not my place. But you look like you haven't slept in ages and you're about to present something you could teach to Harvard professors. Give yourself a break?"

Leah wanted to believe that was possible. She wished she could shake off the relentless urge for perfection, but doubts festered in her mind like this irritating itch. As they gathered their stuff, a wave of nostalgia washed over Leah. She imagined the art room—the colors and shapes so freeing compared to the rigid expectations of academia imposed by her family. It felt like her creativity was tucked away in a dark corner, a distant memory of the daily pressures.

Just then, Mrs. Hayes walked in, overstuffed with graded papers. Her gaze lingered on Leah's carefully crafted poster.

"Girls! You're here bright and early," she said, setting her papers down and studying Leah with that signature teacher's focus—like she had done with a thousand slides before.

"Not surprised, honestly," Mrs. Hayes continued, eyes on Leah. "You ready for the big day?"

"Yep, Mrs. Hayes." Leah's reply was automatic, and she sat up straight, grip tightening around her coffee cup. "I just wanted to do a final review of—"

"She's more than ready," Kate interrupted, ignoring Leah's glare. Leah's cheeks flushed with embarrassment as Kate continued, "She's been ready since last week."

Mrs. Hayes set down her papers, watching both girls with a knowing look.

"You know, Leah, you've already got the highest grade in the class. This presentation isn't going to change that."

"I know," Leah shot back quickly, her voice tinged with anxiety. Those words, which should have been comforting, only amplified her fear of not measuring up. "But I need to make sure it's perfect."

A flicker of something crossed Mrs. Hayes's face—was it concern, or maybe understanding? "Perfection's a tough load to carry," she said, her voice soothed yet sincere. Leah swore she could see Mrs. Hayes reflecting on her own struggles. "I'm looking forward to your presentation. You should head to homeroom—the bell's about to ring."

As they gathered their things, Leah felt that familiar weight in her chest again. Just then, her phone buzzed—another text from Dad.

"Running late. Tell your mom not to wait up."

That knot tightened in Leah's stomach, and she straightened her posture. "What now?" Kate asked, reading Leah's expression.

"Nothing," Leah said, her words tight and clipped. "Let's go—we'll be late."

The hallways buzzed with kids, their voices creating a loud backdrop as Leah moved through the crowd with ease—it was like muscle memory after years of high school. Her heart raced with a mix of nerves and determination as she clutched her presentation poster protectively. Just before she reached her homeroom, Coach Stevens called out to her, clipboard in hand, a jumble of numbers occupying the sheets.

"Miller! Just the swimmer I wanted to see!" he said, drawing the attention of several passing students. His excitement made Leah's heart swell with pride. "Your freestyle's looking strong, but we need to work on your turns if you want to qualify for the state."

"Of course, Coach," Leah said, mentally analyzing her schedule for later. "I can stay late today—"

"You can't," Kate interjected, stepping forward with narrowed eyes. "You have art club today, remember?"

Coach Stevens raised an eyebrow, skepticism clear. "Art club? Miller, state qualifiers are just three weeks away. We need your focus."

"I can handle both," Leah insisted, though a twist of anxiety stirred in her stomach, feeling like two opposing forces. The fear of disappointing one side pulled against the other.

"That's my girl," Coach Stevens said, patting her shoulder. "See you at practice—three-thirty sharp!"

As he walked away, Kate turned to Leah, seeing right through her facade. "You don't have art club today."

"I know," Leah replied, avoiding eye contact as shame flushed through her. "But I need the pool time."

"What you need is sleep," Kate said, stepping into her path. "And maybe a week on a desert island, away from everyone's expectations." There was sincerity in her voice, a friendship thick with the understanding Leah both cherished and resented. Why couldn't Kate see the weight that followed her?

The warning bell rang out, snapping Leah from the moment like a rubber band. She ducked into homeroom, relief washing over her as she escaped Kate's probing look. While Mrs. Peterson droned on about morning announcements, Leah's thoughts drifted back to AP Biology and ran through the presentation points in her head. The idea of having to juggle swimming and art while living under the pressure of perfection had twisted her stomach into knots, and she felt dizzy as the day unfolded like a choreographed chaos of responsibilities and expectations.

In AP Biology, Leah delivered her presentation flawlessly. Her voice didn't waver as she navigated the complex cellular processes. Mrs. Hayes beamed with approval, and the looks from her classmates radiated admiration. But when it had been over, Leah had felt only a sense of hollow relief brewing in her chest—a fleeting victory swallowed by a tide of ongoing struggles.

"Exceptional work, as always," Mrs. Hayes said when Leah returned to her seat, seamlessly transitioning between emotional landscapes. "But I've gotta know—when you said cells under stress can act differently, care to dive deeper?"

At that moment, something shifted in the atmosphere. Leah paused, picking up on the deeper implications of the question. Perhaps Mrs. Hayes sensed something behind her words, some unvoiced invitation for a connection. "So, under intense circumstances," Leah started, her voice gaining strength, "cells might prioritize survival over normal function. They might seem fine while teetering on the edge."

The room held its breath as her peers processed her words. She could almost feel Mrs. Hayes's perceptive gaze weighing on her, probing deeper into her thoughts. Was this still about biology, or was it a subtle nudge for Leah to reflect on her own pressures and expectations? The thought felt unsettling.

"Interesting observation," Mrs. Hayes said, a knowing glint in her eyes as if she had tapped into a hidden truth about Leah.

"Thank you, Leah."

As the bell rang, Leah gathered her materials, still feeling the weight of Mrs. Hayes's perceptive gaze. The hallway bustled with activity as she made her way to AP History, her mind racing between thoughts of cellular structures and her next presentation.

"Hey, Miller!" A familiar voice cut through the chaos. "Nice work in Bio."

Leah turned, and there was Ryan Matthews, his dark hair tousled as if he'd been running his hands through it during class, a faint scent of his cologne lingering in the air. Her heart did a little flip—it always did when he was around.

"You weren't even in Bio," she replied, trying to keep her voice steady despite the flutter in her stomach.

"No, but word travels fast when Leah Miller crushes another presentation." The leftward tilt of his smile, that signature Ryan smile, banished her anxieties, a comforting lightness replacing her tension. "Something about cells under stress?"

"You actually paid attention to hallway gossip about cellular biology?" Leah raised an eyebrow, adjusting her books against her chest.

"Only the interesting bits." Ryan shrugged, his shoulder brushing against hers as they navigated through the crowd. "Besides, we're partners for that history project, remember? I need to know what I'm up against."

Right. The History project. Mr. Peterson had paired them up yesterday for their presentation on the Industrial Revolution. Leah had spent half the class trying not to look too excited about working with Ryan while simultaneously panicking about maintaining her perfect grade.

"Speaking of which," Ryan continued, pulling out his notebook as they entered the History classroom, "want to meet up at the library after school? We could start planning the outline."

"Oh, I—" Leah started, but then remembered swim practice. "I can't today. Swimming."

"Right, state qualifiers coming up." Ryan nodded, looking genuinely disappointed. "Tomorrow maybe? I heard you're pretty amazing in the pool, too."

Heat crept up Leah's neck. "Who told you that?"

"Let's just say I might have watched a few meets," he admitted, running a hand through his hair—a nervous gesture that made him even more endearing. "You're kind of incredible, you know that?"

Before Leah could respond, Mr. Peterson called the class to order. She slipped into her seat, two rows behind Ryan, her heart racing. As he took his own seat, Ryan glanced back at her, that crooked smile making another appearance.

Throughout the lesson, Leah stole glances at the back of Ryan's head, watching as he took notes, the way he tapped his pen when he was deep in thought. With a quick turn of his head, he caught her staring, a playful wink sealing the moment. She quickly looked down at her notebook, pretending to be fascinated by her doodles of historical dates.

When class ended, Ryan lingered by her desk as she packed up. "So, tomorrow? Library?"

"Yeah," Leah heard herself said, surprising even herself. "Tomorrow works."

"Cool. It's a date." He paused, his eyes widening a little. "I mean, not a date-date, unless... I mean, it's just studying, but—"

"Tomorrow," Leah cut in, saving him from his adorable fumbling. "After school."

Ryan's relief was clear. "Right. Tomorrow." He backed away, nearly bumping into another desk. "You're going to rock those qualifiers today, Miller!"

As she watched him leave, Leah felt warmth spread through her chest—a distinct pressure different from what she usually carried. For a moment, she forgot about her dad's expectations, her mom's messages, and the weight of perfection.

But reality crashed back as her phone buzzed with another text from her dad. Looking at the time, she realized she needed to head to the pool. The brief respite Ryan had provided had faded as she thought about her father watching the practice, analyzing her every move.

At three-thirty, the swimming pool loomed ahead, its waters a welcoming comfort Leah needed more than ever. She slipped on her goggles, preparing for warm-up laps, and spotted her dad in the top row of the bleachers, laptop open, peeking at his work while monitoring practice. A mix of relief and anxiety washed over Leah.

"Your dad's here," Jessica whispered, one of the varsity swimmers nodding toward the bleachers. "That's new."

"Yeah," Leah replied, her throat tightening. "He must've finished early," she mumbled, dreading the thought. Would he be critiquing every single move she made, as usual?

As Coach Stevens blew his whistle, Leah dove into the water, grateful for the escape. At sixteen, she'd discovered new layers to this refuge—the pool's embrace now felt less like hiding and more like transformation. Each stroke carved through the water with practiced precision, her body moving through familiar patterns while her mind grappled with the unfamiliar territory of growing up amid uncertainty. No messy emotions here, no complicated family dynamics—just the clean mathematics of speed and distance she'd mastered through countless hours.

"Miller!" Coach Stevens called out after her third lap, his voice booming above the water. "Watch those turns—you're losing precious seconds!"

Leah pushed herself harder, ignoring the burn in her muscles and the fatigue creeping up on her. Her dad's presence felt heavy, like a weight strapped to her chest, lingering like a terrible memory. She knew he'd be timing her laps, calculating each second, scrutinizing numbers like it was some scientific experiment.

After an hour of drills, Coach Stevens gathered the team. "Great job today, everyone. Miller, hang back for a second."

Leah's teammates filed past, some offering sympathetic looks. She swam on, her heart heavy with mixed feelings. As she approached her coach, she saw her dad had closed his laptop and was heading down the bleachers.

"Your times are improving," Coach Stevens began, flipping through his notes. "But you're still about two seconds off where you need to be for state qualifiers."

"I'll work harder," Leah promised instinctively, the words an automatic response molded by years of pressure.

"I was going to suggest—"

"Her turns are the problem!" her dad interrupted, moving closer and instantly commanding attention. "She's taking too long on the wall. And her second lap butterfly? Weak."

For a moment, both Leah and Coach Stevens blinked, surprise etched across their faces. Leah felt her heart race, caught between anger and resignation. She could already feel the weight of doubt creeping in alongside her father's criticism.

"Mr. Miller," Coach Stevens said, eyebrows raised, "I didn't realize you knew competitive swimming so well."

"I've been reviewing Olympic trial videos," John shot back, pulling up a clip on his phone and thrusting it toward Leah. "Look at this technique, Leah. See how the swimmer keeps momentum through the turn? That's the fix."

Leah stared at the screen, droplets racing down her hair and splashing onto the pool deck. Each critique felt like an extra weight piled onto her already heavy load, a reminder of how hard she would need to fight for her dad's approval.

"Well," Coach Stevens stepped in, trying to ease the tension, "those are all great points to think about. But Leah's one of our strongest swimmers, Mr. Miller. She has real talent."

"Talent isn't enough," John countered sharply, still engrossed in the video. Looking at Leah, he added, "It needs refining, perfection. Right, Leah?"

"Sure, Dad," Leah replied flatly, the words tasting bitter, a sting that reminded her of the weight of expectations that weren't hers to carry.

"I've got a late meeting," John said, breaking eye contact. "And don't forget to tell your mom about the mortgage payment."

As he walked away, Leah fought the urge to scream. A retort caught in her throat. Why did everything feel suffocating? Why was perfection always expected?

"Are you okay, Miller?" Coach Stevens asked, concern etched across his face as he stepped closer, breaking Leah's dazed trance.

"Yeah, I'm fine," Leah replied quickly, but the word felt flimsy, splintered under the weight of emotion swirling in her head. "Can I... do a few more laps?"

The coach hesitated before nodding. "Twenty minutes max. Don't wear yourself out."

Alone in the water again, Leah pushed herself harder than before, each stroke a desperate attempt to outrun her father's expectations and her need for validation. The water was a temporary escape, muffling her chaotic thoughts, if only for a moment. Each lap—a test of endurance, both mentally and emotionally.

When she emerged from the pool, her body trembling with exhaustion, she found the locker room empty. Her teammates had scattered, leaving only echoes of laughter behind—a haunting reminder of the normalcy Leah felt so far removed from.

As she reached for her towel, the door creaked open, and Kate stepped in. "Hey, I figured you'd still be here." She leaned against a locker, arms crossed, her expression a blend of determination and concern. "Saw your dad leaving."

"Yeah, he came to watch practice," Leah said, toweling her hair dry, trying to downplay it. "That's a good thing, right?"

"Is it?" Kate pressed, her voice gentle but full of empathy. "Because you kinda look like you just swam the English Channel." Leah bit her lip tightly, holding back the swirl of emotions threatened to spill over.

"I'm fine," Leah insisted, hoped that repetition would convince her, too.

"For someone as smart as you, you sure use that word a lot without meaning it," Kate said, concern laced in her tone.

Leah's hands stilled as she surveyed her friend. "What do you want me to say, Kate? That I'm not fine? That everything's falling apart, and I have no idea how to pull it together anymore?"

"Yes!" Kate stepped forward, fierce sincerity shining through. "That's what I want you to admit! Because it's true! You're my best friend, and I hate watching you kill yourself trying to be perfect for everyone else!"

The words hit Leah like cannon fire, stirring something deep inside her. She felt her chest tighten, struggling to articulate the complex expectations weighing her down. It felt foreign, like trying to speak a language she had only whispered in silence.

"I found your paintings," Kate said, lowering her gaze for a moment before locking eyes with Leah again. "In the art room. I was looking for Mrs. Chen about yearbook photos and saw them behind a cabinet. They're incredible, Leah. And heartbreaking."

Leah's head snapped up, a wave of panic rushing in. "What? "

"Incredible. Heartbreaking," Kate repeated, her tone steady. "They're beautiful. You shouldn't hide them."

The weight of those words crashed down on Leah, and she instinctively recoiled. "You weren't supposed to—no one was meant to see those."

"Why not?" Kate's voice turned gentle, yet a hint of frustration tinged it. "They're beautiful. They're honest. They're the first real thing I've seen from you lately, not filtered through this perfect mask you're trying to keep up."

Leah sank onto a bench, the exhaustion weighing through her bones while grappling with the vulnerability Kate had unearthed. She thought about the paintings—vivid explosions of color, emotions spilling onto canvas in ways words had failed her. At sixteen, she found herself increasingly caught between worlds—the structured perfection her father demanded and the wild, honest expression that called to her soul. She had tucked these pieces of herself beneath layers of practicality, convinced they didn't hold value in her world of academic achievement driven by parental expectations.

"Dad thinks art's a waste of time," Leah admitted, her voice barely a whisper, heavy with hurt. "It doesn't lead to a stable career or have practical uses."

Kate pressed, moving closer and challenging Leah, her voice gentle but strong. "And what do you think?"

Leah stared at her pruned hands, damp from being in the water, feeling the weight of truth growing heavier. "I think... when I'm painting, it's the only time I can breathe. Everything else feels like it's closing in." Her voice trembled, a flood of emotions creeping to the surface.

Kate sighed, an understanding and frustrated sound. "Then why are you letting your dad's opinions dictate your passions? You're gifted, Leah. Art is powerful, and it can set you free. You've picked up this heavy stone and shoved it in your backpack, but nobody asked you to carry it."

Leah squeezed her eyes shut, the urge to defend her dad rising in her throat. But she saw the truth in Kate's words. Her parents' expectations felt like lead, intertwining with her own desires. "I thought... if I made them proud, things would be better," she confessed, bitterness lacing her words. "If I accomplished everything right, they'd stop fighting. They'd be happy."

"And what about you?" Kate asked, resting her hand reassuringly on Leah's shoulder. "You don't owe them this perfect version of yourself. No one can be perfect, Leah—not even your parents. They need to own their happiness, just like you have to own yours. You can't carry their mess and still find room for your joy."

The truth in those words jolted Leah, like a revelation crashing into her consciousness. Why had she tied her identity so tightly to their approval? The suffocating pressures of perfection and unwavering success drowned out everything that made her who she truly was. She envisioned the vibrant canvases tucked away in the art room, pulsing with energy, alive with color, waiting for her—like a part of herself begging to be liberated.

Tears pricked at the corners of her eyes, and she furiously blinked them away, determined not to let her emotions win. "Everything feels so out of control," she admitted quietly, her voice wavering. "I don't even know who I am beyond grades, swimming, and expectations. Painting is my escape—but then I feel guilty for escaping."

Kate nodded, her expression shifting to one of compassion. "Art is good for your soul. So, make time for it. Bring it back into your life and don't let anyone tell you it's not meaningful."

Leah allowed the weight of Kate's words to settle in—a missing piece of her puzzle falling into place. She realized how she had been living in reaction to everyone else's expectations, suppressing her passion and individuality. The world outside felt chaotic and relentless, yet a part of her craved the freedom that came with expressing herself through art.

"Okay," Leah said, feeling a surge of resolve. "I'll think about it."

The next day, Kate invited Leah over to their house for dinner after school, which had been their usual routine since grade school. Leah brought with her the new painting she created in art class that day. Arriving at Kate's house, Mrs. Anderson greeted Leah warmly, with the comforting aroma of baking wafting through the air. "Dinner's almost ready, girls! Go wash up!" she called from the kitchen.

As Leah followed Kate into her room, the familiar space felt like a sanctuary away from the chaos of her reality. Band posters, art club projects, and scattered sketches adorned the walls, each item encapsulating laughter, secrets, and genuine moments of connection that recharged her soul.

"Okay, show me what you created!" Kate urged; her eyes were bright with excitement.

Leah took a deep breath, the familiar twinge of nervousness emerging as she pulled out her latest painting from her backpack. She positioned it on the bed, the array of colors nearly glowing under the dim lighting. "It's about... everything," she said, hesitated a moment before she added, "The struggle, the hidden anger, but also the hope—the part of me that wants to break free from all the chaos."

Kate's eyes widened as she stepped closer to examine Leah's work. "Oh wow," she breathed, clearly captivated. "This is stunning, Leah! The golden streak—it's like light piercing through darkness. You captured so much here."

A swell of pride blossomed in Leah's chest, warming her from the inside out. "Thanks! It feels good to let this out," she admitted, a smile breaking across her face. "I think I've been bottling all of this up for too long."

"Good! You should keep creating, no matter what anyone else says. Art is powerful, just like you," Kate emphasized, her voice firm yet encouraging. "Use it to communicate. Start reclaiming what's yours."

When Mrs. Anderson called them to dinner, Leah realized she was hungry for more than just food; she craved connection, understanding, and the comfort of being with someone who cared—someone who reminded her it was okay to feel, to be imperfect, and to pursue her passions.

As they settled into their seats and ate the steaming lasagna, Leah felt a new resolve settle inside her—a determination to live authentically, to communicate openly with her parents about boundaries, and to embrace both the light and shadows within herself. With Kate beside her and her heart opened to the struggles and joys ahead, she knew she could piece together her fractured self.

The evening unfolded in laughter and conversation, the warmth of companionship wrapping around Leah like a cozy blanket. She noticed Kate picking at her food more than eating it, pushing the lasagna around her plate in careful, measured movements. When

Mrs. Anderson gently urged her to eat more, Kate simply smiled and mentioned not being very hungry lately.

After dinner, once the dishes were cleared away, Kate leaned back in her chair, glancing at Leah with curiosity. "So, what's next for you? Any big plans for your art?"

Leah pondered for a moment, feeling a flicker of excitement at the thought. "I think I want to explore more abstract pieces. Maybe dedicate some time to paint every weekend. And I really want to open up about my art to my parents. Show them... show them what it means to me."

"You totally should!" Kate encouraged. "It's part of who you are. You deserve to share that side of yourself, even if it's scary."

Leah smiled, feeling a mix of nerves and exhilaration bubbling up. "Yeah, I think I will. I want them to see me for who I really am, not just the grades I bring home or the performance in the pool."

"That's the spirit!" Kate grinned, raising her glass of lemonade in a toast. "To being true to ourselves!"

"To being true to ourselves!" Leah echoed, clinking her glass with Kate's.

As the night wore on, Leah felt as if she were stepping onto her own path, free from the constant need to prove herself to others and hide her creativity. She was on her way to finding balance—a blend of her identity as both an artist and a student, a daughter striving to carve out her own space amidst their expectations.

When it was time to head home, Leah felt that familiar knot in her stomach, but this time, it was laced with excitement instead of dread. As she walked home, she reflected on the night, the engaging conversations, and the reaffirmation of her passions.

When she got home, the house was quiet. She crept to her room and glanced at her phone, deliberating whether to check for new texts. Gathering her courage, she opened it to find nothing new—not a word from either of her parents.

Feeling an odd sense of relief, she locked her phone away and turned on her desk lamp, illuminating her workspace. She paused, glancing at the empty canvases stacked against the wall, then grabbed one and set it up on her easel.

As she dipped her brush into vibrant colors, Leah felt a surge of inspiration wash over her. She turned up the music, letting the rhythm fuel her creativity. With every stroke, she poured herself into the painting, weaving her emotions into the canvas, translating everything she felt into waves of color and form.

Tonight, she would create. Tonight, she would reclaim her art and a piece of herself that had long been subdued. For the first time in a long while, Leah felt truly alive. She was not just a student or a daughter; she was an artist, and it was time to embrace that part of her wholeheartedly.

Under the soft glow of her lamp, with the music playing in the background, Leah painted her truth. The brush danced across the canvas, and with it, she felt her burdens lighten.

CHAPTER 3

The Friendship Anchor

The Anderson house looked much the same—warm yellow siding, cheerful flower boxes under every window, and a welcome mat that said "welcome." Leah stood on the porch, inhaled the scent of Susan Anderson's legendary chocolate chip cookies, and felt her shoulders drop after a long day. Everything about this place felt like a warm hug, almost like a balm for her fraying nerves. She hoped a slice of this warmth and stability would trickle into the chaos of her life.

The door swung wide open before she could even lift her hand to knock, and there stood Marcus, Kate's twelve-year-old brother, his glasses askew and a mischievous grin on his face. "Mom! Leah's here!" he shouted, excitement bursting from him. "Can she stay for dinner? She needs cookies!"

Leah couldn't bring herself to correct Marcus's exuberance. In his world, cookies could fix everything, and honestly, sometimes they did. If only adulting was that easy.

"Marcus," Kate's voice floated from inside, "what did we say about commenting on how people look?"

"But she looks like she needs it!" Marcus argued as Leah stepped inside, instantly wrapped in the familiar scents and sounds of the Anderson household.

"Why don't you help me with these cookies instead of critiquing our guests?" Susan Anderson's gentle reprimand flowed from the kitchen as she pulled a fresh batch from the oven.

For Leah, this moment felt like safety in the middle of chaos. At seventeen now, she mapped the geography of comfort with new precision—each visit to the Anderson house a reminder of what stability looked like, felt like, tasted like in the air. The months since her last birthday had brought a sharper awareness of the contrasts: here, where Susan's flour-dusted apron and messy ponytail radiated nurturing authenticity, versus home, where her mother's increasing panic and her father's deepening coldness had transformed familiar spaces into emotional minefields. She followed Marcus into the kitchen, drinking in the predictable warmth of this sanctuary, even as part of her ached knowing she'd eventually have to leave it.

"Perfect timing!" Susan smiled when she spotted the hopeful look on Leah's face. "These need taste testers!"

"Mom makes stress cookies," Marcus explained, snagging one even with Susan warning him about the hotness. "Dad says it's better than when she used to make stress pot roasts."

"Speaking of your father," Susan glanced at the clock, "he should be home early today. Leah, are you staying for dinner?" It felt more like a command than a question; Leah had practically been adopted into the family ages ago.

"If it's not too much trouble," Leah said, those words slipping out before she could stop them. She wasn't used to being a bother, not with all the little sighs of disappointment from her own parents, but she knew that feeling hadn't fit into the Andersons' welcoming vibe.

"Eight years of friendship," Kate sighed dramatically, rolling her eyes. "And she still acts like she needs a formal invite."

"Unlike some people," Susan teased. "Who invited half the soccer team over with no warning?"

"That was one time!" Kate shot back, her cheeks flushing with embarrassment, but the playful banter warmed Leah's heart—a huge contrast to the stilted conversations she dreaded back at home. Not that she'd ever spill her gratitude; that felt weird somehow.

"One time that cleaned out my entire pantry," Susan added, her tone light and bubbling with laughter.

The easy back-and-forth wrapped around Leah like a cozy blanket, inviting her into the moment and easing the weight pressing down on her. She settled at the kitchen table, accepting a still-warm cookie and pulling out her calculus homework, trying hard to anchor herself in this comforting atmosphere. Kate mirrored her actions, though her textbook stayed closed as she studied Leah's face.

"So," Kate said, while Marcus debated the cookie choices with their mother, "do you wanna talk about it?"

As the cookie's warmth left her hand, Leah felt a familiar, icy heaviness settle in her chest, a suffocating pressure that stole her breath. "Nothing to talk about. Just the usual."

"The usual being..." With a gentle touch, Kate pressed, sensing Leah's apprehension through her own fingertips.

"Mom called Dad's secretary again." Leah spoke in a hushed voice, aware of the tension that had crackled in her home. The noise of unresolved issues felt like it hovered under the surface. "Dad stormed out. Mom threw his clothes on the lawn. You know, just a typical Tuesday."

Susan's hand slid between them, placing two glasses of milk on the table, a welcome distraction that helped ease the heaviness in Leah's heart. If she'd caught onto their conversation, she didn't show it, but the gentle squeeze she gave Leah's shoulder conveyed a world of understanding.

"Hey, Leah," Marcus piped up, cookie crumbs dusting his chin, genuine curiosity bright in his eyes, "is it true that when parents fight a lot, they're gearing up to—"

"Marcus James Anderson!" Leah felt her heart race at the boy's bluntness, while Kate leaped in with sisterly protectiveness. "Go do your homework!"

"But—"

"Now." Kate's voice brooked no argument, and Leah silently thanked her for the interruption and her fierce protectiveness.

Marcus shuffled out but not before throwing one last nugget over his shoulder: "I'm just saying, Jenny's parents fought a lot before they—"

"Out!" Kate nearly shouted, a hint of desperation sneaking into her voice.

Once the door clicked shut behind Marcus, Leah let out a shaky breath. "He's not wrong," she murmured, the words feeling heavy.

"He's twelve," Kate stated, folding her arms. "He doesn't know anything except what he sees on Disney Channel."

Leah briefly fell silent, reflecting on the wisdom found within characters like Peter Parker and Ron Weasley. "But what if that's all I see too?" she said, the thought slipping out before she caught it. "All I can see is the fighting, the constant uncertainty about what's next. I'm stuck between my parents' needs and responsibilities, and honestly, finding my way seems impossible."

Susan settled across from her, her gaze warm but focused. "You know, Leah, twelve-year-olds often see things a lot clearer than we give them credit for. They haven't complicated the truth with adult worries yet."

Leah felt a swell of appreciation at Susan's understanding. She realized that the turbulence from her parents created ripples that left her feeling battered.

Her phone buzzed—another message from her mom, likely another mundane worry. "Do you need to get that?" Susan asked, her voice soft and inquisitive, like a gentle breeze.

"No," Leah said, flipping the phone face-down. "She wants me to check with Dad about some insurance papers. I'm just... I can't be their messenger anymore." The words tumbled out, heavy with the weight of finding her voice.

Susan nodded, her expression understanding. "That's a healthy boundary to set," she affirmed.

"So," Kate said, her eyes narrowing a little, "what do you really want to talk about?"

It took Leah a moment to gather herself, the warmth of the cookie fading into her thoughts. "I don't know," Leah replied, her voice softening as she traced patterns in the scattered flour on the counter. "At seventeen, you'd think I'd have figured out how to navigate this by now. But I still feel lost sometimes, like I'm caught in the middle of it all. The fights are different now—more calculated, less explosive. Sometimes I think that's worse."

"Well, you don't have to go through it alone," Kate whispered, her voice filled with sincerity. "You have me and this family. They care about you, you know?"

Leah couldn't help but smile faintly. "Yeah, I know. It's just... hard to reach out sometimes."

"Totally get it," Kate replied. "But you should know, the more real you are with us, the better we can help you. You're not a burden, Leah."

Susan nodded, her eyes shining with understanding. "Yes. And remember, you can always talk about what's going on. You're part of this family. We care about you."

Leah felt warmth envelop her like a thick blanket, and she glanced down at her homework as if her notes could provide the answers to her emptiness. "Thanks, you guys. It really means a lot."

A moment passed in comfortable silence; the kitchen had filled with soft sounds of the world around them. The laughter in the air had hung like a sweet perfume, soothing her heart, if only for a little while.

"Why don't we do something fun?" Kate suggested. "We could binge-watch that new show we were talking about earlier!"

"Yeah! I mean, who doesn't love a good binge-watch?" Marcus piped up from the other room.

"You can join, nerd! Just get your homework done first," Kate teased, throwing a playful grin.

As they cleaned up the remains of dinner, Leah's heart felt a little lighter. It was moments like this that reminded her of the beauty of togetherness—even amidst the chaos.

Later, as they flopped onto the couch, Leah nestled in beside Kate, a bowl of popcorn balanced on her lap. The show began, and they lost themselves in the episodes unfolding before them—laughter and bright moments filling the room like sunlight breaking through a cloud.

After a few episodes, Leah felt the need to breathe, a deep sigh escaping her lips. "It's nice to escape for a bit like this."

"Right?" Kate replied, nudging Leah with her shoulder. "Nothing like losing ourselves in fiction."

"Totally," Leah said, her smile softening as the warmth of the family enveloped her. "I don't know what I'd do without you guys."

"Hey, just remember you're never alone, okay?" Kate said, her voice sincere. "We've got each other's backs, no matter what."

Leah nodded, clutching the popcorn bowl more tightly. "Thanks, Kate. I really appreciate it."

As the evening wore on, the laughter and banter between them flowed naturally, filling the room with a sense of peace that felt like a balm for Leah's weary heart. Even when Marcus chimed in with his classic one-liners, making ridiculous impersonations of the show's characters, Leah couldn't help but laugh alongside Kate and Susan.

The show reached a cliffhanger, and they all groaned in unison. "No way! They can't just leave it there!" Marcus threw his hands up in exaggerated disbelief.

"Right? Not cool at all!" Kate agreed, her eyes wide with faux outrage. "They're totally trying to manipulate us into coming back for more!"

"Guess we'll have to binge it all tomorrow," Susan said with a knowing smile, already gathering empty snack bowls. "But for now, it's time for bed, guys."

"Aww, do we have to?" Marcus complained, a pout forming on his face.

"Yes, you do," Susan replied, yet with a hint of affection in her tone. "And Leah, if you want to stay over, you're more than welcome."

The offer warmed Leah's heart. "I think I might." She looked at Kate, and her friend immediately smiled with enthusiasm.

"Sweet! We can have a sleepover!" Kate exclaimed, jumping up.

"Just keep the chaos down," Susan quipped, her eyes sparkling.

As everyone settled in for bed, Leah couldn't shake the feeling of gratitude that washed over her. The warmth and acceptance she felt within the Anderson household was a stark contrast to her reality at home. It felt like a safe harbor amidst the storm.

Later that night, as they lay in Kate's room under a blanket draped with fairy lights, Leah tossed and turned. Exhaustion clung to her, yet her thoughts raced. "I'm glad I came over," Leah said, breaking the silence. "I needed this. I really did."

"I'm glad too," Kate replied. "Remember, whenever you feel overwhelmed, you can always come here. We've got a couch that can double as a bed anytime."

Leah smiled, feeling comforted by the offer. "You know, it's just hard to reach out sometimes. I feel like... I don't want to be a burden."

"Leah," Kate said, "you're never a burden. You're my best friend, and you need to lean on me sometimes. That's what friends are for. You don't always have to carry everything alone."

Leah's heart swelled with appreciation. "Thanks, Kate. I wish I could be more like you—so confident about everything."

Kate chuckled. "Trust me, I have my moments of doubt too. But it's okay to be vulnerable to those who care about you. Just be real, and all will work itself out."

"Yeah, I guess you're right," Leah said, a small smile on her face. "It's just... hard to let go sometimes."

"Totally get that," Kate said, as she snuggled deeper under the blanket. "We all have our baggage—it's part of being human. Just don't forget that we have each other's backs."

As the two girls drifted off to sleep, Leah felt a flicker of hope burning deep within her. She clung to the promises made amidst the laughter—of support and sisterhood. The chaos that often filled her own home felt distant in this moment; it could wait until tomorrow.

With a newfound determination, Leah let her eyes flutter shut, hope swirling in her dreams—dreams where she could express herself without fear, where laughter and warmth filled her days, and where she never had to carry her burdens alone.

In the days following their art session, Leah felt a subtle shift within her, one that stirred both excitement and hesitation. As she navigated her last few months of high school, her mind often wandered back to the inviting warmth of the Anderson home and the steady momentum of her friendship with Kate. The comfort of distraction wasn't merely about art anymore—it included the quiet exchanges of glances and laughter she often shared with Ryan.

One morning, as Leah strolled through the hallways, Kate walked beside her, animatedly recounting a story about their recent group project in AP History. "And then Ryan said the funniest thing about Lincoln needing to shape up his presidency! I swear, if you had heard it, you would've laughed so hard."

Leah's heart leaped at the mention of Ryan's name, a flutter of nervousness igniting in her chest. "He's funny, alright," she replied, a touch of shyness creeping into her voice.

"Funny? You mean downright charming!"

Kate teased, shooting Leah a challenging glance. "I saw the way you smiled at him during our presentation. You can't deny that he totally makes you blush."

Leah rolled her eyes, attempting to deflect the conversation while her cheeks turned a deeper shade. "Oh, come on! He's just a friend."

"Just a friend who you crush on," Kate teased, smirking knowingly. "I mean, he is cute and kind, and you showed definite signs of enjoying your time with him during our final project."

Leah snorted, trying to brush it off. "Maybe in a general sense." But truthfully, she couldn't help it—Ryan had woven himself into her thoughts more often than she'd like to admit.

As they walked, Leah spotted Ryan chatting with a few guys by the lockers, each laugh punctuated with genuine camaraderie. Leah felt a rush of warmth. She briefly caught his eye, and a smile broke across his face at the sight of her. The moment was brief, but it sent butterflies swirling in Leah's stomach, making her heart race with electric anticipation.

"See! There it is again!" Kate exclaimed, nudging Leah with her elbow as she caught the brief exchange. "You totally light up when he looks at you. You're like a firefly caught in a jar."

Leah chuckled nervously, feeling both flattered and embarrassed. "Fine, maybe I think he's cool. But that means nothing!"

Kate grinned, clearly, she enjoyed teasing her friend. "Cool? He's more than cool! Ryan Matthews is practically the poster boy for charming! You two would be perfect together."

"Perfect, huh?" Leah said, squinting at Ryan from a distance, her heart racing as he laughed at something one of his friends said. "You really think so?"

"Without a doubt!" "Not just in academics, but in art! You both appreciate creativity and—"

"Okay, Kate. Let's not go too far." Leah interrupted, a mix of hope and self-doubt swirling within her as memories of their moments together replayed in her mind.

At that moment, Marilyn, one of their classmates, approached with a wide grin, joining the duo. "Hey, Leah, did you hear Ryan asked about you during lunch yesterday?" she said, her eyes sparkling with excitement.

Leah's stomach dropped. "What? No, I didn't hear that."

"Yeah! He was all, 'Is Leah coming to the party this weekend?' I mean," Marilyn continued, clearly enjoying the gossip as she adjusted her backpack, "he sounded really interested. Kinda cute, right?"

Leah glanced at Kate, who wore an expression of exaggerated glee. "See? You could totally take things to the next level!"

"Okay, so... maybe he's thought about it," Leah said. She laughed nervously as her heart fluttered. Ryan, wanting her to be at a party, felt surreal against the backdrop of her family's chaos.

"Just think," Kate chimed in, grinning ear to ear. "You could go, hang out, let loose a bit! Who knows what could happen? You're ready for this!"

Leah felt a rush of nervous energy. A party? With Ryan?

That sounded perfect. But her excitement was tempered by the nagging fear of being caught in the storm of her family dynamics. Still, the fleeting possibility of something developing between her and Ryan kept the hope alive.

As the day unfolded, thoughts of Ryan hovered at the fringes of Leah's mind, dancing with possibilities and festering insecurities. During the rest of her classes, she doodled his name in the margins of her notes, along with little hearts and stars—a secret manifestation of her growing feelings. Each time she caught sight of him in the hall, it felt like a spark igniting her interest further.

Later that week, Leah couldn't shake her nerves about the rumored party and the potential encounter with Ryan. She paced her room, rehearsing potential conversations in her head. What if he was just being friendly? What if she misread his intentions?

"Just relax, Leah," she told herself one night, staring into the mirror as she adjusted her hair. "It's not a wedding; it's just a party." But even as she said it, the word "just" felt heavy with meaning. A casual get-together could turn into something much more significant if the stars aligned.

The Friday night of the party arrived, and Leah spent what felt like hours picking out an outfit—deliberate but casual, yet playful enough to show off her personality. She finally settled on a floral crop top paired with high-waisted jeans, perfect for a fun evening without stepping too far outside her comfort zone.

"Okay, you look amazing!" Kate gushed when she stopped by to help Leah get ready. "Ryan is going to be blown away."

"I don't want to think too much about that," Leah replied, fidgeting with the hem of her shirt. "What if he's just there for everyone else?"

"Then he's missing out!" Kate declared, her enthusiasm contagious but strategic. "Remember, confidence is key. You just need to be yourself."

As they arrived at the party, the air was thick with the sounds of laughter and music. Leah's heart raced as they entered the living room, the energy palpable. Colors blazed from decorations, and the scent of pizza wafted through the air, mingling with the faint notes of a popular song playing in the background.

"Let's grab some food before it runs out!" Kate said, pulling Leah toward the kitchen. As they helped themselves to snacks, Leah stole a glance around the room, her heart racing at the sheer number of faces.

"Look!" Kate exclaimed, pointing through the crowd. "There's Ryan!"

Leah's breath hitched as she followed Kate's gaze to see Ryan standing by the drink table, animatedly chatting with a group of friends. There was an ease to how he moved, the way he laughed, and the way his eyes sparkled with excitement. Leah's heart raced, a mix of nervousness and exhilaration surging within her as she felt a magnetic pull to him.

"Go talk to him," Kate encouraged, nudging Leah forward. "You've got this!"

"Wait, now?" Leah stammered, hesitating, feeling as if she were about to dive into deep water without a life jacket.

"Yes, now!" Kate urged, her eyes gleaming with anticipation. "What is the worst that could happen? You say hi, he smiles, maybe you two laugh over something. Come on, you both have to start somewhere!"

Leah took a deep breath, summoning every ounce of courage she could muster. "Alright," she said, trying to inject some confidence into her voice. "Let's do this."

With determination, Leah made her way through the throngs of partygoers, navigating the blur of bodies and sounds. She could feel her heart pounding in her ears, but as Ryan came into clearer view, her nerves subsided, replaced by undeniable excitement.

"Hey, Leah!" Ryan called out as she approached, his face breaking into a warm smile that made her heart flutter. "I'm glad you could make it!"

"Wouldn't miss it!" Leah replied, trying to keep her voice steady and casual. "How's it going?"

"Pretty great! Just hanging out, taking in the vibes. Everyone's having a good time." He gestured around him, and Leah caught sight of people dancing and others lounging around in clusters, laughing and sharing stories.

"I can see that," Leah said, shifting her weight from one foot to the other as she fell into step beside him. "Looks like a lot of fun."

"Wanna help me mix up some party drinks?" Ryan asked, his eyes sparkling with mischief.

"Sure! What are we making?" Leah smiled, feeling a rush of warmth from being included in the lighthearted atmosphere.

"Let's go with something classic—fruit punch with a twist!" Ryan grinned, leading her to the small bar set up nearby. The work was simple: jugs of punch and colorful garnishes laid out for mixing.

As they worked together, Leah noticed how easily they fell into conversation; every moment felt fluid and comfortable, like a dance they both knew. He joked about the randomness of high school parties, and she shared stories of her awkward moments in the past, finding comfort in their shared laughter. Ryan's presence was grounding, and with every joke, her nerves dissipated.

"Okay, but have you ever had a punch disaster?" Leah asked, recalling a party mishap she'd overheard where someone had dumped way too much soda into a concoction gone wrong.

Ryan chuckled, shaking his head. "I can safely say no, but now I want to try just to know the thrill of a good party foul."

Their playful banter made the task feel easier, and time slipped away as they mixed drinks and enjoyed each other's company. Leah stole glances at Ryan, catching how his eyes lit up when he talked about his favorite movies or his dreams of engineering—each revelation felt like a peek into his vibrant world.

"Here—try this," Ryan said, handing her a cup filled with their punch. She took a sip, mostly out of curiosity.

"Wow! This is actually good!" Leah exclaimed, impressed. "Who knew we had such mixology skills?"

"Well, now we're the party punch queens," Ryan joked, raising his cup in a mock toast.

As they shared more playful moments, Leah felt a growing sense of connection, realizing that being around him was effortless. They leaned against the table, sipping their drinks, and Ryan leaned in, his expression turning more serious.

"So, Leah, what do you envision for your future? Any grand plans yet?" he asked, genuine curiosity shining in his eyes.

Leah felt a rush of vulnerability wash over her, but there was something in his gaze that encouraged her to open up. "Honestly? I want to go into pre-med and eventually become a doctor—help people and make a difference, you know? But it's kind of a lot of pressure to think about it all at once."

"I totally get that. There's a lot of pressure on figuring out what you want," Ryan replied thoughtfully. "I have my family's expectations hanging over my head too. Engineering feels like what everyone thinks I should do, but sometimes, I wonder if that's what I truly want."

Leah nodded, sensing the weight of both their dreams and uncertainties. The moment felt vulnerable yet grounding, as though their concerns connected them. "We should just set our own paths, you know? It doesn't always have to be about meeting everyone else's expectations."

"That's right!" Ryan exclaimed, a spark igniting in his eyes. "I'm with you on that. We just have to figure it out together."

A comfortable silence settled between them, broken only by laughter from a nearby group. Leah felt a warmth spread through her at the thought of having someone like Ryan in her corner. He was easy to talk to, sincere in a way that made her feel understood, and she could already sense the potential for something more.

"Let's make a deal," Ryan said, breaking into her thoughts. "We'll keep each other accountable for our goals. No secret plans, no pretending to be something we're not."

Leah felt the sincerity in his voice and nodded enthusiastically. "Of Course! I love that idea."

"Great! We can start practicing right now by being honest about our weirdest quirks," Ryan suggested, a playful smile tugging at the corners of his mouth.

"Okay, you first!" Leah's eyebrow arched, curious about what he might reveal.

"Alright, here goes. I talk to my cat like he's a person," Ryan confessed, a hint of sheepishness in his tone. "I swear we have conversations, especially about my day. He's much better at listening than most of my classmates."

Leah burst into laughter, the sound infectious. "That's adorable! I can totally picture it. What's his name?"

"Mr. Whiskers," Ryan said, a proud smile crossing his face. "Very regal, I know."

"Classic cat name!" Leah teased. "Alright, my turn. I can't resist dancing when I'm home alone. I literally cut the rug without a care in the world. It's like my own personal concert."

"Now that I need to see!" Ryan laughed, his eyes sparkling with amusement. "So what you're saying is, next time we hang out, I should catch you dancing it out?"

"Definitely not!" Leah said, blushing a bit, the playful banter easing any previous tension. "That's off-limits."

"Not anymore!" Ryan grinned, leaning in closer. "I might have to sneak a few videos."

Leah felt the butterflies return with a vengeance, but this time, they felt lighter, less about anxiety, and more about excitement. "Well, if you want a dance partner, just know I require snacks as payment."

Ryan laughed, their chemistry simmering in the air. "Deal! I'll bring the snacks if you bring the moves."

Leah felt a genuine warmth settle between her and Ryan as they exchanged playful banter. The laughter did wonders, wrapping around them like a cozy blanket against the chill of the night air. Each joke, each smile, drew them closer, creating a shared space that felt vibrant and alive.

"Okay, now that we've established our quirks," Ryan said, wiping the last remnants of his drink from his lips, "what's the wildest thing you've ever done?"

Leah considered this for a moment, her heart racing as the thrill of revelation danced in her chest. "I once climbed a tree in my backyard to get a better view of the sunrise. My mom thought I was nuts, but it was kind of magical."

"That's awesome!" Ryan exclaimed, leaning in, clearly impressed. "I'd say we're both kind of adventurous. Maybe we need to shake things up a bit and go on nature hikes or something."

"Definitely!" Leah replied, her heart racing with excitement at the thought of embarking on new adventures with him. The chemistry between them crackled like static electricity, and she felt buoyant in Ryan's presence.

As they continued to chat about their experiences and what they hoped to explore together, Leah noticed Ryan's eyes gleaming, reflecting a sense of enthusiasm that felt contagious.

This was the connection she had never expected; the easy laughter and shared dreams felt like a treasure to hold on to tightly.

"I can't believe how easy this is," Ryan said, looking directly at Leah, his expression sincere. "You know? Just being together, chatting about everything and nothing."

Leah's heart fluttered at his words, the enormity of the moment sinking in. "I feel the same way. It's like we can just be ourselves with no pressure."

"Indeed!" Ryan said enthusiastically. "And, you know... I really like you, Leah."

The honesty of his admission sent Leah's heart soaring, a mix of surprise and joy bubbling to the surface. "I like you too, Ryan," she replied, her voice barely above a whisper, but filled with sincerity.

He smiled, the warmth and excitement flowing in the small distance between them; it felt as if they were something more, each moment stitching them together in a tapestry of budding love.

As they lingered in that shared gaze, the world around them faded into a soft blur. For the first time in what felt like months, Leah allowed herself to smile without worry—the genuine smile that came from deep within, one that pushed aside the shadows of her home life and embraced the thrill of potential.

Under the stars, they leaned in closer, their hearts beating in sync, but just as Leah prepared to say more, a vibration pulsed through her pocket, breaking the moment.

Leah pulled out her phone to see a message from her mom. Her heart sank as she read the words: "You need to come home right now. There's been an issue with your father, and I need your help."

The world around her spun, and panic crept in. "Not again," she whispered, swallowing hard. The veil of happiness that had enveloped her throughout the day tore, revealing the jagged edges of her reality.

Taking a deep breath, Leah gathered her thoughts and headed back to the living room, fighting to maintain a brave face. "Um, guys," she said, her voice steady, masking the storm surging inside her. "I think I should head home. My mom needs me."

"Is everything okay?" Ryan asked, his brow furrowing with concern.

"Yeah, I just... I'm not sure," Leah replied slowly, trying to sound nonchalant. "It's probably just some drama at home. You know how it is." But even as the words left her mouth, she felt a wave of despair wash over her at the thought of her parents' chaos waiting to engulf her again.

"Alright, call me if you need anything," Ryan replied, his eyes soft with concern.

"Thanks, I really appreciate it," Leah said, her voice barely above a whisper.

As Leah made her way to the door, she could feel the weight of both worlds pressing down on her—one filled with laughter and love, and the other laden with tension and unresolved issues. With each step she took toward home, she felt the vibrant colors of the day fading, replaced by the heavy gray clouds that loomed in her mind.

When Leah arrived home, her stomach twisted with dread as she opened the door to her darkened house. "Mom?" she called out, the echo of her voice hitting the silence like a stone tossed into still water.

No response.

Panic bubbled inside her as she stepped into the living room, noting the disarray of her father's shoes haphazardly thrown by the door and the flickering light from the kitchen, where she could hear muted voices—one of them undeniably her father's.

"Mom?" Leah's voice trembled as she approached the kitchen.

As she peered around the corner, her heart sank. There in the kitchen stood her parents, faces taut with anger, the atmosphere thick with confrontation. Her mom paced the room, agitation evident in her every movement. Her father leaned against the counter, arms crossed tightly, a storm brewing in his eyes.

"Leah!" her mother snapped, catching sight of her. "Just in time. You need to hear this."

"Mom, what's going on?" Leah asked, her voice barely audible beneath the weight of their tension.

"Your father has some nerve!" her mother responded in frustration. "He's just going to continue to avoid my calls!"

"I told you, Claire, I was busy!" her father retorted, his face flushed with irritation. "You know how my job gets. I can't drop everything for every little thing you want. And now you're dragging Leah into this?"

"Stop it! Stop fighting!" Leah cried out, feeling that all-too-familiar heaviness settle back in her chest. It felt like the walls were closing in around her. "Please, can't we just talk civilly?"

The room fell silent at her outburst, the tension rippling like electricity in the air. For a moment, all eyes were on her—her mother looked stunned, her father's expression hardened.

"Leah, this is between your mother and me," her father said, a cold edge in his voice.

"No! It's not just about you two!" Leah shot back, feeling her voice break with emotion. "You both need to understand how this affects me, too!"

A heavy silence stretched as Leah's heart raced. The sense of safety she felt with the Andersons was a distant memory now, replaced by the chaos brewing at home—chaos she desperately wanted to escape.

"Leah, you don't understand. This is grown-up stuff," her father said dismissively.

But Leah could feel the storm inside her boiling. "No, I understand!" she shouted, feeling her voice rise. "It's not just about you! We're all hurting here, and this constant fighting is tearing everything apart!"

Leah's words hung in the air, a tremor of raw emotion cascading through her. The kitchen, once a backdrop of familial warmth and comfort, now felt like a battlefield where her parents stood on opposing sides, guarded and uncertain.

"Leah, don't do this," John said, his anger cooling into a weariness that twisted Leah's heart. "You don't have to get involved. This is something Claire and I need to figure out."

"But it involves me! Your fights, your problems—they're affecting my world too!" Leah's voice broke, the knot in her throat tightening.

Her frustration surged, a hot wave washing over her. "Why do you both keep saying that? You expect me to just stand here and watch everything fall apart? I want to help! I want my family to be okay!"

As her words left her lips, the air shifted—heavy with unspoken truth. In that moment, Leah felt every unaddressed issue laid bare, every worry and unresolved fear clawing at the edges of her sanity. The weight of it crashed down, suffocating her with the enormity of what lay ahead.

From behind her, a sharp knock rang against the front door, reverberating through the charged atmosphere. The sound startled all three of them, pausing the mounting tension as John's expression shifted from anger to uncertainty.

"Who could that be?" Claire asked, her voice laced with trepidation, glancing at Leah as if searching for guidance.

"I'll check it," John said, his tone now cautious, stepping away from the counter with resolve.

Leah's heart raced as he made his way to the door. She could sense the impending shift in energy—the low hum of worry that buzzed in her chest made her apprehensive. What if this knock was a harbinger of something darker on the horizon?

The door creaked open slowly, revealing a figure Leah did not expect. A uniformed officer stood there, his expression serious and grave. "John Miller?" he called out, the weight of his voice cutting through the air like a knife.

Leah felt a chill run down her spine, the dread solidifying into something tangible. She exchanged glances with Claire, the worry etched into her mother's features.

"Yes, that's me," John replied, his voice steady but edged with unease.

"We need to talk," the officer said, stepping inside without waiting for an invitation. Leah's stomach twisted as she glanced at her parents, both of whom looked like they had just been struck by a wave of ice-cold water.

John's brows furrowed. "About what?"

The officer took a moment, scanning the room, before locking eyes with John. "We have some questions regarding your involvement—"

John immediately interrupted the officer and asked if they could speak about it privately outside to avoid letting Leah hear it.

CHAPTER 4

Chaos Escalates

As Leah leaned closer to her mother, the tension thickened in the air. Everything felt suspended in time, the world outside slipping away as Claire's fingers trembled around the phone. Each breath seemed to catch in her throat, her knuckles whitening as she gripped the device harder.

"Look," Claire said, her voice dropping to a dangerous whisper that made Leah's skin prickle. "I've been putting up with this for too long." The words carried a weight that seemed to press against Leah's chest, heavy with unspoken accusations.

Leah watched as her mother's face transformed—the familiar lines of worry deepening into something darker, more desperate. Claire's free hand pressed against her forehead, fingers splaying across her temple as if trying to hold back a flood of thoughts. Her breath hitched, a small, broken sound that seemed to echo in the kitchen's stillness.

"No..." The word escaped Claire's lips like a plea, her voice cracking. She paced, her movements sharp and erratic. "You can't be—" She cut herself off, jaw clenching as she listened to whatever response came through the phone. Each step seemed to carry her further from the mother Leah knew, transforming her into someone harder, someone shaped by betrayal.

Leah's stomach churned as she watched Claire's shoulders tense, saw the way her mother's throat worked around words she couldn't seem to voice. When Claire spoke again, her tone had shifted from disbelief to something raw and wounded. "I don't care what he said!" The words exploded from her, sharp enough to make Leah flinch. "Just stop defending him!"

Claire's pacing quickened, her free hand gesturing in tight, aggressive movements. "You think I haven't noticed?" Her voice rose, trembling with an emotion that seemed to hover between anger and desperation. "I can't believe you'd choose his side over mine!"

Leah caught glimpses of a side to her mother she had rarely seen—something uncontrolled and dangerous beneath the careful facade of composure. Claire's eyes had taken on a glassy sheen, reflecting the kitchen lights in a way that made them look almost feverish. Her breathing had become shallow, rapid, like she was running from something unseen.

"Mom?" Leah's voice wavered as she tried to catch her mother's attention. "What's going on? Who are you talking to?"

Claire jerked away, her whole body seeming to recoil from the question. She held up one hand, palm out, creating a barrier between them that felt more significant than the physical distance. "Just give me a moment, Leah." The words came out strained, each syllable careful and measured, as if speaking normally might shatter something precious.

"What's happening?" Leah pressed again, anxiety clawing at her throat. "Just tell me!"

Claire moved back to the counter, her spine straightening as if bracing for impact. When she spoke, her voice carried the weight of exhaustion, of too many secrets kept too long. "It's a lot, Leah. I thought..." She paused, her fingers drumming an anxious rhythm against the counter's edge. "I thought I could handle it without you knowing, but it's not that simple anymore."

Leah stepped forward, her heart thundering against her ribs. "You can't just drop a bomb like that!" The words escaped before she could stop them, desperate and raw. "What's going on with Dad?"

Claire's hands moved in restless patterns across the counter's surface, as if trying to grasp at something just beyond reach. Her shoulders curved inward, a physical manifestation of the weight she carried. "Just..." The word hung suspended, fragmenting in the air between them. When she finally turned to meet Leah's gaze, the shadows in her eyes—deep wells of uncertainty—struck Leah; they made her seem years older, profoundly vulnerable, her usual defenses washed away. "It's complications, Leah."

The kitchen light cast harsh shadows across Claire's face as she struggled to weave together the dissolving threads of their reality. Her fingers twisted around each other, a nervous dance that spoke of barely contained anxiety. "John and I..." She swallowed hard, her throat working around words that seemed to resist being spoken. "Your dad and I, we've been going through some things." The admission came out barely above a whisper, as if speaking any louder might shatter what remained of their carefully constructed world.

Just then, the doorbell's sharp intrusion made them both jump. Through the window, a figure stood silhouetted against the afternoon light—official, imposing. John moved quickly to the door, his footsteps heavy with dread. "Stay back," he commanded, the words carrying a weight that made Leah's stomach clench.

When the door swung open, the stranger's voice cut through the tension like a knife. "Detective Rodriguez." The badge glinted under the porch light, its metallic gleam somehow ominous. "I need to speak with John."

Claire's grip tightened on Leah's shoulder, her fingers trembling against the fabric. The pressure felt like an anchor, but one that might break rather than stabilize. "This isn't good," she whispered, fear bleeding into every syllable.

John stepped onto the porch, pulling the door closed behind him. The soft click echoed with a finality that made Leah's chest constrict. Through the window, she could see her father's shoulders hunching forward, his usual confident posture crumbling under the detective's words.

When he returned, the color had drained from his face, leaving him ashen and unfamiliar. "Claire," he said, his voice hollow, "we need to talk. Now." Each word seemed to cost him something vital, as if speaking them drew from some rapidly depleting reserve of strength.

The silence that followed pressed against Leah's ears like cotton, muffling everything except the frantic beating of her own heart. She watched her father's hands—always so steady, now trembling slightly as he ran them through his hair. His wedding ring caught the light, a brief flash of gold that seemed to mock the crumbling foundation of their marriage.

"About what?" Claire's voice had taken on an edge Leah had never heard before—sharp enough to cut, yet fragile as spun glass. "What's this about, John?"

"About everything." The weight of those two words seemed to physically push him down, his shoulders sagging beneath an invisible burden. "And it's not going to be easy."

Leah felt the world tilting beneath her feet, reality shifting into something unrecognizable. "What's going on, Dad?" Small, young, and filled with a childlike vulnerability, the question—a fragile sound—pierced the heavy, oppressive silence, seeking a lifeline of reassurance. "Just tell us!"

John moved closer, his presence carrying none of its usual authority. Instead, he seemed diminished, as if the truth he carried was eating away at him from within. "It's about my work..." His voice dropped to barely a whisper, the words escaping like prisoners breaking free. "I got involved with some people I shouldn't have."

Claire's sharp intake of breath sliced through the air. Her hand flew to her throat, fingers pressing against her collarbone as if trying to hold something back. The gesture was achingly familiar to Leah—the same way her mother used to brace herself before their biggest arguments.

"What kind of people?" Leah demanded, even as dread pooled in her stomach like lead. "What have you done?"

John's eyes darted between them, carrying a haunted quality that made Leah's skin crawl. The kitchen light cast harsh shadows across his face, deepening the lines of worry into canyons of guilt. "There are things happening in my department—things that aren't legal." Each word seemed to physically pain him, dragging themselves out like thorns from a wound. "I thought I could manage it, keep you all safe, but I've made mistakes."

The revelation struck Leah like a physical blow, forcing the air from her lungs into a sharp exhale. The kitchen walls seemed to press inward, the familiar space all of a sudden felt like a trap. Her father—always the pillar of integrity, the voice of reason—stood before them, transformed into someone she barely recognized, his guilt casting shadows that stretched across their family's foundation.

Claire's laugh, when it came, held no humor—just a brittle, breaking sound that seemed to crystalize everything wrong in their world. "Manage it?" The words dripped with disbelief, each syllable sharp enough to draw blood. "Like you've managed everything else?" Her hands clenched into fists at her sides, knuckles white with restraint.

The air between them grew thick with unspoken accusations, years of trust crumbling like sand through their fingers. Leah watched her mother's face transform, witnessed the exact moment when something fundamental shifted in her eyes. It was like watching a door close, but one that had been slowly swinging shut for years—they just hadn't wanted to see it.

"I can't do this anymore." Claire's voice emerged steady, but beneath it ran currents of grief so deep they seemed fathomless. "I won't let your choices destroy me too." Each word fell between them like stones into still water, ripples of consequence spreading outward in ever-widening circles.

The finality in her tone struck Leah like a physical blow. She reached for her phone, fingers trembling as they sought Brian's contact—a lifeline in the storm that was drowning them all. The screen blurred before her eyes as she typed: "Mom's leaving. For real this time."

The message felt inadequate, unable to capture the way their world was splintering apart in this kitchen, how the familiar walls of home had become witnesses to their family's dissolution. But it was all she could manage as she watched her mother gather her keys, her movements precise and deliberate, as if she'd rehearsed this moment in her mind countless times before.

Claire paused at the threshold, her hand resting on the doorframe. For a moment, she looked back—not at John, but at Leah—and her eyes held volumes of unspoken love and regret. Then she was gone, the door clicking shut behind her with a quiet finality that somehow hurt more than any slam could have.

The silence that followed pressed against Leah's ears like a physical weight, broken only by the soft ping of Grace's response: "that sucks. hang in there." The period at the end felt like another door closing, her sister's measured distance a preview of the new normal that awaited them all.

Brian's call came moments later, his ringtone cutting through the heavy silence like a knife through fog. Unlike Grace, who had fled to UCLA's sun-soaked campus, Brian had chosen MIT with careful calculation—close enough to maintain the connection, far enough to claim independence. The familiar warmth in his "Hey, squirt" wrapped around her like a blanket, though now it carried static-filled echoes of guilty distance.

Leah pressed the phone closer to her ear, as if the extra pressure might somehow collapse the miles between her and Brian. His voice carried that familiar warmth that used to make everything manageable, but now it wanted to warm herself with a photograph of sunlight. Words spilled from her in broken waves, each confession carrying fragments of their shattered home.

"Everything's falling apart, Bry." Her voice caught on his nickname—a sound from simpler times. "Dad's wrapped up in something dark at work, Mom can't take it anymore, and I'm just..." she trailed off, the silence speaking volumes about her isolation. "I'm here alone, watching it all crumble."

"You're not alone," Brian insisted, though the words rang hollow against the static of distance. Once, he'd been her shield against their parents' storms. Now all he could offer were digital lifelines, text messages like paper boats on a rising tide. "I can come home this weekend—"

"No." The steel in her voice surprised even her, forged perhaps from months of holding herself together while everyone else fled toward freedom. "You have finals coming up. I know how hard you worked for that scholarship." She swallowed hard, tasting the bitterness of her own sacrifice. "I just... I needed to hear your voice, I guess."

The silence stretched between them, thick with shared memories and unspoken guilt. Through the phone, she heard the familiar rustle of Brian running his hand through his hair—a gesture so achingly normal that it made her chest constrict with longing for simpler times.

"Remember what I told you before I left?" His voice softened around the edges, reaching for the connection across the digital divide. "About being stronger than you think?"

"Yeah." The word came out as barely more than a whisper, heavy with the weight of that last night before he'd driven toward Boston—toward freedom. They'd both known he wasn't just driving to college; he was driving away from the fault lines spreading through their family's foundation. "But I didn't think I'd have to be this strong."

Grace's text buzzed through then, its casual tone another small betrayal: "lmk if u need anything." The abbreviated words felt like emotional shorthand, as if their family's collapse didn't even merit complete sentences. Her sister's escape to California wasn't just geographic; it was existential—each beach photo and study group update carefully edited to exclude the chaos she'd left behind.

"I get it," Leah said into the phone, though part of her wanted to scream about how different "here" felt through a screen, how presence couldn't be replicated through cell towers and Wi-Fi signals. "It's just... everything's different now. You and Grace got out just in time, you know? Before it all exploded."

"Hey," Brian's voice softened with recognition of her pain. "We didn't abandon you, squirt. We just—"

"Had to get out. I know." Leah closed her eyes, remembering how she'd helped Grace pack for California, both of them pretending the distance she craved wasn't personal. How she'd hugged Brian goodbye, understanding his need to build something separate from their family's fault lines. "Sometimes I think you both saw this coming. That's why you went so far."

The silence that followed confirmed what she'd long suspected. Finally, Brian spoke: "Maybe we did. But that doesn't mean leaving you behind was easy."

"Could've fooled me," Leah muttered, thinking of Grace's increasingly curated life—Instagram stories of Pacific sunsets and coffee shop study sessions, each post another brick in the wall between then and now.

A gentle knock interrupted her bitter thoughts, pulling her attention to the bedroom door. Kate's voice filtered through, carrying notes of concern that made Leah's throat tight with gratitude and grief. "Leah? You okay in there?"

"Go away," she managed, the words muffled against her knees as she curled tighter into herself. But even as she said it, she knew she didn't mean it—not really. Kate's presence on the other side of the door felt like the last tether to normality she had left.

"Leah, please open up. Let me in." The genuine worry in Kate's voice cracked something in Leah's carefully constructed walls. She pushed herself up from the floor, legs unsteady as she moved to unlock the door.

Kate slipped inside, her presence bringing an unfamiliar warmth to Brian's distant comfort. She didn't waste time with empty questions, just knelt beside Leah and opened her arms—an invitation to fall apart safely.

"My parents..." Leah's voice cracked around the words. "They're really done this time, Kate. It's over." Speaking it aloud made it real in a way that text messages and phone calls hadn't. The truth of it settled into her bones like a winter chill.

"I'm so sorry, Leah." Kate's voice carried the weight of genuine understanding rather than mere sympathy. She held Leah closer as silent tears tracked down both their faces. "I'm here. Whatever you need."

But beneath the comfort of Kate's embrace, Leah felt something else stirring—a dangerous spark of rebellion, a desire to break free from the suffocating weight of being the good daughter, the last one standing, the keeper of a home that no longer existed. The feeling rose in her chest like smoke, dark and intoxicating.

"What if I don't want to be strong anymore?" The words escaped before she could catch them, carrying hints of a darkness she'd never allowed herself to voice. "What if I just want to break everything apart, like they did?"

Kate pulled back slightly, searching Leah's face with growing concern. "Hey, listen to me. You're hurting right now, and that's okay. But don't let this pain make you into someone you're not."

"Maybe I want to be someone else," Leah whispered, the rebellion in her chest expanding like a storm cloud. "Maybe I'm tired of being the responsible one, the one who holds everything together while everyone else gets to fall apart."

The shadows in her room seemed to deepen as she spoke, as if responding to the darkness brewing inside her. Through her window, she could see the street where her mother's car had been parked just hours ago—now empty, like so many other spaces in her life.

Kate's grip on her shoulders tightened slightly, anchoring her to the present. "I know that feeling. But trust me, running from pain only makes it chase you faster."

Leah met her friend's steady gaze, seeing the worry there, the fear that she might splash too far into these dangerous waters. But the tide of rebellion was already rising, whispering promises of escape, of freedom from the weight of expectations and family legacy.

As they sat together in the growing darkness, Leah felt herself balanced on a knife's edge between the person she'd always been and the one she could become—the obedient daughter and the rebel, the anchor and the storm. The choice stretched before her like a forked path, each direction disappearing into shadow.

Outside, a car door slammed, the sound echoing through the quiet street like a gunshot. For a moment, Leah's heart leaped—but no, it wasn't her mother returning, wasn't her father coming home to make things right. It was just another ordinary sound on an extraordinary night, another reminder that life continued its relentless forward motion even as her world crumbled to dust.

Months later, on a rain-slicked evening that mirrored the turbulence of that fateful night, John sat in his office for the last time. The 'Miller Financial & Accounting' plaque on his desk caught the lamplight, its brass surface reflecting years of carefully built success—and the weight of secrets that had nearly destroyed everything he'd worked for. His fingers traced the edges of a manila folder, thick with documents that told the story of his silent battle.

The Castillo Group had seemed like any other client at first—a growing import-export business that had brought prestige to his firm. But four years ago, during a routine audit, John had noticed discrepancies that made his blood run cold. Hidden beneath layers of legitimate transactions lay a pattern that spoke of something darker—money moving through shadows, profits that didn't quite add up. The cartel's fingerprints, invisible to most, had become glaringly obvious to his trained eye.

He remembered the moment the truth had hit him, sitting at this very desk late one night. The numbers had danced before his eyes, each digit seeming to whisper of violence and threat. His first instinct had been to report it immediately, but then photos of his family had caught his eye—Leah's swim meet victory, Brian's graduation, Grace's artistic performances. The thought of those smiling faces twisted by fear had stayed his hand.

For four years, he'd carried that knowledge like poison in his veins. Each morning, he'd kissed Claire goodbye, swallowing guilt with his coffee. Each night, he'd checked the locks twice, three times, wondering if today would be the day someone noticed his careful documentation, his quiet cooperation with federal authorities. The weight of it had changed him, turned him into someone Claire couldn't recognize—someone who brought work stress home like a contagion, infecting their marriage with unspoken fears.

Detective Rodriguez had been his lifeline, though John couldn't tell Claire that. Their late-night meetings, which she'd suspected were affairs, had been careful strategy sessions. Every document had to be perfect, every move calculated. One wrong step could have brought disaster not just to him, but to everyone he loved.

The final raid had come three weeks after Claire left. The news had painted it as a sudden discovery, but John knew better. Years of careful preparation, of quiet cooperation with authorities, had finally paid off. The Castillo Group's empire had crumbled, and somehow, through a mixture of luck and meticulous planning, John and his family had emerged unscathed—at least physically.

Now, as he packed the last of his personal items, John felt the weight of his choices settle around his shoulders like an old coat. The firm's sale papers lay signed on his desk, a fortune in his account that felt hollow without his family to share it with. He'd protected them from the cartel's threats, yes, but in doing so, he'd lost them, anyway. The irony tasted bitter in his mouth.

His phone buzzed—a text from Leah. These days, their conversations were careful things, fragile as spider silk. She was healing, finding her way through the aftermath of their family's implosion. She didn't know the full truth yet; maybe she never would. But someday, he hoped she'd understand that every decision, every silence, had been wrapped in love—misguided perhaps, but love, nonetheless.

John stood, taking one last look at the office that had been both his pride and his prison. The rain outside painted tear tracks on the windows, nature's own commentary on the end of an era. He'd saved his family from one kind of destruction, only to watch it fracture from within. As he turned off the lights for the last time, he wondered if there had ever been a right choice, or if some situations offered only different flavors of loss.

The door clicked shut behind him with a finality that echoed through the empty corridors. Tomorrow, these halls would belong to someone else. His secrets would be packed away with his degrees and awards, and life would move forward—different, broken, but somehow still continuing. Just as it had that night when Claire had walked away, when Leah's world had shattered, when the careful facade of their perfect family had finally crumbled to reveal the fractures that had been spreading for years.

The familiar creak of the floorboards beneath his feet had whispered decades of memories as John made his way through the darkened office, each footfall stirring dust motes that danced in the wan light like displaced fragments of the past. His shoes had traced paths worn into the carpet over countless late nights and early mornings—grooves that held the invisible weight of client meetings that had built his reputation, devastating realizations that had altered the course of his life, and all the moments in between when he'd convinced himself that silence was a form of love.

The sale papers had been signed the previous week, the numbers more than generous. The buyer, a larger firm from Chicago, had been eager to acquire Miller Financial's sterling reputation and client list—what remained of it after the Castillo Group investigation. But John had known the truth: no amount of money could compensate for the weight of memories these walls held. Every corner had seemed to echo with Claire's accusations, every empty office a reminder of the secrets he'd kept in the name of protection. The conference room still held phantom traces of family celebrations—birthdays and promotions, moments when his professional and personal lives had intertwined in what he'd once thought was perfect harmony.

As he'd reached the building's entrance, John's hand had hesitated on the door handle, cool brass beneath his fingers like the countless times he'd locked up late, phone heavy in his pocket with Detective Rodriguez's warnings. Through the rain-streaked glass, he could see his reflection—grayer now, lines etched deeper around his eyes, wearing the face of a man who had won the war but lost his own peace in the process. The company had been his life's work, built from nothing but determination and Claire's unwavering support in those early years. Now it felt like a museum of his mistakes, each success shadowed by the cost of his choices.

"Sometimes," he had murmured to the empty lobby, his voice barely audible above the rain's gentle percussion against the windows, "starting over means leaving behind the things we built." The words had tasted of both truth and regret, bitter and sweet on his tongue. The divorce papers had sat in his briefcase, another ending wrapped in legal terminology and careful civility. Claire had been surprised when he'd agreed to sell the company—perhaps the first time he'd truly surprised her in years. She hadn't known that every morning, walking into this building had felt like stepping into a mausoleum of their marriage, each room holding echoes of the man he'd been before fear and duty had reshaped him.

Standing there in the growing darkness, John had allowed himself one last moment of acknowledgment. This building, these rooms, had been both his fortress and his prison. They had protected his family while simultaneously destroying the trust that had bound them together. Now, like so many things in his life, it would belong to someone else—someone unburdened by its history, someone who could see only its potential rather than its ghosts, someone who wouldn't check the shadows for threats or hear accusations in the silence.

The rain had softened to a gentle mist as John finally stepped outside, the night air cool against his face. Tomorrow, he would begin looking for a new purpose, something untainted by the shadows of his past choices. But that night, he would carry these last moments with him—a final memory of the empire he'd built and lost, a reminder that sometimes the greatest act of courage was simply letting go, even when letting go meant acknowledging that some broken things couldn't be mended, only mourned.

CHAPTER 5

New Horizons

The "Pool Closed for Maintenance" sign had mocked Leah through the pre-dawn darkness. She stood in the empty natatorium, her swim bag felt heavy on her shoulder as she stared at the still water that should have been alive with morning practice. The air had been thick with chlorine, and without the splash of swimmers and Coach Stevens' whistle, it had felt off—like a theater without actors, just a backdrop to a play that wouldn't happen.

Leah huffed out her frustration, her breath visible in the chilly air, and checked her phone. No email from Coach Stevens and no heads-up about the closure. Just another crack in her meticulously maintained routine. She swallowed her disappointment, scrolling through her calendar for missed notifications, but her screen was blank—a stark reminder of how easily plans could fall apart.

The locker room lights flickered on as she walked in, fluorescent glare bouncing off the metal lockers, making her squint. She caught her reflection in the full-length mirror, taking in the dark circles under her eyes, partly hidden by concealer. Her hair was pulled back into a perfect ponytail, and her outfit was chosen to look effortlessly put-together. Lately, the art of looking fine had become her specialty.

As Leah stood there, her phone had buzzed in the silence. She glanced at the screen, seeing her mom's name. "Can you swing by the lawyer's office after school? Need you to sign some papers."

Another buzz followed quickly from her dad: "You going over college applications tonight?"

She let out a sharp exhale. She swiped both messages away: Delete. Delete. Just breathe, she told herself, taking another deep breath to steady the rising tide of stress within her, feeling the old pressure of expectations weigh on her shoulders.

The hallways were quiet, except for the janitor cleaning up by the senior lockers. College pennants hung above her—Harvard, Yale, Stanford—dreams splashed on fabric, taunting her with their price tags. Her footsteps echoed off the metal and linoleum as she made her way to her locker.

"Well, if it isn't Little Miss Perfect."

Ashley Peters' voice dripped with malice. She leaned against the lockers, her cheerleading uniform spotless, her smile sharp. Two of her usual followers flanked her, their expressions feigned concern.

"Good morning, Ashley," Leah replied, keeping her voice steady as she focused on her combination lock. Each click reminded her of her practiced composure.

"Is it?" Ashley tilted her head like a bird of prey. "I heard it hasn't been great at your house lately. Something about some trouble with the authorities?"

Leah's fingers slipped on the lock. She gritted her teeth, willing herself to stay calm as embarrassment flushed her cheeks. In their small town, news spread like wildfire, especially about the once picture-perfect Miller family's fall from grace. She could picture Ashley's dad relished the gossip over his morning coffee.

"I don't know what you're talking about," Leah said, keeping her voice neutral while she opened the lock.

"No?" Ashley's smile widened, cruel and gleeful. "That's not what my dad says. He says your mom—"

"Your dad should probably focus on his own family." Kate's voice sliced through the tension. She appeared beside Leah, standing strong against Ashley's venom. "Especially after what happened at the country club last month."

For a second, a flicker of uncertainty crossed Ashley's face. "Whatever. Come on, girls."

The trio retreated, whispers trailing behind them. Leah let out a breath she hadn't realized she was holding, a wave of gratitude washing over her for Kate's timely rescue.

"You okay?" Kate asked, helping Leah grab her books.

"Fine," Leah replied, although the word felt brittle on her tongue.

"There's that word again," Kate said, gentle but firm. "You know you don't have to be fine, right?"

Before Leah could answer, the hallway filled with students. The morning crowd brought its usual chaos—laughter, shouts, the clatter of doors and lockers. Every voice felt amplified, every movement too sharp compared to Leah's raw vulnerability.

"We should get to Bio," Leah said, deliberately shutting her locker. "I need to ask Mrs. Hayes about the lab report."

"The one you've already redone three times?" Kate shot back, fully aware of Leah's perfectionist tendencies.

"It needs to be perfect," Leah said, her words weighed down by anxiety.

Kate sighed but followed Leah down the hall, her thoughts lingering unspoken between them. Perfect was all Leah had left. Perfect grades, perfect appearance, perfect facade. If she could keep everything immaculate, everything might eventually fall into place—or at least give the illusion it would. Perhaps she could keep pretending she didn't hear whispers, see stares, and feel her family's implosion pressing down on her shoulders with every step.

The AP Biology classroom smelled of formaldehyde and anxiety—a fitting combo for senior year. Mrs. Hayes was already at her desk, glasses perched on her nose as she graded papers with her signature red pen, a symphony of clicks marking each page. Mrs. Hayes glanced up as Leah approached, her expression softening.

"Leah, you're early again," she remarked, setting her pen aside with a gentle clatter. "The lab report revisions aren't due till next week."

"I know, but I wanted to check something about the mitochondrial function analysis—" Leah's explanation drifted off as Mrs. Hayes gestured toward a nearby stool, inviting her to pause.

"Sit down for a moment," Mrs. Hayes suggested, her tone kind but firm. "And not to discuss anything about cellular respiration."

Reluctantly, Leah perched on the edge of the stool, her perfect posture acting as a shield against whatever was coming next. Through the classroom windows, she could see Ashley and her friends in the courtyard, heads bent together in conspiratorial whispers. She pictured them cooking up more gossip about the latest chapter in the Miller family saga.

"Your last three submissions have been perfect," Mrs. Hayes said, her gaze probing into Leah's. "Every calculation, every citation, every conclusion exactly right."

"Isn't that good?" Leah countered, her voice carrying a defensive defiance that barely masked her fragility.

"Perfection can be a warning sign," Mrs. Hayes replied. "Sometimes it means we're trying to control what we can because other things feel out of control."

The sting of truth in those words caught Leah off guard, hitting home. She looked away, drawn to the DNA model's graceful spin above Mrs. Hayes' desk. Each precisely placed nucleotide seemed to click softly as it turned, a stark contrast to the noisy, hectic atmosphere. Its smooth, plastic surface felt cool under her fingertips as she reached out absentmindedly.

"I'm fine," Leah insisted, even though it felt like a lie.

"You know, the cell membrane has this cool property," Mrs. Hayes continued, as if Leah hadn't spoken. "It's selectively permeable—letting some things in and keeping others out. But if it becomes too rigid and perfect, it can actually damage the cell."

"Mrs. Hayes—"

"The art department tells me you've been spending your lunch periods in the studio," Mrs. Hayes interjected, abruptly shifting the focus and catching Leah off-guard with the unexpected turn.

"I... yeah. It's quiet there," Leah admitted, surprised at how easily this small sanctuary slipped out.

"And your paintings are extraordinary." Mrs. Hayes smiled at Leah's surprise. "Yes, I've seen them. Mrs. Chen is quite impressed."

As other students trickled into the classroom, Leah felt a small wave of relief. She quickly retreated to her usual seat, pulling out her meticulously organized notes, each page a testament to discipline. Yet, Mrs. Hayes' words echoed in her thoughts: Perfection can be a warning sign.

The morning went by in a blur of classes, each one a parade of maintained routines and strategic avoidance. Leah lingered late in classrooms, sidestepped hallways notorious for Ashley's presence, and kept her gaze downcast, focusing intently on textbooks to steer clear of pitying glances. The weight of her parents' divorce lurked like a shadow, gnawing at her concentration and forcing raw thoughts into her otherwise structured mind.

By lunchtime, Leah's muscles ached from the tension of maintaining her hypervigilant state. Instead of the bustling cafeteria, where every voice felt too loud and every glance too probing, she craved refuge in the art room, her haven from the storm of senior-year pressures.

The room enveloped her with its familiar scent of paints and clay, the afternoon sun spilling through paint-splattered windows like a blessing. Her latest work sat on an easel in the corner—an abstract piece full of sharp angles and dark spaces, with a single bright streak of gold cutting through the chaos. But even as she doodled and contemplated her work, fleeting thoughts of her parents' arguments slithered into her focus: accusations, tears, helplessness—everything that had spiraled out of control.

"Hiding out again?" Kate's voice pulled Leah back to the moment. Her best friend appeared at the doorway, a brown bag in hand.

"I'm not hiding," Leah shot back, picking up a brush, grounding herself. "Just working."

"You need to eat," Kate said, stepping closer with purpose, unpacking her bag. "Mom made extra sandwiches. She knows you skip lunch on Thursdays."

"I'm not hungry," Leah replied, her eyes glued to the canvas.

"Didn't ask if you were," Kate retorted, extending half a sandwich to Leah, refusing to take no for an answer.

Leah hesitated, then accepted the offer. The bread felt soft between her fingers. As Kate unpacked her lunch, Leah took a bite, finding solace in the simple act of eating—fuel for a weary mind and body.

The room was quiet except for their soft chewing and the distant ticking of the wall clock, marking time against the backdrop of their habitual routine. Leah added another layer of dark blue to her canvas, feeling the steady rhythm of her brushstrokes helping to calm her racing thoughts. Yet the vibration of Ashley's biting words and Mrs. Hayes' gentle warnings persisted in her subconscious, swirling together like paint on a palette.

"You know," Kate said, breaking the silence with a tone that balanced on the edge of casual and concern, "it's okay to let some of the mess show through."

"What?" Leah paused mid-stroke, the brush hovering in the air, challenged by the thought.

"In the painting. And maybe in life, too." Kate gestured toward the canvas, a tapestry of Leah's emotions overlaid with meticulous precision. "You keep covering up all the rough spots. Sometimes it's the imperfections that give it character."

Leah glanced down at her painting. The bold streaks felt stagnant, almost too rehearsed, as if she were trying to force order amid turmoil. She wanted to dismiss Kate's insight, to pretend her controlled strokes were enough to shield her from her emotional whirlwind.

But before Leah could respond, laughter spilled in from the hallway—Ashley and her crew, drawn by curiosity or malice to the open doorway.

"Oh, look, it's the charity case and her guardian angel," Ashley's voice echoed, dripping with sarcasm as she stepped into the art room, arms crossed and confident. "Wasn't this your mom's favorite hiding spot too, Leah? Before all the drama?"

Leah's heart raced as adrenaline surged through her. She opened her mouth, preparing to fire back, but the words felt elusive.

"Get out," Kate said, stepping in front of Leah, her tone fierce.

Ashley merely smirked, unwilling to back down. "I'm just showing concern. Must be rough watching your perfect family fall apart. Although, I guess it was never really perfect—just good at faking it."

Something snapped within Leah. The walls she had built around her emotions crumbled, exposing the raw vulnerability beneath. Maybe it was exhaustion from maintaining her facade, sleep deprivation, or the simmering resentment she had buried that reached a boiling point.

"You know what's interesting, Ashley?" Leah turned from her canvas, the paintbrush transforming into a weapon of her outrage. "How desperately you need other people's drama to feel important."

Ashley's smug expression faltered as annoyance sparked in her eyes. "Excuse me?"

"It must be exhausting pretending your life is perfect while dissecting everyone else's," Leah said, feeling the words spill out in a steady stream. Her voice remained controlled, a shield against the chaos. "How's your dad's 'special friendship' with his golf instructor?"

The color drained from Ashley's face, a flicker of unexpected vulnerability slicing through her facade. Behind her, joy drained from her friends as anxiety crept into their expressions.

"You don't know what you're talking about," Ashley snapped, a defensive edge entering her tone.

"No? Maybe you should ask your mom about those private lessons. The ones that always run late?"

Silence swallowed the room as Ashley's bravado crumbled. With a hasty gesture, she turned and fled, her entourage trailing in her wake, leaving behind a vacuum of shock.

"Holy shit," Kate breathed, breaking the quiet. "That was... epic."

"Terrible," Leah replied, the weight of her words sinking in. "I'm terrible."

"You're human," Kate corrected, stepping closer to squeeze Leah's shoulder. "And she had it coming."

"I'm supposed to be better than that. Perfect, Little Leah, always doing the right thing."

"Says who?" Kate's question lingered in the air, its truth undeniable.

Leah stared at her canvas again, but now the perfect strokes seemed foreign, almost deceitful. She longed for honesty, yearning to be free from the suffocating expectations that had tightened around her like a vise.

"Maybe," Leah said slowly, picking up cadmium yellow and boldly slashing it across the blues, letting the paint drip in chaotic abandon.

Kate watched as the vibrant yellow blazed on the canvas, its jagged path transforming the painting—raw, unapologetic, and beautifully flawed.

The afternoon unfolded in a blur of classes, but each moment felt heavy with Leah's internal struggle. She tried to focus on her studies, but her mind often clouded with thoughts of her parents' divorce, the tension in their home rippling through her like a storm. Cases of missed calls, silences that stretched too long, and sharp words thrown like daggers echoed in her mind. Despite the normalcy she tried to uphold at school, the emotions from home felt like unwelcome guests, demanding her attention.

The fluorescent lights in the kitchen cast hollow shadows across the scattered papers that night, each bill spread like fallen leaves across the granite countertop. Leah sat with her father, surrounded by the evidence of their life trying to hold together in Claire's absence. The empty chair at the table—her mother's chair—mocked their attempts at normalcy.

His phone buzzed, sharp and intrusive in their careful silence. She watched his face tighten as he glanced at the screen, the blue glow highlighting new lines around his eyes that seemed to deepen with each passing day.

"Richard Peters," he said, the name falling between them like a stone in still water. The phone continued its insistent vibration against the stack of unpaid statements. Leah's stomach clenched—the same Richard Peters whose daughter had tried to wound her with whispered rumors just hours before, whose golf lessons had spawned endless whispers in their small town's gossip circles.

Her father's thumb wavered over the screen before he declined the call, his jaw working silently. "Dick probably wants to discuss the club dues again." His words carried the weight of fading business alliances, of social circles drawing their boundaries in invisible ink. He ran a hand through his salt-and-pepper hair—a gesture that struck Leah with painful remembrance of earlier days, when rejection from country club circles wouldn't have mattered so much.

Understanding settled over her like an evening frost. Ashley's taunts transcended mere high school drama—they echoed their parents' world fracturing beneath polished surfaces and pressed shirts. Her own words in the art room took on new weight, heavy knowing that they'd both fought battles inherited from their parents' carefully constructed facades.

Her father cleared his throat, shuffling papers with forced purpose. "We should finish these before it gets too late," he said, his voice carrying the weariness of a man watching his carefully built world crumble, one declined phone call at a time.

Leah pulled the nearest stack closer, though the numbers blurred before her eyes. In the space where her mother's voice should have offered guidance or comfort, only the soft hum of the refrigerator and the whisper of papers shifting beneath trembling fingers filled the void.

In the following days, her grades remained high, and strangers commented on how well she handled everything, but inside, she wrestled with a heightened sense of fragility. Each swim practice felt endless, the pool a sanctuary and a prison. She would dive into the water, the coolness offering momentary relief, but the pressure of expectations loomed overhead, tugging at her relentlessly—a reminder that perfection was the only option.

One afternoon after practice, Leah changed in the locker room, feeling exhausted. Her phone had buzzed with notifications as she dressed. She glanced at the screen: texts from her parents, each layered with urgency. They didn't discuss their issues with her, but the strain in their messages was palpable, filled with polite neglect and the burden of unspoken troubles.

"Could you call your father tonight?" her mom's message read.

"Did you get my last email? We need to talk," her dad's came moments later, the coldness cutting through the usual warmth of their communication.

Ignoring them, Leah shoved her phone back in her bag and left, desperate to escape the looming discussions about finances and formalities—the facets of their lives that had become increasingly tangled and messy with divorce. She needed to find clarity, to untangle the feelings that suffocated her like a thick fog.

When she returned home, Leah's heart sank at the sight of the piles of papers strewn across the kitchen table—a visual representation of the chaos her family was grappling with. Her parents rarely shared meals together anymore, retreating into opposite corners of the house, their conversations dwindling to exchanges about responsibilities, schedules, and hollow comments about the kids.

"Hey," Leah mumbled as she coasted through the kitchen, trying to ignore their mounting tensions.

"Hi, sweetie," her mom replied vaguely, not looking up from the papers. Her voice sounded tired, fingers skimming the documents with practiced detachment.

"Everything okay?" Leah asked, heart racing as silence filled the space between them.

Her mom sighed, glancing up for a moment. "Just trying to get things sorted."

Leah turned away, the tightness in her throat growing. She wanted to reach out, to break through the static, but what could she say? She was battling her own storm. Pushing back her feelings, she retreated to her room, where the walls felt less confining and more like a canvas upon which she could express herself freely.

Later that night, Leah faced her easel, letting her frustrations flow through the paintbrush. She allowed dark colors to collide with bursts of brightness, mixing her emotions onto the canvas like a cathartic release. Each brushstroke felt like a rebellion against feeling trapped by her parents' decisions, a refusal to carry the weight of their divorce entirely on her shoulders.

After a while, Kate texted, breaking Leah's focus.

Kate: "Want to hit the studio tomorrow? I've got an idea! We can bring in some new themes."

Leah smiled involuntarily. Kate's energy was always infectious—a much-needed respite from her reality.

Leah replied: "Sounds great! I need a distraction."

But even as she typed, Leah felt the nagging voice in the back of her head, reminding her that no amount of art could pull her away from the mess at home.

The following day, while Leah and Kate worked in the art studio, the lingering thoughts of her family loomed like wisps of smoke, curling around the edges of her consciousness. Afternoon light spilled through the paint-splattered windows, casting warm patterns across their canvases as they worked side by side, comfortable in their shared silence until Kate noticed the distant look in Leah's eyes.

"You can talk to me, you know," Kate said softly, setting down her brush. "About whatever's weighing on you."

Leah's hand trembled slightly as she added another layer of dark blue to her canvas. "I keep trying to act like everything's fine, but it's getting harder. My mind's always racing with what's happening at home."

"You don't have to keep pretending," Kate whispered, her voice gentle but firm. "It's okay to not have it all figured out."

"But what if I stop being perfect?" Leah's voice cracked slightly. "What happens then? What if I fail?"

Kate moved closer, her presence steady and grounding. "Look at this piece you've created," she gestured to Leah's canvas, where swirls of dark reds blended into softer blues, streaks of bright yellow cutting through the chaos. "It's beautiful because it's real. You're pouring everything you feel into it."

"I know that," Leah replied, her voice barely audible. "But even art isn't perfect. Some days, I'm just so tired of pretending everything is okay."

Kate pulled Leah into a warm embrace, steady and sure. "You don't have to pretend with me. We can figure this out together."

Something inside Leah softened at Kate's words, a mix of relief and vulnerability washed over her. For the rest of the afternoon, they poured their emotions into their canvases, allowing the chaotic strokes and splattered colors to mirror the complexity of their feelings. As they worked, Leah felt the tension slowly unfurl from her shoulders, replaced by the quiet comfort of friendship and understanding.

Over the following weeks, Leah leaned into her art as an escape from the pressures of her life. Each day brought its own struggles with her family situation, but she found solace in painting, swimming, and Kate's unwavering support. Their friendship became a sanctuary that helped her navigate the uncertainty swirling at home, one brushstroke at a time.

As Leah tackled her homework with determined focus and continued to excel in swimming, the tension in her family life lingered like a stubborn shadow. Yet amid the chaos, a flicker of excitement ignited whenever she received a message from Ryan.

One afternoon, while Leah sat in the library studying for a calculus test, her phone buzzed, pulling her attention away from her notes. It was Ryan.

Ryan: "Hey! Just wanted to check in. How's the studying going?"

Leah couldn't help but smile, feeling warmth wash over her. She quickly typed back:

Leah: "Hey! Not too bad, just stuck on a couple of problems. How about you?"

Ryan: "Same here. Calculus is giving me a run for my money. Want to compare notes later?"

Leah felt a surge of happiness at the thought of working together.

Leah: "Sure! I could use some extra muscle on this. How about the cafeteria after school?"

Ryan: "Sounds perfect! I'll bring snacks—can't study on an empty stomach!"

As the school day wound down, Leah felt both excitement and nervousness. Meeting Ryan outside their usual routine sent butterflies fluttering in her stomach, making her feel lighter. In the cafeteria, she found him already waiting, looking at ease with a plate of cookies and a giant bag of chips.

"You're such a nerd," Leah joked, a grin breaking across her face as she slid into the seat across from him.

"Hey, if I'm a nerd, then I'll take that badge proudly. Snack nerds unite!" Ryan shot back, breaking out a cookie and offering it to her. "Plus, cookies are essential study fuel."

Leah took the cookie, appreciating not just the sweetness of the treat, but the growing rapport between them. As they compared calculus problems, their conversation shifted from numbers to more personal matters.

"So, how are things at home?" Ryan asked, lowering his voice as he noted the strain in Leah's demeanor.

Leah took a steadying breath, grateful for his concern, yet hesitant to dive into the realities of her family dynamics. "You know, it's... complicated. My parents are still navigating that whole mess. It's weird being the one who's supposed to comfort them while grappling with my own feelings about it all."

Ryan nodded, his expression softening. "That sounds tough. If you ever need to talk about it, I'm here for you."

A hint of warmth spread through Leah, knowing that Ryan genuinely cared. "Thanks, Ryan. It helps to talk to you about it.

Honestly, I feel pretty overwhelmed sometimes, but I'm trying to focus on the things I love—like art and swimming."

"That's the spirit," Ryan encouraged, leaning in. "Pour that energy into your art. I can't wait to see what you come up with for the showcase!"

As they continued their study session, mixing calculus with shared laughter, Leah felt a sense of relief washing over her. Each moment spent with Ryan felt like a step toward brighter days, a reminder that she wasn't alone in her struggles.

Later that week, they ran into each other at the school's spring sports exhibition. Leah was bustling around, checking in on the swim team, when she caught sight of Ryan chatting with some classmates by the bleachers. His smile lit up the room as he gestured animatedly, and for a moment, she paused, feeling an inexplicable warmth wrap around her.

"Hey!" Leah called as she approached him, her heart racing. "You made it!"

"Of course! I wouldn't miss the chance to see my favorite teammates in action." He flashed her that dimpled smile that made her stomach flip.

"Just wait until you see us dominate the competition!" Leah teased, her confidence surging at his encouragement.

When the swim team took to the pool for their exhibition glide-through, Leah felt the familiar thrill of adrenaline rushing through her veins. The cheering crowd, combined with Ryan's supportive presence, ignited a spark of determination within her. After the event, as teammates celebrated their efforts, Leah approached Ryan again.

"Thanks for coming to support us! It means a lot," she said, her voice warm and genuine.

Ryan grinned, his eyes sparkling. "I love to see you in your element. You were amazing out there!"

Leah felt a rush of pride at his words, her cheeks flushing. "Thanks! Hopefully, I can keep that energy going for the championships next week. I'm nervous about those."

"You've got this," Ryan said, stepping closer. "You're a powerhouse, Leah. Just think about all the hard work you've put in. When you dive into that water, it'll be just you and your determination."

"Right," Leah replied, feeling the fire of his encouragement light up her spirit. "I really appreciate you being there to cheer me on. It means a lot to have someone in my corner."

Their connection felt electric as they stood there, the chatter of their peers fading into the background, and Leah thought about how seamlessly Ryan had woven himself into her life.

"I'm with you every step of the way," he promised, sincerity ringing through his voice. "And afterwards? We need to celebrate these swim meets properly! Ice cream and a movie marathon?"

"Deal!" Leah exclaimed, excitement bubbling within her. They shared another warm smile, and as they exchanged playful banter, the warmth surrounding them felt unguarded and real.

After the sports exhibition, Leah found comfort in their dynamic. While she sometimes fell back into anxious thoughts, she was always buoyed by Ryan's unwavering support.

Throughout the week leading up to the championships, their text messages became a lifeline, homework questions naturally morphing into heartfelt check-ins.

Ryan: "Hey, how's the undercurrents treating you today? Ready to make waves at the meet?"

Leah: "Just trying to keep my head above water! Feeling the pressure, but I'll be good. How are the engineering designs coming along?"

Ryan: "All systems go! Just finished my prototype, thank goodness. Can't wait to show you!"

Leah felt a swell of pride as she glimpsed what Ryan was passionate about. "I'm excited to see it! Maybe this weekend we can catch up on both swimming and engineering?"

As the championship meet approached, Leah's nerves were palpable—but so was the sense of camaraderie surrounding her, strengthened by knowing Ryan would be present.

Finally, the day of the competition arrived, and Leah felt a mixture of excitement and dread coursing through her veins as she made her way to the pool. The vibrant energy of the crowd filled the air, just as the distinct scent of chlorine hit her nostrils.

Ryan had promised to find her in the stands, and as she scanned the area, her heart swelled at the sight of him near the front row, waving enthusiastically despite the bustling crowd. His smile cut through her nerves like a beacon, grounding her amidst the chaos.

"Hey, you!" he called out, his enthusiasm infectious. Leah felt her heart rate steady as she approached him, practicing the breathing techniques they had discussed during their study sessions.

"You made it!" Leah exclaimed, her voice lifting with genuine happiness. Once they were close enough, Ryan grabbed her hand, squeezing it reassuringly as if to lend her strength.

"Wouldn't miss it for the world," he replied, sincerity shining in his eyes. "You are going to crush it today."

"I hope so," Leah said, her voice a tad shaky despite the confidence she wanted to portray. "Just a little nervous."

Ryan stepped closer, warmth radiating comfort as he leaned in to speak. "Just remember all the hard work you've put in. When you dive in, it's just you and the water, remember? Embrace the moment."

Leah could feel his unwavering support, and she breathed in the moment, letting energy surge back into her. The surrounding air buzzed with anticipation while the announcer called the starting line-ups.

"Alright, I'm gonna head up to the bleachers before it starts," Ryan said, releasing her hand, but the warmth lingered. "Hold on to that positive vibe. I'll be right here cheering for you!"

"Thanks, Ryan—seriously," Leah said, feeling grateful as she turned back toward the pool. The sound of splashing water and cheering spectators rang in the air, and she could feel adrenaline pulsing through her veins.

As Leah positioned herself on the starting block, she surveyed the pool, the blue surface shimmering under the bright lights. She focused, tuning out the noise around her as they counted down. The memories of training, the laughter shared with Ryan, and the support of her friends fueled her determination.

The sound of the starting gun shot through the air, breaking the silence. Leah dove into the water, the cool embrace enveloping her as she kicked off in a blur of strokes, breaking through the surface, focused and determined.

After what seemed like a whirlwind of seconds, she surged toward the finish line, adrenaline coursing through her, propelling her like a comet through the water. She could hear Ryan's voice cutting through the din of the crowd, offering encouragement as she pushed herself harder.

When Leah touched the wall, she emerged from the water gasping for air, exhilaration coursing through her. The sound of clapping and cheers filled her ears, blending with her racing heartbeat as she looked up at the timer. A personal best!

"YES!" she shouted, excitement bubbling up uncontrollably. The mixed emotions swirled inside her, a heady mixture of relief and joy sweeping over her like the waves she had just conquered.

Amid the congratulatory shouts from her teammates, Leah turned her gaze to the stands and caught sight of Ryan jumping up and down, his face a canvas of pride. She felt an electric connection as their eyes met; his enthusiasm ignited something deep inside her—a sense of belonging and comfort that she desperately craved.

After the meet, Leah had a flurry of hugs and congratulations from her teammates, gripping her towel tightly. "You crushed it, Leah! We all knew you could do it!" Kate exclaimed, pulling her into a bear hug that nearly squeezed the breath from her lungs.

"Thanks! I couldn't have done it without all of you!" Leah replied, beaming as she accepted high-fives and encouragement, but her heart surged as she looked for Ryan amidst the crowd.

Soon enough, he wove his way through the excitement to pull her into a hug, lifting her off her feet for a moment. "I told you! You were amazing!" Ryan exclaimed, his voice ringing with excitement.

"Thanks! I can't believe I did it!" Leah laughed, a giddy rush overtaking her. "I've never felt like this before!"

Ryan pulled back, gripping her shoulders with a proud smile. "I knew you could do it. You've worked so hard, and I'm glad I could be there for you."

As the swim season culminated in a whirlwind of competitions, Leah brought home several medals, each one a reminder of her hard work and dedication. Despite the tumult at home, she felt proud of herself—proud that she had made it this far.

But it wasn't just swimming that signified her resilience; it was art. She felt the emotional weight of her experiences manifest in her final projects. Each piece she created for the spring showcase told a different story—of heartache, healing, and hope. They captured the messy beauty of her journey, and for the first time, she was ready to share all of it with the world.

CHAPTER 6

Caps and Gowns

The bathroom mirror showed two Leah Millers—the perfect student in her shiny grad gown and the scared little girl hiding under all that polyester. She adjusted her honors cords for the tenth time, the gold tassels catching the fluorescent light like trophies for her academic wins. But the reflection that stared back felt fractured, like a cool mask over an anxious heart struggling to chill out.

"If you keep messing with those cords, they're gonna hug you tighter than your mom before we even get our diplomas," Kate's voice cut through Leah's doubts, and she found comfort in her friend's teasing grin.

"Right? Sorry," Leah's hands dropped, embarrassed for trying to be perfect. The weight of everyone's expectations was heavy, pulling her down. "Just trying to make everything—"

"Perfect?" Kate jumped in, her smile remained bright but with concern. The medals around her neck for being valedictorian had sparkled, but Leah could see the nerves lurking under her confidence.

They stood shoulder to shoulder, blue-robed figures in the empty bathroom, buoyed by friendship while holding onto their worries. Outside, the world buzzed with energy—parents grabbing seats, siblings calling each other out, and the distant sounds of the band warming up with those familiar notes of "Pomp and Circumstance."

"Hey, let me pin your cap," Kate said, turning Leah to face her in the mirror.

The familiar routine seemed almost sacred as Kate's steady hands adjusted Leah's cap, getting it just right for the cameras outside. Leah closed her eyes for a moment, soaking in the warmth of Kate's support.

"There you go." Kate stepped back and admired her work. "Now, you do mine."

As Leah reached to pin Kate's cap, her friend grabbed her wrist. "Wait! I gotta tell you something," she said.

"Okay..." Leah kept pinning, her stomach fluttering with nerves.

"So, my speech... I borrowed some inspiration from this year. From you," Kate revealed, locking eyes with Leah in the small mirror.

Leah's heart raced. "What do you mean?"

"I mean," Kate went on, her voice steady but eyes flickering with uncertainty, "that some of the best lessons on strength come from watching you tackle the impossible."

"Kate—"

"I didn't say names," Kate explained. "But I needed people to know. For them to see that true strength isn't about being perfect. It's about being flawed and getting back up."

Those words hit Leah hard, almost making her tear up and ruin her makeup. "You didn't have to—"

"Yes, I did," Kate insisted, squeezing Leah's hands. "You're my best friend. Your story matters. Somebody out there needs to know they're not alone."

Just then, a knock at the door shattered the moment. "Five minutes, ladies!" Mrs. Hayes called, her voice a sharp reminder of the ceremony coming up.

They did one last mirror check—caps straight, gowns smooth, emotions barely kept in check. Kate whipped out her phone for a pre-grad selfie, capturing a moment they had dreamed of.

"Ready?" she asked, tucking away her phone with a determined smile.

"Ready," Leah echoed, though her stomach twisted with anticipation.

The hallway became a sea of blue gowns and nervous energy as they joined their classmates. Through the glass doors, Leah saw the football field, now a sea of white chairs, vibrant flowers adorning the stage, and the proud parents filling the bleachers, their murmurs a soft hum.

Her gaze landed on her dad first, sitting stiffly in his expensive suit, checking his phone despite the principal's request to silence all devices. Three rows back, her mom sat with Grace and Brian, laughs spilling easily as they joked about something ridiculous.

"Your mom looks nice," Kate said, leaning toward Leah.

"Yeah." Leah's heart twisted as she saw Claire lean in closer to Grace, laughed like nothing was wrong.

As Leah walked down the center aisle, she pushed back against the weight of every gaze. She raised her chin, remembering her mom's insistence about posture. To her left, the Andersons waved enthusiastically; Tom had his camera out like he was ready for war, capturing every moment.

"Look at the crowd!" Kate said, excitement bubbling in her voice. "They're all here for us!"

Leah stepped forward, adrenaline pumping through her.

Every sign of support felt like an anchor reminding her that while uncertainty loomed at home, this was a celebration—recognizing all of her and her classmates' hard work.

The sun hung low, casting a warm glow over the field as they approached the stage. Leah felt her heart race; each step amplified the swirling thoughts in her head about family, art, and the uncertain road ahead.

When Kate's name was called, she took a deep breath and walked across the stage, shaking hands with Principal Roberts before facing the crowd. For a moment, the world shrank to the blinking camera lights, hushed whispers riding the wind, and the familiar faces she loved.

"Hey, everyone," Kate started, her voice steady despite the jumble of feelings inside. She had practiced for this moment, but standing in front of everyone made her feel exposed—all her fears and hopes tangled together. "I'm Kate Anderson, and I'm proud to be part of this graduating class."

As she spoke, Kate reflected on all the shared moments with her classmates—the sleepless nights, peals of laughter, and quiet reflective times. "But today isn't just about marking our wins. It's also about recognizing that we've all faced struggles, each on our own journeys."

The audience remained silent, rapt, as she pressed on. "We've juggled responsibilities, managed expectations, and confronted fears. And while we've chased perfection—whether through grades, sports, or our own images—it's okay to trip and fall. It's okay to be imperfect."

Kate felt some of the tension in her chest release; the words flowed freely, like water from a fountain. "This past year has shown me that true strength isn't about being perfect. It's about having the courage to stand back up after you fall. It's about trusting ourselves enough to share what we're struggling with, especially with those we love."

Scanning the crowd, Kate caught sight of Leah and smiled, seeing her best friend beaming with pride. "And sometimes, we need the support of friends and family to remind us we're not alone during tough times," she said, subtly pointing to Leah as a source of inspiration. "To recognize we're more than just grades or appearances, but individuals who bring light into each other's lives. It's those connections that help us find strength."

As those words hung in the air, Kate felt the weight lift off her shoulders, becoming lighter with every note of unity she spoke. A spark of hope ignited inside her, lighting a path she hadn't seen before.

"As we step into this new chapter, let's carry with us our dignity and the stories that bind us. Let's celebrate being perfectly imperfect and make connections based on authenticity rather than expectation."

With her speech ending, Kate stepped back and was met with thunderous applause—each clap resonating within her as she returned to her seat beside Leah, her heart soaring. Every cheer reminded her of the transformation they had all undergone together.

Once the ceremony wrapped up with heartfelt speeches and memories shared, Leah felt pumped to embrace this next phase. With Kate by her side, shoulders bumping in playful camaraderie, she knew their paths would intertwine with laughter, love, and powerful honesty.

The graduation caps flew into the air, carrying dreams, determination, and promises for the future. As Leah gazed upward, she felt the weight of her worries slip away, replaced by excitement for what lay ahead—a blank canvas waiting for her story.

Through the swirl of falling caps and rising cheers, Leah spotted the Peters family near the refreshment table. Mr. Peters stood slightly apart, his attention fixed on his phone's blue glow, mirroring the same restless energy that had haunted her father. Mrs. Peters maintained her picture-perfect smile, though it cracked at the edges like old varnish. And Ashley—Ashley stood between them, her graduation gown hanging pristine and pressed, a final armor against the world that had never quite bent to her will the way it seemed to for Leah.

Their eyes met across the celebration's chaos, and Leah felt time slow, the space between them heavy with years of misplaced rivalry. The familiar spark of hostility in Ashley's eyes had dimmed, replaced by something that looked almost like exhaustion—the kind that came from running a race you could never win. In her carefully composed features, Leah recognized the same desperate chase for perfection that had haunted her own reflection countless mornings, though Ashley had never known about Leah's silent battles, the sleepless nights, the weight of expectations that made each effortless-looking achievement feel like lifting mountains.

Ashley's gaze held a flicker of something new—not quite understanding, but perhaps a grudging recognition that they'd been more alike than different, both daughters drowning in their parents' expectations, both trying to stay afloat in the choppy waters of small-town success. The difference lay not in their struggles, but in how they'd chosen to weather them: Leah behind a mask of serenity, Ashley behind a shield of sharp words and sharper ambitions.

Their shared look lasted only seconds, but it carried the weight of every competition Ashley had lost, every achievement she'd watched Leah claim, every bitter word she'd wielded like a weapon against what she'd perceived as effortless grace. Ashley's slight nod, when it came, felt less like surrender and more like exhausted acknowledgment—that perhaps they'd both been fighting battles no one could really win.

As Ashley turned away, disappearing into the crowd of celebrating families, Leah felt the last threads of their antagonism dissolve into the warm afternoon air. Their war had always been one-sided, fueled by Ashley's perception of Leah's perfection rather than the messy reality that lay beneath.

"Everything okay?" Kate appeared at her side, her valedictorian medals catching the sun as she adjusted her cap, eyes bright with the concern that came from years of shared secrets and silent understanding.

"Yeah," Leah replied, surprised by the truth that nestled in her chest like a bird finding its way home. "Just saying goodbye to old ghosts." She smiled, feeling lighter as another chapter closed behind her. Some battles weren't worth carrying forward, especially those born from misunderstanding and the desperate need to prove oneself in a world that demanded perfection from its daughters.

As they made their way through the buzzing crowd, Leah felt the electric energy in the air. Students clapping backs, parents glowing with pride, and the delightful smells of grilled food from nearby stands filled her with joy.

"Leah! Over here!" Tom Anderson called as they approached the Anderson crew, still bursting with excitement. Tom's grin was wide as Susan stood beside him, her eyes sparkling with pride.

"Congrats, Leah!" Susan beamed, wrapping Leah in a warm hug.

"Thanks, Mrs. Anderson." Leah replied, grateful for their unwavering support. She glanced at Kate, who was busy chatting animatedly with her parents, excitement spilling over the conversation.

As the sun set on the picnic festivities and families shared laughter, Leah felt a flutter of anticipation. Everyone seemed engrossed in their conversations, and she noticed Ryan lingering nearby, looking more serious than usual. She felt a mix of excitement and nerves as he caught her gaze, a shy smile breaking across his face.

"Hey, Leah," Ryan said, casually moving closer as he held a plate of food. "Can we talk for a sec?"

Leah's heart raced at the sudden attention. "Yeah, sure! What's up?"

Ryan glanced around to make sure they had a moment alone, then leaned in closer, his expression shifting to one of determination. "I was just thinking about the fun we had at the beach last week. I enjoyed our time together—and I'd like to take you out for ice cream sometime. Just the two of us."

Leah's heart fluttered, surprise mingling with delight as she processed his words. "You mean, like a date?"

Ryan's cheeks flushed, but he held her gaze. "Nothing too fancy, just us hanging out. You know, more of those conversations we had."

Leah felt a smile spread across her face. "I'd love that!"

"Really? Awesome!" Ryan exclaimed, clearly relieved. "Let's look at our schedules and pick a day. I promise I'm a fun date—no pressure or anything!"

As they shared their first blush of excitement, Kate's voice chimed in from a few paces away. "What's going on over here, lovebirds?" She had that teasing sparkle in her eyes, which only made Leah laugh even harder.

Leah felt her cheeks heat up. "Nothing! Just talking about... ice cream!"

Kate raised an eyebrow. "Ice cream? Is that code for a first date? Because it totally sounds like code for a first date!"

Ryan grinned at Leah, his eyes twinkling with mischief. "I might have been working up the courage to ask."

"Well, a round of applause for Ryan for finally making his move!" Kate clapped her hands, drawing amused looks from nearby family members. "I'm so thrilled for you both!"

Leah felt the warmth of Kate's enthusiasm wrap around her. A rush of affirmation encouraged her excitement. "Thanks, Kate! I didn't know you were such a cheerleader."

"And you know it," Kate replied, winking. "Now, can we discuss what you're going to wear on your first date? You have to look fabulous—no pressure, though!"

Ryan chuckled at their playful banter. "No pressure whatsoever," he said, smirking at Leah. "Just ice cream and your fabulous self."

Leah's heart swelled at the casual ease they shared as she looked back at Ryan. "I'll make sure it's something special."

"As long as you don't turn into an ice cream cone yourself," Kate teased, her eyes sparkling with mischief. "That would be the ultimate fashion statement—Leah, the edible sundress."

"Kate!" Leah laughed, shaking her head. "You're impossible."

Their playful dynamic felt comforting, allowing Leah to embrace the excitement of her new relationship with Ryan amidst the chaos of family celebrations. Ryan's smile was infectious, and with Kate's enthusiastic support, the atmosphere felt ripe with potential and joy, setting the perfect foundation for their budding romance.

"Okay, enough about fashion," Ryan said, stepping back with a mock-serious look. "Shall we get back to enjoying that delicious food before it disappears?"

Leah grinned widely, feeling lighter at the thought of the impending feast. "Totally! We need to get some now before Marcus finishes it all!"

"Lead the way, Leah," Ryan said, determination in his tone as they made their way side by side toward the food table.

With each step, Leah felt her excitement bloom. Ice cream and pizza aside, this was the beginning of something special—a new adventure unfolding as they embraced the uncertain, thrilling path ahead of them.

As they moved closer to the food stalls set up for the celebration, Leah's stomach grumbled, responding eagerly to the delicious smells wafting through the air. "What's the move? Pizza or nachos?" she asked, glancing at Kate, who was already scoping out the options.

"Pizza! But only if we order enough to last through our next week-long movie marathons," Kate declared, giving Leah a playful nudge. "Let's start a tradition!"

"Agreed!" Leah laughed, her earlier tension washing away with each passing moment. She peeked back at her parents, who were still in a quiet conversation. The change in the surrounding atmosphere was almost palpable—a chill in her dad's demeanor and a softness in her mom's eyes.

Ryan joined them, sliding up beside Leah with a bright smile. "Did someone say pizza?"

"Yes!" Kate exclaimed, her eyes lighting up as she welcomed Ryan into the conversation. "We're planning a feast!"

"I'm all in," Ryan said, glancing at Leah. "What's your favorite topping? Because I'm about to represent Team Pizza here."

Leah felt a smile tug at her lips. "I'm a pepperoni gal, but I'm open to suggestions."

"Pepperoni it is, then!" Ryan declared, nudging Leah as they stepped toward the pizza stand. "But we better get some with extra cheese. You can never go wrong with cheese."

All around them, families dove into laughter and stories, soaking up the moment as young lives began their bright futures. Leah's hope flickered with each cheer and clap, a reminder that resilience was key, even amidst adversity.

When it came time to chow down, they all gathered around a gigantic table draped in a red and white checkered tablecloth—the classic picnic vibe like something out of a movie. Leah felt like it didn't matter how many slices she had; all she needed to focus on were the memories they were making.

Tom started slicing the pizza into huge portions, and the towering stacks of food vanished before they even hit the table. Leah helped herself to a slice, feeling a surge of camaraderie as they shared stories and jokes that filled the air with echoes of happiness.

"Okay, okay! Let's do a toast!" Kate shouted, trying to rise above the chatter. "Here's to us! To fresh starts and messy lives! May we always make time for laughter and a little imperfection!"

A rush of warmth spread through Leah as they raised their cups. At that moment, she felt free. Together, they embraced the imperfect moments ahead—college, messy family dynamics, and the unpredictable paths they would take.

As the evening spiraled into light banter, Leah caught sight of her family from a distance. Claire was deep in conversation with Grace, while John seemed to listen intently. The charged air around them felt softer in the golden glow of the setting sun. Leah noticed her dad nodding thoughtfully; his expression was less defensive this time. Maybe they were wrapping their heads around everything that had happened.

With every minute, the warmth of the community wrapped around Leah like a cozy blanket. Laughter erupted as Marcus made a goofy pizza impression, parodying a famous food commercial. Leah took a moment to appreciate the swirl of emotions around her, realizing how beautiful gatherings like this could be—the tangible joy, cherished memories, and laughter filling the spaces where silence used to be.

A sudden nudge at Leah's side startled her; something soft and furry brushed against her. She turned to see Kate holding up her phone, winking at her while making an exaggerated gesture toward the group. "Selfie time! We gotta capture this moment!" Kate exclaimed, taking center stage at the table, her energy contagious.

"Ready?" Leah said, a soft smile breaking through as she scooted in closer.

"Wait! Here's the plan—we need a dramatic pose—something creative and eye-catching!" Kate shouted, flapping her arms dramatically.

As Leah grinned and struck a goofy pose, the moment felt like an emblem of their shared journey—a reminder that life didn't have to be perfect to be meaningful.

"Got it!" Kate exclaimed, the sound of her laughter punctuating the click of her camera.

After scrolling through the photo, Kate burst into more giggles. "Oh wow, this is gold! Look at us—we look ridiculous!"

"Okay, I'll admit my hair was wild," Leah said as she tried to smooth it down.

"Who cares? It's just a snapshot of us being us!" Kate replied, her voice thick with enthusiasm. "And it's perfect—you should celebrate that!"

Their playful dynamic felt comforting, allowing Leah to embrace the excitement of her budding romance with Ryan amidst the chaos of family celebrations. Ryan's smile was infectious—he could light up any room. With Kate's enthusiastic support, the atmosphere felt ripe with potential and joy, setting the perfect foundation for Leah and Ryan's relationship.

As the food settled, Leah caught a glimpse of Ryan across the crowd. He was laughing and sharing a joke with some friends, and she couldn't help but grin. Their chemistry was undeniable, and every moment spent with him felt like an adventure waiting to unfold.

After some time, Ryan made his way over to Leah and Kate, his eyes bright with excitement. "What did I miss?" he asked, feigning ignorance. "Just a game of 'who can embarrass themselves the most'?"

Kate chuckled while Leah felt a rush of warmth at Ryan's approach. "Oh, you know, we were just sharing the latest gossip about graduation drama," she said with a smirk.

Ryan raised an eyebrow, leaning in closer. "Is it about the legendary Balloon Incident? Because I need in on that."

"Not yet, but you should dig into the high school archives," Kate teased. "What are you doing here anyway? I thought you had like, a billion things to handle as chief engineer of the universe."

Ryan shrugged, unfazed. "It can wait. Watching you two party is much more important."

"Aw, what a charmer!" Leah teased, nudging him. "But you better step it up later; we can't let you off too easily!"

As the celebration continued, Leah felt her heart fluttering at the idea of Ryan being around in the days to come. They exchanged banter and laughter, adding to the joy of the moment.

The night unfolded with playful challenges, where they raced to see who could build the tallest cookie tower—a hilarious endeavor that resulted in crumbs dusting everyone involved. Laughter filled the air, and Leah felt a sense of belonging she had craved for so long.

Later on, when they gathered around a bonfire for s'mores, Leah caught Ryan's eye from across the flames. He smiled, that genuine, infectious grin that made everything else fade away.

"You know," Leah began, her voice rising above the crackling fire, "I can't remember the last time I had this much fun. It feels like we've really clicked."

Ryan leaned closer, tossing a marshmallow onto his stick and keeping his gaze steady on her. "I know what you mean. I wasn't sure how this summer would go, but hanging out with you has been the highlight."

Leah felt a warmth spread through her at his words. "Same here. You're easy to be around."

As the fire flickered, they fell into a comfortable silence, the warmth wrapping around them like a cozy blanket. Leah thought about what Kate had said about embracing imperfection—how freedom lay in letting go of the need to be perfect and just being real.

Ryan turned toward her, a thoughtful look in his eyes. "Hey, can I ask you something?"

"Sure," Leah replied, a flicker of curiosity dancing in her chest.

"What's your biggest dream? Like, if you could do anything without worrying about what others thought—what would it be?"

Leah paused, her heart racing at his question. For so long, she had only focused on expectations—on grades and on becoming a doctor. But Ryan's sincere curiosity opened up a path to something deeper. "Honestly? My ultimate dream is to become a doctor. I love the idea of saving lives and putting others first. That's what truly brings me joy."

"That sounds incredible," Ryan replied, his eyes brightening. "You should totally pursue that. You have the passion and dedication to make it happen."

Leah felt a rush of gratitude. "Thanks! It's just hard to break away from everyone's expectations. But maybe this summer, while we're both figuring out who we really are, I can find a way to embrace that dream."

Ryan smiled, his expression earnest. "I believe in you. You don't have to fit into anyone else's mold. You can create your own path, and I'll be right there cheering you on."

Their connection deepened in that moment, and Leah felt as if they were forging a bond that could withstand the challenges ahead. "You're really inspiring, you know that?" Leah replied, her voice softening as she felt the weight of his words. "I hope I can find that kind of courage to be true to myself without all the noise."

"We'll figure it out together," Ryan said, squeezing her hand reassuringly. As the fire crackled, sending sparks soaring into the night sky, Leah felt something shift within her—a resolve to embrace who she really was, imperfections and all.

As the evening wore on and the laughter continued, Ryan leaned closer, a mischievous grin on his face. "So, what's next for us? More adventures, or perhaps we dive into the art scene you're so passionate about?"

Leah felt a surge of excitement at the prospect of sharing her art with Ryan. "Actually, I was thinking about planning a group art day where we could invite some friends to come paint by the lake. It's such a relaxing spot, and I would love to showcase my work!"

Ryan's eyes sparkled with enthusiasm. "That sounds amazing! Count me in! I could use a break from studying, and I want to see how talented you really are."

The thought of Ryan experiencing her creative side gave Leah butterflies. "I'd love that! It'll be fun to share that experience with you."

As they wrapped up the night, feeling the warmth of camaraderie and connection, Leah couldn't help but look forward to what the summer would bring. With their friendship blossoming, she wanted to explore not just her dreams, but also take a leap toward something more meaningful with Ryan.

"Ready to head back?" Leah suggested as the evening settled into a warm, friendly calm.

"Yeah. Let's go celebrate!" Kate chirped, linking her arm with Leah's as they navigated their way through the crowd, a festive spirit alive around them.

They found their families mingling, the joyful atmosphere wrapping them in a cozy embrace. Together, with laughter still echoing, they stepped forward into the bright promise of tomorrow—a new beginning waiting to unfold, one imperfect adventure at a time.

CHAPTER 7

Summer of Change

The sundress had lain on Leah's bed like a question mark—yellow cotton with tiny white flowers, just right for a first date, but cute enough to show she cared. Kate lounged next to it, cross-legged, and watched Leah cycle through the outfit combos with growing frustration.

"Seriously, the sundress is perfect," Kate said for the third time, her voice a mix of encouragement and impatience.

"You're overthinking this."

"I'm not overthinking," Leah shot back, holding up dark jeans and a blue top. "I just wanna look..."

"Perfect?" Kate raised an eyebrow, aiming for a laugh. "What happened to embracing the messiness?"

Leah dropped the jeans with a sigh, letting them land in a heap. "This is different."

"Ryan Matthews," Kate chimed in, and just hearing his name made Leah's heart do a little flip. She forced a smile, but butterflies kicked up in her stomach. "The guy you've had a crush on since forever."

"Come on, I have not—" Leah protested, but Kate wasn't having it.

"Please." Kate flopped back on the bed dramatically. "You turned red every time he walked by in AP History."

That memory made Leah smile despite the nerves. Ryan was two rows ahead—his dark hair always messy, thoughtful with his answers. She spent ages pretending not to notice him while soaking in all the little things—like how he tapped his pen when he was deep in thought or how his smile tilted to the left, and his laugh during group chats was pure gold.

"The sundress," Kate decided, standing up like it was settled. "With your silver sandals and that bracelet I got you for Christmas."

"Are you sure it's not too—"

A knock at the door interrupted them. Grace leaned against the doorframe, amused.

"Mom wants to know why there's a fashion show going on in here." She glanced around at the clothes strewn everywhere. "Ah, the big date."

"It's not big," Leah protested, wringing her hands, nerves bubbling up. "It's just ice cream."

"Sure, with Ryan Matthews." Grace rolled her eyes, half-smirking but also protective. "Mr. Perfect, himself."

"What's that supposed to mean?" Leah shot back, trying to shake off the creeping sense of inadequacy.

"Nothing." Grace shrugged, but she lingered, her expression a mix of mischief and caution. "Just... be careful, yeah?"

Before Leah could respond, their mom's cheerful voice floated up from downstairs, laced with urgency. "Leah? Ryan's here!"

Oh God. Leah felt her stomach drop. She turned to Kate, who was already nudging her toward the door, adjusting the straps on Leah's sundress.

"Go! You got this!"

With a deep breath, Leah stepped into the foyer, where Ryan stood waiting, looking handsome in the warm light. Dark jeans and a fitted blue button-down made him look good, and as he turned, a smile spread across his face like the sunrise.

"Hey," he greeted, leaning casually against the wall, the vibe between them electric. "You look beautiful."

Leah felt her cheeks heat up, warmth flooding through her like sunshine. "Thanks." The word came out almost shy, but she met his gaze, trying to act cool despite the nerves bubbling up.

"Ready to go?" he asked, offering his hand. That casual move sent her pulse racing, a mix of anticipation and nerves.

"Yeah," Leah nodded, taking his hand as they walked out together. His grip felt warm, igniting sparks of excitement she'd kept hidden.

They stepped outside into the early summer evening, Leah sneaking a glance back at her family. Claire was animatedly chatting with Grace, and Leah felt a pang—longing mixed with uncertainty.

As they slid into Ryan's sleek car, the weight of expectations settled on Leah's shoulders. The classroom drama, the gossip about Ashley and her perfect crew swirled in her mind, but she tried to focus on what was happening right now—her date with Ryan.

The car smelled like a mix of leather and fresh air, a glimpse into Ryan's confident lifestyle.

"Where to?" Ryan asked, glancing at her as they pulled onto the main road.

"Uh, I thought we'd just grab ice cream?" Leah said, though dread was creeping in. "I mean, if that's cool with you?"

Ryan chuckled. "Ice cream? Pssh, I thought we'd celebrate your graduation with something more... special."

"Oh?" Leah felt her stomach flip. "What do you mean?"

"Well," Ryan said, glancing over with a playful smile, "there's this cute little spot outside town. The best homemade ice cream ever, and I thought we could do a picnic afterward."

"A picnic?" Leah's heart raced at the thought. "Outside? Like, at the park?"

"Just grab a blanket, chill, enjoy the sunset, and maybe some snacks—if you're down for it."

Leah could hardly contain her excitement. The idea of a picnic under the sunset with Ryan felt thrilling and nerve-wracking all at once. This differed from their usual hangouts, and being alone with him felt intoxicating. But a flicker of doubt crept in. "What if it's too much? I mean, it's just ice cream..."

Ryan's laughter broke through her thoughts. "C'mon, just ice cream with fresh air and good vibes is never too much. It'll be fun, trust me!"

Leah felt herself relax a little; Ryan's energy was contagious. As they drove, the world outside became a blur of summer greens and golden fields, the sunset throwing a warm glow on everything. It reminded her of those carefree days when ice cream and laughter were all that mattered.

When they arrived at the park, Leah felt a rush of sweetness. The picnic area buzzed with families and friends, laughter ringing through the air. Ryan found a cozy spot under an enormous oak tree, where the grass made for a perfect picnic blanket, and they spread out the blanket.

"How's this?" he asked, throwing a cheeky glance over his shoulder, his eyes sparkling.

"Perfect!" Leah beamed, settling down and soaking in the lively atmosphere. The park was alive with sounds—the joyful shouts of kids at play, the distant laughter of friends—it all felt freeing.

After heading to get ice cream, they plopped down together, savoring their cones in comfortable silence at first, trying to one-up each other with ridiculous drips and goofy flavors. Ryan chose a mint chocolate chip, while Leah went for a chocolate fudge swirl, fully aware of the impending sticky mess.

"Alright, let's see who can finish theirs first," Ryan teased, a competitive glint dancing in his eyes.

"Oh, you're on!" Leah laughed, instinctively pushing aside her nerves as they dove in for big bites.

As she enjoyed the sweet treat, Leah felt the carefree vibe of the whole moment wrapping around her. The sun cast warm rays on her skin, making her feel alive and inspired.

In between bites, they shared stories—funny high school moments, embarrassing swim meet fails, and their hopes for the future. The conversation flowed easily, no pressure, just laughter and chatter, shedding the weight of Leah's worries.

As the sun dipped lower, the sky painted with soft pinks and oranges, Leah glanced at Ryan, who was now staring off at the horizon. In that moment, she felt a spark—something special forming between them through shared dreams and uncertainties.

"Hey, Leah," Ryan said, breaking the peaceful silence. "After all this graduation stuff calms down, want to study together? Maybe hit the books and share some ideas?"

"Really?" Leah's heart leaped at the idea. "You'd want to?"

"Certainly!" He smiled like he'd just suggested a fun game. "We could prep for college or even brainstorm ideas for projects in med school."

The excitement bubbled inside her. "I'd love that," Leah replied, feeling the thrill of having someone who believed in her. "That way, it's not so intimidating."

"Totally! Let's team up and make a plan," Ryan said, brimming with enthusiasm.

Leah felt a surge of gratitude, watching him light up with ideas. "It's a deal," she said, grinning. "I'll even bring my notes next time we hang out."

The sky glowed with fiery colors as they finished their ice cream. As Leah savored the last bites, she felt the warm glow of the moment and the latent connection growing stronger between them.

"So, how's it feel to be done with high school?" Ryan asked, glancing sideways at her, a smile playing on his lips.

"It's... kind of surreal, honestly," Leah replied, leaning back on her hands. "Graduation was wild. I mean, part of me is excited about what's next, but part of me is freaked out about college."

"Same here," Ryan said, nodding. "With all the pressure to jump into the next phase, it can feel overwhelming."

"Right?" Leah sighed. "Sometimes it's like everyone's holding their breath, waiting to see what I'm gonna do next. My parents have this idea of who I should be, and it's just exhausting."

Ryan's expression softened, and he leaned in a little closer. "I get that. My folks are the same way. They're all about striving for greatness—especially with my engineering degree."

"That's correct!" Leah exclaimed, her eyes lighting up at their shared experience. "It feels like they've got this checklist of achievements they want me to hit. Sometimes it's suffocating."

Ryan nodded again. "They mean well, but it's like there's no room to just figure things out. I feel the pressure, too, to be that perfect student with a secure future in engineering."

"Right!" Leah said, feeling a rush of camaraderie. "I want to make them proud, but I also want to explore what I really want without all the pressure."

"Totally." Ryan smiled, his gaze meeting hers. "Sometimes I feel like my whole life has been planned out for me. They expect me to go into engineering—it's what everyone else wants."

Leah leaned her head on her chin, diving deeper into the conversation. "Do you think that's what you want, too?"

"I don't know," Ryan admitted, running a hand through his hair, making Leah's heart flutter. "I like math and physics, but sometimes I wonder if it's really my passion or just what's expected."

"Same here," Leah confessed. "I care about wanting to help others, but I also want to find what truly excites me, you know?"

They shared a moment of understanding, and Leah felt that stronger connection forming—one built on shared experiences and the unique pressures from their families.

"Maybe we can figure it out together?" Ryan suggested tentatively, a hopeful glint in his eyes. "You know, support each other this summer as we transition into college? Professionals in progress?"

Leah chuckled. "Yeah, I like that idea. We could use all the help we can get!"

Ryan smiled, "Deal. And if you ever feel overwhelmed, just remember—you're not alone in this. I get what it's like to want to break free from those expectations sometimes."

"Thanks, Ryan," Leah replied, feeling grateful for his kindness. "Honestly, having you by my side makes it a little less scary."

"Same here," he said, leaning back against the tree as the last rays of sunlight painted the sky in dusky purples. "I'm glad we're doing this."

As they continued talking, their conversation drifted toward light topics—favorite books, goofy sports moments, and their go-to snacks. Laughter filled the space between them, and Leah felt the last remnants of nervousness fade away.

After a while, the sky darkened, and the stars twinkled overhead. It was a magical night, and Leah felt as though the connection between them had solidified. She glanced over at Ryan, who was admiring the night sky, his face illuminated by starlight.

"This is kind of perfect, isn't it?" Leah said, breaking the serene silence.

"Yeah," Ryan replied, his gaze still on the stars. "It really is. I feel like we're lucky to have this moment... and each other."

Leah's heart raced. She couldn't believe how easy it felt to be with him, how well they understood each other. The weight of their families' expectations felt a little lighter, and the bright future ahead appeared less daunting.

"Hey," Leah hesitated and then continued, "we should definitely keep doing this. Hanging out, supporting each other through the summer—we could really help each other out."

"I like that," Ryan grinned, his eyes sparkling with optimism. "I see many more late-night talks and study sessions in our future."

As they wrapped up their picnic and began packing their things, Leah felt something shift inside her. She had spent so long feeling burdened by expectations, but with Ryan, it felt like she could breathe. She had enjoyed their picnic more than she had ever expected, and as they gathered their things, a smile crept onto her face, thinking about spending more time with him.

As they packed up, Ryan glanced over and smiled. "So, what's next? Got any wild summer plans?" he asked, his tone light.

"Honestly, I just want to enjoy the downtime before college starts," Leah replied, brushing off bits of grass from her sundress. "Catch up on reading, maybe hit the beach a few times. You?"

"Pretty much the same," Ryan said. "I want to hang out with friends and maybe tackle a couple of projects before classes kick off. But I'm definitely making time for more evenings like this."

"Yeah, me too," she said, her heart fluttering at the thought. The light breeze stirred, and she tucked a loose strand of hair behind her ear, glancing shyly at him.

The moment hung between them, electric with possibilities. "What do you think about grabbing dinner?" Ryan asked, breaking the tension with a grin. "You know, to celebrate our newfound freedom?"

Leah's heart raced. "Like an actual date?"

"Yeah, a real one," he replied, his eyes sparkling with interest. "We could hit that new taco place downtown. I hear their spicy shrimp is amazing."

"Count me in for tacos!" Leah exclaimed, excitement filling her voice. "As long as you promise not to steal all the spicy ones."

"Oh, I can't make that promise," he joked, pretending to think hard. "It's just too tempting."

They both laughed, and Leah felt a rush of warmth at the playful banter. As they walked back toward the car, the air felt charged, almost electric. Ryan reached out, brushing his fingers against hers, their laughter fading into a comfortable silence. Leah's heart raced at the tiny touch.

Arriving at Ryan's car, he opened the door for her with practiced ease. "After you, milady," he said, bowing in a mock knightly gesture. Leah giggled as she slid into the passenger seat, feeling both giddy and nervous.

Ryan hopped in next to her and started the engine. "So, what are you looking forward to most about college?" he asked, keeping his gaze on the road but stealing glances at her from time to time.

"I think just meeting new people and figuring out who I really am," Leah said, her voice thoughtful. "I want to dive into my classes and see if pre-med is really what I want. What about you?"

"I can't wait to build stuff and work on projects," Ryan replied. "Engineering is like this puzzle to solve. I love figuring out how things work; it's super satisfying."

As they drove, they talked about their hopes, their expectations, and even their fears about college. The more they shared, the more Leah felt a sense of safety in their growing bond.

They reached the taco place. "Here we are!" Ryan said, pulling into a spot. Leah hopped out excitedly, admiring the colorful decor and the lively atmosphere.

Once inside, they placed their orders, and as they waited, Leah couldn't help but admire how relaxed Ryan seemed, how he engaged with the staff effortlessly. She found herself drawn to him more than ever, enjoying the way he animatedly talked about the different taco options.

When their food arrived, they grabbed a cozy booth toward the back. As they dug into the tacos, laughter filled the surrounding air. Leah delighted in Ryan's playful teasing about her choice of toppings, and he challenged her to try the spiciest salsa.

"Okay, but if I pass out from heat after this, it's your fault," Leah said dramatically, her eyes watering from the heat of the salsa.

Ryan chuckled, leaning closer, their shoulders bumping. "I'll be here to revive you with ice cream afterward," he replied, a teasing grin on his face.

Leah felt a warmth blossom in her chest at their closeness, at how easy everything felt. They devoured their food, trading bites and suggestions, and with each laugh, the walls they had built around themselves slowly faded away.

After finishing their meal, Ryan suggested they grab dessert. "How about we go for ice cream again? It's the perfect ending to this feast," he said, winking.

"Lead the way!" Leah said, her heart racing as they left the taco place. The summer night air was warm, and they strolled down the sidewalk together, their hands brushing against each other occasionally, igniting sparks.

At the ice cream shop, the mouth-watering scents filled the air. They browsed the flavors, laughing over ridiculous combinations. Leah settled on a chocolate fudge brownie swirl, while Ryan opted for mint chocolate chip.

"Two classics!" Ryan declared as they walked out, holding their cones like trophies. The night was alive with the sound of laughter and chatter from other patrons enjoying their late-night treats, and the city lights twinkled like stars overhead.

As they strolled along, Leah took a moment to savor her ice cream, the rich chocolate melting blissfully on her tongue. "This is so good!" she exclaimed, glancing over to see Ryan practically licking his cone in joy.

"Right? I have no regrets," Ryan replied with mock seriousness before taking another enthusiastic bite. "Ice cream is basically a food group."

Leah laughed, feeling a rush of happiness. It was refreshing to just enjoy the moment. They made their way to a nearby park, where fairy lights strung through the trees created a whimsical atmosphere.

"Let's sit on that bench," Ryan suggested, pointing toward a cozy spot under a canopy of lights. They made their way over and plopped down, the soft sound of leaves rustling in the night breeze surrounding them.

Once seated, they settled into the rhythm of sharing stories about their favorite moments from high school. Leah couldn't help but open up about her love for painting and how, despite the pressure from her family, she dreamed of creating something meaningful.

"I had this idea for a mural at school, but I was too scared to pitch it," Leah admitted, doodling in her ice cream with her spoon. "I figured, with no one expecting it, it'd be silly to bring it up."

Ryan's expression turned serious. "You should've totally gone for it! Your art could inspire so many people. You shouldn't let anyone else define what you can achieve."

"They'd probably just roll their eyes," Leah said, shrugging. "It's like every time I try to step outside the box, I feel like I'm being pulled back in."

"That's what makes it tough for us perfectionists," Ryan said, tilting his head. "I get that, too. I want to build things that matter, and I feel pressured to stick to the traditional paths in engineering, but I just... sometimes I want to create something unexpected, you know?"

Leah nodded, appreciating his honesty about the internal struggles. "Totally! It feels like there's so much pressure to be perfect—to not make any mistakes."

Ryan turned toward her, his expression earnest. "But what if we gave ourselves permission to mess up? To explore and take risks? We're only in our first summer after high school. We've got time to figure it all out."

Leah's heart swelled at his words. "You're right. I guess we don't have to have things figured out right away." She paused, searching for his gaze. "Thanks for being so understanding."

"Anytime," he replied sincerely, a gentle smile spreading across his face. "We make a pretty good team—it's nice to know we're not alone in all this pressure."

As the evening continued, they took turns teasing each other about silly high school moments and dream careers, their laughter echoing in the night. With each shared story, Leah felt the bond between them deepen, like they were weaving threads of a shared adventure together.

After finishing their ice cream, Ryan wiped his hands on his jeans and glanced at Leah. "How about we take a walk? The park is really pretty at night."

"Sure!" Leah agreed, her heart racing with excitement. They rose from the bench and began wandering, the lights sparkling above them like stars on Earth.

As they meandered through the paths, they explored the night, pointing out little things—a couple holding hands, children playing catch with a glow-in-the-dark ball, and the gentle swaying of branches in the breeze.

Ryan stopped and pointed toward a small hill nearby. "Hey, wanna climb that? I bet the view from the top is amazing!"

Leah laughed, feeling adventurous. "Sure, why not?"

They made their way up the hill, the soft grass underfoot feeling delightfully cool. When they reached the top, they both paused, taking in the spectacular view of the city skyline illuminated by the night sky.

"Wow," Leah breathed, feeling her heart soar. "This is incredible."

"I know, right?" Ryan said, his voice filled with awe. He stepped closer to her as they stood side by side, their shoulders brushing together. The moment felt perfect, and Leah couldn't ignore the thrill of being next to him.

As they gazed at the view, Ryan turned toward her, a more serious expression crossing his face. "Leah, I know we've only been getting to know each other, but I really enjoy spending time with you. Like, a lot."

Leah's breath caught. "Me too, Ryan. I didn't expect this summer to be so... meaningful, but it feels special."

Ryan looked into her eyes, his gaze sincere. "I'd like to do this more. As in, officially hang out—go on more dates if you're up for it."

Leah felt her heart leap at his words, a smile spreading across her face. "You mean, like, you want to make this official? I'd love that!"

"Really?" Ryan's eyes lit up, a wide grin breaking across his face. "Awesome! I mean, we already get each other, and I'd love to see where this goes."

"Same," Leah replied, excitement bubbling within her. "There's something different about us, like we really understand each other. I think we can make it work, even with college starting soon."

They stood there for a moment, looking out at the city lights, both feeling the weight of the moment. Leah couldn't believe how quickly things had shifted. Just a few weeks ago, she was nervous about starting college, and now here she was, standing on a hilltop with her new boyfriend, with the world stretching ahead of them.

"Let's promise we'll make time for each other when college kicks off," Ryan said, turning to her, his voice earnest. "I don't want to lose this. It feels too important."

"Agreed," Leah said, her heart racing. "We've waited too long for this moment, and I believe we've got what it takes to weather whatever comes our way."

Ryan stepped closer, the intimacy of the space between them growing as the moment deepened. "I feel the same. College is gonna be a challenge, but facing it together? That sounds like a plan."

Leah nodded, grinning from ear to ear. She felt a thrill run through her as Ryan leaned in, and they shared a gentle kiss under the starlit sky. It was soft and sweet, a promise of what was to come. When they pulled away, both smiled shyly, knowing their relationship had just taken a significant leap.

As they made their way back down the hill, their hands brushed occasionally, electric and warm. The rest of the night unfolded with more laughter, more deep conversations about their hopes for the future, and dreams of what college life would hold for them.

As the summer rolled on, they spent countless evenings together, making memories that they both knew would strengthen their bond. Whether they were tackling summer assignments at the park, sharing more ice cream dates, or exploring local hangouts with friends, the connection they shared grew stronger.

When the day arrived for them to move into college, nerves tingled in the air. Leah stood outside her dorm, surrounded by boxes, feeling both apprehensive and excited. Ryan pulled up in his truck, ready for the big day.

"Hey!" he called out, a relaxed smile lighting up his face as he hopped out. "Ready to conquer this?"

"Ready as I'll ever be!" Leah replied, feeling a rush of relief and excitement wash over her at seeing him. They exchanged hugs, full of support for what lay ahead.

Together, they moved Leah's things into her dorm room, their laughter echoing through the hall, easing their nerves. As they unpacked, they shared little secrets about their expectations for college—the freedom, the workload, and the challenge of balancing everything.

Once Leah's room was set up, they took a moment to sit on her bed, gazing around her new space. "Wow, it's all happening," Leah said, glancing over at Ryan, who was leaning back with a smile.

"Yeah, and I think it's gonna be amazing," Ryan replied. "You know, we still need to keep our promise to be there for each other, right? No matter how crazy things get."

"Definitely," Leah said, her tone serious. "We'll make it work. We're a team now. I won't let anything distract us from that."

Ryan nodded, extending his pinky finger. "Pinky promise?"

Leah giggled, hooking her pinky around his. "Pinky promise."

The days that followed were a whirlwind of new experiences—meeting new people, navigating classes, and adjusting to college life. They both worked hard, but whenever they could, they made time for each other. Late-night study sessions turned into long talks about their days, and weekends were filled with adventures exploring campus.

While challenges arose, like busy schedules and the occasional long-distance weekend, Leah and Ryan leaned on one another. They communicated openly, laughing through awkward moments, celebrating victories, and sharing the weight of each other's frustrations.

One evening, as they sat on Leah's dorm bed, surrounded by textbooks and snack wrappers, Ryan looked over at her, his expression more serious. "Hey, I really appreciate how much you put into this, especially with all the craziness college brings."

Leah felt warmth fill her chest. "Thanks, Ryan. It's not always easy, but I want this—as in, you and me. We'll get through whatever comes our way together."

Ryan grinned, his eyes sparkling with admiration. "I feel the same. I didn't expect my first year of college to include the best teammate ever. You keep me grounded."

Leah smiled, tucking a loose strand of hair behind her ear. "And you challenge me in ways I never thought I'd appreciate. I'm really excited about everything ahead."

As the semester wore on, they navigated the ups and downs side by side. Late-night study sessions morphed into spontaneous ice cream runs, and study breaks became opportunities for long talks about their dreams. On weekends, they ventured out to local cafes or parks, soaking up the summer's final days, creating memories that would last a lifetime.

But they also supported each other through stressful moments. When Leah struggled with a tough exam, Ryan was right there with her, offering encouragement and study tips. And when Ryan had late-night engineering projects due, Leah would bring him coffee, sharing late-night snacks and jokes to keep his spirits up.

"Here you go, caffeine king," Leah teased one evening, sliding a steaming cup of coffee across the table to him.

"Just what I needed," Ryan replied, taking a grateful sip. His eyes sparkled with gratitude as he looked up at her. "You're the best."

"Just trying to keep my favorite engineer awake," Leah said with a playful wink.

As October rolled around, they celebrated their three-month anniversary and made it special. They planned a date night at the local fair, filled with laughter, games, and a few thrilling rides. Leah wore a cute sundress that Ryan had complimented the first time he saw it, giving her a boost of confidence.

"This is gonna be awesome!" Ryan exclaimed as they entered the fairgrounds, excitement radiating from him.

"Totally! I want to try everything!" Leah replied, her eyes sparkling with joy.

They wandered through the fair, exploring game booths, indulging in cotton candy, and testing their bravery on rides that made them scream with laughter. When they reached the Ferris wheel, Leah's breath caught at the sight.

"Let's do it!" she said, grabbing Ryan's hand and leading him toward the line.

As they ascended to the top, with the fair lights twinkling below, Leah felt a sense of exhilaration. "This is beautiful!" she exclaimed, looking out at the city illuminated beneath a blanket of stars.

"I know! And we're up here together," Ryan replied, leaning closer. Feeling the rush of the moment, he took her hand, intertwining their fingers.

Leah turned to look at him, heart racing even faster. "This has been the best night," she said, her voice barely above a whisper.

Ryan smiled, his gaze steady on hers. "You make everything better, Leah. I'm really glad we're doing this."

Before Leah could respond, Ryan leaned in, capturing her lips in a soft kiss. It was sweet and tender, a perfect moment against the backdrop of the night sky. When they pulled away, both were grinning like the sun.

"I could get used to this," Leah said, her heart soaring.

"Me too," Ryan replied, squeezing her hand. "I want to make more moments like this happen for us."

As they reached the bottom of the Ferris wheel, they held hands as they continued exploring the fair, taking pictures, playing games, and winning stuffed animals for each other. That night solidified their relationship, a reminder that they were stronger together and had built a bond that could withstand anything.

As midterms approached, life got busier, and stress levels rose, but Leah and Ryan never lost sight of each other. They worked hard but always made time for small pockets of joy—whether it was a quick coffee date before class or a cozy movie night in her dorm after a long week.

One chilly evening, as they huddled on her bed, wrapped up in blankets and watching a movie, Ryan turned to Leah. "I just want you to know how much you mean to me. It's easy to get lost in everything else, but you make it all worthwhile."

Leah's heart swelled, and she nestled closer to him. "You mean a lot to me too, Ryan. I couldn't have gotten through this without you. You keep me grounded."

He smiled at her, and with determination in his eyes, he added, "No matter how this semester goes, I want us to keep this—we can meet the challenges head-on together."

"Absolutely," Leah said, feeling a sense of resolution. "We're in this together."

As they continued through their college journey, Leah and Ryan weathered every challenge that came their way. Their communication grew stronger, their feelings deepened, and every moment spent together wove them closer as a couple.

By the end of the semester, they were not just partners; they had become each other's greatest support system. They made it through finals, celebrated their achievements, and learned to balance their individual responsibilities with their growing relationship.

During winter break, as they spent time with their families, they often texted and called each other, sharing stories about their holiday experiences and counting the days until they would be back together.

"Five more days!" Leah texted Ryan one evening, excitement bubbling in her chest. "I can't wait to see you!"

"Same here! I've missed you like crazy," he replied almost instantly. "Let's have a movie marathon when you get back. I'm bringing all the snacks."

With each passing day, Leah felt more certain that Ryan was someone she wanted to keep in her life for the long haul. Their connection had blossomed in ways she hadn't expected, and she was grateful for the love, support, and laughter he brought into her world.

Once they reunited after the break, they slipped back into their comfortable routine, blending their time between studying, hanging out with friends, and enjoying spontaneous adventures together. One Saturday, they took a day trip to the nearby beach, reveling in the sun and surf that reminded them just how delightful their summer had been.

After splashing in the waves, they settled onto a big blanket spread out in the sand, soaking in the sun's warmth. Ryan lay back, propping himself up on his elbows, and watched Leah as she doodled in her sketchbook. She glanced up; her heart warmed at the sight of him.

"What are you thinking about?" he asked, his tone light.

Leah smiled. "Just sketching out a few ideas. I want to paint something big—something that represents us, you know? The journey we've been on together."

"I love that idea!" he replied, excited. "Let's make it happen. I can even help if you want!"

"Really?" Leah asked, doing her best to hide her surprise. "You want to get artsy with me?"

"Who wouldn't want to create something beautiful with their favorite artist?" he teased, making her laugh.

Leah's heart soared. The fact that Ryan encouraged her to pursue her passions meant everything to her. After enjoying the beach some more and light conversation, they took a stroll along the shore, collecting seashells and laughing as the surf lapped at their feet.

As the sun set, they made their way back to their blanket. Ryan turned to Leah with a more pensive expression. "You know, I was thinking... we've been through so much already, and I just want you to know I'm all in with this relationship. I really care about you, Leah."

Leah felt a surge of emotion. "I care about you too, Ryan. I love what we have, and I can see us tackling whatever comes next together."

Ryan took her hands in his, the warmth radiating between them. "I know we're still figuring things out, but I can honestly see a future for us. I want to keep building this connection, no matter the challenges."

"I feel the same way," Leah said, her voice steady and sincere. "We've built something special. I want to grow with you, both in our relationship and as individuals."

The golden hour cast a warm glow around them, and as they leaned in, Ryan kissed her, a perfect promise under the fading sunlight. As their lips met, Leah felt more certain than ever that this was right—the two of them together, supporting each other's dreams and navigating life as a team.

As the new semester approached, both Leah and Ryan felt ready to face whatever challenges lay ahead, strengthened by their relationship. Classes resumed, bringing fresh pressures, but they continued to prioritize their connection. Study dates became rituals, and they learned to celebrate even the small victories.

By the end of the academic year, their bond had withstood the test of time and circumstance. With finals behind them and summer on the horizon, they took a moment to reflect on everything they had accomplished together.

"You know," Leah said one evening as they stargazed from her dorm roof, "I never imagined I'd find someone like you who gets it—who challenges me and supports me at the same time."

Ryan turned, looking genuinely touched. "And I never thought I'd find someone I could connect with and share so much with. You've really changed my life for the better."

"Here's to us," Leah said, raising her imaginary glass in the air as they shared a smile.

"To us," Ryan echoed, his warm eyes sparkling with love and promise.

As the summer began, they planned a season full of adventures—road trips, camping under the stars, and even exploring the art scene that Leah was so passionate about. They knew there would still be challenges ahead, as college often introduced new obstacles, but with each passing day, they felt even more inseparable, buoyed by shared dreams and newfound joys.

One evening, as the sun set in a glorious blaze of color, Leah and Ryan found themselves at their favorite park. They sat on a blanket, the warmth of late afternoon wrapping around them, and Leah reflected on everything they had built together. With laughter echoing in the air, she felt a tinge of contentment; life was good, and love felt secure.

"Can you believe how far we've come since that first date?" Ryan said, scooping a handful of popcorn from the bowl between them.

"Not at all," Leah replied, a soft smile spreading across her face. "I thought I was going to crumble under all that pressure, but you made everything feel so much lighter."

"Me?" Ryan raised an eyebrow, a mock look of disbelief. "Nah, it's all you. You've grown so much this year. It's been amazing to watch."

Leah beamed with pride at his words, soaking in the moment's warmth. "Thanks. I couldn't have done it without you by my side."

As the sky darkened above them, stars twinkling into view, a sense of peace enveloped Leah. She felt so grateful for Ryan—their connection felt strong and real. But in the back of her mind, a flicker of apprehension stirred. She thought about how easily things could change and how relationships could shift, especially in the unpredictable world of college.

"Hey," Leah said, turning serious, trying to shake the feeling. "Promise me we'll always be open with one another, no matter what happens? I don't want any secrets between us."

"Of course," Ryan replied, looking her in the eyes, sincerity coloring his voice. "We're solid, Leah. Our bond is strong enough to weather anything."

Leah nodded, her heart swelling with affection, but she felt the flicker of unease come back again. She tried to brush it off, reminding herself how much faith they had in each other. What could possibly go wrong?

But deep down, shadows were gathering—shadows that Leah couldn't yet see. As the summer days faded into nights filled with laughter and kisses, she couldn't shake the feeling that something was lurking beneath the surface, hidden behind the smiles.

CHAPTER 8

Shattered Innocence

Winter break of their sophomore year arrived, blanketing the campus in soft snow and a sense of renewal. Leah and Ryan had made plans to spend the holidays together, eager to share cozy nights and winter festivities. On the surface, everything felt perfect. They had settled into a rhythm, and Leah believed their love could weather any storm.

But as they returned to campus after the break, Leah sensed things weren't as rosy as she hoped. It started small—Ryan was more distracted than usual, often checking his phone during dinner or brushing off her questions with a smile. It should've been minor, but Leah couldn't shake the feeling that something was off.

One afternoon while studying in the library, Leah noticed a group of girls laughing loudly at a distance, stealing glances at Ryan. He was focused on his work, but when he caught a glimpse of them, a chuckle escaped his lips. Leah's heart sank at the sight.

"You good?" she asked, trying to mask her unease, but Ryan was oblivious as he turned back to her, engrossed.

"Yeah, I'm fine! Did you see my last text?" he replied, swiping at his phone.

"Uh, no," Leah answered, trying to stay calm. "Thought you caught that. Those girls seem really into you."

Ryan shrugged, a dismissive wave of his hand showing it didn't matter. "Whatever, they're just messing around."

But Leah couldn't extinguish the nagging anxiety in her gut. Later that night, she tried to convince herself it was nothing, that perhaps she was being paranoid. With each passing day, more shadows had loomed over her thoughts.

One evening, as they lounged on the couch with a movie playing in the background, Leah noticed Ryan typing on his phone. His face shifted, a brief tension crossing his features before he smiled and turned the device face down on the coffee table.

"What's up?" Leah asked, raising an eyebrow. "You've been kinda glued to that thing lately."

"Just group messages for class prep," he replied casually. "You know how it is."

"Right, sure," Leah said, forcing a smile. But inside, her heart raced—her intuition couldn't shake the feeling that things had felt "too good to be true." This wasn't the Ryan she knew.

Another week passed, and Leah's internal turmoil compounded. Conversations had felt hollow. His laughter lacked its usual warmth. The nagging feeling escalated into something unbearable. Leah found herself plagued by memories of their early days—a time when she never second-guessed his devotion. But now, something hung in the air, a separate reality she hadn't wanted to face.

"Am I being ridiculous?" Leah pondered one night, staring at the ceiling in her dimly lit room. "Why can't I shake this feeling? What if I'm just being naïve?"

What if he doesn't really care as much as I thought?

The reality had felt like a punch in the gut. She tried to brush off the doubts, insisting to herself that it was a phase, that everyone went through awkward times.

But when one of Leah's friends, Sophie, made a seemingly casual comment, it shattered the little peace she had left. "Hey, Leah, I saw Ryan at that off-campus party last weekend. He seemed pretty chummy with some girls. Nothing serious, though, right?"

Leah felt her heart drop. "What are you talking about?" she asked, panic lacing her voice.

"Just heard he was getting a little flirty, maybe it was nothing," Sophie replied, her tone light, but Leah felt a chill race down her spine. "But you know how college parties can be, right?"

Before Leah could respond, the words hung heavily in the air. The shadows of doubt slithered into her mind and closed in on her. How could she have been so blind?

Finally, one evening in early February, Leah's patience snapped. She confronted Ryan in the coffee shop they visited often. Her heart pounded and the tension in the air was thick.

"Can we talk?" she began, her voice trembling. "Sure, what's up?" he asked, glancing up from his coffee, that familiar charm on display.

"Ryan, I need to know something," Leah said, gathering her courage. "Did something happen at that party... did you cheat on me?"

His expression faltered for a split second—just enough for Leah to catch it. "What? No, of course not! What makes you think that?"

"Because things have felt off lately," she admitted, her heart racing as she pressed on. "You've been distant, and I've seen you acting weird around other girls."

Ryan leaned back, his confidence slipping. "Leah, come on," Ryan said, his voice growing uneasy. "I told you, it's just been a busy semester. I've got a ton on my plate. You're reading too much into this."

"Busy or not, I feel like you're hiding something. You've been secretive, and I can't ignore that. Just tell me the truth!" Leah's voice rose, desperation clawing at her throat.

"Okay, okay," Ryan replied, running a hand through his hair. His nerves were clear. "I just... it was a mistake. I got drunk at that party and... I slept with someone."

Leah's breath caught in her throat, a wave of nausea hitting her. "You did what?" she repeated, unable to process the words spilling out. "When? How could you do that to me?"

"I didn't mean for it to happen! I was drunk. I swear, it didn't mean anything to me. I was just—" he faltered, his eyes pleaded as they searched hers. "It was stupid; I messed up."

Leah felt her heart shatter, reality collapsing around her. "So, that's it, huh? You get drunk and throw everything we have away? How could you even think that's okay?"

"I didn't think! I was overwhelmed and caught up in the moment. I never wanted to hurt you, Leah. You have to believe that!"

Tears spilled down Leah's cheeks as the betrayal clawed at her insides. "I trusted you! I defended you when people told me to be careful. And this is how you repay that?"

Ryan reached out, trying to take her hand, but she instinctively pulled away, the distance between them feeling vast. "Please, don't. I can't just let you brush this aside. You don't get to say, 'I messed up' and expect things to go back to normal."

"I know I don't deserve your forgiveness. I've screwed up," Ryan admitted, his voice pained. "But Leah, you mean everything to me. I don't want to lose you. We can work through this!"

"Work through this?" Leah echoed, her heart aching with disappointment. "You've broken my trust. How do you expect me to trust you again? I don't even know if I can talk to you without waiting for the next shock."

"Just give me a chance," Ryan begged, desperation creeping into his tone. "Let's talk about it, figure it out. I don't want to lose what we have!"

Leah shook her head, feeling a mix of anger and heartbreak. "What we had? It's not what we had; it was fragile, built on honesty and trust. You broke that. And now... all I feel is doubt and betrayal."

For a moment, silence enveloped them, heavy with all that couldn't be unsaid—the weight of unfulfilled promises and a love tarnished by deceit. The hurt in Leah's heart felt overwhelming, and she could sense Ryan's tension grasping desperately for a lifeline that felt impossibly far away.

"Leah, please don't do this. I care about you more than anything. I—I love you," he said, conviction lacing his words.

But Leah felt a deep pit rise within her, the words just another layer of hurt. "You love me, but you broke my heart anyway. How do I know it's not just convenient for you to say that now?"

"I didn't want this to happen! You have to believe that!" he exclaimed, exasperation mingling with sorrow. "I made an awful decision, and I hate myself for it. But I still want you."

Tears streamed down Leah's cheeks as she fought back the waves of emotion. "Wanting me isn't enough now, Ryan. You had me, and you threw it away. What's the point of continuing when I'll always wonder if I'm not enough for you?"

"Leah, please," he pleaded, anguish creeping into his voice. "I want you to know you are enough. You're amazing, and I don't want to let this one mistake ruin everything."

As the weight of his words sank in, Leah realized the truth: she didn't want to be with someone who could easily throw away their relationship. Her heart felt constricted, a cold emptiness settling in. In that moment, she knew she could no longer ignore the truth.

"Then maybe we need to end this," Leah whispered, the words tasting bitter as they left her lips.

"You—what?" Ryan's voice broke, shock and disbelief filling his face. "Leah, don't say that! Please!"

But Leah stood firm, shaking her head as fresh tears welled in her eyes. "I can't keep pretending everything's fine, Ryan. I can't stay in a relationship built on this kind of betrayal. It's too painful." Leah's voice trembled, filled with anguish, but there was also clarity in her resolve.

"Please, don't do this," he urged, his eyes wide with desperation, realizing she might mean it. "I'll do anything to fix it. Just tell me what I need to do !"

She swallowed hard, trying to collect herself, but the hurt felt massive, like a tidal wave she couldn't fight against. "You can't fix this with a few kind words or promises. You've hurt me, and I don't think I can ever trust you again. It's not fair to either of us to keep dragging this out."

Ryan reached out once more, and this time Leah didn't pull away, but his fingers barely grazed her arm. "I care about you, Leah. You know that. It's just... I messed up. But I don't want to lose you—I want to be better. I can be. Just give me a chance."

Tears spilled over again, and Leah felt her heart breaking in two. "You had your chance, Ryan. You had plenty of chances, and you threw them away. I feel like I'm never good enough—like I wasn't enough for you to think twice before going after someone else."

He looked stricken, as though her words were cutting deep. "That's not true! I was stupid and drunk, and it meant nothing to me. You are more than enough, Leah. It was a mistake that I regret every single day."

"Regret doesn't fix what's been broken," she replied, shaking her head slowly. "What's the point of us continuing if I'm just going to live in fear that you'll do it again?"

"I won't! I swear I won't!" Ryan insisted, his voice rising, panic shadowing his features. "I can't believe I'm saying this, but I was an idiot. I don't want to lose you, Leah. I can't bear that thought!"

Leah took a step back, allowing the gap between them to widen, wrapped in heartache. "Maybe you deserve to lose me after everything you've done," she said, her voice trembling. "And maybe it's what I need for myself—some space to heal from this."

Ryan's face fell, and Leah could see the tears building in his own eyes. "But I love you. I don't want to let this moment be the end for us."

"But it already is," Leah whispered, her heart breaking at the pain on his face. "I can't keep waiting for you to prove what you say when your actions tell me otherwise."

The air was heavy with a suffocating silence, the weight of their shared moments echoing around them. Everything felt wrong, and Leah could feel the tight knot in her stomach as she faced a reality she hadn't wanted to accept.

"I thought we were forever," Ryan said, almost as if trying to grasp something slipping away too quickly.

Leah felt herself shatter at his words. "I thought so too, but forever can't be built on broken trust and fear. I'm sorry, Ryan. I really am."

"Don't say that, please..." he begged, his voice trembling with emotion. "Please don't walk away. I made a mistake. We can figure it out together!"

But Leah felt defeated. She took a deep breath, letting the warmth of their time together wash over her one last time, and tried to etch that memory into her heart before letting it go. "I need to prioritize myself for once. I need to let you go."

Ryan's expression contorted from desperation to despair as the weight of her words sank in. "Leah..." he murmured, voice trailing off as if he couldn't believe the reality facing him.

"I wish things were different," she said, tears spilling onto her cheeks. "I wish it didn't have to come to this. I just can't stay in a relationship that feels like it could break me."

As Leah turned to leave, each step felt heavier than the last, the haunting ache of goodbye gnawing at her insides. She glanced back one last time, meeting Ryan's sorrowful eyes, and felt a pang in her chest that felt like loss.

He stood there, looking utterly broken, the weight of his choices hanging over him. "I'm so sorry, Leah," he whispered into the silence.

And with that, Leah walked away, leaving behind a piece of her heart, feeling the reality of their relationship shatter like glass—memories, laughter, and love slowly fading as she stepped into a future she now had to face alone.

The days following the breakup felt like a haze. Leah tried to go through the motions of her daily life, attending classes and keeping up with her assignments, but the weight of heartbreak pressed heavily on her chest. The laughter and joy she once felt were replaced by a suffocating sense of emptiness. Each time she saw someone who reminded her of Ryan, a fresh wave of pain washed over her.

It wasn't until the following weekend when she found the courage to reach out to Kate. They hadn't seen each other much since the breakup, but Leah knew her best friend would understand what she was going through. Kate had always been there through the ups and downs, and Leah needed that support now more than ever.

"Hey, can we hang out?" Leah texted Kate, her heart racing.

She needed this.

"Of course! Miss you! Want to come over?" Kate replied instantly.

With a deep breath, Leah agreed, feeling a small flicker of hope as she made her way to Kate's apartment. Upon arrival, she was welcomed with an embrace that felt like home.

"Hey, you," Kate said, studying Leah's face. "You okay? You look... exhausted."

"Yeah, it's just been a rough few weeks," Leah admitted, her voice barely above a whisper. "Can we talk?"

Kate nodded, her expression serious. "Of course! Let's get some cocoa and settle in."

They tucked themselves into the cozy blanket on Kate's couch as steam swirled from their mugs. The warmth helped soothe Leah's nerves, but the shadows of her heartache still loomed large.

"So, what's been going on, really?" Kate asked, concern etched across her brow. "I want to hear everything."

With a shaky breath, Leah opened up, pouring her heart out. "I thought Ryan was the one, you know? But then... everything fell apart. He cheated on me, Kate. He slept with someone while he was drunk, and I can't wrap my head around how he could do that to us."

"No, he did not! Oh, that jerk!" Kate reacted, pulling Leah into another tight hug. "I'm so sorry. You deserve so much better than that. It's heartbreaking."

Leah nodded, tears threatened to spill again. "I just feel so foolish, like I should have seen the signs. He seemed so distant, but my instincts were telling me it was nothing."

"Don't blame yourself. You trusted him, and that's not a weakness; it's a strength," Kate reassured her, taking Leah's hand in hers. "It just shows how deeply you connect with people. But this is definitely on him."

"Yeah, I know," Leah said, looking down at her cocoa. "It still hurts. I feel like I'm never good enough for anyone, that maybe I was naïve for believing we could make it."

Kate squeezed her hand tighter. "You were never naïve to believe in love, Leah. It's brave! But you can't let his mistakes cloud your view of yourself. You are incredible and deserving of someone who sees all of that."

Leah glanced up, meeting Kate's gaze, grateful for her friend's unwavering support. "I just... I don't know how to move on. I feel so lost."

"Take it one step at a time," Kate suggested. "You're allowed to feel sad and hurt, but don't let it consume you. Let's make plans to do fun things together—get out, meet new people, find outlets that can help mend your heart."

Leah managed a small smile. "I'd like that. Maybe a weekend getaway or just nights out to distract me?"

"Yes! How about we head to that pop-up art exhibit downtown next weekend? It's supposed to be amazing," Kate proposed with a bright smile.

"Yeah, I'd love that!" Leah responded, feeling a flicker of excitement. "It'll be nice to immerse myself in the art scene again. It always makes me feel alive."

"Perfect! And remember, I'm here. You're not alone in this," Kate said, leaning closer and tucking her arm around Leah's shoulder. "You'll heal, I promise."

As the evening continued, Leah felt lighter. The burden of heartbreak was less heavy with Kate beside her. They talked, laughed, and reminisced about their college adventures—powerful moments when life was filled with possibilities.

In the following weeks, Leah allowed herself to lean on Kate, embracing her friend's steadfast support. Together, they embarked on little adventures, taking pottery classes and attending local theater performances, slowly rekindling Leah's spark.

But even with the distractions, inevitable moments would hit hard. In class, she'd catch glimpses of Ryan's friends, or her phone would buzz with reminders of shared plans, and each time, the ache would resurface. The memories felt relentless, each one a reminder of what she once had and the pain that now filled that space.

One afternoon, they were sitting in a café, Leah absently stirring her coffee while the scent of pastries filled the air. Kate was animatedly recounting a funny moment from their pottery class.

"...and then I dropped the entire bowl I was working on! It shattered everywhere. Prof. went totally pale, but I couldn't help it—I just started laughing!" Kate chuckled, her face lighting up.

Leah smiled weakly, trying to focus on her friend's laughter. "That sounds like a disaster."

"But a hilarious one! You should've been there!" Kate said, her infectious energy drawing Leah in. Yet Kate could still sense Leah's lingering sadness beneath the surface.

"Hey, it's okay to feel that way," Kate whispered. "You're allowed to have those moments. Just don't let it pull you down."

"I know, it's just... it's hard," Leah admitted, her voice shaky. "I thought we had something special. But when he threw that away, it made me feel like I was never enough. Like, why wasn't I worth sticking around for?"

"You are enough, Leah. Never forget that," Kate reassured her, squeezing Leah's hand. "Ryan messed up. His actions don't define your worth. You are amazing—creative, smart, and kind. You deserve someone who will recognize that and never even think about betraying you."

"Thanks," Leah murmured, feeling warmth spread through her at Kate's supportive words, but the doubt still gnawed at her. "I just keep wondering if I missed the signs, if I was blind to what was right in front of me."

"Don't go down that road," Kate warned, a serious tone in her voice. "You know how easy it is to fall into the trap of self-blame. You weren't naïve for loving him. You were brave for giving him your heart."

Leah took a deep breath, digesting her friend's advice. "You're right. I need to focus on healing and reclaiming who I am, not on what went wrong."

"That's right!" Kate exclaimed, her smiled returned. "So, what do you say we head to that art exhibit this weekend? Art always helps clear the mind."

"I'm in," Leah replied, a genuine smile crossing her lips. The thought of immersing herself in something she loved felt like a breath of fresh air.

As they finished their coffee, Leah felt a mix of determination and hope flicker inside her—a small spark, the first signs of healing, even in the face of pain. She knew it wouldn't happen overnight, but she could feel the shift starting.

The following weekend, Leah and Kate made their way to the art exhibit. The vibe was electric; colors danced across canvases in vibrant strokes, and the atmosphere buzzed with creativity.

Leah couldn't help but feel alive as they explored the exhibit, discussing the artwork and their interpretations.

"This one is amazing!" Kate said, gesturing toward a canvas splashed with bold colors. "I love how the chaos feels so intentional."

"It's beautiful," Leah agreed, excitement washing over her. "It's like all these artists are pouring their emotions out for everyone to see."

Their chatter filled the void left by Ryan, allowing Leah to embrace her passion for art again. As they moved through the gallery, Leah felt herself relaxing into the moment, discovering joy amidst the chaos of her heartache.

Later, as they approached a striking piece—a huge mural filled with intricate patterns and vivid colors—Leah paused, studying it intently.

"You okay?" Kate asked, noticing Leah's expression.

"Yeah, I just..." Leah started, then sighed. "I was thinking about how art tells stories, you know? Each painting is like a glimpse into someone's heart."

Kate nodded, understanding the weight of Leah's words. "Yup! And just like these artists, you're also crafting your own story. No one has the power to rewrite that for you."

Leah smiled, touched by her friend's insight. "Thanks, Kate. I needed to hear that."

As Leah stood before the mural, its vibrant colors swirling together in a beautiful chaos, she felt a shift deep within her. The pain of the breakup still lingered, a haunting reminder of trust shattered, but for the first time in weeks, Leah held a glimmer of hope.

"Art is all about transformation," she whispered to Kate, her voice filled with newfound conviction. "Just like life, it's messy and beautiful. And I think it's time for me to focus on my story, to transform this pain into something that pushes me forward."

"I love that," Kate beamed, wrapping her arm around Leah's shoulders. "You're stronger than you know. And remember, your story is not finished yet."

Leah took a deep breath, looking at the mural once more. After Ryan's betrayal, her heart had been chaotic, but she realized that chaos could also lead to creativity, growth, and clarity. Maybe this was the moment to embrace her artistic passions once again—to channel her heartbreak into something beautiful.

"Let's make a pact," Leah said, facing Kate. "Let's both prioritize our passions this semester. I want to dive into art like I used to, and I want you to keep aiming for your goals, too."

"Definitely!" Kate replied, her eyes dancing with excitement. "We'll both reclaim what we love! You'll rise—stronger and more amazing than ever."

As they left the exhibit, Leah felt a weight lift from her shoulders. The heaviness that had shadowed her for too long dissipated, and a renewed sense of purpose propelled her forward. Deep down, she understood that moving on wouldn't happen instantly, but she had faith that she could navigate through it—one brushstroke at a time.

In the following weeks, Leah threw herself into her classes and art. She started sketching again, pouring her emotions onto the page, using colors and forms to express the tumult of feelings inside. Each piece she created felt like a step toward healing, a way to reclaim her identity that Ryan had shaken.

Her friendship with Kate flourished through their shared creativity and spontaneous adventures, whether it be late-night movie marathons or exploring new cafés across town. She surrounded herself with the support she needed, turning to her friends when the echoes of doubt crept back in.

By the time spring arrived, Leah felt lighter. It was a bittersweet reminder of how much had changed, but she was ready to embrace this new chapter in her life. The warmth of the season mirrored the burgeoning strength she felt within herself.

One sunny afternoon, while alone in her favorite park, Leah set up her easel and painted a large canvas. With every stroke of the brush, she felt herself breaking free from the shackles of her past. She painted fiercely, blending colors into a gorgeous display of emotion, transforming her pain into a vivid portrayal of renewal.

As she stepped back to admire her work, a satisfied smile broke across her face—this was her story, one of resilience, creativity, and the strength to move on.

In that moment, Leah understood that heartbreak was just a chapter, not the end of her story. She was reclaiming her narrative, transforming the pain into possibilities. Her past didn't define her; she was reborn through it.

With her heart slowly mending, Leah knew she was ready for whatever came next—ready to embrace life and its beautiful complexities, with or without Ryan. She was stronger than she had ever realized, and now she was determined to face the world on her own terms.

As the sun began to set, casting warm golden hues across the sky, Leah packed up her supplies, feeling a sense of accomplishment and clarity. The lingering shadows of doubt had faded, replaced by a vibrant resolve. She left the park that day with a sense of freedom, one brushstroke at a time, ready to create the next chapter in her life—this time, on her own terms.

CHAPTER 9

The Unexpected Journey

L eah stared blankly at her organic chemistry textbook, the usual coffee shop noises merging into a dull hum. The barista's chatter, the clinking of cups, and the soft jazz didn't bring her the usual comfort. Normally, this little coffee shop had been her go-to retreat at Northwestern, but today, it felt like a trap. The sweet vanilla, bitter espresso, and frothy milk that usually soothed her had all just made her stomach turn today.

Absently tracing her finger along the pages, Leah tried to focus on her notes, but the words blurred together. Glancing outside, she watched snowflakes fall against the backdrop of brick buildings, a cozy blanket of white covering the campus. It all looked peaceful, yet each flake that hit the ground felt too permanent for her liking right now.

"You look rough," Kate said, stumbling into view and plopping down in the chair across from Leah. Kate's messy bun, with stray wisps circling her face, was a beautiful mess—something Leah envied. She could tell Kate had been worried about her.

"Thanks," Leah replied, mustering a weak smile that didn't reflect her feelings of dread. "Just what every girl wants to hear, right?"

Kate leaned in, eyes narrowed. "When's the last time you actually slept?" She reached over, closing Leah's organic chemistry book. "Or eaten anything that isn't coffee and protein bars?"

Leah's first instinct was to defend herself. "I eat!" But even as she said it, the protest felt lame. "I'm just busy, okay? These MCAT practice tests are killer." The anxiety throbbed inside her like a bad song on repeat.

"Busy isn't a good excuse for not eating," Kate shot back. "You remember how easily you get dizzy when you skip meals?" She studied her with concern swimming in her brown eyes. "And when was your last period?"

Leah blinked, confusion washing over her. "What?" The abrupt change in conversation had caught her off guard; her breath hitched in her throat, an icy wave of surprise washing over her.

"Your period, Leah. When was it?"

A chill swept through her. Honestly, she couldn't recall. "I dunno," she murmured, reaching for her planner, her heart racing. "You know how irregular they are." Flipping through her color-coded notes gave her a little structure at this dizzying moment. "Maybe... October?"

Kate's eyes widened, like she was putting two and two together. "It's February."

"So what?" Leah snapped back, defiance bubbling up as she glanced at her hands. "I've gone longer without one. Remember junior year of high school? The doc said it was stress—"

"Leah," Kate interrupted, her voice softer but still sharp. "That was different. This? It's different."

"Different how?" Leah snapped again, defensive walls going up against a truth she didn't want to face.

"Because this time, you're always exhausted. You were throwing up in the mornings, and you nearly passed out in Bio lab last week."

Leah's stomach churned at the recollection. She'd chalked it up to skipping breakfast and too much coffee, but now, looking at Kate, something deeper was clawing at her inside.

"No," she mumbled, shaking her head, as if that could erase the reality creeping in. "That's not... I can't be..."

"Leah," Kate leaned closer, concern mixed with determination. "When's the last time you were with Ryan?"

The question hit Leah like a punch to the gut. It brought back memories of heartbreak, stress, and non-stop studying. Their last weekend had been in October, just before everything fell apart—right before she discovered he had cheated. Their second anniversary was a bittersweet memory now.

"October," she whispered, the realization crushing down on her. "Right before..."

Kate finished her sentence, "Right before you found out he was cheating," her touch gentle as she squeezed Leah's hands, offering silent comfort. The word "betrayal" hung between them like a heavy cloud.

"No. No, I—I can't be pregnant." Just the thought sent panic surging through her body, her heart racing. "I can't! I'm trying to get into med school. I'm finally learning to live for me without him. I can't..." Her voice trailed off, fear curling tight in her stomach as if it wanted to push her away from the truth.

"First things first," Kate said, her voice gentle. She stood, taking charge of the situation. "We're going to the health center."

"No!" Panic shot through Leah, hotter than before. Her breath quickened as the walls felt like they were closing in. "I've got class in an hour. I've got a study group—"

"You've got a situation that's bigger than a study group," Kate shot back, determination in her eyes. "The study group can wait."

Overwhelmed by the force of Kate's insistence, Leah stumbled out of her chair as if it had protested. The frigid February air hit her like a splash of ice water when they stepped outside, starkly contrasting the warmth of the coffee shop. Snowflakes whirled around them—delicate crystals reflecting the streetlamps—while Leah's heart felt as heavy as the textbooks stuffed in her backpack. Each step toward the student health center felt like marching into the unknown, swirling memories of frantic studying, pressure to excel, and the sting of Ryan's betrayal flying around her head.

Nurse Thompson's office welcomed them with a clinical warmth, the bright walls and posters contrasting with the storm brewing in Leah's mind. Colorful posters about sexual health, pregnancy, and mental wellness lined the walls—a calm facade that felt almost cruel. The nurse's knowing look made Leah shrink deeper into her plastic chair.

"Four months, you say?" Nurse Thompson asked, her calm demeanor never wavering. As she took notes on her tablet, Leah felt the urge to squirm. "And you've been having morning sickness and fatigue?"

"I thought it was just stress," Leah said weakly, pleaded for understanding. "With finals and MCAT prep..." Realizing how far beyond normal that stress could be.

"And your periods have always been irregular?" the nurse continued, fixing her gaze on Leah with an understanding that both reassured and terrified her.

"Yeah," Leah responded, an old fear creeping back in—one she'd battled since high school. "The doc said it was normal with my activity level and stress..."

Nurse Thompson nodded, her voice kind but firm. "It can be. But let's do some blood work to be absolutely sure."

Leah felt her heartbeat quicken, the drum pounding harder in her chest as the weight of getting tested sank deeper. The next hour dragged on in a haze of needle pricks and gentle questions, with each moment feeling like it took forever. While Kate attempted to keep Leah distracted with stories of silly high school mishaps, Leah fought against the rising tide of uncertainty that felt like it would swallow her whole.

The office door swung open, and Nurse Thompson came in with a tablet and a gentle smile that felt like it was prepping her for news she didn't want to hear.

"The blood test confirms it," she said. "You're approximately 16 weeks pregnant." The finality of those words echoed in Leah's mind, crashing into her thoughts, wrapping around her breath until it felt hard to exhale. Four months. A third of a pregnancy that she'd somehow overlooked until now.

"I'll give you some time to process," Nurse Thompson continued, the crinkle of the folder's many papers filling the silence as she handed it to Leah. The weight of the options, resources, and pamphlets pressed heavily into Leah's hands. "But we should talk about your options soon. At this stage..."

"I need to call my mom," Leah blurted out, desperation creeping into her voice—filling her mouth with a bitter taste. "I need... I can't..."

"Of course," Nurse Thompson replied with a nod. "Take all the time you need."

Once they were alone, Kate pulled Leah into a fierce hug, grounding her in the chaos. "I'm right here," she whispered, her grip unyielding. "Whatever you decide, I'm right here."

Leah's phone felt massive in her hand as she dialed home, dreading the conversation. Each ring felt like a heartbeat, echoing like a frantic reminder that her world might be shifting. Each ring counted down to a reality she wasn't ready to face.

"Mom?" The word escaped her lips barely above a whisper. She could picture Claire settled in the kitchen, warm light streaming through the window. But Leah knew this chat might shatter that peaceful image.

"Leah?" her mom's voice came through, disoriented from sleep yet filled with concern. "Honey, what's up?"

"I need..." The words snagged in Leah's throat, heavy as boulders. Taking a deep breath, she forced herself to speak. "I need you not to freak out."

"Okay," Claire replied, her tone steady—a lifeline in the chaos. Leah could hear her mother processing, piecing together her worries and the gravity of the situation.

"I'm pregnant," Leah blurted out, the truth crashing over her like a tidal wave.

Silence enveloped the call, stretching unbearably, each heartbeat echoing like thunder in Leah's ears. She could visualize her mom's reaction—the sharp intake of breath, the shock rendering her mother immobile.

Claire broke the silence. "I'll be on the next flight out."

"Mom, you don't have to—" Panic surged through Leah again, desperate denial flooding her senses.

"Yes, I do," Claire's voice regained strength, sounding resolute. "You're my daughter, and you need me. Everything else can wait."

The call ended, and as Leah sat in the waiting room, Kate buzzing with purpose, she felt the reality of it all settle uncomfortably in. The folder of brochures and information lay heavy in her lap, a tangible representation of the choices looming ahead.

"What am I going to do?" Leah whimpered more to herself than to Kate, the weight of it all feeling overwhelming.

"First," Kate said, sliding into the seat beside her, fierce determination lighting up her face, "you're gonna breathe. Then we'll get you some proper food—no more coffee shop stuff. We'll wait for your mom and Marina, and we'll figure this out together."

"I can't have a baby," Leah muttered, as if saying it aloud could change anything. "I'm supposed to be applying to med school. I'm supposed to be everything I've planned." Tears threatened again, crashing down like the weight of this revelation.

"Perfect?" Kate asked. "Maybe it's time to let go of 'supposed to' and figure out what you really want."

As they walked back to Leah's dorm, the silence hung thick between them—each step weighed down with the implications of a future that felt utterly unwritten. Inside her tiny room were remnants of what had once felt real: neatly organized study guides, med school brochures, and notebooks filled with all she envisioned for herself.

Now, the same space felt suffocating and chaotic—everything in disarray.

"What will people think?" Leah sank onto her bed, still clutching the folder like a lifeline. She glanced around the room, searching for answers among the remnants of her old life.

"Since when do you care about what people think?" Kate began gathering the scattered study materials, organizing Leah's space in a way that brought her a bit of control. "The Leah I know has been through her parents' divorce, a cheating boyfriend, and pre-med biology while holding up a 4.0 GPA. She can handle anything."

"Yeah, well, that Leah was striving for perfection," Leah admitted, her voice thick with realization. The admission was uncomfortable, a jagged truth that left a pit in her stomach. "And look where that got me."

"It got you exactly where you needed to be," Kate said, sitting on the edge of Leah's bed, shoulder brushing against hers. "Strong enough to face this, whatever you choose to do."

At that moment, Leah's phone buzzed with a text from Marina: "On my way! Don't make any decisions until I get there. Love you."

Another buzz vibrated against her bedside table. It was from Claire: "Landed, flight in two hours. We'll figure this out together."

The thought of facing her mother filled Leah with a mix of dread and warmth. They had been through so much together; she couldn't help but wonder if this would be any different.

As dusk painted the sky with muted pastels, Leah reflected on the past four months—the grind for academic excellence had consumed her, a desperate distraction from the heartbreak of Ryan's betrayal.

Each symptom had been part of her coping mechanism, dismissed as stress until now.

"I should have known," Leah whispered, regret weighing heavily on her heart. "How did I not know?"

"Because you were busy surviving," Kate said, her soft tone wrapping around Leah's turbulent thoughts like a warm blanket. "You were caught up in the pain and the exhaustion, pushing through to meet everyone's expectations. Sometimes, you don't see what you're not ready to face."

Leah bit her lip; the sharp edge of self-realization stung. She'd always sought perfection—an admirable GPA, a stellar resume, and a life that looked good from the outside. But now, sitting amidst uncertainty, she grasped the consequences of that pressure. It had left her blind to the truth growing inside her.

Then, a knock at the door startled them both. Nurse Thompson stepped back into the room holding a stack of pamphlets and a warm smile that suggested she was ready to help.

"I thought you might have questions," she said, pulling up a chair across from Leah. "About your options."

Options. The word resonated in Leah's mind, weighted by expectations and realities that felt unanticipated. She stood at a precipice, the view below obscured by fog. Leah glanced at Kate, who offered an encouraging nod, then turned her gaze back to the nurse, searching for a lifeline.

"Take your time," Nurse Thompson offered warmly. "This is a lot to take in." She tapped her fingers on the folder resting on Leah's bed. "You've got support, and we can go at your pace."

Leah's pulse drummed in her ears as she considered the implications of those words. It felt surreal—the realization that she was now responsible for not just herself, but for another life. The enormity of that thought weighed on her as she began listing questions to regain control of this spiraling situation.

"What are my options?" Leah asked, her voice steadier than she felt. She'd always been the one with answers; now, she was desperate for clarity.

Nurse Thompson leaned in, her expression attentive. "There are a few paths to think about—parenting, adoption, or termination. Each choice has its own set of implications, so it's important to ponder what feels right for you."

Leah's heart raced as she absorbed the weight of those words. "I want to apply to med school," she murmured, struggling to make sense of it all. "How can I do that with a baby?"

"Many women go back to school or even start careers while raising children," the nurse reassured her. "It can be tough, but your goals don't have to fade away. Finding support is key, and figuring out what you genuinely want for your future is critical."

Kate squeezed Leah's hand, offering her steady presence. "You're not alone in this, Leah. Whatever you decide, we'll figure it out together."

Leah locked eyes with the nurse, feeling a deep well of concern reflected on her. "What about my mental health?" she pressed, anxiety gnawing at her thoughts. "What if I can't handle it all?"

Nurse Thompson nodded, her expression softening. "That's a valid concern. You might experience a whirlwind of emotions—fear, anxiety, excitement, and even sadness. All those feelings are normal and can coexist. Seeking counseling can provide valuable support as you navigate this journey."

"I just... I don't want to fail again," Leah whispered, tears pooling in her eyes. The weight of her past was heavy. Memories of Ryan's betrayal still stung deep. "I thought I was finding myself. I was learning to live for me."

"Finding yourself isn't about one decision; it's a journey," Kate reminded her, brushing a stray hair from Leah's tear-stained cheek. "This is just one part of your story. You are so much more than your grades or a ticking clock. You have the strength to handle this, no matter what."

A silence settled around them, filled only by Leah's breathing, punctuated by the reality of her situation. It was hard not to visualize the life she'd dreamed of—a powerhouse student prepping for med school and piecing her heart back together. But now, a new life demanding her attention—a tiny flicker of possibility nestled within her—was at the forefront.

As the minutes ticked by, Kate's presence felt like an anchor, steady and unwavering. The thought of finding a way forward gnawed at Leah with budding clarity. Could she balance a career and raise a child, or would one have to give way?

"Are there resources for single mothers at med schools?" Leah asked, her heartbeat rising again as she voiced her fears aloud, realizing how serious the situation had become.

Nurse Thompson nodded, tapping the edge of the folder. "Many schools offer resources specifically for parents or expecting students. There are childcare facilities, support groups, and financial aid options that acknowledge the unique challenges you might face."

Leah took a shaky breath, picturing the logistics—the long nights of studying with a baby in her arms, the exhaustion that would surely accompany it. Could she manage the burden of her dreams alongside another life's needs? The earlier resolve faltered, uncertainty creeping back in. "But what if I can't do it all? What if I drop the ball?"

"Then you adjust," Nurse Thompson replied, her demeanor steady and reassuring. "There's no perfect way to navigate this. Both motherhood and education are challenges, but countless women have walked this path before you. They've found their way—and you can too."

Slowly, Leah's emotions aligned; the wheels in her mind shifted toward a new direction. She felt Kate's hand grip tighter around hers—a grounding force in the whirlwind of thoughts.

"Before we dive deeper, is there anything you need from us right now?" Nurse Thompson asked, inviting Leah to lean on the available support. "We can connect you with counseling or parenting classes if you think that would help."

Taking a deep breath, Leah considered her options. "I think I need to talk it out with my mom when she gets here. I have a lot of questions and fears; I can't do this without her. She's always been my guide."

Nurse Thompson nodded in understanding. "That sounds like a solid plan. Having family support can make a significant difference during this time."

As the conversation shifted back to practical steps, Leah felt the tension in her shoulders ease. She may not have all the answers today, but she could take things one step at a time. After all, she wasn't alone in this; Kate, her mom, and many resources were available.

Minutes later, the familiar buzz of her phone interrupted the silence. A text came in from her roommate, Marina: "I'm outside!"

Leah's heart swelled with appreciation. Their tight-knit friendship felt like solid ground—Marina was practical, organized, and always ready to offer a helping hand.

"Just in time," Leah said, rising from her seat. She felt a flicker of nerves, but recognized that those nerves were part of a shift occurring within her.

As they awaited Marina's arrival, a shared sense of camaraderie enveloped the room, soothing Leah's tumultuous thoughts. Memorable moments flashed through her mind—the countless late-night study sessions, the heartbreak discussions, and the laughter and tears that formed the very fabric of their friendship.

A moment later, Marina burst through the door with infectious energy. "You two look like you just survived a natural disaster. What happened?"

Leah met Marina's gaze, a mix of fear and determination bubbling to the surface. "I'm pregnant," she blurted, her words tumbling out before she could second-guess herself.

To Marina's credit, she didn't recoil or question her. Instead, she stepped forward, unfazed. "Okay, let's talk about this. What's next?"

With Kate's comforting presence and Marina's practical mindset, Leah began reciting everything that had happened—the test results, the waiting room, and her conversation with Nurse Thompson. As she spoke, the weight of her thoughts coalesced, morphing fear into a narrative—a story where she was still the protagonist.

"First off, you're not alone in this. I'm coming with you to see your mom," Marina said fiercely. "We'll map out a plan together and figure out what that looks like."

"I really appreciate that," Leah replied, emotional gratitude swelling within her. "It means everything to have you by my side."

"Seriously, Leah," Kate chimed in. "This is a journey of discovery, and you've got so much support. We're all going to help you navigate this."

Leah closed her eyes, allowing their words to wash over her like a warm wave of comfort. The shock was still there—raw and unsettling—but now a flicker of something brighter emerged, a small ember of resolve igniting beneath the surface. She wasn't just facing the storm; she was about to step into the light, her friends beside her.

After discussing immediate options and the next steps, a rough plan took shape, and Leah felt a renewed sense of agency. They would meet her mom at the school, sit with her, lay everything on the table, and work through fears and uncertainties. For the first time since receiving the news, Leah felt a little more grounded—the chaos of her thoughts slowly aligning like a jigsaw puzzle coming together.

As her mother's arrival approached, Leah paced her small dorm room, anxiety and excitement swirling within her. The familiar walls felt stifling, reminders of the future she had envisioned solo. But they also held memories of laughter and strong friendships with Kate and Marina.

"What if she's disappointed in me?" Leah voiced her fears, glancing at Marina, who was perched on the edge of her bed, a look of fierce determination on her face.

"Don't you dare think that way," Marina countered, sitting up straight. "You're her daughter. No matter what happens, she's gonna love you and support you."

"But what about her dreams for me?" Leah asked, her voice wavering like her confidence. "I was supposed to be the perfect daughter—getting into med school, living out my dreams. What if this changes everything?"

"Perfect is overrated," Kate chimed in, her arms crossed. "You've already been through heartbreak and setbacks. This just adds another layer to your journey. Trust me, most parents want what's best for their kids, even if it doesn't look like what they originally envisioned."

Leah frowned, mulling over her friends' encouragement while trying to push down her creeping doubts. "I just wish I knew how to talk to her about this."

"Start with honesty," Marina suggested, her tone softening. "Tell her how you feel—the fear, the uncertainty—everything. She'll appreciate your honesty."

The conversation shifted from speculation to strategies, further bolstered by the comfort of their friendship. They discussed how Leah might frame the news, what potential questions her mom might have, and reactions they should prepare for. It was all a whirlwind, but the support of her closest friends made it feel less daunting.

A text pinged through Leah's phone—"I'm here!" It was her mom, signaling her arrival.

Leah stood at the threshold of her dorm room, feeling a knot form in her stomach as that familiar warmth and anxiety collided. "Okay, here we go," she muttered, bolstered by Kate and Marina's solid presence beside her. Their support felt unbreakable, anchoring her to the moment.

They met Claire at the bustling entrance of Leah's dormitory. As her mom stepped inside, Leah's stomach twisted tighter. Claire's face held a mix of weariness and concern. But as their eyes locked, that unmistakable, unconditional love washed over Leah.

"Leah!" Claire rushed forward, wrapping her in a hug that felt both safe and suffocating. Leah breathed in her mom's familiar scent, a comforting piece of home amidst the uncertainty. "I'm so glad to see you!" The rush of relief in Claire's voice set the scene for what awaited them.

"Hi, Mom," Leah managed, the warmth of the embrace igniting a mixture of comfort and anxiety within her. They pulled apart, and Leah caught a glimpse of her mom's expression—worn but loving, eyes sharp and alert, ready to face whatever storm might brew between them.

"Let's sit down," Leah said, motioning toward the student lounge. It was cozy, adorned with mismatched couches that seemed perfect for heartfelt conversations.

Leah took a deep, fortifying breath. "Mom, I found out today... I'm pregnant."

A heavy silence enveloped the room, feeling louder than anything that could be said. Leah braced herself for her mom's reaction, anticipating disappointment or disbelief.

Claire's gaze softened as she processed the reality of the moment. "Oh, honey..." she murmured, a mix of concern and understanding in her voice. "How are you feeling?"

"I don't know," Leah admitted, her voice dropping to a whisper. "I'm scared. I've worked so hard to get here, and now everything just feels flipped upside down."

Leah's emotions crashed over her like waves, and she let her fears spill into words. "I thought I was finally taking control of my life after everything with Ryan. And now... this."

Claire reached across the space between them, her hand cradling Leah's. "Sweetheart, it's completely understandable to feel overwhelmed right now. This is a huge change, and being scared is okay." Her voice was steady but warm, the sounds from the lounge fading into nothingness.

"But what about med school?" Leah's voice wobbled with desperation. "I can't just put everything on hold. I don't want to throw away my dreams."

"Leah," Claire said, locking eyes with her daughter. "You're not throwing anything away. This is part of your journey, not the end. People live their dreams while raising kids every day. It will be challenging, but you have a support system right here."

The warmth of her mother's words eased some of Leah's fears, serving as a lifeline she desperately needed. "I don't want to disappoint you," she confessed, tears prickling her eyes. "I wanted to make you proud."

"You are my daughter, and nothing will change that. You don't have to be perfect to earn my pride—just be yourself," Claire said, squeezing Leah's hand tightly. "I'll always love you, no matter what you choose. This does not define you."

In that moment, Leah felt a flicker of validation ignite within her; perhaps there was room for her aspirations along with whatever path lay ahead. She glanced over at Kate and Marina, who were close by, their expressions attentive and encouraging, silently supporting her in this raw moment.

As they sat together, the conversation deepened. Claire asked Leah about her feelings regarding the pregnancy, anticipated challenges, and her thoughts on the future. Each question felt more like an intimate exploration rather than an interrogation—an unearthing of Leah's hopes and fears.

"I was so focused on being perfect," Leah admitted, her voice earnest and vulnerable. "Setting high standards for myself and trying to control every little detail—but now it feels like that ideal is slipping through my fingers."

"Perfection is a myth, Leah," Kate chimed in, her tone gentle yet firm. "Real life isn't a perfectly-organized planner; it's messy and complicated—and that's totally okay. It's how you navigate through those messes that truly define you."

Tears pricked at Leah's eyes, a mix of relief and sorrow washing over her. "But I feel so overwhelmed. I never expected this, and I don't know if I'm ready to be a mom."

"You're not alone in feeling that way," Claire reassured her, her voice a soothing balm. "That's totally normal. Not everyone feels ready to become a parent, and it's a significant life change. But your instincts will kick in, and you will learn as you go. Just remember to lean on us when you need to."

Leah wiped her eyes with the back of her hand, the tremors of uncertainty slowly settling. "I guess I just need space to process everything and decide."

"Of course," Marina piped up from her seat. "We can look for resources together—parenting classes, support groups for student parents, whatever you need. You're not expected to have it all figured out right now."

"What if I decide to keep the baby?" Leah asked quietly, her words hanging heavily in the air. "What if I want to do this?"

"Then that's your choice, and we'll all be beside you," Kate assured her, her expression unwavering. "You have a tribe, Leah. We'll make this work together."

Leah breathed deeply, glancing around the circle of supportive faces—her mother, her closest friend, and her well-organized confidante. They were her lifeline at a time when she felt adrift.

"Okay, I think I need to explore what it means to be a parent while pursuing my dreams," she murmured, reflecting on her thoughts. "It might not look like I imagined, but maybe that's okay."

A small smile broke across Claire's face, pride shining in her eyes. "That's a healthy approach. It's all about being adaptable, honey. Life is full of surprises, and your happiness matters most."

As they continued discussing options and resources, Leah felt glimmers of possibility cutting through some of the fog of anxiety. Each question and prospect they explored felt like a step toward clarity, pulling away some of the fear and uncertainty clouding her vision. With every word, Leah felt herself reclaiming her strength, embracing the unexpected path that lay ahead.

When the conversation wound down, Leah felt lighter, as if a burden she hadn't fully realized she was carrying had lifted. Her mom had her arms around her, and Kate and Marina were right there beside her. She knew she could lean on them in the days and weeks to come.

As evening fell, the indigo sky outside her dorm window grew deeper, sprinkled with stars that gradually pierced the twilight. Leah walked her mother to her hotel, feeling the echoes of their conversation settle in her heart. Claire hugged her tightly, a reassuring presence filling Leah with comfort.

"Remember, whatever you decide, you're not alone," Claire whispered, her words a promise.

Leah watched her mother walk into the hotel, feeling the weight of friendship and support lingering in the air. Turning back toward campus, the familiar paths and brick buildings she'd walked countless times seemed to glow with new meaning. Every snow-covered step felt like a move toward something new—an unfamiliar future that she was welcoming.

Kate and Marina lingered in Leah's dorm room, reluctant to leave her alone. They sprawled on her bed and flipped through the stack of pamphlets Nurse Thompson had provided, adjusting to this new normal with their usual banter and seamless support for Leah.

"What are you thinking about?" Kate asked, nudging Leah gently.

"I'm thinking about everything," Leah replied, a hint of wonder infusing her tone. "It's like my life flipped upside down, but I'm not scared anymore. I think maybe I'm actually excited."

"Excited is good," Marina said, closing a pamphlet and exhaling in relief. "Excited means you're ready for what could come next."

Leah nodded, soaking in their warmth and support. As snowflakes danced outside, the wind spiraling, Leah realized she was just at the start of a new story. Each uncertainty was now an opportunity to build a broader, more intricate life than she had ever envisioned.

Later, as Leah lay in bed, staring at the ceiling in the dim light, she traced her fingers over her stomach. The sensation felt no longer threatening, but promising. For the first time in a long while, she didn't feel the pressure of perfection crushing down on her. Instead, a quiet resolve settled inside her, rooted not in certainty but in embracing the unexpected.

She picked up her phone one last time that night to text Ryan, the only loose end she felt obligated to tie up.

"I'm starting a new chapter," she typed before pausing. She thought of the empathetic closeness of her friends, her mom's unwavering support, and the promise of new beginnings. But then she deleted the message with a small, serene smile before sending it.

Leah knew the journey ahead wouldn't always be easy. There would be hurdles and heartaches, challenges and triumphs. But she also understood that she hadn't been alone, which filled her with profound comfort.

As the night deepened, Leah placed a gentle hand on her stomach, acknowledging the life that would soon change hers in ways she couldn't even imagine. With each measured breath, Leah accepted the beauty of imperfection, releasing the rigid expectations of what her life was "supposed to" look like and opening herself up to what it could become.

The next few days passed in a blur—calls with her mom, long talks with Kate and Marina, and research into resources for expectant students. Each meeting and conversation helped Leah piece together a plan, one that hadn't existed before but now felt like a canvas waiting for her to paint it.

During lunch one day, Leah and Kate huddled over laptops in the dining hall, flipping through various websites about parenting resources available for student moms.

"Look at this place," Kate said, pointing excitedly at her screen. "They offer parenting classes and support groups, and I think they even have scholarships for student parents!"

"They really pack a punch with their programs," Leah nodded, her excitement building. "This could be a tremendous help!"

As they navigated websites, a new sense of purpose blossomed in Leah. Instead of overwhelming anxiety, she felt a surge of hope coursing through her—a guiding light illuminating her path forward.

"I never thought I'd be in this situation," Leah admitted, her tone thoughtful. "But maybe this is actually an opportunity. I get to shape my future, even if it's not how I pictured it."

"You're gonna crush this, Leah," Kate said with a grin, leaning over to squeeze her friend's shoulder. "You've already handled so much. This is just a new adventure."

And Leah started believing that maybe it could be. She had surrounded herself with a solid support system—Kate, Marina, her mom, Nurse Thompson, and an entire community of resources. They would walk this journey together, and Leah could forge her own path, one step at a time.

With renewed energy, Leah focused on her studies while balancing her coursework and preparing for the MCAT. She filled her planner not just with study schedules but also with classes she planned to attend and meetings with counselors. The structure helped her regain a sense of control amidst the uncertainty swirling in her life.

Days turned into weeks, and Leah settled into her new rhythm. She still had moments of doubt and fear flickered at the edges of her consciousness, but they were fewer and farther between. Every time she felt the nagging worry creeping back in, she'd take a deep breath, remind herself of her goals, and remember all the people who believed in her.

Her conversations with her mom became more open and honest. They discussed everything from practical arrangements to Leah's fears and dreams for the future. Claire's unwavering support showed Leah how she could still pursue her ambitions while embracing the idea of becoming a parent.

One evening, while Leah was prepping for an upcoming midterm, a wave of exhaustion hit her. She leaned back in her chair, rubbing her eyes, and sighed. Just as she was about to dive back into her notes, Kate popped her head into the door.

"Hey, study queen! You've been at it for hours. How about a break?" Kate suggested, a playful glint in her eyes.

"I could use one," Leah replied, her smile breaking through the fatigue. "What do you have in mind?"

"Let's hit up that new coffee shop down the street! They have the best hot chocolate," Kate proposed, her enthusiasm infectious.

"We can celebrate your progress with some sweet treats."

Leah laughed, the heaviness of studying lifting. "Okay, but I need to finish a few things first."

"Just a few, huh?" Kate teased. "Make it quick! I'm craving that hot chocolate."

After a few more minutes of cramming, Leah wrapped up her study materials and joined her friend. As they strolled down the street together, snowflakes fell again, illuminating the evening with a magical glow.

As they settled into their cozy corner booth with steaming mugs in hand, something shifted in Leah. Surrounded by the warmth of her friend and the comforting scent of chocolate and coffee, she felt a surge of hope mixed with anxiety.

"So," Kate began, leaning forward, her grin bright. "What's the latest on the baby front? Have you thought more about how you'll balance everything?"

Leah took a sip of her hot chocolate, savoring the rich flavor as she contemplated her response. "I have. I still have a lot of questions, but

I'm starting to feel like I can handle this. Like, I can really figure out a way to do both—school and being a mom."

"You totally can!" Kate said, her enthusiasm was infectious. "You've got an amazing support system—don't forget that. Plus, you've always been the most organized person I know. It's gonna be full-on, but totally doable."

"Yeah, I'll just have to adjust some of my plans along the way," Leah agreed, her confidence growing. "But here's the thing... I think I need to talk to Ryan."

Kate raised an eyebrow. "Ryan? You mean the ex?"

"Yeah," Leah said, already feeling a knot form in her stomach. "I have to let him know... about the baby."

Kate looked at her, surprise flickering across her face. "Are you sure? That's a big step."

"I know," Leah replied, taking a deep breath. "But he has to know. It's his child too, and he deserves to be part of this conversation, whether he wants to be involved later on. I don't want to keep this from him."

Kate nodded slowly, the seriousness of the moment sinking in. "That's really brave, Leah. But are you ready for whatever reaction he might have?"

"Honestly? No," Leah admitted, her voice shaky. "But I can't let fear keep me from doing what's right—and I need to be upfront about this, especially since I plan to keep the baby."

"I get that," Kate said, her eyes filled with understanding. "You need to be true to yourself and your situation. Talking to him might bring some clarity."

As they chatted about how Leah might approach the conversation, her resolve built. "Maybe I can message him tonight," Leah said, feeling a mix of anxiety and empowerment. "I'll just be honest. I owe him that."

Kate leaned in, her expression supportive. "Whatever you decide, just know you're strong enough to handle it. You've tackled so much already, and you can navigate this too."

As they left the coffee shop, Leah felt lighter, buoyed by their support. The cold air was invigorating, and the laughter they shared made her heart feel warm. The knot in her stomach remained, but she realized it was tied to excitement too—a readiness to face the challenges ahead.

When they reached Leah's dorm, the weight of her decision pressed down on her shoulders, but it no longer felt paralyzing. It felt like a fresh beginning.

"Thanks for the pep talk," Leah said, pulling her friend into a quick hug. "I'll keep you posted after I talk to Ryan."

"Absolutely," Kate replied, her smiled unwavering. "You got this, Leah."

As Leah entered her room, she felt a renewed sense of purpose. She was nervous about reaching out to Ryan, but the decision was made. With each step she took, Leah felt more empowered to navigate this new reality—shaping the journey ahead while embracing the twists and turns along the way.

CHAPTER 10

Bitter Truth

T he mid-March air carried winter's chill as Leah waited outside the coffee shop where she and Ryan had agreed to meet. Her stethoscope still hung around her neck from her morning clinical rotations, and she tucked it into her bag with trembling hands. The early spring sunlight felt bright, promising warmth it couldn't quite deliver—much like her hopes for this conversation. Her stomach churned with morning sickness and anxiety as she checked her phone for the hundredth time. The weeks since discovering her pregnancy in February had blurred into doctor's appointments, sleepless nights, and endless debates about whether she should tell him.

She spotted Ryan's familiar figure approaching from down the street, but he wasn't alone. A tall, slim girl with styled blonde hair walked beside him, their fingers intertwined. Leah's heart sank. She had prepared for many scenarios, but this wasn't one of them.

"Hey," Ryan said, as if they were acquaintances passing by. "Um, this is Jessica. She's in my advanced robotics class."

Jessica's lips curved into what seemed like a practiced smile. "Hi! Ryan's told me so much about you. You're the pre-med student, right?"

Leah managed a tight nod, trying to keep her composure. "Ryan, could we maybe talk privately for a minute?"

"Whatever you need to say, you can say in front of Jess," Ryan replied, his arm wrapped around Jessica's waist. "We don't keep secrets from each other."

Leah recognized the irony in his statement. She shifted uncomfortably, aware of how her oversized sweater draped over her growing belly. Her mind flashed to the organic chemistry textbook in her bag—another reminder of all she stood to lose.

"I... I really think this should be private."

"Look," Jessica interjected, "if this is about getting back together with Ryan, you should know that—"

"It's not," Leah cut her off, her voice sharper than intended. She took a deep breath, knowing there was no easy way to do this. "Ryan, I'm pregnant."

The words hung in the air like smoke. Ryan's face went blank while Jessica's eyes narrowed.

"I'm about four months along," Leah added quietly.

"Four months?" Jessica scoffed, gripping Ryan's arm tighter. "And you're just telling him now? That's convenient. How do we even know it's his?"

Leah felt her cheeks burn. "Because, unlike what you might think, I'm not that kind of person. And trust me, I wasn't planning on telling him at all."

"Then why are you?" Ryan spoke, his voice cold.

"Because..." Leah's voice cracked. "Because no matter how things ended between us, you deserve to know. I couldn't... I couldn't live with myself knowing I kept this from you."

"Look," Jessica stepped forward, "Ryan's busy with his engineering senior project, his internship at Tesla, and graduate program plans. He can't throw all that away because of a mistake—"

"Mistake?" Leah's voice trembled. "Is that what you're calling it, Ryan? A mistake?"

Ryan ran his hands through his hair, frustration clear. "What do you want me to say, Leah? That I'm ready to be a father? I've got my engineering degree to finish, my certification exams are coming up. This isn't part of the plan."

"The plan?" Leah laughed bitterly. "You mean like how I planned to start medical school next fall? You think this was part of my plan? To jeopardize everything I've worked for?"

"At least he's not trying to trap someone with a baby," Jessica snapped.

"Trap him?" Leah's eyes widened. "You think I wanted this? You think I planned to get pregnant at twenty-one? To have morning sickness so bad I can barely make it through my clinical rotations. To explain to my parents why their straight-A daughter might have to put her med school plan on hold?"

"Nobody's asking you to keep it," Ryan muttered, staring at the ground.

The words hit Leah like a physical blow. She stared at him, this boy she thought she knew, this boy she had loved, and saw a stranger.

"I am keeping it," she said, her hand instinctively moving to her stomach. "With or without you. I just... I thought you should know."

"Well, now I know," Ryan said flatly. "And I can't be involved in this, Leah. I'm sorry. I've got my whole future planned—the engineering program at Tesla, maybe grad school after that..."

"Don't be sorry," Leah replied, surprised by her steadiness. "I don't need your money, I don't need your support, and I certainly don't need your pity."

Jessica tugged at Ryan's arm. "We should go. We've got that engineering lab meeting."

Ryan hesitated for a moment, and Leah saw a flicker of something—regret? fear?—crossed his face. But then it was gone, replaced by that same blank expression.

"Good luck, Leah," he said, turning away. "I mean it."

The following weeks passed in a blur. Leah threw herself into her studies, trying to maintain her near-perfect GPA while battling constant fatigue and morning sickness. Her lab coat felt tighter each week, and standing for hours during clinical rotations became increasingly challenging. The formaldehyde smell in the anatomy lab, once merely unpleasant, now triggered waves of nausea.

One evening, she sat in her dorm room, staring at her biochemistry notes while absently rubbing her growing belly. Her MCAT prep books were stacked neatly on her desk, a stark reminder of the future she'd planned. Her back ached from today's eight-hour hospital rotation, and she could barely focus on the enzyme pathways she needed to memorize.

"You okay?" her roommate, Marina, asked from across the room. "You've been staring at the same page for an hour."

Leah closed her textbook with a sigh. "I don't think I can do this anymore."

Marina set aside her own genetics homework. "The studying?"

"All of it," Leah gestured vaguely. "The pre-med track, clinical rotations, MCAT prep... I almost fainted during rounds today. Dr. Matthews had to send me home early."

"Have you thought about what we talked about?" Marina asked. "About taking a break? Med school will still be there in a few years."

Leah nodded slowly, her hand still resting on her bump. "I had this whole timeline planned out, you know? Graduate this spring, start med school in the fall. Now..." She trailed off, fighting back tears. "Now I can barely make it through a hospital shift without getting dizzy."

"Being a doctor is still possible," Marina reminded her. "Just... maybe not on the timeline you originally planned."

"My advisor said there are plenty of non-traditional medical students," Leah added. "People who had careers or families first. I just never thought I'd be one of them."

"And you're not giving up," Marina said firmly. "You're just adapting."

Leah picked up her stethoscope, running her fingers over the smooth metal. "The irony is, being pregnant has taught me more about medicine than some of my classes. Every appointment, every ultrasound... I ask questions about everything. My OB-GYN probably thinks I'm crazy."

"Sounds like you're still meant to be a doctor," Marina smiled. "Just taking a scenic route to get there."

The next morning, Leah walked into the pre-med advisor's office. Her decision was made, but that didn't make it any easier.

"Are you sure about this?" Dr. Peterson asked, looking over Leah's withdrawal forms as early April sunshine streamed through his office window. "Your academic record is outstanding. We were planning to write you a strong recommendation for medical school for next year's cycle. Perhaps we could look into part-time options to finish the spring semester?"

"I need to be realistic," Leah said, her voice stronger than she felt. "I can't keep up with clinical rotations while preparing for the baby. And the MCAT... I can barely stay awake long enough to study these days."

Dr. Peterson nodded thoughtfully. "Some of our most successful medical school applicants have taken non-traditional paths. One of our graduates last year was a mother of three."

"That's comforting to hear," Leah managed a small smile. "I'm not giving up on becoming a doctor. I'm just... postponing it."

"Well, when you're ready to come back, your track record here will speak for itself. And this experience..." Dr. Peterson gestured to Leah's belly, "might give you a unique perspective as a physician someday."

As she left the office with her withdrawal forms processed, Leah felt a strange mix of sadness and relief. Her phone buzzed with a text from her mom: "How did it go? Want me to come help pack up your lab equipment this weekend?"

Leah typed back a quick "Yes, please" before stopping in the middle of the medical sciences building. Students rushed past her, heading to labs and lectures, living the life she thought she'd have. But as she felt a small flutter in her belly—the first definite movements she'd felt from the baby—she realized she wasn't saying goodbye to her dreams, just redrawing the map to reach them.

That evening, as she began packing her dorm room, Leah wrapped her microscope—a high school graduation gift from her parents when she'd announced her pre-med aspirations. Her lab coats hung neatly in the closet, and her medical dictionary sat dog-eared on her desk, filled with highlighted terms and margin notes.

"Want me to box up the MCAT books?"

Marina asked, gesturing to the stack of prep materials.

"No," Leah decided after a moment. "I'll keep those. Maybe I can start reviewing them during late-night feedings." She managed a small laugh. "Organic chemistry might be better than lullabies."

As she sorted through her desk, she came across an old photo of her and Ryan tucked into her anatomy textbook. They were at the engineering department's spring showcase, where Ryan had presented his robotics project. She was wearing her clinical rotation scrubs, having rushed straight from the hospital to support him. Both were smiling as if they had their whole lives figured out.

"Want me to throw that out?" Marina asked, noticing what Leah was looking at.

Leah considered it for a moment before sliding the photo back into the book. "No," she said. "I think I'll keep it. Not because I miss him or want him back, but because someday, when my kid asks about his or her father, I want to show him or her he wasn't always the person he chose to be that day. That once, he was someone who stayed up all night helping me study for my anatomy finals, who brought me coffee during my morning clinicals."

Marina squeezed her shoulder. "You're gonna be a great doctor someday, and an even better mom."

"I hope so," Leah whispered, her hand finding its way to her bump again. "Because right now, being a good mom is the only thing I'm sure about."

The next few days were a whirlwind of packing, paperwork, and goodbyes. Leah's mom arrived that weekend with their family's minivan, ready to help move her daughter back home before the spring term ended. The early April breeze carried the scent of blooming dogwoods as they loaded the last box of medical textbooks—a bittersweet reminder of the season's promise of renewal.

"It feels weird," she admitted to her mom. "Like I'm giving up on my dream."

Her mom pulled her into a hug. "You're not giving up, sweetheart. You're just taking a different route to get there. Some of the best doctors I know had families first. Remember Dr. Williams? She had three kids before she even started med school."

As they drove away from campus, Leah caught a glimpse of Ryan heading toward the engineering building, blueprints tucked under his arm. He didn't see her, and she was glad. She had said everything she needed to say that day outside the coffee shop.

Her mom noticed her tense up. "You okay?"

Leah took a deep breath and nodded. "Yeah, I am. You know what's funny? A few months ago, I thought Ryan breaking up with me was the worst thing that could happen. Now... now I think it might have been the universe's way of showing me who he really was before it was too late."

"The universe has a funny way of working things out sometimes," her mom said wisely. "And hey, maybe this little one will grow up to be a doctor like their mama."

Leah smiled, feeling the baby move again. As they merged onto the highway, leaving campus behind, Leah felt a strange sense of peace settle over her. Her medical textbooks might be packed away for now, but they weren't gone forever. Her dream of becoming a doctor wasn't ending—it was just being reimagined with a new character in the story.

She might not have Ryan's support, and her medical school plans would have to wait, but she had something more important: the strength to make difficult choices, the courage to face their consequences, and the wisdom to know that sometimes life's biggest challenges lead to its greatest rewards.

The baby kicked again, stronger this time, as if in agreement. Leah smiled, placing her hand over the spot. "Just you and me, little one," she whispered. "And someday, when I'm doing my residency, you'll know that dreams don't have expiration dates. They just need a little patience sometimes."

Her mom reached over and squeezed her hand, and Leah felt tears slip down her cheeks—not tears of sadness or regret, but of hope. Because sometimes the hardest choices lead to the most beautiful outcomes, and sometimes the longest paths lead to the best destinations.

Later that evening, Ryan sat at his desk in his apartment, staring blankly at the engineering drawings spread before him. The CAD software on his laptop remained untouched, the cursor blinking accusingly. His senior project deadline loomed, but all he could think about was the look on Leah's face when he'd walked away.

"You're being quiet," Jessica said from his bed, where she was scrolling through her phone. "Still thinking about what happened?"

"Just stressed about this project," he lied, closing his laptop. But Leah's words echoed in his head: "I'm pregnant." Two simple words that had the power to derail everything he'd worked for.

After Jessica left, Ryan paced his room, running his hands through his hair—a nervous habit he'd never broken. He picked up the Tesla internship offer letter from his desk, the words "Graduate Engineering Program" jumping out at him. Everything was falling into place just as he'd planned—the internship, his upcoming graduation, the promise of a six-figure salary.

"Fuck," he muttered, dropping onto his bed. He pulled out his phone and looked at his last text conversation with Leah from months ago. Their exchange had been about returning each other's things after the breakup. Now she was carrying his child, and he'd treated her like she was trying to ruin his life.

"Maybe I should call her," he said to the empty room. His thumb hovered over her contact information. But what would he say? That he was sorry but still couldn't be involved? That he felt guilty but not guilty enough to change his mind?

He thought about his own father, who'd always pushed him toward engineering, toward success, toward putting career first. "Don't let anything distract you from your goals, son," he'd always said. Ryan had followed that advice religiously.

Opening his laptop again, he found himself typing "parental rights and responsibilities" into Google. The search results made his stomach churn. Child support calculations. Custody agreements. Legal obligations. His planned future seemed to blur before his eyes.

"She said she doesn't need anything from me," he reminded himself, closing the browser. But he knew Leah—she'd rather struggle alone than ask for help. It was one thing he'd admired about her, back when they were together. Her determination, her independence, her drive.

His phone buzzed—a text from Jessica about meeting up later. Ryan stared at it for a long moment before responding. Jessica was uncomplicated and fun, aligned with his plans. She understood his ambitions because they matched her own. No messy emotions, no life-altering surprises.

But that night, sleep wouldn't come. He kept seeing Leah's face, the way her hand had instinctively moved to protect her belly—their baby. The thought made him break out in a cold sweat. Their baby. He was going to be a father, whether he stepped up or not.

"I can't do this," he whispered to his dark room. "I'm not ready." But another voice in his head whispered back: "Neither is she, but she doesn't have a choice."

The next morning, he threw himself into his project work with renewed determination, trying to drown out his conscience with equations and design specifications. When friends from campus mentioned seeing Leah, he changed the subject. "It was easier this way," he told himself. Better to make a clean break now than to be a half-hearted father. Better to focus on his career, on his future. Better to ignore the guilt gnawing in his stomach, the voice in his head that called him a coward.

But sometimes, late at night when he couldn't sleep, he'd look up local OB/GYN offices, wondering which one she went to. He'd catch himself calculating due dates in his head, imagining what the baby might look like. In those moments, the hollow sound of his own justifications echoed in his ears. The weight of his ambitions felt less significant.

Then he'd remember his plans, his goals, his father's expectations, and he'd push those thoughts away. He'd text Jessica, or work on his project, or do anything to avoid thinking about Leah facing this alone because of his choice.

"It's better this way," he'd repeat to himself, like a mantra. But each time, the words sounded less like conviction and more like cowardice. He opted for his well-charted, ambitious future, ignoring the uncertain road of fatherhood. He told himself that someday, when he felt powerful enough, wealthy enough, and emotionally prepared enough, perhaps he would rectify his decision.

But deep down, he knew that day would probably never come, and that knowledge would become yet another thing he'd have to learn to live with.

As the weeks passed, Ryan became more skilled at avoidance. He switched to his usual coffee shop when he learned Leah had morning clinical rotations nearby. He took longer routes to his engineering labs to avoid the medical sciences building. But despite his best efforts, reminders of his impending fatherhood seemed to lurk everywhere.

During his spring semester robotics lecture, a classmate showed ultrasound pictures of his sister's baby. The warm April sunlight streamed through the engineering building's windows, catching dust motes as the black-and-white image passed around, making Ryan's chest tighten with unwanted thoughts.

"Earth to Ryan," Jessica nudged him during their study group. "The Tesla project specs? You were about to explain the thermal management system?"

"Right, sorry," he mumbled, forcing himself to focus on the technical drawings. Lately, Jessica's conversations had been filled with the details of their future: the perfect apartment near the park, their joint career goals, a life of shared dreams and ambitious plans. It was everything he'd wanted, yet something felt hollow about it now.

One afternoon, he ran into Marina, Leah's roommate, in the campus bookstore. She gave him a withering look as he feigned interest in an engineering textbook he already owned.

"She's leaving school, you know," Marina said flatly, not bothering with pleasantries. "Putting her medical school dreams on hold because she can barely make it through clinical rotations with the morning sickness."

Ryan's grip tightened on the book, and he tried to remain calm. "I didn't... I mean, that's her choice, right?"

Marina's laugh was sharp. "Yeah, keep telling yourself that. Must be nice to have a choice."

The encounter haunted him for days. He looked up medical school acceptance rates, calculating how many years it would take Leah to get back on track. His father's voice echoed in his head: "Focus on your future, son. You can't let anything derail your plans."

But what about her plans?

During his internship at Tesla, he excelled at designing systems and solving problems. In engineering, everything had a solution if you applied the right principles. But this... this had no elegant solution, no simple formula to follow.

One evening, he overheard two engineers discussing their kids' college funds. They spoke with pride about sacrifices made, about balancing career and family. Ryan wondered if he'd ever have that—quiet pride in putting someone else first. Right now, all he had was the gnawing knowledge that he'd chosen the easier path.

"You seem distracted lately," Jessica commented over dinner. "Is it the senior project? Or..." she hesitated, "is it about Leah?"

"Just stressed about graduation," he lied smoothly, the words coming easier each time. Jessica smiled, satisfied, and launched into her plans for their post-graduation move to California.

But later that night, alone in his apartment, he pulled up his email and began typing: "Leah, I've been thinking..." He stared at the cursor for twenty minutes before deleting it. What right did he have to reach out now? To disturb whatever peace she'd made with his absence? His fingers hovered over the keyboard again.

"I'm sorry..." Delete.

"I want to help..." Delete.

"I'm a coward..." Delete.

Finally, he closed his laptop and pulled out his phone, scrolling through old photos he hadn't had the heart to delete. There was one of Leah in her first set of scrubs, beaming with pride. Another of them at his engineering showcase, her head resting on his shoulder after pulling an all-night study session. They looked so young, so certain about everything.

The next morning, he saw her across the quad. She was walking slowly, one hand resting on her now-visible bump, the other clutching her medical textbooks. For a moment, their eyes met, and Ryan felt the weight of everything he was running from.

She didn't smile or wave. She just looked at him with a mixture of disappointment and resignation before turning away. He realized then—she'd already accepted his absence. She'd figured out how to move forward without him, while he was still struggling with the guilt of letting her do it alone.

That evening, he threw himself into his senior project with renewed determination. This was one thing, at least, he could control. This followed the rules of physics and engineering, unlike the messy, complicated reality of impending fatherhood.

Jessica came over with takeout and plans for apartment hunting in California. As she chatted excitedly about their future, Ryan nodded and smiled at all the right moments. But part of him wondered if, years from now, he'd look back on this time and realize he'd engineered the perfect escape from the greatest responsibility of his life.

"You made the right choice," he whispered to himself that night, staring at his ceiling. But the words rang hollow, and somewhere across town, his child grew stronger under the heart of a woman who'd found the courage to face everything he'd run from.

As weeks turned into months, Ryan mastered the art of compartmentalization. He focused intensely on his senior project, threw himself into his Tesla internship, and convinced himself that his relationship with Jessica was everything he wanted. But sometimes, reality would crack his carefully constructed facade.

During a dinner with Jessica's family, her young nephew toddled over to their table, and Ryan automatically reached out to steady the child. The simple action sent a jolt through him—somewhere out there, his own child would soon take first steps, speak first words, reach similar milestones.

"You're good with kids," Jessica's sister commented.

Ryan withdrew his hand as if burned. "Just good reflexes," he mumbled, avoiding Jessica's curious glance.

Later that night, Jessica brought it up. "You know, someday, after we're established in our careers, we could think about having a family."

He didn't miss the irony. "Let's focus on California first," he deflected, kissing her to change the subject. She seemed satisfied with his response, but something in him felt increasingly hollow.

His decision to stay away became easier to justify with each passing day. He'd already missed the pregnancy, he reasoned. He'd already chosen his path. Breaking his silence now would only complicate everything—his relationship with Jessica, his career trajectory, his planned future.

During his last semester, he accepted a full-time offer from Tesla. The salary was impressive, the benefits exceptional, the career path clear. When he called his father to share the news, the pride in his father's voice confirmed he'd made the "right" choice.

"This is why you can't let distractions derail you," his father said. "Focus on success first. Everything else comes later."

Ryan didn't mention Leah or the baby. He'd never told his parents about the pregnancy, adding another layer to his web of avoidance. It was easier this way, he told himself. Cleaner.

The day before graduation, he overheard some pre-med students talking about Leah—about how she'd left school, about her plans to return, eventually. One mentioned seeing her at the grocery store, visibly pregnant now, still carrying her medical textbooks.

"She's crazy determined," one student said. "Said she'll still study whenever the baby lets her sleep."

Ryan hurried past them, his carefully maintained walls threatened to crack. That night, he dreamed of a small child with his eyes and Leah's smile, asking why he'd never been there. He woke up in a cold sweat, but by morning, he'd pushed the dream away, filed it under things he couldn't change.

Jessica started talking about engagement rings, about their future home in California, about building their life together. Ryan played along, ignoring the voice in his head that reminded him he already had a future out there, one he'd chosen to abandon.

The day he packed up his apartment to leave for California, he found an old notebook from his sophomore year. Inside was a sketch he'd made of a baby mobile, designed when Leah had mentioned how much she loved the engineering side of medical devices. He'd planned to build it someday, combining their interests into something unique.

For a moment, his resolve wavered. He could stay, could try to make things right, could face the responsibility he'd run from. But then Jessica called, excited about the apartment she'd found in San Francisco, and the moment passed.

He threw the notebook away.

On the flight to California, as Jessica slept against his shoulder, Ryan made the final decision. He would never look back, never check in, never try to be part of the life he'd helped create. It was better this way, he told himself. The child would have Leah—strong, determined, loving Leah—and that would have to be enough.

He'd chosen his path, and now he would walk it, carrying the weight of his choice like a secret beneath his success. Sometimes, the right engineering solution meant cutting off a failing component entirely. That's what he told himself this was—a clean break, a necessary sacrifice for optimal performance.

But late at night, when Jessica talked about their future children, he would think about the one he'd never know and wonder if all his carefully engineered justifications would ever be enough to fill the void he'd chosen to create.

CHAPTER 11

A New Path

"Everything's in order." Amanda Williams, the family law attorney, slid the document across her desk. "The voluntary termination of parental rights agreement is straightforward. Once he signs, it's permanent."

Leah nodded, her hand resting on her barely visible bump. "And after he signs?"

"Once the baby is born, the court will finalize it. He'll have no legal rights or responsibilities." Amanda's voice remained professional but kind. "Are you sure this is what you want?"

"He made his choice." Leah's voice held firm. "He doesn't get to change his mind later."

The certified letter went out that afternoon. Leah watched the postal worker scan it, tracking number recorded in her phone. No more uncertainty. No more waiting for Ryan to step up.

[Two days later in Ryan's apartment...]

"Just sign it." Jessica paced Ryan's apartment, the legal document open on his coffee table. "This is what you wanted, right? Clean break?"

Ryan stared at the signature line. His hands shook. "Once I sign..."

"You're free." Jessica stopped pacing. "No responsibility, no child support, no complications. Isn't that better?"

Guilt churned in his stomach. Images of doctor appointments, first steps, bedtime stories flashed through his mind. But terror followed—screaming babies, endless demands, a life derailed.

"She'll be better off," he whispered, more to himself than Jessica. "I'd just mess it up anyway."

Jessica handed him a pen. "Then make it official."

His signature looked shaky on the paper. Jessica immediately grabbed the document, sliding it into the return envelope. "I'll mail it on my way home." She kissed his cheek. "You did the right thing."

But as the door closed behind her, Ryan sat alone in his apartment, the finality of his decision settling over him like a heavy cloud.

The fluorescent lights of the ultrasound room hummed overhead, a sound that usually irritated Leah, but today, it seemed to pulse in rhythm with her racing heart. The paper crinkled beneath her as she shifted on the examination table, trying to find a comfortable position while her growing belly made simple movements challenging.

"The gel will be cold," Dr. Chen warned, her voice carrying the warmth the gel lacked. "Though I suppose you're used to that by now."

"You'd think," Leah laughed, then gasped at the cold sensation. "Nope, still shocking every time."

Kate sat beside her, one hand clasped in Leah's, the other holding her phone, ready to record the moment. The room smelled of antiseptic, fresh paper, and possibilities, an oddly comforting combination that reminded Leah of her former medical school dreams.

"Alright," Dr. Chen said, moving the wand across Leah's belly. "Let's see what your little gymnast is up to today."

The screen flickered to life, and suddenly, the room filled with the rapid whoosh-whoosh of a heartbeat. Leah felt tears form before the image cleared—this sound had become her favorite melody over the past few months.

"There we are." Dr. Chen smiled as the fuzzy image resolved into distinct shapes. "Look at that profile—it resembles Mom's bone structure."

"Oh my God," Kate whispered, squeezing Leah's hand tighter. "Look at those tiny fingers!"

The baby on the screen moved as if on cue, one small hand seeming to wave at them. Leah couldn't breathe, watching this tiny person stretch and turn.

"Would you like to know for certain what you're having?" Dr. Chen asked, though her smile suggested she already knew.

"Yes," Leah managed, then laughed through her tears. "Though I think I've known all along somehow."

"Mother's intuition is already working," Dr. Chen nodded. "Well, you're right. A girl, and quite an active one. Look at these movements—she's going to be a handful."

"Like mother, like daughter," Kate grinned, wiping her eyes. "Your mom says you never stopped moving, either."

Dr. Chen took measurements, explained each with the patience of someone who understood this moment's significance. "Strong heartbeat, perfect size for twenty-two weeks; all organs are developing beautifully."

"She's okay?" Leah couldn't stop staring at the screen, at this miracle she'd carried for months without knowing. "Even with... everything?"

Dr. Chen understood the unspoken worry—the stress of Ryan's betrayal, the weeks of not knowing, the coffee and minimal sleep that had fueled Leah's first trimester.

"She's more than okay," the doctor assured her. "She's thriving. You've done everything right since finding out, and babies are remarkably resilient. Would you like to hear something amazing?"

At Leah's nod, Dr. Chen adjusted something on the machine. A strange, rhythmic humming filled the room, unlike a heartbeat, more intricate and unsettling.

"What is that?" Kate asked, the phone still recording.

"That's her moving," Dr. Chen explained. "You can sometimes hear them swimming in the amniotic fluid at this stage. Listen—there's a kick, and... there, she just turned."

Leah closed her eyes, letting the sounds wash over her—her daughter's symphony of movement and life. When she opened them again, Dr. Chen was watching her with understanding.

"Have you thought about names?" she asked, giving Leah a moment to compose herself.

"Louise," Leah said without hesitation. "After my grandmother."

"The nurse?" Dr. Chen smiled at Leah's surprise. "I noticed her photo in your medical history file—Louise Miller, Army Nurse Corps, World War II. Quite a woman."

"Sounds like the perfect namesake for a strong girl," Dr. Chen said, printing several images. "Something tells me this little Louise will need that strength."

"She already has it," Kate declared. "Look at that right hook she's throwing."

They all laughed as the baby on screen indeed seemed to punch at nothing, her tiny fist clear against the dark background.

"Fighting spirit," Dr. Chen nodded. "You'll need that too, Mom."

The word still felt strange—mom. Mother. Parent. Leah touched her belly where Louise continued her gymnastics routine, feeling the flutter of movement that matched the image on the screen.

"I have something for you," Dr. Chen said as she helped Leah clean off the gel. "Usually, we save this for later, but given your interest in medicine..."

She retrieved a distinctive instrument from her bag, resembling a specialized stethoscope. "This is a fetal Doppler," she explained. "It enables you to listen to the baby's heartbeat in the comfort of your own home. Are you interested in learning how to operate it?"

Leah's eyes lit up with both personal and professional interest. "Really? I mean, yes!"

Dr. Chen smiled knowingly. "I thought so. Once a medical student, always a medical student. Here, let me show you..."

She showed the proper placement, explained the technical aspects that made Leah's inner pre-med student thrill. "The trick is finding the sweet spot... there, hear that?"

The familiar whooshing filled the room again, this time through the handheld device. Leah's hands trembled as she took hold of the Doppler, following Dr. Chen's guidance.

"Oh wow," she breathed, adjusting the position. "That's... amazing. Wait, is that... is that arrhythmic?"

Dr. Chen chuckled. "Already diagnosing, are we? No, that's perfectly normal. What you're hearing is, actually..."

"The placental blood flow mixed with the heartbeat?" Leah finished eagerly, then blushed. "Sorry, I just... I was reading about it in my old obstetrics textbook last night."

"Don't apologize," Dr. Chen said warmly. "Your medical knowledge will be incredibly valuable during this journey. Though maybe ease up on the late-night medical reading—you need your rest."

Kate, still recording, laughed. "Good luck with that! Yesterday I caught her watching a C-section video at 3 AM while eating ice cream."

"It was educational!" Leah protested, then winced as Louise delivered a powerful kick. "Oof! Okay, apparently someone agrees with Aunt Kate about my study habits."

Dr. Chen watched the interaction with amusement. "The Doppler's yours to keep. Just promise me you won't obsess too much—once a day is plenty for monitoring."

"Thanks, Dr. Chen," Leah said, placing the Doppler in her bag. "For everything. I know I probably ask way more questions than your usual patients..."

"Are you kidding? It's refreshing! Most of my patients don't want to discuss the intricate details of fetal development or ask about the latest research in maternal-fetal medicine."

As they prepared to leave, Dr. Chen paused. "Leah, I know this isn't the path to medicine you planned, but sometimes the detours teach us the most valuable lessons. My best obstetrics resident was a mother of two who didn't start medical school until she was thirty-five."

Leah felt tears threatening again—damn hormones. "Really?"

"Really. She said experiencing pregnancy and motherhood first made her a better doctor later. Something to think about."

In the car afterward, Kate noticed Leah was quiet. "You okay? That was a lot to process."

"Yeah, I just..." Leah absently rubbed her belly, where Louise continued her acrobatics. "It's weird, you know? Like, part of me is still mourning the life I thought I'd have, the medical school track I was on. But then I hear her heartbeat or feel her move, and suddenly... suddenly I can't imagine any other path."

"Who says you can't have both?" Kate pointed out. "Maybe not right now, but someday. And hey, at least you'll have firsthand experience with the miracle of life, or whatever they call it in those textbooks you're always reading."

Leah laughed, then grew serious. "Kate? Thanks for... for being here. For not bailing when everything got complicated."

"Are you kidding? And miss my chance to be the cool aunt who teaches your kid all the bad words? No way!"

They both laughed, and Louise kicked again, as if joining in.

The bell chimed softly as Leah and Kate entered Little Treasures Baby Boutique, a converted Victorian house where each room showcased different baby essentials. The hardwood floors creaked beneath their feet, and the air smelled of lavender and fresh linens.

"Welcome back, Leah!" Mrs. Bennett, the silver-haired owner, called from behind the antique counter. "How's our little medical prodigy today?"

"Currently using my bladder as a trampoline," Leah laughed, one hand resting on her bump. "We're here for the big nursery shopping trip."

"Perfect timing! I just got in some gorgeous custom bedding sets. And that ergonomic glider you were eyeing last week is still available."

Kate watched in amusement as Leah pulled out her phone. "I can't believe you made a color-coded spreadsheet for baby shopping."

"Hey, organization is key!" Leah protested. "Okay, so according to my research—"

"Of course you researched," Kate rolled her eyes fondly, grabbing a handwoven basket. "Lead the way, Dr. Mom."

They wandered into what used to be the house's dining room, now filled with well-curated clothing displays. Mrs. Bennett followed with a knowing smile.

"How many onesies does one tiny human need?" Kate asked, watching Leah methodically sort through the options.

"Well," Leah started, shifting her weight to ease her back pain, "considering the average newborn goes through 8-12 outfit changes a day because of spit-up, diaper blowouts, and general mess—"

"Oh my god, stop with the statistics!" Kate laughed, holding up a hand-embroidered onesie with tiny medical symbols. "But this one's non-negotiable. Look, they even got the caduceus right!"

"Actually, it's an Asclepius staff," Leah corrected automatically. "The caduceus is often mistakenly... and I'm doing it again, aren't I?"

Mrs. Bennett chuckled, bringing over a cushy ottoman. "Here, dear. Rest a bit. Now, tell me about your nursery plans. Sally—you remember my daughter, the interior designer? She just did the most beautiful medical-themed nursery for another doctor's baby."

"That sounds amazing," Leah sank gratefully onto the ottoman. "We've already painted the walls mint green, but we need everything else."

"Including this," Kate announced, added the medical onesie to their basket. "Non-negotiable."

They moved through the converted house, each room revealing new treasures. In the former library, now the furniture showroom, Mrs. Bennett showed different gliders.

"This one's handcrafted by local artisans," she explained, "with extra lumbar support and a wider seat for nursing."

"Perfect for those late-night study sessions," Kate teased. "You know she'll be reading medical journals while feeding the baby."

"Speaking of reading," Mrs. Bennett led them to a corner displaying hand-painted bookshelves. "These are designed to grow with the baby—you can see how the lower shelves are perfect for board books, but the upper ones can hold textbooks later?"

Leah ran her hand over the smooth wood, imagining Louise's books filling the spaces. "It's beautiful."

In what used to be the sunroom, now transformed into a bedding boutique, Kate grabbed a display blanket. "Feel how soft this is! And look—it's got little DNA helixes embroidered on the border!"

"That's from our 'Future Scientist' collection," Mrs. Bennett noted. "The matching mobile has molecules and atoms..."

"No mobile," Leah said quickly, her hand instinctively moving to her bump. "We're... still deciding on that."

Kate smoothly changed the subject, steering them toward the custom nursing pillows. But in the quiet moment that followed, Mrs. Bennett touched Leah's arm.

"You know, dear, my husband left when I was pregnant with Sally. I thought my world was ending. But sometimes..." she glanced around her successful boutique, "life has better plans than the ones we made."

Leah felt tears prick her eyes—damn hormones. "Thank you," she whispered.

"Now then!" Mrs. Bennett clapped her hands briskly. "Let's talk about that glider. And I have some lovely organic cotton sheets that would match your mint walls perfectly..."

As they finished their shopping, Mrs. Bennett insisted on having everything delivered. "The last thing you need is heavy lifting, dear. Tommy will bring it all by tomorrow morning."

The total made Kate's eyes widen, but Leah just nodded. She'd been saving her internship money, and her parents had helped. Besides, the quality was worth it—especially that glider.

"You sure you don't want the mobile?" Kate asked, as they headed to the car. "That DNA one was pretty cool."

"No, I..." Leah trailed off, remembering Ryan's detailed sketches. "Maybe I'll find something else later."

That evening, they worked on organizing the nursery, putting away tiny clothes and arranging books on the new shelves. Leah sat in the glider, supervising, as Kate attempted to assemble the crib.

"You know," Kate grunted, wrestling with a side rail, "for someone who builds rockets, Ryan really missed out. This is definitely rocket science."

"Here, let me see the instructions," Leah laughed, then suddenly stopped, her hand flying to her side.

"What? What's wrong?"

"Nothing, she's just... really active tonight. Different from usual, though." Leah frowned. "More... patterns to it?"

"Maybe she's practicing for her grand exit," Kate joked, but observed her friend closely. "You okay?"

"Yeah, just tired. And my back's been killing me all day."

They worked for another hour until Kate insisted Leah get some rest. "Everything else can wait. You look exhausted."

That night, Leah couldn't sleep. Louise's movements felt stronger, more purposeful somehow. She pulled out her pregnancy app, checking her countdown. "Three weeks to go, little one. No rush."

She dozed off around midnight, her medical textbooks scattered across the bed. The last thing she remembered was a sharp twinge in her lower back.

At 3 AM, she woke with a start. Something felt... different. The moonlight streamed through the nursery window across the hall, illuminating the half-finished room. As she stood to use the bathroom for what felt like the hundredth time that night, she felt it—a distinct tightening sensation wrapped around her middle.

"No, no, no," she muttered, grabbing her phone to time it. "You're not ready yet. I haven't finished the nursery, I haven't packed my hospital bag, I haven't..."

Another wave hit, stronger this time. She gripped the bedpost, breathing through it like she'd practiced. When it passed, she looked down at her phone's stopwatch.

Seven minutes apart.

"Oh shit," she whispered into the quiet house. "This is really happening."

The moment her fingers brushed her phone to call Kate, a warm, viscous liquid streamed down her legs, its unexpected warmth shocking her.

And then the actual pain began.

CHAPTER 12

Resilience Born

T ime seemed to bend and warp around Leah as she fumbled with her phone, another contraction building like a wave. Her medical knowledge felt useless in the face of actual labor–knowing the stages and experiencing them were entirely different things. "Come on, come on," she muttered, trying to dial Kate's number. The phone slipped from her trembling fingers, clattering to the floor.

When she bent to retrieve it, another contraction hit–harder, longer, more intense than the others. She gripped her desk chair, breathing through clenched teeth. "Not yet, Louise. Please, not yet." Finally, she managed to call Kate.

"Mmph... hello?" Kate's voice sounded thick with sleep. "Kate? I think... no, I know I'm in labor." There was a crash on the other end–presumably Kate falling out of bed. "What? Now? But you're not due for three weeks!"

"Tell that to your niece," Leah gasped as another contraction built. "My water broke and... oh god... they're getting stronger."

"Okay, okay, don't panic. Well, don't panic more than usual. I'm on my way. Have you called your mom?"

"Not yet. I was going to pack my hospital bag first—"

"Forget the bag! Call your mom. I'll be there in ten minutes. Don't you dare have that baby without me!"

Leah's laugh turned into a groan as another contraction peaked. After it passed, she called her mother, who somehow sounded calm.

"Time the contractions, sweetheart. I'll be right there. And Leah? Breathe."

The next twenty minutes were blurred with pain and preparation. Kate arrived first, bursting into the house like a whirlwind.

"Okay, I grabbed some stuff from my place," she announced, dumping an armload of supplies on Leah's bed. "Comfy clothes, hair ties, snacks... why are you standing?"

Leah was swaying by the window, hands braced against the wall. "Helps with the pain. Read about it in... unngh... chapter seven of the labor preparation guide."

"Of course you did," Kate muttered, quickly throwing essentials into an overnight bag. "Only you would quote textbooks during labor."

Leah's mom arrived moments later, calm and efficient. "Six minutes apart," she announced after timing a contraction. "We should go."

The drive to the hospital involved breathing and cursing. Every bump felt like torture, and Leah regretted every medical text she'd ever read about labor.

"Did you know," she said between contractions, "that the pain signals during childbirth travel through the..." she trailed off, gripping the car seat as another contraction built.

"Maybe save the anatomy lesson for later?" Kate suggested from the front seat, breaking several speed limits.

They reached the hospital just as Leah's contractions hit five minutes apart. The fluorescent lights of the emergency entrance felt harsh after the pre-dawn darkness.

"My daughter's in labor," her mom told the nurse at reception. "She's three weeks early."

The nurse looked up, recognition crossing her face. "Oh, Dr. Martinez's patient! The medical student, right?"

"Former... medical student," Leah managed through gritted teeth. "Current human incubator about to evict her tenant."

Things moved quickly after that. Dr. Martinez was called. A room was prepared, and Leah found herself in a hospital gown, hooked up to monitors that beeped steadily.

"Six centimeters already," the nurse announced after checking her. "This little one's in a hurry."

"She gets that from her father," Leah mumbled, then immediately regretted mentioning Ryan as another contraction crashed over her.

Kate squeezed her hand. "Hey, none of that. Focus on you and Louise right now. Although..." she grinned, "I notice you're still wearing your 'Future Doctor' socks."

Leah looked down at her feet in the stirrups, where indeed, her favorite socks peeked out. "Never hurts to manifest..." Her words cut off as the strongest contraction yet gripped her.

The monitors showed the baby's heart rate speeding up. "Something's wrong," Leah said immediately, her medical training kicking in as she watched the numbers. "Her heart rate's too high, and the pattern's..."

Dr. Martinez rushed in, already checking the readouts. "I think the cord might be compressed," Dr. Martinez said. "Leah, I need you to turn onto your left side."

The next few moments were blurred with activity. Nurses rushed in, responding to Dr. Martinez's calm but urgent commands. Leah's mind raced between her medical knowledge and raw maternal instinct as she turned to her side, fighting through another contraction.

"Heart rate's still elevated," a nurse called out.

"I know what this means," Leah said through gritted teeth, her hand clutching Kate's. "The cord—"

"Take a break from being a medical student for a moment," Dr. Martinez interjected in a gentle yet firm tone. "Right now, you're a mother. Let us handle the medical part."

Kate brushed Leah's sweat-dampened hair from her forehead. "Yeah, this is probably the one time you should stop analyzing everything."

Another contraction hit, stronger than before. The monitors beeped more urgently.

"The baby's showing signs of distress," Dr. Martinez announced. "Leah, we might need to consider an emergency C-section."

"No," Leah gasped, tears mixing with sweat. "Please, I can do this. Just... just let me try."

Dr. Martinez checked her again. "Eight centimeters. If we can get her heart rate stabilized..."

Leah's mom stepped forward, taking her other hand. "Breathe, sweetheart. Remember what we practiced."

The next hour was the most intense of Leah's life. Each contraction felt like it would tear her apart, but between them, she focused on the monitors, watching Louise's heart rate like a hawk.

"It's stabilizing," she muttered, more to herself than anyone else. "Come on, Louise. We can do this."

"Nine centimeters," Dr. Martinez announced. "The position change helped. You're almost there."

Kate's rapid-fire commentary, a blur of words designed to distract Leah, abruptly stopped, the hush heavy with unspoken tension. "Oh wow," she whispered, looking at the monitors. "Is that...?"

"Time to push," Dr. Martinez confirmed. "Leah, on the next contraction..."

What followed was a blur of pushing, breathing, and more colorful language than the delivery room had probably ever heard.

"Did you know," Leah panted between pushes, "that the pressure on the pelvic floor during delivery equals... oh GOD!"

"Less talking, more pushing," her mom advised, hiding a smile.

"I can see the head!" Kate exclaimed, then immediately appeared to regret looking. "That's... definitely something I can't unsee."

"Crown's presenting," Dr. Martinez said calmly. "One more big push, Leah."

Gathering every ounce of strength she had left, Leah pushed. The pressure built to an impossible peak, and then...

A clear, powerful cry, brimming with life, cut through the quiet. "She's here," Dr. Martinez announced, lifting a squirming, dark-haired bundle. "And she's beautiful."

Time seemed to stop as they placed Louise on Leah's chest. All the medical knowledge in the world couldn't have prepared her for this moment–the weight of her daughter against her skin, the perfect tiny fingers grasping at nothing, the dark eyes blinking up at her.

"Hi," Leah whispered, tears flowing freely now. "Hi, Louise. I'm your mom."

Kate openly sobbed, trying to film with shaking hands. "She's perfect. Look at those lungs–definitely takes after you in the vocal department."

Leah couldn't take her eyes off her daughter's face. She saw traces of Ryan there–the shape of the nose, the curve of the lips–but mostly, she saw new life, pure possibility.

"Seven pounds, eight ounces," a nurse announced. "Great APGAR scores."

"Of course they're great," Leah murmured, counting fingers and toes. "We studied for this, didn't we, Louise?"

As the early morning sun peeked through the hospital windows, Leah held her daughter close, marveling at how complete she felt despite everything that had led to this moment. No, this wasn't the life she'd planned. It wasn't the perfect medical school trajectory she'd mapped out.

It was better.

Louise wrapped her tiny hand around Leah's finger, and in that grip, Leah felt her future reshape itself. Maybe she wouldn't be Dr. Leah Miller, M.D. right away. But she would be Dr. Mom for now, and somehow, that felt like the most important title in the world.

The hospital room settled into a quiet rhythm after the intensity of delivery. The monitors now beeped softly in the background, and Louise dozed against Leah's chest, wrapped in the DNA helix blanket Kate had insisted on buying.

"Fair warning," the nurse said as she checked Leah's vitals. "She's going to want to feed soon. First-time latching can be tricky."

"I've read about the proper techniques," Leah started, then caught herself. "But I'm guessing it's different in practice?"

The nurse smiled knowingly. "Just a bit. Don't worry, I'll help you through it."

As if on cue, Louise stirred, her tiny face scrunching up in what would soon become a cry. The nurse helped Leah position her, and after some awkward moments and frustrated tears (from both mother and daughter), they finally got it right.

"Look at you two," Kate whispered, having returned from a coffee run. "Already in sync."

Leah couldn't take her eyes off Louise's face. "This is surreal. An hour ago she was inside me, and now..." She traced her daughter's eyebrow with a gentle finger. "Her eyebrows arch just like Ryan's."

"Hey," Kate whispered, "none of that. This moment is about you and her."

The pediatrician came in for Louise's first check-up, and Leah switched between a worried mother and a curious medical student.

"Her Moro reflex seems strong," she observed as the doctor tested Louise's responses. "And her grasp reflex..."

The pediatrician chuckled. "Dr. Martinez warned me you'd be thoroughly informed. Yes, all her reflexes are perfect. Would you like to go through the neurological assessment together?"

Leah's face lit up, even through her exhaustion. "Could we?"

After the examination, as Louise was being weighed again, Leah's mom returned with a surprise—the tiny lab coat from the boutique.

"For her first photo shoot," she explained, laying it across the hospital bassinet. "Though maybe we should wait until she's not quite so..."

"Squishy?" Kate supplied helpfully. "Who knew newborns looked so much like angry potatoes?"

"My daughter does not look like a potato," Leah protested, then looked more closely at Louise's scrunched face. "Okay, maybe a very cute potato."

The next few hours passed in a blur of feedings, diaper changes (which Kate documented with perhaps too much enthusiasm), and visitors. Marina arrived with more baby clothes and tears of joy. Even Dr. Chen stopped by with a gift—a children's book called "My Mom is a Doctor."

"For future inspiration," she winked.

As evening approached, Leah's mom insisted Kate go home to rest, promising to stay the night. Once they were alone, she watched her daughter expertly swaddle Louise after another feeding.

"Look at you," she whispered. "Already a natural."

"I don't feel natural," Leah admitted, settling Louise in the bassinet. "I feel... terrified. Excited. Overwhelmed. Is that normal?"

"That's motherhood, sweetheart." Her mom smoothed Leah's hair back. "The fact that you're worried about doing it right means you're already doing it right."

Louise made a small sound in her sleep, and both women turned to watch her.

"She has your chin," her mom observed. "And your determination–did you see how she powered through that delivery? Pure Miller stubbornness."

Leah laughed, then winced at her sore muscles. "I keep waiting for it to hit me–that I'm actually someone's mother now. That this tiny person depends on me completely."

"Oh, that'll hit you around 3 AM when she's screaming and you can't figure out why," her mom said dryly. "But you'll handle it. Just like you've handled everything else."

A nurse came in to check their vitals again, smiling at Louise's peaceful face. "First night's always interesting. Try to rest while she does."

But Leah couldn't sleep. She sat in the hospital room's rocking chair, watching her daughter's chest rise and fall, memorizing every perfect detail of her face.

"I have so many plans for us," she whispered to her sleeping daughter. "So many dreams. And maybe they're different from my old ones, but..." She touched Louise's tiny hand, marveled at the perfect fingernails. "Maybe they're better."

Just as Leah's mom predicted, the 3 AM feeding struck, the baby's hungry wails a stark contrast to the quiet house. Louise's cry started soft, but quickly escalated to an impressive volume that had Leah fumbling in her hospital gown.

"Okay, okay," she murmured, lifting her angry daughter. "I know, everything's weird and new and... oh god, which side did we start with last time?"

Her mom stirred in the recliner. "Left side, honey. And don't forget to support her head like—"

"Got it," Leah managed, getting Louise positioned. The room fell quiet except for tiny nursing sounds and the ever-present monitor beeps.

"You know," Leah whispered, tracing Louise's ear with her finger, "in medical terms, this is called the rooting reflex, where babies instinctively..." She caught her mom's amused look. "And I'm doing it again, aren't I?"

"You wouldn't be you if you didn't analyze everything," her mom smiled. "Just wait until she starts crawling–you'll probably make a PowerPoint about gross motor development."

"Already have one started," Leah admitted sheepishly.

The night passed in three-hour increments, each feeding session a new learning experience. By morning, Leah had mastered one-handed diaper changes and could swaddle Louise in record time.

Dr. Martinez came by for their discharge check around noon. "Everything looks perfect. How are you feeling about going home?"

"Terrified," Leah admitted. "The hospital has monitors and nurses and emergency equipment..."

"And you have medical training, incredible instincts, and our direct line if you need anything," Dr. Martinez reminded her. "Plus, I hear you've got quite the support team."

As if on cue, Kate burst in with a car seat and what appeared to be enough supplies for a month-long expedition.

"Okay, I got everything on the list, plus some things I saw on TikTok that looked useful, and — oh my god, she's doing the thing with her hands!"

Louise had indeed discovered her hands, staring at them in fascination as she waved them randomly.

"That's normal infant behavior," Leah explained, then caught herself. "Sorry, you probably don't want the developmental psychology lecture."

"Are you kidding? Your random medical facts are the best part!" Kate set down her bags. "Now, let's get this little future doctor ready for her first car ride."

Getting Louise into her going-home outfit proved to be a team effort. The tiny lab coat made an appearance for photos, though Louise seemed unimpressed with her first professional attire.

"She's definitely giving you that 'really, Mom?' look," Kate laughed while snapping pictures.

The car seat challenge came next. Despite having read the manual three times, Leah still fretted over every strap and buckle.

"The angle needs to be exactly 45 degrees," she insisted, while Kate and her mom exchanged knowing looks.

Finally, they were ready. A nurse wheeled Leah down to the hospital entrance while Kate brought the car around. The morning sun felt surreal after two days in the hospital room.

"Ready?" her mom asked.

Leah looked down at Louise, sleeping peacefully in her car seat, tiny fingers curled around the strap. "No," she admitted. "But yes?"

The drive home was possibly the slowest in history, with Kate obeying every traffic law while Leah sat in the back, one hand constantly on Louise's car seat.

"She's still breathing, right?" Leah asked for the tenth time.

"Still breathing," her mom confirmed from the passenger seat. "Though I think you might not be if you don't relax a little."

They pulled up to Leah's apartment, now transformed by "Welcome Home Baby Louise" banners and pink balloons–clearly Marina's work.

"Oh god," Leah said, halfway up the front walk. "The nursery isn't done yet. The crib isn't even fully assembled—"

"Already taken care of," Kate assured her. "Marina and I finished it yesterday while you were in labor. Though I can't guarantee the mobile is hanging at a mathematically perfect angle."

Stepping into the nursery, Leah gasped. The transformation was apparent; the room was no longer the same. The DNA helix bedding completed the assembled crib. The medical-themed prints were hung with precision, and the glider sat ready in the corner, a soft blanket draped over its arm.

"We figured you'd spend a lot of time in that chair," Kate explained, setting down the diaper bag. "Oh, and look what Marina found..."

She pointed to a delicate mobile hanging above the crib. The mobile displayed intricate glass sculptures, not of traditional baby designs, but of medical symbols and mathematical equations, each piece cool to the touch and precisely crafted; it was just like Ryan's sketch, but far more exquisite.

"How did you..." Leah trailed off, emotions overwhelming her.

"Marina found an artist on Etsy who specializes in science-themed baby stuff," Kate explained quickly. "We thought... well, we thought Louise should have something that represents both sides of her heritage, even if..."

"It's perfect," Leah whispered, tears falling as Louise stirred in her arms. "Everything's perfect."

Meanwhile, across the country in San Francisco, Ryan sat at his desk at Tesla, staring at his phone. The text from a mutual friend burned into his retinas:

"Thought you should know–Leah had the baby. Little girl. Both are doing well."

His daughter was here. Actually here, breathing the same air, existing in the same world. He found himself opening Google, fingers hovering over the keyboard. What would he even search for? Birth announcements? Local hospital records?

"Hey, ready for the team meeting?" Jessica appeared at his cubicle, then noticed his expression. "What's wrong?"

"Nothing," he said quickly, locking his phone. "Just... project stress."

But throughout the meeting, his mind wandered. Was the baby healthy? Did she look like him? Like Leah? He imagined tiny fingers and toes, first cries, new parent moments he'd never experienced.

During his lunch break, he found himself in the company's parking garage, sitting in his car with his phone out again. He pulled up Leah's contact information–still saved after all this time. His thumb hovered over the call button. He could congratulate her, at least. Ask about the baby. Their baby. His daughter.

The thought sent a wave of panic through him. Daughter. He was a father. The weight of that reality crashed over him, suffocating in its intensity. What would he even say? "Sorry I abandoned you, but hey, congrats on the successful delivery"? "Hope single motherhood is treating you well while I'm out here living my best life"?

His phone buzzed with a text from Jessica about dinner plans. Normal life. Safe life. Uncomplicated life.

With trembling fingers, he closed Leah's contact info. Instead, he opened his work email, throwing himself into project specifications and engineering problems he could actually solve. That night, lying awake while Jessica slept beside him, he allowed himself one moment of weakness. He searched "newborn baby care" on his phone, reading about the first days and milestone moments. For just a minute, he let himself imagine being there, holding his daughter, being the father she deserved.

Then Jessica stirred, mumbling something about their weekend plans, and reality snapped back. He was Ryan Matthews, a rising star engineer at Tesla, with a perfect girlfriend and a perfect future. Not Ryan Chen, unexpected father at twenty-one, responsible for a tiny human's entire existence.

He deleted his browser history. The next morning, he threw himself into work with renewed intensity. If anyone noticed the dark circles under his eyes or the way he flinched when a colleague showed pictures of his newborn nephew, they didn't mention it.

He made it through the day, through dinner with Jessica, through normal conversation about normal things. But that night, he dreamed of tiny hands reaching for him, of a baby with his eyes and Leah's smile, of opportunities lost to cowardice.

He woke up sweating, relief and regret warring in his chest. Relief won. It always did.

Back at Leah's apartment, the reality of being alone with a newborn hit around midnight. Leah's mom had reluctantly gone home, promising to return first thing in the morning. Kate had been convinced to leave after setting up what she called "Mission Control"–a station next to the glider with water, snacks, burp cloths, and every supply Leah might need.

"Text me if you need anything," Kate had insisted. "I mean it. Even if it's just to tell me random medical facts at 3 AM."

Leah sat in the glider, Louise sleeping peacefully against her chest. The mobile cast gentle shadows on the walls, its scientific symbols dancing in the soft nightlight's glow.

"Okay, Louise," she whispered, "it's just you and me now. No nurses, no monitors, no—"

Louise's face scrunched up, and within seconds, her cry pierced the quiet.

"Right on schedule." Leah glanced at the clock. She'd been tracking feeding times in an app, her scientific mind needing to find patterns in the chaos of newborn care.

As she nursed Louise, she studied her daughter's features more closely. The shape of her eyes was all Ryan, but the determined set of her jaw was pure Miller stubbornness.

"You know," Leah whispered, "your dad would probably love how timed your feeding schedule is. He always appreciated good engineering." Her voice caught. "And he would've thought this mobile was pretty cool..."

Louise responded by grunting and squirming.

"Yeah, you're right. Enough about him. Let's talk about more important things, like how the oxytocin release during breastfeeding promotes maternal bonding through neurochemical..." She laughed at herself. "Or maybe we should just work on this whole eating thing first."

The night progressed in a blur of feedings, diaper changes, and brief moments of sleep. Leah found herself grateful for all those late-night study sessions–they'd apparently been good practice for newborn care.

Around 4 AM, during a fussy period, Leah paced the nursery, patting Louise's back and reciting from memory.

"The infant digestive system takes approximately six weeks to fully mature, which explains the frequency of..." She stopped as Louise let out an impressive burp. "Oh! Good job! See? Everything's better with scientific explanation."

Dawn found them in the glider, Louise sleeping after a marathon feeding session. Leah was exhausted but couldn't bring herself to put her daughter down. Instead, she watched the sunrise paint the nursery walls in soft pinks and golds, highlighting the medical prints and making the mobile's equations glitter.

"Your first sunrise," she murmured to Louise. "Did you know the human circadian rhythm develops in the first weeks of life? Though right now, yours seems to operate on its own unique schedule."

A text buzzed on her phone–Kate checking in. "How's our future doctor doing?"

Leah smiled, typing one-handed: "Currently showing excellent reflex responses and consistent feeding patterns. Mom is sleep-deprived but functioning. Did you know newborns spend approximately 16-17 hours a day sleeping?"

"Only you would turn sleep deprivation into a teaching moment. Need coffee? I can be there by 8:00."

Before Leah could respond, Louise stirred, her tiny face scrunching up in what Leah was learning to recognize as her pre-cry expression.

"Actually, yes," she typed quickly. "Coffee would be amazing. And maybe you can help me document her first morning weight? I've got the scale ready."

"OMG, you're already collecting data. Be there soon, you beautiful nerd." Leah smiled, setting down her phone as Louise fussed. "Okay, little one. Let's review your morning vital signs while we wait for Aunt Kate. And maybe we can work on perfecting that latch technique."

Kate arrived with coffee and breakfast sandwiches, finding Leah in full research mode. A notebook lay open beside the changing table, where she was meticulously recording Louise's morning statistics.

"Time of feeding: 6:15 AM. Duration: 22 minutes. Diaper output: normal color and consistency..."

"Oh my god," Kate laughed, setting down the coffee. "You're literally taking clinical notes."

"It helps me feel more in control," Leah admitted, swaddling Louise. "Besides, tracking patterns is important for—"

"For optimal infant development, I know," Leah finished, as she snapped a picture of Louise's grumpy morning face. "But maybe take a breakfast break? You can't survive on medical knowledge alone."

Louise dozed in her bassinet while Leah devoured her sandwich. The early morning sun streamed through the windows, making everything feel softer, more manageable.

"So," Kate said, watching Leah check the baby monitor for the fifth time, "how was your first night as a solo mom?"

"Terrifying. Amazing. Exhausting." Leah smiled tiredly. "Did you know newborns have a startle reflex that—"

"Nope, no medical lectures until you finish your coffee," Kate interrupted, then softened. "But seriously, you're doing amazing. Look at her–she's very content, well-fed, loved..."

Louise chose that moment to let out a squeaky noise in her sleep, making both women laugh.

"I keep waiting to feel completely overwhelmed," Leah admitted, cradling her coffee. "Like, shouldn't I be more freaked out? I'm twenty-one, technically a college dropout, single mom..."

"And you're crushing it," Kate insisted. "Look at your notebook–who else makes spreadsheets for diaper changes? This kid's going to grow up thinking data collection is normal parenting."

"Is that weird?"

"It's perfectly you," Kate smiled. "And that's what Louise needs."

Their conversation was interrupted by Louise's hungry cries. Leah scooped her up with growing confidence, settling into the routine they were building together.

"Want me to time this feeding too?" Kate teased, reaching for the notebook.

"Actually..." Leah looked down at Louise, who had latched on the first try. "Maybe we can just enjoy this one."

As morning turned to afternoon, Leah settled into a rhythm that felt surprisingly natural. Yes, her path had diverged dramatically from her original plans. No, she wasn't in medical school as scheduled. But watching Louise discover her own tiny fingers, recording each small milestone, finding the science in everyday moments of motherhood–it felt right.

That evening, after Kate left and Louise was fed and changed, Leah sat in the nursery glider, her daughter sleeping peacefully against her chest. The mobile spun slowly above them, its equations and symbols casting patterns that seemed to map out infinite possibilities.

"You know what, Louise?" she whispered, running a finger along her daughter's perfect cheek. "We've got this. It won't be easy, and it definitely won't be traditional, but..." She smiled as Louise's tiny hand gripped her finger in her sleep. "Some of the best scientific discoveries came from unexpected experiments."

The future stretched out before them, full of challenges but also possibilities. There would be sleepless nights and difficult moments, milestones missed by an absent father but celebrated by a fierce support system. There would be time for medical school eventually, but for now, Leah had the most fascinating research subject: watching her daughter grow.

She pulled out her notebook one last time that day, but instead of clinical observations, she wrote: "Day One: Learned that love can be measured in tiny fingers and toes, in perfect feeding schedules and midnight cuddles. Hypothesis: We're going to be more than okay."

Louise sighed in her sleep, as if in agreement.

Outside, the sunset painted the nursery in soft colors that promised new beginnings. Leah held her daughter close, ready to face whatever came next—not just as a mother, not just as a former medical student, but as both, and something entirely new altogether.

They had their own path to forge, and for the first time since leaving school, Leah felt certain about her direction. It wasn't the life she'd planned, but maybe it was the life she had all along.

CHAPTER 13

Finding a Community

The evening sun cast long shadows through St. Mary's garden, and the string of lights twinkled like early stars above the gathering crowd. Leah adjusted Louise on her hip, feeling an unexpected flutter of nerves about this first church social. At six months, Louise was a warm, solid weight against her chest, drooling on the shoulder of Leah's chosen sundress, its vibrant pattern reflecting her hopeful outlook.

"It's just a potluck," Leah whispered, smoothing Louise's wild curls while glancing at the crowd mingling nearby. "There's nothing to be nervous about." Yet her heart thrummed with a mix of excitement and uncertainty. She could see children playing tag between the tables, parents engaged in animated conversations, and laughter floating through the air like music. The scene was inviting, yet Leah felt like an outsider looking in.

"Talking to yourself?" The warm voice jolted her from her thoughts. It belonged to Grace Thompson, the community outreach coordinator who also happened to be a good friend of Mrs.

Anderson, Kate's mom. Grace's friendly demeanor and genuine smile eased Leah's nerves. "Or is Louise offering commentary?"

"Both, maybe." Leah smiled, grateful for the familiar face in the sea of new ones. "I made my grandmother's banana bread." The sweet aroma of cinnamon and bananas filled the air as she recalled comforting memories attached to the recipe—rainy Sundays spent in the kitchen, her grandmother's laughter, and that warm coziness that always filled her home.

"Perfect!" Grace exclaimed, expertly guiding them toward the buffet tables lined with an enticing variety of dishes. "And don't worry—everyone's a little nervous their first time. But St. Mary's is different. You're going to see."

The garden was beautiful, blooming with vibrant roses, climbing trellises, and fairy lights illuminating the space. It felt magical, yet Leah felt anticipation settle in her chest. She inhaled deeply, savoring the mingling scents of grass, flowers, and the delicious offerings around her.

"Over there is the children's area," Grace pointed out, her expression brightening as she showed a nearby corner where several babies and toddlers played on colorful blankets under careful supervision. "Louise can make some friends while you—"

She paused, a knowing smile crossing her face as she looked beyond Leah's shoulder. "And here's our music director now. Chris! Come meet our newest members!"

Leah turned, and her world shifted imperceptibly. There stood Chris Johnson, the church's music director, his tall frame backlit by afternoon sun streaming through stained glass. Something in his warm brown eyes caught her off guard - a depth of kindness she hadn't expected to find here, hadn't prepared herself to face. His gentle smile carried none of the judgment she'd grown accustomed to, and the flutter it sent through her stomach was both welcome and terrifying. She found herself frozen in that moment, struck by how a stranger's gaze could feel so inexplicably familiar, so safe, when she'd trained herself to expect anything but.

"Chris!" Grace called out, waving him over with an infectious enthusiasm that made Leah both excited and bashful.

"Hey there!" Chris approached them, his demeanor casual and welcoming. "Is this little one waiting for me?" He looked at Louise, soothingly cradling the stuffed elephant she had dutifully hung onto.

"This is Louise," Leah found her voice, feeling warmth. "And I'm Leah. Leah Miller." She couldn't help but notice how, at that moment, her nervousness about the potluck melted away as Louise's fascinating smile brightened her spirits.

"Ah, the famous Louise!" Chris grinned, expertly reaching out to catch the elephant as it dropped from the baby's grasp. He returned it, his fingers brushing against Leah's in a sweet, fleeting moment that sent a spark of electricity up her arm. "Grace mentioned you might join us. She said you're an artist?"

"Only part-time," Leah replied, her modesty bubbling up despite the unmistakable warmth pouring in from his attention. "I work in art therapy at the community center. It's a little different from painting pretty pictures."

"Not at all! Sounds incredibly valuable," Chris replied earnestly, his gaze steady. Then Louise, apparently boldly, reached for Chris's tie, her tiny fingers grasping the fabric like an exciting toy.

"Louise." Leah gently disentangled her daughter's fingers, shaping her response into a quiet laugh. "I'm so sorry! She's very curious."

"Curious minds are the best," Chris stated as he smiled at Louise. "It's what makes talented artists and musicians."

Before Leah could redirect the conversation back to safe subjects, Louise let out a delightful squeal, sending Chris into an infectious fit of laughter. The sound filled the space with warmth, further easing Leah's apprehensions.

"Speaking of which," Grace cut in, "Chris leads our children's music program. Would you like to sign up Louise for the next session? They often incorporate art so it could blend both of your talents!"

Leah hesitated, glancing down at Louise, who was starting a playful battle with Chris's tie. Enrolling her little girl in a music program was tempting, but the idea of social commitments made her feel anxious.

"I don't know if we're ready for that yet," Leah began, but Louise's joyful babble filled the air, and Chris swooped in, effortlessly distracting her with the gentle hum of a familiar children's tune.

"This one loves music, it seems," he observed, a playful glint in his eyes. "She'd be an instant star."

"Perfect pitch," Leah chuckled as Louise's babbles synchronized with the playful notes. It was delightful to see Louise so animated, and Leah's heart warmed at the connection forming before her eyes.

"Can't resist sweet sounds," Chris teased, his smile infectious. "And if she's anything like her mom, she will have the gift."

The timeline of their conversation shifted, and for Leah, it felt seamless—effortless even—as Chris described his role in the choir and how he fostered creativity through music. His enthusiasm was palpable, and it felt easy to be swept along.

As the sun sank lower in the sky, Leah noticed how the garden illuminated with new life—children playing tag, parents laughing, familiar scents swirling around them in a comforting dance. It was the evening that built the community, and Leah wanted to be a part of that vibrant orchestration even more.

"She's as much an artist as any of us," Leah said, a wide smile on her face. "She'll create her passions. Who knows where that will take her?" In that moment, her heart brimmed with possibilities, forging a path for herself and Louise—a path of creativity, expression, and community.

"So true," Chris agreed, his gaze drifting to the children playing nearby. "The arts can be such a wonderful outlet, especially for kids. It's fun to see how they react to music and how it encourages them to express themselves differently."

"It's also therapeutic," Leah added, her voice lifting with enthusiasm. "Art and music therapy—it's amazing how they can help children process their emotions, especially through tough times. Just like little Tommy with his paintings."

"Seems like you're pouring a lot into this community," Chris remarked, gesturing around him. "Bringing healing and creativity to others. It's inspiring."

"Thanks," Leah replied, feeling a swell of pride. "I've found that art can bridge the gaps left by unspoken emotions, especially for kids. I want to give them a safe space to explore that part of themselves."

"I think music can do the same," Chris said, nodding in agreement. "When I teach the kids, I encourage them to find their voices, to express what they feel rather than just learn the notes."

"That's right!" Leah's excitement surged. "A melody can convey what words sometimes can't. It's all about connection—helping them communicate feelings when lost."

Chris' eyes sparkled with admiration. "You have a knack for it. Maybe your talents could intersect with the music program. We'd love to have you join our team sometime."

"Oh, I don't know about that," Leah replied, a nervous tremor in her voice betraying the secret hope blossoming in her chest. The idea of collaborating on a project excited her, but also terrified her. "I have my hands full with Louise."

"If you ever decide to, we'd love to have you," Chris reiterated, then looked over at Louise, who was now very much awake, her curious eyes scanning her surroundings. "And if she's anything like you, I can already tell she will be a force of nature."

"Let's hope so!" Leah laughed, still shy yet encouraged by the ease between them.

"Just let me know if you ever want to brainstorm ideas together," Chris said, his tone was encouraging. "We could create something awesome."

Leah's heart raced with a mix of excitement and apprehension. "I will," she promised. The prospect of collaboration bloomed in her mind, along with the fear of stepping outside her comfort zone.

Before she could ponder it further, Grace beckoned from across the garden with a plate of food. "Come on! You must try the lasagna! It's incredible!"

As they made their way toward the buffet, Leah felt a sense of community surrounding her, wrapping around her like a comforting embrace. The garden, filled with laughter and connection, became a temporary haven where she could let her walls down, share stories, and allow Louise to be part of something bigger than herself.

The bite of lasagna was savory, and Leah relished her meal while listening to others share their experiences—mothers recounting their birthing tales, fathers discussing their first moments with their newborns. Each story painted a picture of love mingled with chaos, a beautiful tapestry of shared humanity.

"Are you ready for this?" Grace asked, her expression earnest as she glanced at Leah while they sat on a bench surrounded by friends.

"I think so," Leah replied, feeling the gentle weight of Louise nestled in her arms. "Having Louise has already opened my eyes to so much. It's like the world looks different now."

"You're right. It does." Grace's eyes sparkled with wisdom. "Being a mother is transformational. It's a mix of love, joy, pain, and growth wrapped into one."

"I just want to make sure she feels supported," Leah mused, glancing down at her daughter, exploring the folds of her sundress. "I want her to know she's loved, no matter what."

"She will," Grace reassured, her voice steady. "You're going to be an incredible mom, Leah. Just remember to take care of yourself, too. Allow yourself to feel it all."

The moment settled into a peaceful rhythm, and Leah found herself absorbed in the warmth of shared laughter and stories. With every passing minute, the garden transformed into a sacred space where her life, her daughter's life, and her sense of community intertwined.

As the sun dipped lower, casting a golden hue over the gathering, Leah felt a shift inside her—a steadfastness founded in newfound strength. The lingering fear of the past faded, replaced by the hope and possibilities of their future.

"Louise," she whispered while cradling her daughter, "this is just the beginning. We're embarking on a journey full of beauty, love, and the unexpected."

With a contented sigh, Louise snuggled closer to Leah, her tiny fingers curling around the fabric of her mother's sundress as if sensing the warmth of reassurance in Leah's voice. There was something so reassuring in her daughter's weight against her—a physical reminder of their profound connection.

"Your first of many potlucks," Leah continued, silently sharing her dreams with Louise. "And look at all these people who love you already, who care for you. One day, you'll have your friends, your adventures."

As the sun set, tinting the sky with glorious hues of orange and pink, Leah felt an overwhelming sense of gratitude fill her heart. The surroundings shifted in their radiance, a reminder that her journey was as captivating and multifaceted as the colors streaking across the sky. She savored every moment, from the gentle sounds of laughter to the delicate softness of Louise's breaths.

"Wow, look at those colors!" Grace remarked, her voice vibrant with excitement. "Nature knows how to put on a show. Just like you and Louise."

Leah turned her gaze toward Grace's beaming face, appreciating the warmth and support radiating from her. "It does. And I'm so glad to share this with you. I never imagined I could feel so connected to a community, especially after everything that's happened."

Grace placed a reassuring hand on Leah's shoulder, her expression mirroring Leah's thoughts. "You belong here, and you always will. Just wait until Louise runs around, making friends of her own—it'll be even more special."

As they watched the sun dip below the horizon, Leah felt the fear and burdens of her past gradually loosen their grip. The weight of judgment dissipated with every story told and every laugh shared. She was not just Leah, the single mother; she was the artist, the friend, the daughter, and now—a part of something bigger.

"Speaking of friends," Grace said, her voice enthusiastic. "I think I just spotted a few more church members arriving! Let's meet them! They're part of the playgroup I mentioned earlier. New friends for you both!"

"Okay!" Leah exclaimed, surging with newfound confidence. With Louise securely nestled against her shoulder, Leah followed Grace into the crowd.

As the night wore on, Leah immersed herself in conversations with other parents. They shared stories of sleepless nights and the joy of first smiles, bonding over the collective experience of being in the trenches of parenthood together.

"Have you been hit by the colicky phase?" one mother asked, eyes wide with sympathy and understanding.

"No, not yet. But I'm braced for it," Leah replied, smiled knowingly. "At least I have plenty of company if it happens. If tonight was any indication, I'm lucky to have support."

Observing the lively chaos, Louise cooed as if joining in on the surrounding conversations. Each sound sent a wave of joy rushing through Leah; her daughter was already integrating into this vibrant community.

Finally, Leah sat at a small table with several other new parents crowded beneath the soft glow of the string of lights. The air was now filled with the comfort of shared stories and laughter, a sense of belonging orchestrating itself beautifully among them.

"Next time," one mother suggested, her voice carrying the warmth of newfound friendship, "let's do a talent show! We can showcase the kids' musical skills, maybe?"

Leah felt the earlier conversation with Chris resurface, his gentle encouragement about Louise's musical instincts echoing in her mind. She watched her daughter's tiny fingers curl against her dress, remembering how naturally they had reached for Chris's tie, keeping time with his hummed melody.

"Count me in," she said softly, the words carrying more weight than mere social agreement. The music program he'd described suddenly felt less like an abstract possibility and more like a tangible future—one where Louise might find her voice among these people who had already felt like family. "Though we might need a few lessons first."

The gathered parents laughed, the sound harmonizing with the evening's gentle whispers, and Leah joined in, surprised by how easily joy bubbled up from a place she'd thought long sealed. Louise stirred against her shoulder, making one of those sweet baby sounds that seemed to bridge the gap between coo and song.

"Already practicing," Chris commented as he rejoined the group, his presence added another layer to Leah's growing sense of possibility. The knowing look they shared spoke of their earlier conversation, of potential collaborations and shared creative dreams that now felt closer than ever.

Leah's heart lit up at his arrival, a spritz of excitement coursing through her veins. His easy laughter filled the space, drawing her in as she realized how much she appreciated his company.

"Do you play any instruments?" Leah inquired, eager to learn more.

"Just about everything," Chris replied, a hint of pride in his tone. "I can play the guitar and the piano and even dabble in drums. But I wouldn't say I'm a pro at all!"

"I'd love to hear you play one day," Leah said, her voice soft but sincere. Sharing that moment gave her butterflies—a new dream blossoming.

As the vibrant conversations flowed and laughter erupted, Leah felt a renewed sense of purpose. This gathering was no longer intimidating; it had transformed into a canvas of connection where she could breathe, belong, and forge memories for herself and Louise.

"I'm glad you came, Leah," Chris said, his gaze earnest. "It's been great getting to know you more. I can show you around the music program next week if you'd like. I think you and Louise would enjoy it."

Leah felt a rush of warmth at his invitation, her nervousness giving way to excitement. "I'd love that," she replied, allowing herself to envision them exploring together, filled with music and creativity. "And maybe we can even create special songs for the kids."

"That sounds fantastic!" Chris' enthusiasm matched her own, and Leah couldn't help but smile. The prospect of weaving her artistic skills into the music program felt like a beautiful opportunity taking root and flourishing.

As they continued to talk, the evening unfolded with conversations that ebbed and flowed around them. Laughter echoed through the garden, and Louise cooed contentedly in her mother's arms, her tiny face lighting up with every familiar sound.

Time passed quickly, and Leah found herself comfortable in this new role—not just as a mother, but as a member of a community that rallied around her. It felt like a significant shift from her life just a few months ago, when she had felt fragmented and alone.

"Hey, let's take a picture to celebrate your first church social," Grace suggested, pulling out her phone and gathering the group close.

"Everyone smile!" Leah grinned, holding Louise in her arms. Chris leaned in on the other side, his arm casually draped over her shoulder. The warmth of his presence felt comforting, and Leah felt a pulse of joy as they all crowded together, laughter blending with the sounds of nature around them.

After several snaps, Grace reviewed the photos, laughing at the silly expressions captured in real time. "This is going in the album of memories! Just look at that little face," she said, pointing at Louise, mirroring the group's laughter, her eyes sparkling with innocent joy.

As the evening ended, starlight twinkled above, and the air cooled, bringing with it the scent of blooming flowers and fresh earth. Leah felt an overwhelming sense of contentment wash over her—a deep, abiding joy in simply being present in this moment, surrounded by people who cared for and loved her.

"Thank you for including us tonight," Leah said, sincere gratitude filling her voice as she addressed her new friends. "I didn't think I could feel this connected so soon."

"You're part of the family now," Chris replied, his eyes glinting warmly. "We're so glad you and Louise are with us. It's a journey we're all on together."

"Yes, and if you need anything, all you have to do is ask," Grace added, her tone earnest. "Seriously. We support one another here."

As Leah and Louise headed toward the car, the garden's fairy lights created gentle halos in the gathering darkness. Louise had finally surrendered to sleep, her warm weight both comfort and anchor against Leah's chest. Each step across the lawn felt like crossing a threshold—leaving behind the cocoon of community they'd found tonight, yet carrying its warmth with them.

The soft crunch of footsteps on the garden path made Leah pause. She turned to find Chris approaching, his movements deliberately quiet, a consideration that touched something deep within her. The string lights caught the edges of his silhouette, softening him into a figure that seemed to belong to this liminal moment between evening and night, between what was and what could be.

"Hey," he called softly, his voice barely above a whisper. In his hand, a business card caught the ambient light. "I wanted to give you this." He extended it toward her, and Leah shifted Louise carefully to free one arm, the practiced movement of a mother who had learned to navigate the world while keeping her child close. "For the music program, of course. And maybe..." His pause held a universe of possibility. "Coffee sometime? To discuss collaboration ideas?"

The card felt warm against her palm, as if it had absorbed some essential heat from his hand. Louise stirred slightly at the exchange, not fully waking but adjusting against Leah's shoulder with one of those fluttering sighs that always made her heart contract with love. In this suspended moment, Leah felt the weight of potential—of music and connection, of creativity and community.

Then her phone buzzed.

The harsh vibration against her hip seemed to fracture the gentle twilight atmosphere. Still holding the card, Leah reached for her phone, an instinct she couldn't quite suppress. The screen's blue glare cut through the garden's soft illumination, stark and demanding:

"Heard you're going to St. Mary's now. I'm in town next week for work. Think we should talk..."

Ryan's words landed like stones in still water, ripples of tension spreading through her body. Louise, attuned to her mother's sudden stillness, shifted again, small fingers curling more tightly into Leah's dress. The business card in her other hand seemed to take on a different weight now—no longer just an invitation to possibility, but a choice. A crossroads.

"Everything okay?" Chris's voice carried genuine concern, and when Leah looked up, she found his expression had shifted from hopeful to protective, as if he'd sensed the subtle change in her demeanor.

"I... I don't know," she answered truthfully, unconsciously drawing Louise closer, seeking comfort in her daughter's steady breathing. The weight of her past and the possibility of her future seemed to converge in this moment, leaving her suspended between what was and what could be.

As she drove home that night, the rhythmic thump of the tires on the highway a counterpoint to Louise's soft breathing in her car seat, Leah weighed her options—should she text Ryan and relive old wounds, or call Chris and embrace the unknown? The streetlights blurred past, mirroring the hazy uncertainty in her mind. The business card sat on her dashboard, catching the streetlight's glow, while her phone remained heavy in her pocket, Ryan's message unanswered.

"What do you think, little one?" she whispered to her sleeping daughter. "Should Mommy be brave?"

Louise sighed in her sleep, and Leah smiled despite her uncertainty. Whatever she decided, one thing was obvious—nothing would be the same after next week.

She felt the excitement and apprehension mingle within her, both possibilities laden with potential. The warmth of her community, the promise of new friendships, and the encouraging presence of Chris made her heart swell. At the same time, the shadow of Ryan loomed, a reminder of past struggles, leaving her torn.

As the car rolled through familiar streets, Leah's mind flashed back to the night's events—the warmth of laughter, the sense of connection, and the budding opportunities for creativity. The memories ignited a fire within her, urging her to let go of the fears that had held her back.

"Maybe I don't have to choose just one path," Leah mused, a plan forming in her mind. "Maybe I can embrace both sides of my life."

With newfound resolve, she took things step by step. Each decision would build her future, and she wouldn't let her past define her. Leah felt a sense of liberation wash over her, a gentle reminder she was stronger than she'd believed.

Arriving home, she unbuckled Louise, cradling her daughter as they walked inside. The warmth of her home enveloped them, a stark contrast to the swirling uncertainties of the outside world.

"Let's rest, my love," Leah whispered, the quiet hush of the room broken only by Louise's gentle breathing as Leah placed her in the crib, tucking her in before watching her drift back to sleep. "We have a big week ahead."

With Louise resting peacefully, Leah took a moment to reflect on her choices and the friendships that were sprouting anew. As she sat on the edge of her bed, she pulled out Chris's business card, running her fingers over the information.

"Maybe I'll text Chris tomorrow," she thought, a ripple of excitement coursing through her. "I could use a friend who understands this journey."

Leah nibbled her bottom lip, fighting back the urge to pull out her phone immediately. "One step at a time," she reminded herself. "One day at a time."

With a heart full of hope and determination, Leah slipped under the covers, letting the events of the evening wash over her. She closed her eyes, envisioning the possibilities unspooling ahead of her: moments of laughter, creativity, and the mother-daughter bond thriving amidst the beauty of the community.

"Tomorrow will be a new day," she thought, a serene smile gracing her lips as she drifted off to sleep. "And whatever comes next, I'll face it head-on."

CHAPTER 14

Seasons of Healing

The text from Ryan cast a cold glow across Leah's phone screen, his words burning into her consciousness: "Heard you're going to St. Mary's now. I'm in town next week for work. Think we should talk..."

Leah stared at the message, the darkness of her living room pressing in around her like a physical weight. Down the hall, Louise slept peacefully in her crib, her gentle breathing a counterpoint to the thundering of Leah's heart. The business card Chris had given her earlier that day lay on the coffee table, his carefully penned number a stark contrast to Ryan's digital intrusion. Two possibilities stretched before her like diverging paths in the growing darkness.

She traced her fingers over Ryan's message, remembering his last words, the dismissive wave of his hand that had reduced their unborn child to an inconvenience. Then came the unbidden memory of Chris's warm smile that afternoon, the natural way he'd knelt to Louise's level, how his words 'for the music program, of course' had carried the whisper of something more.

With trembling fingers, Leah deleted Ryan's message. The screen's brief flash illuminated the tears she hadn't realized were falling. Instead, she reached for Chris's card, her fingertips following the precise strokes of his handwriting. The hour was late—too late for a proper call—but perhaps not too late for something new to begin.

She typed carefully: 'Hi Chris, it's Leah. About that coffee... is tomorrow too soon?'

His response arrived with a swiftness that made her breath catch: "Never too soon. 10 AM at The Daily Grind? They have great highchairs for little ones."

The simple thoughtfulness of his response, putting Louise's comfort first, drew a smile through her tears.

The next morning dawned with an autumn clarity that seemed to mock Leah's jangled nerves. Sunlight streamed through the café windows as she maneuvered Louise's stroller through the door of The Daily Grind, each movement deliberate, as if she could steady her racing thoughts through the simple mechanics of motherhood. The familiar scent of coffee and warmth wrapped around her like a promise, and there, in the corner, sat Chris.

He had claimed a quiet table, angled perfectly to catch the morning light while staying clear of the busiest walkways. A highchair waited, already wiped clean, its presence speaking volumes about the attention he paid to details that others might overlook. The sight sent an unexpected warmth through Leah's chest, different from the anxious flutter that had accompanied her through her morning routine.

"I got here early," Chris explained, rising to help her with the stroller. His movements were unhurried but purposeful, each gesture calibrated to put her at ease. "Wanted to make sure we had a quiet spot for Louise." The words carried the weight of consideration, so different from the hasty afterthoughts she'd grown accustomed to from Ryan.

When they ordered, Chris's quiet observation that their oat milk alternative would be better for her while nursing caught her off guard. It wasn't just the thoughtfulness that struck her, but the easy way he acknowledged her reality as a nursing mother without making it feel like an inconvenience to be managed.

Their conversation found its rhythm as naturally as leaves falling outside the window. Chris began with "So, about the music program," but the discussion meandered like a gentle stream, touching on childhood memories, favorite lullabies, and the small moments that shaped them. Between them, Louise contentedly reduced her banana to a sweet, sticky mess, occasionally offering soggy pieces to Chris with the solemn ceremony that only toddlers could manage. He accepted each offering with genuine delight, his eyes crinkling at the corners in a way that made Leah's heart twist with an emotion she wasn't quite ready to name.

"You're good with her," Leah found herself said, the words carrying more weight than their simple syllables suggested.

Chris's response came with a quiet certainty that seemed to fill the sunlit space between them: "She makes it easy." Then, after a pause that held volumes, he added, "You both do."

The words settled around them like autumn leaves, gentle but undeniable in their accumulation. Leah watched as Louise reached for Chris again, her small fingers sticky with banana, and felt something shift in her chest—not the sharp pain of old wounds, but the tender ache of new growth, like shoots breaking through frost-hardened ground.

FALL

The weeks melted into a comfortable routine. Every Wednesday, Leah brought Louise to the children's music program at St. Mary's, where Chris incorporated age-appropriate instruments for the babies.

"Music and movement are crucial for development," he said one crisp October afternoon, demonstrating a rhythm game. Louise watched from Leah's lap, entranced by the wooden blocks Chris tapped together.

"Like neural pathway formation in early childhood," Leah added, then caught herself. "Sorry, the medical student in me sometimes comes out."

"Never apologize for that," Chris smiled. "I love learning the science behind what we're doing. Besides," he winked at Louise, "someone here inherited her mother's curiosity."

As fall deepened, so did their connection. Chris started staying after sessions, helping Leah pack up Louise's things while sharing stories about his day. He made even mundane moments feel special.

One particularly windy afternoon, Louise was inconsolable during the music session. Without missing a beat, Chris switched from "The Wheels on the Bus" to a soft melody in D major. Louise's cries softened immediately.

"How did you know that would work?" Leah asked afterward, amazed.

"I've been paying attention," he said. "She responds best to D major when overtired. Just like her mom relaxes when we play in G."

The fact he noticed such details about both of them made Leah's heart skip.

WINTER

December transformed St. Mary's into a wonderland of lights and carols. The children's Christmas program meant longer planning sessions, which often turned into casual dinners with Louise dozing in her carrier nearby.

"Tell me about medical school," Chris asked one evening over Chinese takeout. "Is it still part of your plan?"

Leah paused, chopsticks midair. No one had asked about her dreams since Louise was born.

"Honestly? I don't know anymore. Sometimes I feel like I'm letting go of who I was supposed to be."

"Or maybe," Chris suggested, "you're becoming who you're meant to be. Different doesn't mean lesser."

His words stayed with her, offering comfort during late-night feedings and quiet moments when doubt crept in.

The Christmas program was a chaotic success, with Louise sporting tiny angel wings as Chris led the children in carols. Afterward, helping her buckle Louise into her car seat in the snowy parking lot, he whispered, "You're incredible, you know that?"

"For what? Keeping a baby quiet during Silent Night?"

"For everything. For being both mother and father, for not giving up on your dreams even if they've shifted, for letting people in even after..." he trailed off, but they both knew he meant Ryan.

SPRING

Cherry blossoms dusted the church garden like pink snow, and their post-session coffee meetings became a highlight of Leah's week. Chris began bringing educational toys and instruments specifically chosen for Louise's developmental stages.

"This helps with fine motor skills," he explained, or "The vibration patterns here support sensory integration."

"Someone's been studying," Leah teased, noting the familiar terminology from her child development textbooks.

"Well," he grinned, "I might have borrowed some of your books. Plus, I have this amazing friend who keeps teaching me about neural pathways."

Their conversations flowed effortlessly between professional and personal. Chris never pushed for more than friendship, but his actions spoke volumes. He automatically packed extra wipes for Louise's messy moments, remembered Leah's coffee preferences, and always knew which song would make Louise smile.

One rainy April afternoon, he asked about Ryan.

"Does he ever..." Chris hesitated, then continued, "reach out?"

"He texted once," Leah admitted. "The night you gave me your number, actually. I chose not to respond."

Chris was quiet for a moment, then said, "That must have been a hard decision."

"Actually," Leah realized, "it wasn't. Some choices are hard because they're wrong. Others are hard because they're right."

SUMMER

The garden parties at St. Mary's became weekly events, with fairy lights strung through the trees and music floating on warm evening breezes. Chris suggested combining music with art therapy, knowing Leah's interest in both.

"We could create something special," he said one evening, strumming his guitar while Louise played on a blanket between them. "Music, art, movement – all working together to help kids express themselves."

"Like a holistic approach to emotional development," Leah added, watching Louise bounce to the rhythm. Chris naturally included her professional interests in their programs, making her feel seen in a way she hadn't since leaving school.

Their planning sessions often extended into the twilight hours, Louise exploring the garden grass while they brainstormed ideas. Grace sometimes found them still there at sunset, lost in conversation that flowed from curriculum planning to personal dreams.

"You three look good together," Grace commented one evening, causing Leah to blush. "Like a perfect harmony."

The changing dynamic didn't go unnoticed by the community. Parents started calling Chris Louise's music teacher, then her friend, then simply "Chris"—as if he'd always been part of their story. Unlike

Ryan's abrupt departure, Chris's presence felt like a gradual sunrise, warming everything it touched.

One memorable evening in late June, during a music session, Louise pulled herself up using Chris's guitar case. Everyone watched as she stood wobbling for a moment, then took three determined steps toward him before tumbling into his arms.

"Did you see that?" he exclaimed, scooping her up with pride. "You're walking!"

Leah felt tears prick her eyes, but not from sadness. For the first time, watching Chris celebrate this milestone with joy, she didn't feel Ryan's absence as a void. Instead, she felt the fullness of what was present—community, support, and something growing between her and Chris that felt both exciting and safe.

"She knows who her biggest fan is," Leah said, watching them together.

As summer progressed, their relationship deepened. Chris never tried to replace Ryan or push for a role he hadn't earned. Instead, he built his place in their lives through countless small moments of care and connection.

By August, when the evening air turned golden and crisp, Leah realized something had shifted in her heart. The pain of Ryan's abandonment had faded, replaced by the warmth of new possibilities. She no longer felt like a single mother struggling alone, but part of something larger—a community, a friendship, and perhaps something more.

The seasons had painted their story in shifting colors - fall's tentative beginnings, winter's quiet nurturing, spring's tender awakening, and summer's full-hearted blossoming. Now, as August drew to a close, the late afternoon light filtered through St. Mary's stained-glass windows with the particular golden quality that marked time's passage like illuminated pages in an ancient manuscript. In this light, their story seemed to pause, suspended in amber, ready for its next chapter to unfold.

The music room held the day's accumulated warmth like a treasured secret, its hardwood floors reflecting rainbow patterns that danced and shifted with each passing cloud. Chris sat with his guitar, Louise propped securely in the circle of his arms, her small fingers reaching for the strings with the uninhibited joy that only children could manifest. The scene before Leah crystallized into something so achingly perfect that she held her breath, as if the slightest movement might disturb the delicate balance of this moment.

"That's it," Chris murmured, his voice carrying the gentle cadence that had become as familiar to Leah as her own heartbeat. He beamed as Louise produced a simple note, the sound hanging in the air like a question waiting to be answered. "Every guitarist starts somewhere, you know."

Leah lingered in the doorway, allowing herself to fully inhabit this moment that seemed to exist outside of ordinary time. The past year unspooled in her mind like a ribbon of memory - each Wednesday session, each shared laugh, each quiet moment of understanding building toward this particular configuration of light and sound and feeling. The scene before her bore no resemblance to the future she'd imagined twelve months ago, yet it held everything she hadn't known to wish for.

"Your love for music is clear," she finally said, her voice carrying the weight of everything still unspoken between them. She stepped into the room properly now, crossing the threshold that separated their carefully maintained friendship from something deeper, something that had been growing in the spaces between notes and words and glances.

"Leah!" Chris's face lit up, the warmth in his eyes making her pulse skip. He adjusted Louise, ensuring she was secure while still able to reach the guitar strings. "We were just working on her first composition."

"Oh, I heard," Leah chuckled, moving closer as Louise's tiny fingers brushed against the strings again, creating a surprisingly harmonious sound. "Very avant-garde."

"Just wait until she discovers chord progressions," Chris quipped, his simple manner making everything feel natural. "For now, I think she's more interested in the tactile experience."

As if to prove his point, Louise lunged for Chris's tie, determined to explore this new texture. Chris caught her hand with practiced ease, the movement so paternal it made Leah's heart twist with unexpected emotion.

"Easy there, little one," he whispered, redirecting her fingers back to the strings. "We want to keep the guitar intact for future concerts—right?"

The scene was so different from the life she'd imagined when she first learned she was pregnant. Back then, she pictured Ryan teaching their daughter music, sharing his engineering mindset. Instead, here was Chris, with his gentle patience and genuine love for both music and teaching, showing Louise a different harmony.

Grace appeared in the doorway; her timing was perfect as always. "I just got the set list for the upcoming children's performance! Are you prepared to see Louise's first concert?"

"Concert?" Leah echoed, maternal anxiety mixing with pride. "Is she ready for that?"

"Of course!" Chris winked at Grace. "With the right encouragement from her favorite music teacher, she'll be ready to steal the show."

The way he said it—with confidence in Louise's abilities and sensitivity to Leah's concerns—reminded her of how far they'd come from that first coffee meeting. How naturally he'd become essential to their lives, not by demanding a place but by earning it, moment by moment.

Grace stepped into the room, her presence always bringing warmth to their interactions. The late afternoon sun filtered through the stained-glass windows, casting a kaleidoscope of colors across the hardwood floors, making the moment feel almost magical.

"Speaking of concerts," Chris said, still holding Louise securely, "I was thinking we could do something special for her part." His eyes met Leah's, filled with that mixture of enthusiasm and caring that had grown so familiar. "Maybe incorporate some of those developmental activities we've been working on?"

Leah felt a rush of warmth at how naturally he included her professional interests. It differed from Ryan, who dismissed her medical knowledge as merely academic. Chris respected her expertise and actively sought to incorporate it into their shared projects.

"I'd love that," she replied, moving closer to adjust Louise's position. Her hand brushed against Chris's as they both steadied the baby, and the brief contact sent a familiar flutter through her chest. "We could focus on sensory integration through music. The combination of sound, movement, and touch..."

"Perfect!" Chris's face lit up. "And look—she's showing us how it works." He nodded toward Louise, who was now alternating between strumming the strings and patting the guitar's smooth surface, engaged in the sensory experience.

"She gets that curiosity from her mother," Grace remarked with a knowing smile. "Always exploring, always learning."

The comment hung in the air for a moment, and Leah caught Chris watching her with an expression that made her heart skip. It wasn't just admiration in his eyes—it was understanding. He saw her not just as Louise's mother, but as a whole person with dreams, knowledge, and aspirations of her own.

Louise chose that moment to let out an enthusiastic squeal, reaching for Chris's tie again. This time, he let her grasp it, supporting her as she used it to pull herself into a more upright position.

"Look at that core strength!" he exclaimed, his voice full of genuine pride. "Dr. Miller, would you say we're hitting those gross motor development milestones?"

The casual use of her title—acknowledging her medical background even as she'd put those dreams on hold—made Leah's throat tight with emotion. Here was a man who celebrated not just who she was but who she could still become.

"Definitely exceeding expectations," Leah managed, trying to keep her voice steady. "Though her musical talents might surpass her motor skills at this rate."

Chris laughed, the sound rich in the room's acoustic space. "With genes like hers, how could she not be talented? She's got her mother's brains and determination..."

He trailed off, perhaps realizing he was close to mentioning Ryan, but Leah found she didn't mind. The pain of Ryan's absence had dulled over the months, replaced by the steady warmth of Chris's presence and the support of their church community.

"And she's got quite the support system," Leah added, acknowledging what they'd built together over the past year. Louise, sensing the emotional undertone, reached one hand toward her mother while keeping her other firmly gripped on Chris's tie.

"Speaking of support," Grace interjected, "the parents have been asking about expanding the music program. They love what you two have created here." She gestured to Chris and Leah. "The way you've combined music education with developmental milestones... it's what our community needed."

Chris adjusted Louise in his lap, his movements natural and practiced after months of holding her during their sessions. "We do make a good team," he said, his eyes meeting Leah's with that blend of certainty and questioned that had been growing between them.

"We do," Leah agreed, surprised by how easily the admission came. A year ago, she would have hesitated to acknowledge any kind of partnership, still raw from Ryan's abandonment. But Chris had earned her trust gradually, building it through countless small moments of reliability and care.

Louise started bouncing in Chris's lap, reaching for the guitar again. Her enthusiasm for music had blossomed under his guidance, just as Leah's confidence in her new life had grown with his support.

"Here, sweetie," Chris repositioned the guitar. "Let's show Mama what we learned today."

He started strumming, and Louise immediately quieted, her face taking on that serious look she got when concentrating. It was the same expression Leah saw in photographs of herself during her clinical rotations—complete focus on the task at hand.

"Amazing how she responds to the D major chord," Grace observed. "Just like her mother."

Leah felt her cheeks warm. She hadn't realized others had noticed how she relaxed when Chris played in that key, how her shoulders would lower and her breath would deepen. He'd picked up on it months ago and incorporated more songs in D major during their evening planning sessions.

"Music speaks to the soul," Chris said, his voice gentle. "Sometimes it says things we can't express in words." His fingers glided over the strings, transitioning into a melody Leah recognized—the lullaby he'd composed for Louise during one of their late-night sessions when she was teething.

The familiar tune brought tears to Leah's eyes. She remembered that night clearly: how helpless she'd felt with Louise crying inconsolably, how Chris had shown up at their door with his guitar and gentle determination, how he'd sat with them until Louise drifted off to sleep.

"You've given us so much more than music," Leah said, the words coming from somewhere deep inside her.

Chris's playing faltered for just a moment, his eyes meeting hers with an intensity that made the rest of the room fade away. "You've given me more than you know," he replied, his voice rough with emotion.

Grace cleared her throat. "I should check on the preparations for Sunday," she said, backing toward the door. "Louise's debut performance needs to be perfect, after all."

As Grace's footsteps faded down the hallway, the music room fell into a gentle silence broken only by Louise's contented babbling and the soft resonance of guitar strings. The late afternoon sun had shifted, casting long golden shadows across the floor, and the stained-glass windows painted Chris and Louise in gentle hues of rose and amber.

"You know," Chris said, his fingers still moving absently over the strings, "I've been thinking about something Grace said months ago, about harmony."

"Oh?" Leah moved closer, drawn by the quiet intimacy of his tone.

"She said sometimes the most beautiful music comes from notes that don't seem to belong together at first." He looked up at Leah, his eyes full of meaning. "How they create something unexpected and wonderful when they find each other."

Leah's heart thundered in her chest. "Like a modern composition instead of a traditional arrangement?"

"Precisely." Chris smiled, understanding her need to process emotions through metaphors. "The original song you planned might get interrupted, but sometimes..." he strummed a gentle chord, "sometimes, the new melody is even better than the one you imagined."

Louise chose that moment to reach for her mother, and Chris stood to help with the transfer. As they moved together, the space between them charged with unspoken feelings, Louise settled naturally between them—a bridge rather than a barrier.

"Chris," Leah began, her voice barely above a whisper, "I need you to know something." She took a deep breath, gathering courage. "This past year, watching you with Louise, seeing how you've supported both of us without trying to replace what was lost... you've shown me what genuine love looks like. Not the kind that demands or takes, but the kind that nurtures and grows."

Chris's hand found hers, warm and steady. "Leah," he said her name like a prayer, "loving you—both of you—has been the most natural thing I've ever done. I didn't plan it. I didn't expect it. But watching you rebuild your life with such grace and strength, seeing you pour love into Louise while still holding onto your dreams... how could I not fall in love with such beautiful courage?"

Tears spilled down Leah's cheeks as years of built-up emotion finally found release. Louise reached up to pat her mother's face, making them both laugh.

"See?" Chris smiled, wiping away a tear with his free hand. "Even Louise knows this is right. We've created our own kind of family here, haven't we? Different from what any of us expected, but somehow perfectly us."

"Perfectly imperfect," Leah agreed, leaning into his touch. "Like a jazz improvisation instead of a classical piece."

"I love how you always understand music metaphors," Chris chuckled, then grew serious. "Leah, I don't want to rush this. I know you and Louise are a package deal, and I treasure that. I want to keep building this, note by note, day by day, if you'll let me."

Louise snuggled between them, her small hand still gripping Chris's tie as she lay her head on her mother's shoulder. The setting sun caught the mobile Chris had made her months ago, sending rainbow patterns dancing across their faces.

"I think," Leah said, her voice strong despite her tears, "that some songs are meant to be sung together. Even if it takes time to learn all the verses."

Chris's smile was radiant as he leaned forward, pressing his forehead against hers. "Then let's write our own music," he whispered. "All three of us."

The final sunbeams, painting the room in hues of gold, bathed Louise's face in a warm glow; her gentle rhythm of breath created a comforting silence, and Leah felt her heart finally unlock. This wasn't the life she'd planned, but standing here, held in the love of a man who had chosen them both, who had earned his place in their story through patience and unwavering support, she knew this was the life she was meant to have.

Their first kiss, when it came, was soft and sure—like resolving a complex chord progression, like coming home to a melody you've always known but just discovered. It was a promise, a beginning, a new verse in their ongoing song.

And somewhere in the garden, as evening fell, the church bells chimed, their sweet harmony floating through the air like a benediction.

CHAPTER 15

Hearts that Bind

As twilight settled over the garden, the day's joy crystallized into something more urgent, more electric. The crowd's chatter receded like an ebbing tide, leaving Leah acutely aware of Chris beside her, of the precise distance between their bodies as they walked the meandering path. Each step seemed to carry them further from the familiar world and deeper into a space where only they existed, where even the air felt charged with possibility.

The stone fountain beckoned them to pause, its gentle music a counterpoint to Leah's thundering heart. Moonlight caught in the water's dance, fracturing into countless silver threads that matched the nervous energy coursing through her veins. Chris stood close enough that she could feel the warmth radiating from him, could catch the faint scent of cedar and coffee that she associated with safety, with home.

"You've been quiet," he said, his voice carrying that note of gentle concern that always slipped past her defenses. When she looked up, the tenderness in his eyes made her breath catch.

"I've been thinking," she admitted, watching ripples disturb the moon's reflection in the fountain. "About how everything feels different now. How I feel different." The words came slowly, weighted with truth. "It's like... like I've been reading a familiar story in a foreign language, and suddenly the words make sense."

Chris shifted closer, and the garden's various fragrances—jasmine, mint, evening primrose—seemed to intensify with his proximity. His hand found hers, thumb brushing across her knuckles in a gesture so tender it made her throat tight. "Different how?"

The space between them hummed with unspoken words, with possibilities that had been building since that first day at St. Mary's. When Chris's free hand rose to cup her cheek, Leah leaned into his touch, drawn by a force as natural and inevitable as gravity.

Their kiss blossomed slowly, like a flower opening to moonlight. Chris's lips met hers with exquisite gentleness, as though she were something precious and rare. His fingers threaded through her hair, cradling the back of her head, and Leah's hands found their way to his chest, feeling the steady drum of his heartbeat beneath her palms. The kiss deepened naturally, tasting of mint and promise, and when they finally parted, their foreheads resting together, the world seemed to have rearranged itself around this new reality.

"Leah," Chris breathed, her name carrying the weight of everything unsaid between them. His hands had moved to her waist, thumbs drawing small circles that sent shivers along her spine. The moonlight painted silver highlights in his dark hair, caught the mix of wonder and desire in his eyes.

She kissed him again, this time with more urgency, letting months of longing and hesitation dissolve in the heat between them. The garden blurred around them, its shadows offering gentle sanctuary as Chris guided them toward a secluded alcove lined with fragrant lilacs. Each step, each touch, felt both inevitable and extraordinary—the natural progression of something that had been building between them since the moment they met.

"Are you sure?" Chris asked, pulling back just enough to search her eyes. His voice carried equal measures of desire and reverence, of wanting and waiting.

"Yes," Leah whispered, the word carrying all her certainty, all her trust. "I want this. Want you."

The night wrapped around them like a velvet embrace as they explored this new intimacy, each touch a discovery, each kiss a conversation without words. The distant sounds of the gathering faded entirely, leaving only their shared breaths, the whisper of fabric, the subtle symphony of two people learning each other's rhythms for the first time.

Later, when reality seeped back in with the distant sound of laughter and Louise's name on the wind, they slowly disentangled themselves, though something essential remained connected between them. Chris helped brush the grass from Leah's dress, his touch lingering with newfound familiarity.

"We should head back," he said softly, though his eyes still held the heat of moments before. "Before we're missed."

Leah nodded, smoothing her hair and trying to slow her racing heart. The world felt simultaneously sharper and dreamlike, as though they'd crossed some threshold into a new version of reality where everything held a deeper meaning, where even the moonlight seemed to pulse with the rhythm of possibility. Leah chuckled, a blend of relief and disappointment washing over her.

"Yeah, I think our first moment shouldn't end up as church talk," Leah joked, her cheeks flushing at the memory of what they had just been sharing. But there was a lightness in her heart, the thrill of possibility lingering even amidst the realization of their surroundings.

Chris smiled, a hint of playful mischief returning to his expression. "No need to add ourselves to the list of evening gossip just yet," he said, brushing a few blades of grass off his jeans as they sat up. "Though it could make for an interesting story at the next potluck."

Leah laughed, shaking her head. "I think I'd prefer to control the narrative a bit more. Something like 'how a single mother rediscovers her rhythm' sounds better."

"Absolutely," Chris agreed, his brow furrowed. "And it will undoubtedly be a hit in our budding careers as artists and musicians."

The warmth twisted around them in the cooling evening air, a tangible reminder of their shared moment. Leah felt the flutter of unease ebb away as they transitioned from the edge of intimacy to the comforting camaraderie they had developed.

Still, she couldn't shake the magic of their kiss, the promise of connection that flooded her senses. It made her reflect on the seamless way Chris had slipped into her life, transforming what once felt lonely into a vibrant tapestry rich with connection and creativity.

As they walked back to the main group, Leah's heart raced, knowing that their relationship was growing. Despite the uncertainties and challenges that lay ahead, she felt an unwavering sense of hope. She wasn't just being a single mother; she was building something beautiful, surrounded by a supportive community and a man who saw her for who she truly was.

"Let's regroup next week," Chris suggested, his voice filled with promise. "We can work on some songs together with the kids. You bring your art supplies, and I'll bring my guitar—maybe a proper children's music jam."

Leah grinned at the idea. "That sounds perfect! I'm all in, as long as I get to paint something in the process."

"Yes! A masterpiece in the making," he cheered, jostling her shoulder. "I can't wait to see what we create together."

As they reached the gathering, Louise awoke, her little yawn breaking into a delighted grin when she spotted her mom. "Hey there, sunshine," Leah said, picking her up from the blanket she had been resting on. "Did you have sweet dreams?"

Louise cooed in response, leaning into Leah as Chris grinned at them. The warmth in his expression made Leah's heart swell once more.

"Looks like someone's excited about joining the party," Chris said, his voice filled with delight. "It's the perfect time for her to meet her extended music family."

Together, they rejoined the lively scene, laughter reverberating amidst friendships and shared experiences. Leah immersed herself in conversation, feeling the connection deepen among them all—the church community blossoming into a more significant part of her life, embracing change and support together.

Later, as they prepared to leave, Chris waved goodbye to fond acquaintances, his presence radiating comfort and familiarity. Leah noticed the little things—the way he engaged directly with others, his warmth shining through. It made her heart flutter, a blend of admiration and budding affection.

Finally, watching the stars emerge in the night sky, Leah felt a longing wash through her—an understanding that this was just the beginning of something beautiful and profound. As they walked back to the car together, discussing the week ahead and sharing ideas, she looked forward to what was yet to unfold between them.

They walked together to the car, hands brushing against one another, a promise of everything that lingered unspoken between them. There was a sweet anticipation in the air, the knowledge that this was just the beginning of many beautiful and messy shared moments.

As Leah settled Louise into the car seat, she felt the joy of being a parent, the nervous excitement of a new relationship, and the warmth of being surrounded by community. She and Chris exchanged a glance from across the car, a silent agreement passing between them—a hidden understanding that this bond was growing, marked by trust, hope, and the promise of shared adventures.

Once Louise was securely buckled in, Leah climbed into the driver's seat, taking a moment to collect her thoughts. The hum of the engine broke the quiet of the night, and Chris settled into the passenger seat, his presence a comforting weight beside her.

"Are you ready for tomorrow?" Chris asked, turning to Leah with an earnestness that reflected the sincerity he brought to everything.

"Yes, I am," Leah replied, excitement bubbling up as they drove through the quiet streets. "I've been looking forward to our music jam for weeks. Everything feels like it's coming together."

"I think it's going to be amazing," Chris said, glancing out the window as they passed illuminated houses and families settling down for the night. "And after this week... I think we both deserve this."

Their eyes met instantly, and Leah felt the warmth of a shared connection, the recognition of something forming deeper than friendship. The drive home seemed fleeting yet eternal, filled with unspoken possibilities.

When they finally arrived at Leah's house, the night had settled into a gentle hush around them, broken only by Louise's soft breathing from the backseat. Leah turned off the engine, letting the quiet envelop them as she caught Chris's eye in the dim light. Something unspoken passed between them—an acknowledgment of the evening's transformation, of boundaries crossed and new territories discovered.

Inside, Leah moved through familiar motions with heightened awareness, settling Louise into her crib while Chris waited in the doorway. The soft glow of the nightlight cast gentle shadows across her daughter's peaceful face, and Leah felt the weight of the moment settle around her—this threshold between what was and what could be.

"She's beautiful," Chris whispered, his voice carrying a tenderness that made Leah's heart constrict. He stepped closer, close enough that she could feel the warmth radiating from him, could catch that familiar scent of cedar and coffee that had become synonymous with safety.

They gravitated toward the living room, where Leah wrapped them both in a blanket, creating a cocoon of shared warmth on the couch. The faint scent of baby shampoo lingered in the air, a reminder of the delicate balance they were all navigating.

"I never expected this kind of connection," Leah confessed, her voice barely above a whisper. The words seemed to hang in the space between them, weighted with months of gradually building trust. "Finding you, having the community's support, feeling so much joy with Louise—it's like I've been reading a familiar story in a foreign language, and suddenly the words make sense."

Chris's hand found hers beneath the blanket, his thumb tracing patterns across her knuckles that sent shivers of awareness through her body. "Sometimes the best things come when we least expect them," he said, his dark eyes holding hers with an intensity that made her breath catch. "You've been so brave, Leah. Taking risks, rebuilding, pouring your whole heart into Louise's world—I've watched you become more yourself with each passing day."

The truth of his words settled into her bones like warm honey, sweet and overwhelming. Tears pricked at her eyes as years of carefully constructed walls dissolved. "Chris," she breathed, her voice thick with emotion. Her fingers tightened around his, anchoring herself in the reality of this moment. "I'm falling in love with you. It terrifies me how much, but it also feels like coming home."

His free hand rose to cup her cheek, and Leah leaned into the touch, drawn by the same force that had pulled them together in the garden. "I'm falling in love with you too," he whispered, each word deliberate and charged with meaning. "Not just with the artist who brings color to children's lives, or the mother who creates magic for Louise. I'm in love with all of you—your strength, your vulnerability, the way you've rebuilt yourself piece by piece."

When their lips met this time, it felt like sealing a promise. The kiss was both an echo of their garden encounter and something entirely new—deeper, richer with understanding. Leah melted into it, allowing herself to pour everything she couldn't say into the connection between them.

Chris drew back slightly, his eyes holding hers with an intensity that seemed to still the very air around them. In that suspended moment, the soft shadows of evening wrapped around them like a tender embrace, and the familiar sounds of their shared space—the gentle hum of the heating system, the distant ticking of the kitchen clock—seemed to fade away, leaving only the sound of their synchronized breathing.

"I love you, Leah Miller," he whispered, each word carrying the weight of months of unspoken longing, of careful restraint finally giving way to truth. His voice held a tremor of vulnerability that made the declaration even more precious, even more real.

Leah felt the words resonate through her entire being, like the perfect note struck on a well-loved instrument. Tears pricked at her eyes as she reached up to trace the curve of his jaw with trembling fingers. "I love you too, Chris," she breathed, her voice thick with emotion but steady with certainty. The truth of it settled into her bones, as natural and inevitable as dawn following darkness.

"Partner," she murmured after a moment, testing the word that seemed to encompass everything they were becoming. "In music, in raising Louise, in whatever life throws our way."

"In everything," Chris affirmed, drawing back just enough to meet her gaze. His eyes held a mix of wonder and certainty that made her heart flutter. "The good days, the challenging ones, the moments when inspiration flows and the times when we're struggling to find the right note—we'll face it all together."

Leah nestled closer, letting her head rest against his chest, where she could hear the steady drum of his heartbeat. Outside, the stars wheeled overhead, witnesses to this quiet transformation. Inside, Louise slept peacefully, unaware that her world was expanding to embrace new possibilities. And here, in this space between what was and what would be, Leah felt the last pieces of her hesitation dissolve into certainty.

They were writing the beginning of a new song—one composed of love, trust, and the beautiful chaos of building a life together. Whatever tomorrow brought, they would face it as a team, their melody strengthened by the harmony they'd found in each other.

CHAPTER 16

Borrowed Time

The call came on a Tuesday morning while Leah was helping Louise practice walking. Her daughter's tiny hands gripped her fingers as they paraded around the living room.

Sunlight streamed through the windows, illuminating dust motes dancing in the air. The smell of pancakes lingered in the background, mingling with their tiny laughter. When Kate's name appeared on the caller ID, Leah smiled, but her best friend's tremor quickly snuffed out that warmth.

"Leah?" Just that one word, broken and scared, made Leah's heart stop. "I need you."

Louise protested as Leah scooped her up; the little girl wriggled in her arms, still trying to take shaky steps. "Where are you?" Leah asked, her voice steady despite the panic swelling within.

"Northwestern Memorial." Kate's voice wobbled; Leah heard the muffled sounds of beeping machines in the background.

"Hematology-Oncology department. They found... they think... can you come?"

The urgency in Kate's tone steeled Leah's resolve. "On my way." She was already dialing Chris with her free hand, her heart pounding as she fought against the shadows of dread. "Don't move."

"Not going anywhere," Kate attempted. Her laugh came out more like a strangled sob. Leah could picture her friend vividly: the radiant energy dimmed; her smile replaced with an anxious twist. "They're pretty insistent about that. My blood counts are... well, just come."

The drive to the hospital surged like a high-speed chase through traffic lights and prayer. Leah's knuckles turned white as her grip tightened on the steering wheel. Louise, usually a bundle of energy, sensed the urgency and remained quiet in her car seat, perhaps sharing in the moment's gravity. Raw thoughts spiraled through Leah's mind—fears pushing against her walls of composure.

When they arrived, Chris stood waiting at the hospital entrance, his tall frame casting a reassuring shadow that anchored Leah in the storm of fear. She felt a rush of relief; he always sensed when she needed a steadying presence.

"Go," he said, taking Louise in his arms. "We'll be right here when you need us."

The oncology department's waiting room smelled antiseptic and the palpable anxiety clung to the air like fog. Its mint-green walls did nothing to soften the weight of worry in the atmosphere. Leah's eyes immediately landed on Kate, who sat between her parents, looking frail in her UCLA sweatshirt, a stark reminder of an everyday life that felt increasingly distant.

"Stage 4 Chronic Lymphocytic Leukemia," Kate said before Leah could speak, her voice clinical, as if discussing someone else's life.

"I've had it for a while without knowing. The fatigue I blamed on finals? The bruises, I thought, were from yoga. All symptoms."

As Kate listed her overlooked symptoms, a haunting recognition stirred in Leah's chest, memories unfurling like pressed flowers between the pages of their shared history. The weight of guilt settled heavily in her stomach as she remembered their high school sleepovers, where Kate would push food around her plate, claiming fullness after just a few bites, her collar bones casting deeper shadows with each passing month.

Leah had been too wrapped up in her own world then—the echoing emptiness of her parents' divorce, the relentless pursuit of perfection that had seemed so vital, concerns that now felt gossamer-thin in the harsh fluorescent light of this hospital room.

The bruises that would appear on Kate's arms and legs, dismissed as clumsy accidents during P.E., had painted a canvas of purple and yellow against her increasingly pale skin. The way she'd curl up in their blanket fort, energy depleted long before their midnight conversations began, her voice growing softer as fatigue pulled at her edges.

Kate herself had laughed it off, attributing everything to stress and late-night study sessions, and Leah—caught in the swirling undertow of what she'd thought were life-shattering problems—had been grateful for the simple explanation.

Now, sitting in this sterile hospital room with the brutal clarity of hindsight, questions clawed at her consciousness: If they had noticed sooner, if they had pushed harder for answers, if they hadn't been so young and convinced of their own invincibility, would the story unfolding before them have a different ending?

Each dismissed signal carried the weight of desperate hindsight, leaving Leah's throat tight knowing that they'd all been blind to the whispers of Kate's body, too caught up in the ordinary chaos of growing up to recognize the extraordinary battle brewing beneath her skin.

Leah took a sharp breath, swiftly joining her on the couch, squeezing Kate's hand. "Okay. Then we'll fight it. Together."

"Just like that?" Kate's incredulous laugh held a hint of hysteria. "No 'oh my God' or 'I'm so sorry' or—"

"Oh my God," Leah obliged, squeezing her hand tighter, feeling the warmth of her friend's skin beneath her fingers. "I'm so sorry. Now, what's the treatment plan?"

That startled Kate, who laughed genuinely, easing some tension in Susan Anderson's shoulders. Tom Anderson managed a weak smile, his hand steady on his daughter's shoulder, exuding the steadfast love of a devoted father.

"Intensive chemotherapy first," Kate recited, clearly having memorized the doctor's words. "Then we'll look into bone marrow transplants and see if we can find a match. They're testing Grace and Brian tomorrow."

"I want to be tested too," Leah interjected, urgency lacing her voice. It was the only lifeline she could offer in this moment of turmoil.

"I'm your sister in every way that matters." Leah's voice remained soft yet firm. "Let them test me." A part of her thought absurdly that maybe, just maybe, this very act could bridge the unbridgeable gap between life and death.

The oncologist arrived then, Dr. Martinez, with compassionate eyes betraying the gravity of her words. She explained medical terms as if reading a critical report, mentioning white blood cell counts and bone marrow function, treatment protocols, and devastating survival statistics. Leah took notes, her hands trembling with the weight of the knowledge. Kate asked questions, their roles reversed from countless study sessions where Kate had organized while pulling Leah through life's hurdles before they arrived at this moment, a surreal standoff with the unimaginable.

"The good news," Dr. Martinez said, her tone careful, "is that you're young and otherwise healthy. The bad news is that the disease is advanced. We need to start treatment immediately."

The words hung in the air like lead, each syllable weighing heavily on Leah's heart. "I was supposed to finish my degree," Kate murmured, her voice cracking. "I was supposed to graduate next spring. I was supposed to start my career. Not... this."

"So we adjust the timeline." Leah's voice held unexpected steadiness, a resolve blossoming within her even as panic clawed at her insides. "You've helped me adjust mine often enough." She glanced at Kate's parents, who wore expressions clouded with fear and sadness. They endured this storm with equal worry for their daughter and pain over the news they couldn't fix.

Hours later, Chris found them in the hospital cafeteria, where the fluorescent lights felt harsh and unyielding. Louise was napping in her stroller, blissfully unaware of the turmoil surrounding her. Chris silently placed two cups of coffee in front of them, his presence a quiet promise of support. Leah felt warmth radiating from the cup; it was a slight comfort compared to their cold reality.

"You know what's funny?" Kate stirred her coffee absently, watching the dark liquid swirl before meeting Leah's gaze. "I always thought if something like this happened, I'd be the strong one. The one with the plan, positive attitude, and color-coded treatment schedule."

"Give it time," Leah smiled through her well of emotions, knowing Kate would likely find her footing again despite everything. "I'm sure you'll have us all organized by tomorrow."

"Speaking of organized," Chris interjected, as though sensing the precarious emotional tightrope they were walking. "I called Grace at the art center. She's covering your classes this week. And Mom's cooking enough to feed an army." His nonchalance disguised the underlying strength of his support—a reassured anchor for both women.

The simple practicality of his words loosened the tension coiling on Kate's shoulders. "You've got a good one here, Leah," she said, a hint of warmth breaking through the icy dread that had enveloped her moments ago.

"We've got a good one," Leah corrected, feeling the truth of her words resonate. "He's part of our village now, remember?"

As the days turned into weeks, a new routine fell into place—an uncharted territory they navigated together. Daily treatments filled their calendars, each session a poignant reminder of the fragility of life. Leah sat by Kate's side through the chemotherapy, recounting stories about Louise's latest adventures as powerful drugs dripped into her friend's veins, their conversations punctuated by the rhythmic beeping of machines and the faint sounds of distant laughter echoing through the sterile halls.

Chris took charge of the art therapy classes, blending music and creativity into the program. The children adored him; his tender affection and soothing melodies filled the art center with an unexpected energy. Meanwhile, Louise spent cherished hours with Chris's mother, Mary Johnson, learning to garden while singing hymns—discovering life in innocent wonder.

The hospital morphed into a second home, a strange blend of comfort and fear. They learned the rhythms of the place, which nurses gave the gentlest needle sticks, which vending machines stocked the best snacks, and where to find sunlight in the treatment room.

"You don't have to come every time," Kate said one morning, her voice fragile yet filled with conviction as she settled back in the hospital chair. Losing her hair from chemotherapy was still fresh, and the bold purple scarf wrapped around her head was a fighting distraction against the hospital's sterile palette.

"Try and stop me." Leah arranged a soft blanket over Kate's fragile legs, remembering the countless times Kate had taken care of her during her pregnancy. "Besides, who else will appreciate my Louise stories?"

"Speaking of stories," Kate's smile turned mischievous despite the exhaustion lining her face, "when's Chris going to propose?"

"Kate—"

"Don't 'Kate' me! I see how he looks at you and how he is with Louise. That man is in it for the long haul." The intensity in Kate's voice demanded Leah's attention, making her heart flutter with conflicting emotions.

"We're taking it slow," Leah replied, fidgeting with the edge of the blanket, though her mind raced back to Ryan—the man who had once left scars buried beneath her heart. "After everything with Ryan..."

"Chris isn't Ryan," Kate stated firmly. "And you're not the same person you were then, either. Promise me something?"

"Anything." Leah's resolve was instant.

"Don't wait too long. For anything. Life's too short to waste time being careful." Such pointed words held a weighty truth, resonating within Leah. As she internalized Kate's insistence, the moment's urgency felt impossibly tangible. It sparked a flicker of life, overshadowed by their current reality yet still trying to break free.

Before Leah could respond, the nurses arrived to start Kate's treatment. In perfect synchronization with her friend's desire for distraction, the rhythmic hiss of the IV machine began, accompanied by the gentle hum of hospital chatter in the background. Kate closed her eyes, allowing the medication to wash over her like a thick tide, her face paling against the brightness of the scarf.

"Tell me about Louise's first steps again," Kate requested quietly, her voice a plea amid the clinical surroundings. "The part where she face-planted into Chris's vegetable garden."

Leah grinned, buoyed by the shared memory, as she launched into the story of Louise's remarkable determination interwoven with the hilarity and tenderness of motherhood. She painted vivid pictures with her words—the sun-drenched afternoon, the sweet smell of the garden, Chris laughing as he assisted, only to find himself knee-deep in dirt and giggles later.

The recounting transported them both away from the sterile medical room, weaving a tapestry of family warmth amidst the weight of shared hardships and unwelcome realities. Each laugh and every memory exchanged heightened their connection, a lifeline binding them against the oncoming assault of illness.

Some days flowed smoothly, while others tested their resolve. The day Kate's hair fell out in clumps, they turned her childhood bedroom into a sanctuary of laughter rather than despair. Surrounded by photographs of happier times, Leah had brought scissors. With humor as their armor, they cut away what remained of Kate's hair, playing with different styles until they finally surrendered and shaved it all off.

"Look," Kate said, examining her reflection in the small oval mirror, her expression caught between absurdity and acceptance. She turned her head at various angles, the mirror capturing her likeness under its cool glass. "I have your dad's hairline!"

The unexpected joke startled a laugh from Leah, the sound breaking through the heavy fog that had settled around them. Soon, both women sat giggling, the room littered with remnants of hair—clippings scattered like confetti, celebrating their defiance against fear. The absurdity of the moment became cathartic, a sacred space where laughter could coexist with pain.

"We should do something crazy," Kate declared, her eyes gleaming with mischief. "Like get matching tattoos."

"Your blood counts are too low for tattoos," Leah replied, but Kate was already grinning like a cat with a new toy.

"Fine, then you get one for both of us." Her eyes sparkled with vibrant energy. "Something meaningful and profound."

"Like what?" Leah chuckled, her heart lighter from the earlier bout of laughter.

"Like 'Kate is awesome' in fancy script," Kate joked, flashing her friend a toothy grin that bridged the gap between bravado and vulnerability.

Their laughter echoed through the room, a sweet rebellion against the surrounding shadows. For a moment, they were not a cancer patient and her caregiver but simply best friends sharing jokes, fighting back against the unwieldy path stretching ahead.

On other days, the weight of reality descended, suffocating and relentless. Leah would come home to find Chris waiting, his presence an anchor as she let her facade crumble. One particularly rough night, she poured her heart out, the tears soaking into his shirt as he held her tightly.

"You're allowed to break sometimes," he whispered, the warmth of his breath soothed her. "You're allowed to be scared."

"I have to be strong for her," Leah protested weakly, piercing through the fog of emotion. "She's always been strong for me."

"Being strong doesn't mean never showing weakness." Chris tightened his arms around her as she let the tension coalesce into fresh tears. "Sometimes it means letting others help carry that weight."

The community rallied around them in ways Leah could never have anticipated. Moments of unexpected love filled the cracks of their heavy hearts. The art therapy kids, united in thoughtfulness, made Kate a quilt adorned with cheerful drawings radiating warmth and childhood joy. Chris's choir recorded her favorite hymns for treatment days, their harmonious gift a gentle caress, lifting spirits in despair. In her vibrant fashion, Mary Johnson kept a constant supply of homemade soup and fresh bread flowing to both households.

One tough evening, after a punishing treatment session that left Kate nauseous and too weak to keep even the ice chips down, Leah ventured into the hospital chapel. She found Susan Anderson there, her usually steady hands shaking as she lit a candle, a flickering light of hope dwindling like her daughter's strength.

"I keep thinking," Susan said without turning around, her voice quaking as she ignited another candle, the flame flickering like her spiraling thoughts. "About all the times I worried about ordinary things. Her grades, her dating life, whether she ate enough at college."

She paused; her breath hitched; an emotional weight too heavy to bear. "Such normal fears seem like luxuries now."

Leah stepped closer, lighting her candle and watching the flames dance beside Susan's. Warmth filled the air, mingling with profound sorrow. "Kate says you're her rock," Leah acknowledged, feeling the bond of shared grief threaded between them.

"I'm trying to be," Susan said, finally turning to face Leah. Her eyes glistened with unshed tears, reflecting a mixture of anguish and determination. "But sometimes... sometimes I look at her sleeping in that hospital bed, and all I can see is my little girl in her first ballet recital, so brave and determined even when she fell."

"She's still brave," Leah whispered, the words tumbling from her heart, wrapping around them like a protective shield. "Still determined."

"Yes." Susan straightened, taking a deep breath, the Anderson strength reasserting itself with quiet dignity in the face of calamity. "And she has you. I always prayed she'd find a friend like you—someone who'd love her through anything."

"She found me first," Leah corrected, compelled by the truth of those words. "When everyone else saw the perfect student, the perfect daughter, Kate saw... me. Just me."

They stood together in the chapel's quiet darkness, sharing a moment that transcended language—an understanding rooted in love and maternal instinct, a mutual recognition of the healing power contained within shared grief.

The anticipation for the bone marrow testing results loomed heavily in the air, each day stretching longer than the last. The news came rushing in like a flash flood, overwhelming in its swiftness—neither Grace nor Brian was a match. The weight of the diagnosis seemed to settle deeper, like a boulder anchored to their hearts. When Leah received the news of her test, she felt her hopes dashed again, the ground beneath her trembling and unsteady.

"Well, there goes my plan to have a piece of you inside me forever," Kate quipped, forcing a smile as she twisted the hospital blanket nervously around her fingers, her bravado a thin veil over the anxiety that creased her brow. "Very 'Grey's Anatomy' of us, though, right?"

"We'll find a match," Leah promised, taking Kate's hand and smoothing the blanket back into place, feeling the pulse of her friend's anxiousness. "There are donor registries, international databases..."

"Leah." Kate's voice was gentle yet unyielding. "We need to talk about... what if we don't..."

"No." Leah's heart clenched, panic rising in her throat. She refused to think about a world without Kate in it, as if uttering the words aloud would turn that horror into reality.

"Yes." Kate caught her hand, her grip surprisingly strong despite her frailty. "I need you to listen, okay? Just listen."

So Leah listened, with an open heart and heavy soul, as Kate outlined her wishes—the practical, the impossible, and everything in between. She spoke of her fears, hopes, and simple things—her favorite songs at her funeral, the memories that filled her heart, and the memories she wanted to leave behind. "I want you to sing 'Heaven' by DJ Sammy," she said slowly, and Leah's heart ached at the implications of those words. "And what to do with my UCLA sweatshirt collection... you know, Louise will eventually grow into them."

"Most importantly," Kate's voice grew serious, anchoring Leah's attention back to her. "I need you to promise me something."

"Anything," Leah whispered, her throat tight.

"Promise me you'll live." Kate's eyes bore into Leah's, urgent and pleaded. "Live, not just survive. Promise me you'll marry Chris, have more babies, make amazing art, and laugh at stupid jokes. Promise me you won't let this break you."

The tears spilled from Leah's eyes, heavier than before, imbued with the weight of desperate love for her friend. "I promise. But only if you promise to fight. Fight, not just for us, but for yourself."

"Deal." Kate managed a courageous smile, her dimples appearing briefly as a reminder of the boundless joy they had often shared. "Now, tell me about Louise's latest musical masterpiece. Chris says she's showing a genuine talent for percussion."

Leah took a steady breath, grateful for the topic shift. "If by percussion you mean banging everything in sight, then yes." She picked up the threads of laughter, thankful for the warmth in her chest. "She's particularly fond of using Mary's soup pots as drums."

"That's my girl," Kate giggled, a joyous light flickering in her eyes. "Teaching her chaos theory early on."

The days blurred into a rhythm that melded sickness with moments of levity, marked predominantly by blood counts and treatment cycles rather than ordinary calendar dates. Leah absorbed medical terminology she had never wanted to know, learned to read infection risk levels through the subtle shifts in Kate's expression, and became intimately familiar with every creak of the treatment room's worn tile floor.

Chris continued to be their unwavering anchor, effortlessly managing everything from Louise's daily routine to Leah's work schedule while showering them with love and patience. He brought his guitar to the treatment sessions, the gentle strumming a welcome balm against the sharp sting of reality. The notes floated through the air, wrapping around them like a comforting hug and easing some of Kate's nausea. On tough days, he would bring Louise along, her toddler energy filling the sterile room with laughter and light, eliciting genuine smiles from Kate.

"She's going to be amazing," Kate observed one afternoon, her voice brightening as she watched Louise "help" Chris tune his guitar, wielding a plastic ukulele of her own. "This little family you're building."

"We're building," Leah corrected, feeling each word resonate within her. "You're part of it too."

"Different part now." The weight of reality shifted as Kate's voice became contemplative. "More like... guardian angel in training."

"Kate—"

"It's okay." Kate squeezed Leah's hand, the contact lingering like a lifeline tethering them both. "Really. I'm not giving up, but I'm also not blind. The last round of chemo didn't work as well as they hoped. Dr. Martinez is talking about experimental treatments..."

"Then we'll try those," Leah insisted, the determination in her voice unwavering.

"Of course we will." Kate's smile, a fragile but fierce thing, crept across her features. "But in the meantime, I need you to know something. Having you as my best friend? Being Auntie Kate to Louise? Watching you find real love with Chris? That's been the best part of my life."

Leah felt fresh tears welling up in her eyes. "Stop talking like you're saying goodbye."

"Not goodbye," Kate corrected. "Just... making sure you know. Sometimes, we wait too long to say the important things."

That night, after Louise was sound asleep and Chris was at choir practice, Leah was drawn to the nursery. The mural she had painted months ago, depicting a vibrant tree with sprawling branches, caught her eye. Those branches held painted promises: strength, hope, love, and courage. She stepped closer, taking a steadying breath, and added a new leaf, delicately painting Kate's name in purple, the color of her defiant headscarves.

"Mama sad?" Louise's small voice startled Leah, drawing her out of her thoughts. She turned to see her daughter standing in the doorway, a teddy bear clutched tightly in one hand.

"A little," Leah admitted as she lifted Louise into her lap, feeling the softness of her daughter's hair against her cheek. "But also grateful. For you, for Chris, for Auntie Kate..."

"Auntie Kate sick," Louise said solemnly, a frown marring her innocent features. "But Daddy Chris says God makes sick people better."

The unwavering faith in her daughter's words made Leah's throat tighten. "Sometimes," she said, her heart aching with the truth. "And sometimes... sometimes God has different plans."

Louise considered this weighty thought with impressive toddler gravity before pointing at the mural. "Tree pretty. Like Auntie Kate."

"Yes," Leah whispered, holding her daughter close, the warmth of their shared connection enveloping them in an unforgettable embrace. "Just like Auntie Kate."

As the experimental treatments kicked in, they entered a new phase—one filled with both hope and anxiety. Kate's hospital room transformed into an informal gallery adorned with vibrant artwork from Leah's therapy kids, heartfelt cards, and photographs, capturing snippets of their lives together. The walls blossomed with life, all the while Kate fought fiercely for her own.

"It's like having a piece of everyone with me," she said one morning, her voice thick with gratitude as Leah filled the room with fresh drawings and bright colors.

"The kids miss you at the center," Leah said, adjusting another finger painting to catch the morning sunlight streaming through the window. "Tommy asks about you every session."

"Ah, my favorite angry artist." A fond smile graced Kate's lips as she leaned back against her pillows. "How's his blue period coming along?"

"Moving toward purple, actually," Leah replied warmly at the thought of the children rallying around Kate. "Chris has him incorporating music into his painting sessions. The combination seems to help."

"Of course it does." Kate's pride shone through, illuminating the somber atmosphere. "You are quite the therapeutic dream team. Promise me you'll keep that going. The art and music therapy combination?"

"Kate—" Leah started, but Kate cut her off gently.

"Promise me," Kate said, her eyes earnest and resolute. "Some of our best work needs to outlive us."

The word "outlive" hung in the air, heavy and foreboding, threading a silent agreement between them. Leah felt the weight of the despair that wafted around them. Before she could respond, Louise burst into the room, all bubbling joy with Chris close behind, her little face lighting up at the sight of her aunt.

"Auntie Kate!" Louise squealed, climbing onto the bed with an exuberant clumsiness that reflected her boundless energy. "Look! I drew you a picture!" She held up a scribbled masterpiece featuring large blocks of color, curlicues, and simplistic shapes—an abstract homage to their love.

"Drew," Leah corrected automatically, but Kate was already examining the colorful scribbles with exaggerated interest, her smile was radiant.

"This is a masterpiece," she declared, laughter spilling from her lips. "The use of color, the bold strokes... your mama is clearly rubbing off on you!"

Louise beamed with pride, enthusiastically reaching for Chris's guitar case. "Music time?" she asked, her little voice bubbling with excitement.

Chris nodded, understanding the importance of this shared ritual. "Sure! Let's make some noise!" He settled onto the floor, and with Louise perched beside him, he began strumming a soft melody that filled the room with warmth.

Kate leaned back, her head resting against the headboard, her expression melting into contentment despite underlying fatigue. "You know," she said, her voice carrying a hint of introspection amid the cheerful music, "I want to remember moments like these. All of us together, creating chaos... like a beautiful mess."

"Yes," Leah agreed, watching the interaction unfold and feeling an ingrained sense of gratitude wash over her. "This is our family."

As the evening wore on, the familiar rapport enveloped them—Louise happily banging on a makeshift drum made from pots and pans while Chris played melodic tunes on his guitar. The laughter spilled over, intertwining with the music; for that fleeting moment, the hospital vanished and was replaced by the haven of their shared lives.

As Leah tucked Louise into bed that night, the stars blazed brightly outside the nursery window, painting the walls in soft, flickering light. She couldn't shake the lingering worry that hovered above their little paradise. After ensuring Louise was comfortably tucked in, her eyes remained fixed on the ceiling, thoughts racing faster than the soothing rhythm of the world outside.

With a deep inhale, Leah stepped out into the hallway, her mind still a swirl of emotions. She went to Kate's room, unsure of what she would find. She paused at the door, the faint sound of Kate's laughter drifting out into the corridor, comforting and inviting.

Peeking inside, Leah saw Kate sitting up, dressed in a hospital gown and a vibrant scarf. The room was livened with colorful art plastered on every wall. Chris was there, coaxing smiles from Kate as they exchanged stories and laughter. It was an image of resilience that washed over Leah like a balm.

"Hey, you," Kate said, her smile radiant even in its fragility. "Come join us!" Leah stepped inside, feeling the warmth envelop her as she settled into the chair next to Kate's bedside. "What are we laughing about now?"

"Oh, I took down those nurses during my last blood draw." Kate made a mock punching motion. "They didn't stand a chance!"

Leah chuckled, warmth blooming in her chest as she leaned in. "They wouldn't dare come at you, that's for sure. I mean, everyone knows you've got the superhero cape on!"

Chris grinned, ending the melodious strumming for a moment. "Who knew Kate had a secret life as a superhero?"

Leah watched as Kate's laughter echoed, weaving through the air, stitching together the broken pieces of the day. One joyful note at a time.

"Speaking of secret identities," Kate mused, her eyes twinkling with mischief, "what's in that bag you've been carrying around?"

Leah glanced down, surprised by the question. "Oh, this is just my bag of tricks—the things I thought might keep us entertained."

"Show me," Kate urged with a glimmer of curiosity.

With a smile, Leah pulled out whimsical items—a pack of markers, a smooth stack of drawing paper, and a tiny travel-sized game. "We could make some art today or start a collaborative project together. I could draw something, and then you can add your touches. We'll see what kind of masterpiece we can create as a team!"

Kate's eyes sparkled with interest, a familiar flicker of joy breaking through the shadows that loomed over them. "I love that idea! Let's make it a true collaboration," she said, enthusiasm in her voice. "How about you sketch something simple, and I can turn it into something wild and colorful? Like a warrior princess fighting a dragon... but, you know, maybe the dragon is a giant pizza!"

"Haha, now that's a battle I'd pay to see!" Leah laughed, feeling her heart swell with love for Kate's indomitable spirit. The laughter that filled the room wrapped them all in a comforting embrace, erasing the weight they had carried for so long.

As Leah pulled out the markers, she glanced at Chris, who sat quietly, observing with a knowing smile. The interplay of laughter and creativity filled the sterile air, transforming the hospital room into a haven of warmth and friendship—a sanctuary where love thrived.

With the markers in hand and laughter carrying their worries away, they began their artwork—a tapestry of colors, a chaotic blend of dreams and imagination that stood as a testament to their journey together, each stroke a promise of defiance against the darker days ahead.

The scene melted into a serene tableau, the three of them together—fingers stained with ink, hearts open with hope. At that moment, the hospital faded away, and Leah knew beyond doubt that love, joy, and laughter would always hold their circle tight, no matter what storms might come.

"Here's to our masterpiece!" Kate declared, raising one marker like a wand, a grin stretching across her face.

Leah reciprocated, a surge of gratitude washing over her as they clinked their colorful tools together. "Here's to us—our love, art, and fight!"

CHAPTER 17

Ghosts of the Past

The morning had begun in the familiar confines of the hospital, where the blend of antiseptic and muted conversations formed a soundtrack to which Leah had become accustomed. She sat beside Kate during her latest treatment, encircled by the vibrant hues of fall. The sunlight filtering through the window painted colors across the sterile room, softening the stark lines of medical equipment and machinery that hummed in the background.

Louise nestled in her portable crib beside them, occasionally stirring with soft baby sounds that merged with the hum of the hospital. Each tiny noise reminded Leah of innocence and joy, a stark contrast to the heaviness that enveloped the space.

"You're worried about something," Kate observed, her voice tired yet alert. Her hazel eyes, sometimes dulled by pain, flickered with the sharpness Leah had always admired. "Spill it."

Leah adjusted Kate's blanket, the motion a futile attempt to create some semblance of normalcy, an effort to distract from the emotional turmoil inside her. "I saw Ryan yesterday. At the grocery store. He didn't see me, but..."

"But he's back in town." Kate's hand found Leah's; her grip weakened but full of the fierce affection they had shared for years. "And you're worried about what that means."

"I shouldn't be," Leah sighed. Anxiety prickled at her thoughts, casting shadows over her heart. "Chris is... he's everything Ryan wasn't. Everything Louise needs in a father. Everything I need..."

"But ghosts are scary," Kate finished, her tone grave. "Even when we know they can't hurt us anymore."

Louise stirred again, preventing an ocean of despair from swallowing Leah whole. She smiled through her swirling emotions, marveling at the happy sounds escaping the toddler's lips. Kate watched her goddaughter with an intensity of love, her face shifting into fierce protectiveness—an instinct that resonated within the two friends.

"You know what's funny?" Kate said after a brief pause, her words presented as a gentle musing instead of a declaration. "When I first got sick, I was terrified about not being here to protect you both. But now I see... you don't need protection anymore. You've built something stronger than any ghost from the past could touch."

Leah felt her heart swell, warmth spreading through her chest at Kate's faith in her. The truth settled on her like a warm blanket. She thought about Chris that morning, making breakfast for Louise in his light-hearted way, humming their song as if the world were right. He patiently encouraged Louise to help pour her juice, indulging her endless curiosity with unwavering love.

"Kate—"

"No, listen." Kate's voice gained strength, cutting through the haze of Leah's worries. "You're not the same person Ryan knew. You're stronger, wiser, and loved in ways he could never understand. And Louise?" She smiled at the sleeping toddler, her face lighting up with pride. "She has the father most kids dream about—one who chose her, earns her love every day, and puts her needs before his."

The weight of Kate's words sank in, settling comfortably in Leah's chest. At that moment, she felt reassured, like a gentle breeze pushing back against the storm clouds hovering ominously above her.

"You did that?" Leah asked, tracing patterns on Kate's blanket, aching slowly as the revelation sank deeper. "Even while dealing with everything else? You made sure the past wouldn't hurt us?"

"Protecting you and Louise has been the easiest part of being sick," Kate said simply, as if it was self-evident. "Because I know that even when I'm gone, I'll still watch over my girls."

Tears threatened to spill, but before they could, Chris appeared in the doorway, fresh from church, the golden rays of the morning sun illuminating him just so. He carried coffee and the cheese Danish Kate had mentioned craving earlier, and the timing of his arrival marked his attentiveness. He was like a lighthouse when the sea storm raged, bringing safety to their treacherous journey.

"Ladies," he smiled warmly, distributing treats as if delivering gifts. "How's treatment going?"

"Better now," Kate accepted her Danish, her face lighting up with genuine pleasure at the thoughtfulness. "Though I'd feel better if you'd play something. The usual soundtrack here lacks artistic merit."

Chris nodded, retrieving his guitar from the corner where he had propped it, ready for the perfect moment to rely on its soothing presence. As he began strumming, the notes spilled into the air, wrapping around them like a gentle embrace, lightening the burden in the room.

"He's a keeper," Kate whispered across the room, her eyes sparkling with the knowledge of love. "The kind worth fighting for."

Later that week, the church community center buzzed with the animated energy of Sunday morning, children racing between the adults' legs while the aroma of fresh coffee mingled with cheerful chatter. Leah leaned against the wall; her eyes filled with warmth as she watched Chris lead the children's choir through their vocal warm-ups. From her perch on Chris's lap, Louise was the picture of delighted concentration, her little eyebrows furrowed in determination as she mimicked the warm-up scales.

"They're good together," Grace Thompson remarked, appearing beside Leah, her hands cradling a steaming cup of coffee. "Like they were always meant to be father and daughter."

"They are," Leah agreed, unable to pull her gaze away from the scene. "Sometimes I forget she's not biologically his." The bond between Chris and Louise felt so organically woven, as though it had existed long before they all came together.

"Family isn't about biology," Grace replied knowingly, sipping her coffee, her eyes twinkling with understanding. "It's about love, presence, and choosing each other daily."

As she spoke, the cheerful bustle of the community center was interrupted. The door swung open, letting in an unexpected gust of fall air that rustled nearby leaves, and Leah felt a chill crawl up her spine. There stood Ryan Matthews in the doorway, looking exactly as she remembered, yet somehow different—his expression was an unsettling blend of familiar charm and a newly forged resolve.

Time seemed to suspend, the joyful noise of the Sunday gathering fading into a distant hum as the moment's gravity settled around her like a dense fog. Ryan's eyes locked onto hers immediately, betraying an emotion she refused to name—regret and hope swirling together in a glance that once would have captivated her heart.

"Leah." His voice sliced through the tension, drawing the attention of congregants nearby. The sudden shift in the atmosphere was palpable. It felt like the walls were closing in.

Louise's delighted squeal erupted before Leah could gather her thoughts, cutting through the awkward tension. "Daddy! Look!" She had engaged the entire children's choir in an impromptu, delightful cacophony of off-key singing and uninhibited giggles.

Chris looked up at Louise's exuberant call, his smile faltering as he assessed the situation. He shifted Louise closer to his side, his presence a powerful barrier between her and the stranger who once claimed to be her father.

Leah caught her breath, feeling a surge of protectiveness towards Louise. The combination of emotions quaking within her—fear, anger, and that long-seated worry—begged for release. She didn't want Ryan's past to intrude upon their present.

Within moments, Kate appeared, her wheelchair moving with purposeful speed despite her weakened state. The church's morning light caught the shadows under her eyes, but her gaze remained fierce.

"Ryan," she said, her voice carrying across the quiet space. "Never thought I'd see you here."

"Kate." Ryan's polished exterior cracked. "I... I heard about the diagnosis. I wanted—"

"To what? Show up now? When it's convenient for you to care?"

"That's not fair," Ryan stepped forward. "Jessica... she follows Leah's social media. When she saw the posts about your treatment—"

"Stop," Leah cut in, anger rising. "You don't get to use Kate's illness as an excuse to force your way back in."

"I'm not," Ryan's voice softened. "Kate, we were friends once. Before everything... I just wanted..."

"To ease your conscience?" Kate's laugh was sharp. "Or to play the hero now that I'm sick? Which is it, Ryan?"

Chris shifted Louise in his arms, his protective instinct visible. "Whatever your intentions, this isn't the place."

"I have rights," Ryan insisted, but the words lacked conviction. "And Kate, you of all people know how much I regret—"

"No," Kate's voice could have cut glass. "You don't get to use my illness to manipulate your way back into their lives. You lost that right when you walked away."

The tension crackled as Ryan struggled visibly with his response. Louise stirred against Chris's shoulder, sensing the shift in atmosphere.

"Look," Ryan ran a hand through his neatly styled hair, "when Jessica showed me those hospital posts... Kate, we all used to be friends. The four of us, before—"

"Before you suggested my goddaughter wasn't yours?" Kate's words were precise, surgical. "Before you told Leah to 'deal with it' because fatherhood wasn't in your five-year plan?"

"I was scared then. Immature. But seeing you sick, Kate... it makes you realize—"

"What?" Kate wheeled closer, her illness making her words more potent, not less. "What life's really about? Funny how my cancer suddenly made you develop a conscience."

Louise reached for Chris's collar, a self-soothing gesture they all recognized. Chris automatically started humming her favorite lullaby while maintaining his protective stance.

"It's not just that," Ryan's voice dropped. "Seeing the posts... the way everyone rallied around you. The community you've all built. I realized..."

"That you missed out?" Leah stepped forward. "That's what this is really about, isn't it? Not Louise, not Kate's illness. You saw what family really looks like and suddenly wanted back in."

"Jessica left," Ryan admitted quietly. "Said I was empty. Seeing Kate's situation, how everyone came together... she was right."

"So Kate's illness is your wake-up call?" Chris's voice carried quiet anger. "Her suffering is your convenient pathway to redemption?"

Kate laughed; the sound was surprisingly genuine. "Oh, Ryan. Still making everything about you, aren't you? Even my cancer becomes your character development moment."

Kate's words hung in the air for a moment before Ryan shifted his attention to Leah, his expression changing to something more calculated.

"Leah, could we talk?" His voice dropped, attempting intimacy. "Privately? About Louise. There are things we should discuss—"

"No." Leah's response was immediate, firm. "Anything you have to say about Louise, you can say right here. In front of the people who've actually been raising her."

"This is between us—"

"There is no 'us', Ryan." Leah stepped closer to Chris and Louise. "There hasn't been since you made your choice two years ago. You don't get to use Kate's illness or private conversations to work your way back in."

"I have legitimate concerns about her future—"

"Her future?" Kate's sharp laugh cut through his words. "The future you walked away from? The one Chris stepped up to provide?"

Louise chose that moment to lift her head, blinking sleepily at the surrounding tension. "Daddy," she reached for Chris, "sing more?"

Ryan flinched at the word 'daddy', his practiced composure cracking further. "Leah, please. Just five minutes—"

"The answer is no." Leah's voice was steel. "You lost the right to private conversations about Louise when you suggested she wasn't yours. When you left us to 'figure things out' and never looked back. Whatever you're selling now, I'm not buying. So please, do us all a favor and just go... please, leave..."

Ryan took one step back, then another. No dramatic gestures, no final declarations. Just the quiet acceptance of a door closing permanently.

"Kate," he whispered, "I hope... I mean, with your treatment..."

"Don't," Kate cut him off. "Don't make my illness part of your redemption story."

He nodded once, glancing one last time at Louise, who was now wide awake and watching the adults with curious eyes. For a moment, something like genuine grief crossed his face—not for the child he'd abandoned, but for the man he might have been.

After Ryan's departure, the atmosphere shifted, but still carried the residue of confrontation. The children's choir resumed their practice, their cheerful cacophony returning to an earthen rhythm, yet the shadow of unease settled over the space.

Later that evening, in the quiet sanctuary of Kate's hospital room, the natural process of healing and confronting began as the door clicked shut behind them. The soft beeping of machines and the faint hum of the hospital's ventilation system enveloped them, creating a bubble of intimacy against the outside world.

Kate was propped up in her bed. The evening light filtered through the window, casting long shadows that danced across the walls. Leah sat beside her, her heart still racing from the tension of the earlier encounter. The room's stillness contrasted with the tumult of emotions still swirling within her.

"You should have seen your face," Kate said, breaking the silence, her eyes sparkling with humor and admiration. "When Ryan made that threat about legal rights. You didn't even flinch."

"Because I know the truth now," Leah replied, the weight of her resolve solidifying within her. "About love, about family, and about what matters." A wave of emotion created within her as the day's memories washed over her, a blend of fear and clarity that had emerged from the storm Ryan's visit had conjured.

"And what's that?" Kate inquired, her voice soft yet probing, eager to delve into the depths of Leah's thoughts.

"Real love shows up every day," Leah said, her heart expanding with the certainty of her words. "In hospital rooms and choir practices, during midnight fevers, and all those ordinary moments that speak to devotion far more than any grand gesture could."

Kate's smile was proud, though tinged with exhaustion. "Look who got wise while I wasn't looking."

"I had an excellent teacher," Leah admitted, squeezing Kate's hand. "Several."

The sound of a soft knock drew their attention to Chris, who entered carrying a sleeping Louise draped lovingly in his arms. The sight was heartwarming—the little girl nestled against him, her round cheeks flushed with sleep, completely unaware of the confrontation that had just taken place.

"Hey, how's my favorite ladies?" Chris greeted cheerfully, despite the residual heaviness lingering in the air. He settled into a chair nearby, positioning Louise in his lap, the protective instinct he exuded unmistakably.

"Better now," Kate answered, her eyes softening as they landed on her goddaughter.

"Isn't it crazy how things change?" Kate said. "Just a few months ago, we were worried about my treatments and what they'd mean for you and Louise. Now, it's like the universe has reshuffled our priorities."

"It makes you see things differently," Leah replied, reflecting on the journey that had unfolded before them. She felt a profound appreciation for the life she had built—the unexpected twists that, while painful, had led her to this moment of understanding, joy, and unwavering support. "I used to be so concerned with the past and what Ryan was doing, but now..."

"Now you see how irrelevant that is," Kate interjected, her gaze steady and encouraging. "Love is right here. It's in Chris, it's in Louise, and it's in us right now. The ghosts of the past? They're just that—ghosts."

"Exactly," Leah affirmed, the power of those words resonating deep within her. She watched Chris as he played, his brow furrowed in concentration yet filled with tenderness as he occasionally glanced at them, as if he wanted to capture the moment in his heart forever. "The past doesn't dictate my future anymore. I have to focus on building something bright for Louise."

"And that's the point," Kate smiled weakly but brightly, her strength shining through the veil of her illness. "You've chosen love over fear, presence over perfection. That's the legacy we'll carry—one built on choice."

There was a soft stir from the sleeping toddler in Chris's lap. Louise's tiny fingers reached up and stretched toward her aunt. Chris adjusted her so that she could see Kate, and a quiet smile spread across Kate's face at the sight of her goddaughter's sleepy affection.

"Mommy?" Louise mumbled as she gradually woke, still caught between dreams and reality.

"Hey, sweet pea," Leah murmured, brushing her fingers along Louise's soft curls. "Want to come say hi to Auntie Kate?"

Louise blinked sleepily, her face lighting up as she focused on Kate. "Auntie Kay!" she exclaimed, her voice filled with innocent joy as she raised her arms, reaching for Kate.

Kate's heart swelled at the sight. "Come here, little one," she said, her voice thick with affection. Chris placed Louise in Kate's arms, creating an unbreakable circle of love—a constellation of connection that defied logic and time.

Leah watched as Kate cradled Louise against her, the deep bond of love and family shining brightly. "You're my brave little warrior," Kate cooed, her voice gentle. "You're going to keep showing the world just how extraordinary you are."

"Like you, Auntie Kay!" Louise replied, snuggling into Kate's embrace. "You're the best!"

A single tear rolled down Leah's cheek as she witnessed the tenderness wrapped in that moment—the grip of fear soothed by the warmth and love radiating between them. She realized this was what Kate had fought for: the tangible love that knew no bounds.

"I'm so proud of you, my sweet girl," Kate whispered, conviction ringing through her words. "You be brave, and remember that love always wins."

The three of them savored a quiet moment, basking in the shared embrace of familial love—Leah holding Kate's hand, Chris resting nearby, watching the connection unfold with a heart full of gratitude.

After a little while, Chris cleared his throat, breaking the tender spell. "I think I need to bring more snacks for this dynamic duo," he said, a smile lighting his face. "What do you think, Louise? Should we get some cookies?"

"Yes!" Louise giggled in delight, clapping her hands together with innocent joy.

"Alright, let's make this a cookie mission," Chris said, rising from his seat without disturbing Kate and Louise. "I'll be back shortly." He cast a lingering glance at Leah, a silent promise passing between them.

As Chris exited the room, Leah settled beside Kate, feeling the warmth radiating from her friend. Another wave of gratitude washed over her. "You're amazing," Leah murmured.

"Just doing what I can," Kate replied, her bright yet weary eyes filled with a fierce light that refused to wane despite her weakened state.

"You're doing amazing work too. Watching you take charge during the whole situation with Ryan? That was inspiring."

"Honestly, I couldn't have done it without you giving me that push," Leah admitted, a mix of admiration and gratitude swelling in her chest.

The pair sat together in comfortable silence, the hum of the hospital fading into the backdrop as they breathed in the extraordinary nature of their friendship. For every challenge, there was also a moment of beauty—a reminder of the profound strength in their shared experiences.

Louise was half asleep in Kate's arms, her tiny figure radiating warmth and safety. Kate stroked Louise's hair, the intimacy of the gesture manifesting countless "I love you's." "What if I wrote her a letter?" Kate asked, her brow knitting in concentration as she planned her thoughts. A love letter for her future, to be read when she's older and to show her how much she's loved.

Leah's heart fluttered at the idea, its poignancy sparking a rush of emotion. "That's a beautiful idea, Kate. She would treasure it," she replied, imagining the treasure trove of wisdom and love Kate would impart through words. "What would you want her to know?"

Kate paused, her voice softening as she gazed lovingly at Louise. "I want her to know she is brave beyond measure. She has the power to change the world. I want her to know about her roots—where she came from, the love that surrounds her, and that family isn't defined by blood but by the love and choices we make daily."

Tears brimming in Leah's eyes, she nodded in agreement. "You should do it. Please write it down. She'll cherish those words for years to come."

Just then, Kate's eyes brightened with an idea. "I could write her a series of letters. You know, milestones. Like, a letter for her first day of school, her sweet sixteen, graduation... stuff that resonates with different points in her life."

"Certainly!" Leah encouraged, feeling the weight of excitement grow. "Louise will need those reminders of your love as she navigates through life's ups and downs."

Kate smiled, renewed energy flickering within her as she envisioned her letters. "This could be my legacy. Growing with her in all these moments, reminding her she is loved every single day."

"Let's get a pretty notebook," Leah suggested, her heart swelling as she watched the fire reignite in Kate's spirit. "Something special just for that."

"Yes! Let's do it," Kate said, her resolve firm as she leaned forward in her chair. "I want Louise to have reminders—guidance whenever she needs it."

Leah felt a swell of pride at Kate's determination, her friend's fierce love glowing brightly amid the uncertainty. "You're the strongest person I know," she declared.

Just then, the door creaked open, and Chris returned with a tray laden with cookies, fruit, and a steaming cup of tea. "I present to you," he announced with a grin, "the Sugar Boost Brigade! Optimal for combating hospital fatigue!"

"Perfect!" Kate replied, her earlier enthusiasm shining through with laughter.

Chris set down the tray and pulled up a chair next to them, his presence radiating calm reassurance. The aroma of fresh-baked cookies and simmering tea wafted through the space, mingling with the familiar antiseptic scent. Their makeshift family gathered around the snack-laden tray, the mood lifting instantly.

"Okay, a quick break for cookie tasting and brainstorming letter ideas!" Chris declared, reaching for a chocolate chip cookie that crumbled in his hand. The texture was inviting.

They took turns passing around cookies, Louise's sleepy eyes fluttering open at the prospect of sweetness, her tiny hands reaching for a cookie as big as her face. Leah offered Kate a cookie while Chris leaned closer to cuddle Louise, his voice playful. "I think that might be a bit too big for you, tiny dancer! How about just half for now?"

"More cookie!" Louise giggled, her baby-like enthusiasm erupting into the air like fireworks, reminded them how precious and fleeting joy could be, even in tough times.

Leah couldn't help but chuckle at the sight—their community, their family, forged through circumstances far from perfect, yet vibrant and full of life. It was a moment of pure love that had the power to erase their worries.

As evening crept closer, the sun began its descent, casting a warm glow across the hospital room. They sat together, sharing stories and ideas, the atmosphere radiating comfort and familiarity. In these moments—woven with laughter amid the strife—Leah understood they were creating a legacy, a tapestry of love and resilience that would serve as a guiding light for Louise, even in the face of hardships.

Finally, as laughter settled into a peaceful silence, Leah glanced at Kate, whose eyes reflected determination and sweetness. "What do you think about setting aside specific times to write these letters together? We can brainstorm ideas for each milestone and record them. It'll be our little project."

"I love that idea," Kate said, her enthusiasm bubbling back to life like a fizzing soda. "Let's make it a monthly ritual. Something to look forward to amid everything."

"Perfect! I'll bring the snacks every time," Chris said, saluting them both as if they were officers in his brigade of cookie warriors.

"I'll hold you to that," Leah teased, her heart buoyed as she imagined a future filled with laughter and sharing hopes and dreams. "And I'll do my best to keep up with you both. I want to be part of that as much as possible."

Kate leaned in closer, determination shining through her fatigue. "No matter what happens to me, I want Louise to have a collection of my love poured into these letters—a roadmap for her life, guiding her through every turn."

After some time, Leah lifted her hand, brushing the hair back from Kate's forehead. "How about we open today's letter by discussing what makes Louise who she is? Her quirks, little giggles, the way she dances whenever music plays—those precious details matter, and we must capture them."

"Yes!" Kate exclaimed, her spirit buoyed by the idea. "Let's include her fascination with colors and animals and her ability to light up a room just by being in it. And her endless questions—that's a keeper!"

"'Why is the sky blue, mama?'" Leah teased, her expression mimicking Louise's childlike curiosity. "That one always gets me!"

"Or, 'Can we eat ice cream for breakfast?'" Chris added, his laughter tying them closer together. "The innocence of her musings is so beautiful."

As they shared laughs and stories filled with sincere joy, a knock at the door pulled focus, and Dr. Martinez stepped in. Her demeanor was always professional, yet imbued with gentleness.

"Good evening, everyone," she greeted, offering a warm smile as she surveyed the cozy camaraderie.

"Hi, Doctor," Leah replied, her heart tightening as she prepared for whatever news the doctor might bring.

"How are we feeling today, Kate?" Dr. Martinez asked, a slight lilt in her voice as she approached the bed.

"Much better—thanks to the sugar brigade over here," Kate replied with a hint of her trademark humor, nodding toward Chris.

"Glad to hear it. They're proving to be quite the supportive team," Dr. Martinez observed, her gaze shifting warmly between them, clearly nourishing the bond that had formed amid trials.

Kate smiled, but Leah noticed the flicker of vulnerability across her friend's face—a subtle reminder of the battles still waging behind the scenes. "Any updates? Anything new?"

Dr. Martinez sat on the edge of Kate's bed, adjusting her glasses. "Well, your treatment continues to respond positively, but I need to discuss a couple of options and make sure we're aligning with your goals," she stated, her tone shifting to one of serious intent.

Leah caught the slight tension in the air as Kate's expression subtly shifted from cheerful to attentive, her body language showing the shift in gravity. "Okay," Kate said, her tone resolute, yet tinged with concern. "I'm ready to hear what you have to say. We're still focused on quality of life, right?"

"Of course," Dr. Martinez affirmed reassuringly. "My priority is to ensure you remain comfortable while exploring additional treatment options. We've seen some positive responses in similar cases, and we want to align our efforts with your wishes and your family's needs."

Kate listened intently, her fierce spirit shining through despite the tenuous nature of her health. Leah's heart ached at the sight, but she felt unwavering hope. They had built a community around love and support, and together, they would navigate whatever lay ahead.

"Thank you," Kate said, gracefully receiving the doctor's words. "It's a lot to consider, but I'm grateful for your honesty."

"Anytime," Dr. Martinez replied with a warm smile. "You know the door is always open for questions and discussions. You're not alone in this."

Leah felt grateful for the medical staff's unwavering support as the doctor prepared to depart. They had become integral to their journey, guiding them through unpredictable waters with steady hands.

CHAPTER 18

Memories that Bind

The walls in Kate's room are adorned with many photos, artwork, and artifacts of a well-lived life and love. Each piece was a fragment of their shared history—laughter caught on film, a crayon drawing made by Louise's tiny hands, notes filled with encouragement and dreams. Kate sat propped against pillows, her laptop open despite her fatigue, a steely determination shining in her fierce blue eyes.

"Operation Time Capsule," she announced as Leah entered the room, her heart lifted by Kate's words. Louise was nestled in her portable crib, surrounded by colorful toys that clinked and clattered as she stirred. "That's what we're calling it. Has a nice secret agent vibe, don't you think?"

Leah smiled, her chest swelling with admiration and love. "What kind of operation?" she asked as she settled Louise with her toys, making sure the little one was comfortable and safe.

"The kind where we make sure certain people," Kate's eyes turned toward Louise, "never forget how much they're loved. Even when some of us are watching from a better view."

The gravity of Kate's words settled heavily in the air, reminding them of the fragility of life amidst a sea of affection. Leah felt the sharp prick of tears, but Louise provided a perfect distraction before sadness could entirely take hold. She held up her latest masterpiece—a finger painting resembling Chris's musical notes, vibrant and chaotic, just like toddler creativity.

"Ah, abstract expressionism!" Kate exclaimed, her eyes sparkling with delight. She examined the painting as if it were a priceless work of art displayed in a gallery. "Influenced by your father's musical notation. The blue makes the crescendo pop."

"Blue pretty," Louise confirmed, her tiny voice laced with a seriousness beyond her years. "Like Auntie Kate's eyes."

Leah felt something catch in her throat at the innocent observation. Despite her illness, Kate's eyes were remarkably vibrant, sparkling with mischievous wisdom. They carried a depth that told stories of love and laughter, juxtaposing their current reality.

"Speaking of pretty things," Kate returned to her laptop, her fingers moving over the keys with renewed purpose. "I've been making lists. Things Louise should know, stories she should hear, moments that need preserving. But I need help with the execution."

As Kate launched her plan, Leah felt swept up in the moment's energy—a sense of purpose that cut through the heaviness of grief. Kate outlined a vision filled with creativity: videos, letters, and memory boxes for different ages and occasions. With every detail, Kate's determination shone through the cracks of her illness, illuminating a fierce desire to leave a legacy of love for Louise.

"Mom's bringing family recipes tomorrow," Kate continued, her enthusiasm clear. "The secret ones passed down through generations. Louise must know how to make those chocolate chip cookies that got us through finals."

"Kate—" Leah's voice cracked as she tried to process the weight of Kate's plans, the enormity of the task ahead.

"No crying," Kate ordered, though Leah could see the shimmer of tears in her friend's eyes, reflecting the fragile thread that bound their hearts together. "This is happy stuff. This is making sure love outlasts everything else. Speaking of which," she turned her attention back to Louise, who was conducting an imaginary orchestra with her paintbrush, her tiny body swaying to a rhythm only she could hear. "Come here, sweetie. Auntie Kate needs your help with something special."

Louise climbed onto the bed, their frequent practice of "gentle hospital visits" now second nature. Kate pulled out a fresh piece of paper and some vibrant paints, eyeing Louise eagerly.

"We're going to make handprints," she explained, the idea illuminating her features. "Yours and mine, together. So you'll always remember how your hand fit with mine, even when you're all grown up." The thought was bittersweet, a reminder of the transient nature of childhood but also a celebration of their unbreakable bond.

As the next hour unfolded, the room filled with laughter and bright colors. They created handprint art, Kate narrating the entire process for the camera she'd set up, capturing both the vibrant moments and the quieter ones full of love. Her hands shook, revealing the fatigue hidden beneath her determination, but each giggle from Louise energized her further.

"Now the secret," Kate directed Louise as they dipped their hands into the paint. "Is to add glitter. Everything's better with glitter—ask your mom about junior prom."

"No glitter stories," Leah protested, laughter breaking the tension as they indulged in joyous reminiscing about their past adventures.

The door swung open, and Chris stepped in, instantly brightening the room like the sun breaking through overcast skies. He carried a small tray with snacks—cookies, grapes, and a steaming cup of Kate's favorite herbal tea. The teasing smile on his face radiated warmth and confidence, bringing a sense of comfort to Leah and Kate's bustling creativity.

"Ladies," he greeted with a grin as he set the tray on the bedside table, glancing at the vibrant chaos they had created. "How's today's masterpiece coming along?"

"Better now with snacks!" Kate declared, accepting the tea with genuine pleasure. The rich scent wafted up, blending with the faint aroma of paints and the hospital disinfectant, creating an oddly comforting atmosphere. "Though I think we need some real artistry here. Can you play something while we work?"

Chris nodded, retrieving his guitar from its corner like a long-lost friend and settling into the chair with practiced ease. As he strummed a gentle melody, the sound wrapped around the room, weaving through the air like a warm embrace. It served as a backdrop, allowing laughter and love to flourish around them.

"Now, this is a proper soundtrack!" Kate smiled, her spirit visibly lifting as Louise clapped her hands to the rhythm, her delightful giggles echoing through the room.

"Perfect inspiration for our handprints!" Leah chimed in, excitement bubbling in her chest. She admired how seamlessly Chris and

Kate co-created these moments. Their connection felt like a shield, surrounding Louise in warmth and security, a fortified circle of love that shrouded her from the worries and uncertainties of the outside world.

As they painted their handprints, the process became a celebration of life—their collective laughter intermingled with Chris's music, resonating with genuine joy. They painted vibrant colors, adding handprints to form a blooming tree, a living testament to their intertwined stories.

"This tree represents our love—growing and changing, always reaching for the sky," Kate said proudly, her determination shining through even as her voice wavered with fatigue.

"Just like you," Leah murmured, her heart swelling with admiration for Kate's unwavering spirit, even in her most challenging moments. "You always reach higher, pushing us all to do the same."

The softness in Kate's gaze turned to mischief. "And you, my friend, have the best taste in partners and snacks, if I say so myself," she teased lightly before redirecting attention to Louise, sprawled out in adorable concentration, attempting to mix colors on the page.

"Sweetheart, do you see all these colors?" Kate asked, her eyes twinkling despite the fatigue lacing her features. "Each one tells a story! This one here," she pointed at a vibrant red, "is about all the hugs you give. And this blue is about your giggles that fill the room with sunshine!"

Louise's face lit up with understanding, her tiny fingers now covered in a bright medley of colors as she felt the moment's music. "I like blue!" she declared. "It's pretty like Auntie Kate's eyes!"

Leah's heart twisted, warmth washing over her at Louise's innocent connection. In these small moments, stitched together through laughter and imaginative storytelling, the true essence of life revealed itself.

Before too long, Chris finished his song, and the atmosphere breathed with contentment. The cookies were devoured, the handprint art completed, and Louise's creative spirit flourished. The sunlight softened, casting a golden hue across the room as they captured the essence of the day.

"Let's take a picture!" Leah suggested, quickly capturing the moment with her phone. "This day deserves to be immortalized!"

"Say 'cheese!'" Kate said enthusiastically, her smiled brightening.

"Cheese!" Louise chirped, her face lighting up as the camera clicked. The single frame captured their joy, which would speak volumes in the coming days.

As the sun set and the warmth of the afternoon melted into evening, Chris helped to settle Louise in her portable crib. Leah took a moment to observe the smooth and tender care he provided, a silent testament to the love that had blossomed between them—a reminder that family is crafted through commitment rather than mere circumstance.

As Chris and Leah exchanged glances, Leah felt the flickering candle of hope reigniting within her, promising new beginnings. Each shared moment, formed through laughter or quiet assurance, fortified everything they built together.

"Thanks for today," Kate said as Chris returned to her side, the tenderness in her voice mingling with the fatigue etched upon her features. "This has made everything feel lighter. You both do not know how much these moments mean to me."

"We're just doing what we can," Leah responded, squeezing Kate's hand. The warmth of the gesture spread between them like a lifeline. She felt the weight of the world lifted as they shared these precious moments.

"That's the magic of being together," Chris added, drawing closer to Kate's bedside, where he could keep her hand securely in his. "We're a team, and teams lift each other."

Kate smiled, her strength reflected in her eyes, which sparkled with determination. "You know, we should make this a weekly thing—art sessions filled with laughter and creativity—a time for us to create fresh memories and preserve them, too."

Leah nodded enthusiastically. "Yes! We can keep adding to our project, capturing what makes our family unique. Story times, music, cooking—everything interwoven together."

With Louise nestled contentedly in her crib, dimming the glow of her radiant energy for the evening, the three of them settled into a comfortable rhythm. They discussed their favorite memories and orchestrated plans for future art projects. They laughed over the whimsical notion of creating a "family cookbook" that included Kate's recipes alongside the memories behind each dish. Leah visualized them cooking together, Louise "helping" with flour-covered hands while they made a mess in the kitchen—barefoot and happy.

As the hours melted away, the mood in the room became more reflective. The sunlight receded, replaced by the soft glow of the bedside lamp, giving the space a cozy ambiance. Leah could feel the peace settling over them, a welcome reprieve from the weight of reality outside the hospital walls.

"Here's a thought," Chris said, glancing at both women. "What if we create time capsules for specific milestones? For Louise's birthdays, for school achievements, and important family gatherings? We could have a designated spot at home where they're kept until she's old enough to open them."

"I love that idea!" Kate exclaimed, her excitement clear, igniting renewed energy in the room. "We could each write letters to her that she can read at key moments. It'd remind her of how loved she is, no matter where life takes her."

"Perfect!" Leah said, feeling her heart swell with anticipation of making memories that would last.

With the idea solidified, they began discussing potential milestones, mapping out birthdays, graduations, firsts of all kinds, and even simple moments that deserved to be cherished. Each memory was assigned a future date, a promise of love waiting to be unearthed once Louise was ready to embrace them.

As they spoke, laughter grew, mingling with heartfelt confessions. Kate shared stories from their childhood—tales of silly antics that had everyone laughing, including the day they'd attempted to bake a cake that turned into a gooey disaster. Leah couldn't remember laughing so hard that her face hurt, but she could vividly recall the joy they shared that day.

The warmth of those memories enveloped them like a blanket, wrapping around their hearts and holding them tight against the chill of reality. Moments like these reminded Leah why she had fought so hard for her present and future with Louise.

Eventually, as the evening wore on and Louise stirred in her sleep, Kate looked at Leah earnestly, her expression serious despite the loving atmosphere. "Can I ask you something?" she whispered.

"Of course," Leah replied, sensing the gravity in Kate's tone.

"Are you okay? I mean, with everything. I know you've been through a lot with Ryan, and I just..." Kate paused, searching for the right words. "I don't want you feeling alone in this."

The sincerity in Kate's voice sent a surge of emotion through Leah. Tears pricked at the corners of her eyes again, but they felt different this time—more like gratitude than fear. "Honestly? I'm still processing everything," Leah admitted, feeling the weight of her truth. "But being here with you and Chris, and knowing that Louise is surrounded by so much love... it helps."

"Good." Kate nodded, her voice steady. "You deserve to have that, Leah. Your past does not bind you. You have a beautiful future, and I want you to embrace it."

Leah met Kate's gaze, and for a moment, everything seemed to crystalize around them. The air was thick with understanding, trust, and the love that could withstand any storm. "Thank you for believing in me, Kate. I'll carry that with me always."

"And I'll always be here, watching over you both," Kate promised, her eyes bright despite the fatigue beneath the surface. "Everything we've built—our memories, art, love, and laughter—all lives on. You have to believe that."

Louise sighed, pulling them from their reverie. She turned in her sleep, her tiny hand reaching out to grasp the love surrounding her. Leah leaned closer, brushing her fingers across Louise's forehead, tucking a stray curl behind her ear—a comforting gesture that felt entirely instinctive.

"Look at that," Kate said with a smile, her voice barely above a whisper so as not to disturb the sleeping toddler. "She's already in tune with the love in the room. Kids are so wise."

Leah watched her daughter, her mind swirling with emotion. Louise's serene expression reflected the peace that permeated their little sanctuary, a reminder that love could exist even amid uncertainty and strife.

"Sometimes, I still find it hard to believe," Leah confessed, her heart aching with depth. "That life has led us here, that we're building this beautiful family, and that our pasts haven't completely overshadowed the present."

"And that's why we're creating these experiences, right? To show her the strength of our love, to remind her of who we are," Kate replied. She looked at Leah firmly, her determination palpable. "That's the beauty of our journey. It's messy, it's complicated, but there's love at its core."

"I love that," Leah said, her heart swelling with gratitude for Kate's unwavering wisdom. "It's about embracing the messiness and weaving the fabric of our lives together with love."

They settled into a comfortable silence, the soft notes of Chris's guitar wafting through the air like a warm embrace. The music was a soothing reminder of their bond, a sound that anchored them amidst the uncertainties still looming on the horizon.

As the evening deepened, Leah noticed the flicker of fatigue in Kate's eyes. "You should rest, Kate," she suggested, aware of the toll the day had taken on her friend. "You've been brave today. You deserve to relax."

A smile spread across Kate's face, the corners of her mouth lifting despite the clear weariness. "I don't think I'll ever tire of seeing you and Louise together. It fills my heart with peace. I could use some of that warmth right now."

As Chris adjusted his guitar, he caught Leah's eye with a nod and a soft smile, sensing the moment's weight. "I can play something light for you while you rest, if you'd like," he offered, his tone gentle and caring.

"Oh, yes, please!" Kate replied, her spirit rejuvenated by the idea of music washing over her like a comforting wave.

Chris began strumming a soothing lullaby, the notes flowing smoothly like water—a graceful dance enveloping the room in tranquility. Leah settled closer to Kate, brushing her hand through Kate's hair, feeling her friend's chest rise and fall as she drifted.

"I'm here," Leah whispered, quiet assurance as she marveled at the strength of Kate's peaceful presence. "You're safe, and you're loved. Always."

As the song played on, adding warmth to the room, Leah embraced the evening, absorbing these precious shared moments. She watched as Louise stirred again, her eyelids fluttering before settling into a peaceful slumber.

Chris paused, his eyes flicking between the two women, capturing the reflection of love radiating in the room. "You know," he whispered, "Kate, you'll always be a part of everything we do. You have created a legacy that will outlast any fear of the past."

The minutes drifted slowly, each moment a graceful note in a symphony that celebrated their intertwined lives.

The room remained hushed, their breathing mingling with the distant whir of hospital machinery. Outside the window, the late fall sky shifted into deeper shades of indigo, the first stars appearing like diamonds scattered across velvet.

Leah turned back to Kate, who lay peacefully asleep, an angelic calm painted across her features. It struck Leah how lucky she was to have shared so much with Kate—a bond transcending the typical bounds of friendship. She resolved to honor that bond, to ensure that Kate's legacy—her unwavering love, her fierce spirit—would live on through each cherished memory and heartfelt moment they crafted together.

Chapter 19

Final Gifts

Part One: Farewell

A few weeks later, Kate's health declined rapidly. The treatments that had kept hope alive now seemed to drain what little strength she had left. Yet she remained determined to finish her letters to Louise, to capture every bit of love and wisdom she could leave behind.

"Just a few more," she insisted when Leah tried to make her rest. "There's so much she needs to know."

The hospital room became their sanctuary. Chris brought his guitar daily, filling the sterile space with melodies while Louise played at the foot of Kate's bed. They created moments of joy even as shadows deepened—Kate teaching Louise silly songs, sharing secret jokes with Leah, planning for a future she knew she wouldn't see.

Then one fall evening, as the sunset painted the hospital windows gold, everything changed. Louise had just left with Mary after delivering her latest batch of finger paintings. The walls were covered with her artwork now, transforming the room into a gallery of love.

Kate's breathing had grown more labored, her consciousness drifting. But when she opened her eyes, they held the same fierce love they always had.

In those last weeks, Kate seemed to glow with an inner light, as if her spirit burned brighter even as her body weakened. She insisted on being part of every moment she could manage—watching Louise's music classes through video calls, writing her letters whenever strength allowed.

The day everything changed started normally enough. Louise had come for her daily visit, bringing a new finger painting of what she called "Auntie Kate's rainbow garden." Kate smiled, truly smiled, as Louise explained her color choices with toddler logic.

"The pink is for love," Louise declared, "and the blue is like your eyes, and the yellow is for happy..."

After Mary took Louise home, Kate turned to Leah with that familiar intensity in her tired eyes. "She sees the world just how I hoped—full of color and meaning."

Chris played in the corner, his music a constant comfort. The sunset filtered through the windows, turning Kate's hospital room golden. Her collection of Louise's artwork glowed like stained glass.

That's when Kate's breathing changed, becoming softer, more measured. As if she was finally allowing herself to rest.

The end came quietly, like sunset fading to twilight. Kate had been peaceful all day, her consciousness flickering between sleep and awareness, embraced by the gentle melodies that filled the air. The guitar chords and delicate strumming echoed like a lullaby against the sterile walls, transforming the hospital room into a haven of warmth. Earlier, Louise had danced through the threshold, her tiny hands clutching colorful finger paintings and her innocent chatter creating a symphony that made Kate smile for the last time.

As evening approached, Leah sat beside her best friend's bed, her fingers entwined with Kate's as Chris played gentle melodies on his guitar. The room felt transformed, no longer a space filled solely with the scent of antiseptic and the hum of machinery. Instead, it had become a sanctuary of love—walls adorned with children's artwork, photos depicting moments filled with laughter and memories, and the setting sun painting everything in soft shades of gold.

"Hey," Kate's voice, though soft and fragile, pierced through the stillness, drawing Leah's attention as her friend focused on her with an intensity that felt profound. "Remember what I said about not being sad?"

"I remember," Leah managed, a knot tightening in her throat as she squeezed Kate's hand. "But I reserve the right to ignore that request."

"Stubborn as always." The corners of Kate's mouth lifted into a smile; fatigue etched across her features, but her spirit was unyielding. "Promise me something else, then?"

"Anything," Leah replied, her heart fluttering with unspoken fears.

"Live beautifully." Kate's fingers tightened in Leah's grasp, a gesture that felt like a lifeline amidst the turbulence of emotions swirling around them. "Love completely. Let Chris take care of you—both of you. And tell Louise... tell her Auntie Kate will always watch over her."

Chris's music flowed through the room's quiet moments, each strum offering solace, anchoring them amid heartache. As tears trickled down Leah's cheeks, she felt the warmth radiating from Kate's hand, grounding her in the shared love that enveloped them.

The sun continued its slow descent, casting the room in deeper shades of farewell—a reflection of the quiet storm brewing within.

"One more thing," Kate's voice grew softer, as if each word were precious, chosen. "The letters... when it's time..."

"I know," Leah whispered, feeling the weight of Kate's careful planning behind every letter she had hidden. "We'll find them."

"Good." Kate's eyes drifted toward Chris, who maintained a steady rhythm, pouring love into every note. "Keep playing? I always loved your music..."

The following hours passed in a gentle blur of love and letting go. Susan and Tom arrived, taking their solemn places in the vigil while nurses crept in, adjusting to ensure Kate remained comfortable. Chris's music provided a gentle river of grace that flowed into every heart present, guiding them toward the inevitable shore.

As night fell, Kate opened her eyes one last time. "Love you all," she whispered, her voice brave yet tender in the face of her impending departure. "See you in the morning light..."

As her hand grew still in Leah's grasp, the last note of Chris's song faded into a poignant silence. Outside, stars emerged one by one like eternal promises against the darkening sky, and somewhere in the distance, church bells chimed the hour, invoking a sad sense of transition.

The following days flowed in a fog of arrangements, grief threading through every moment. The church community enveloped them, handling details with quiet efficiency while the Andersons navigated the profound loss that had touched their lives. With a toddler's intuitive wisdom, Louise seemed to sense the fundamental shift in their family dynamic.

"Auntie Kate with angels now?" she asked one morning, her tiny voice breaking through Leah's quiet contemplation as she sipped her morning coffee. The bitterness served as a reminder of reality.

"Yes, baby," Leah said, pulling her daughter close and breathing in the sweet, innocent comfort she provided. "She's with the angels."

"Does she still love us?" Louise's big, questioning eyes searched her mother's, their innocence piercing through Leah's barriers of sorrow.

"Always," Leah whispered, her heart tightening as she tried to keep her composure. "That kind of love never ends."

The funeral service filled St. Mary's Church with a bright atmosphere, creating an ambiance heavy yet buoyant with love and reflection. Photos of Kate over the years adorned the walls—glimpses of childhood adventures, jubilation on graduation days, and cherished moments with Louise that illuminated her enduring spirit.

When it came time for the music, Leah felt a knot of nerves twist within her as she stepped forward, steeling herself as she looked out at the gathered mourners. Each familiar face carried a quiet resignation, yet their eyes glistened with stories and shared memories, weaving a collective tapestry of care that had sustained them throughout Kate's illness—the realization of the love encircling her filled Leah with a bittersweet strength.

When Chris took his place at the piano, his fingers poised to create the soundtrack to their grief and celebration, Leah inhaled deeply, feeling the cool air coincide with the moment's warmth. As the first poignant notes rang out from the keys, an air of peace enveloped her, providing solace amidst the chaos of emotions.

With the congregation quietly attentive, Leah gathered her resolve, her heart racing in rhythm with the music. Clearing her throat, she stepped forward, allowing the melody to guide her.

"This song always reminded us of Kate," she began, her voice steady despite the tremor of sadness running through her. "It reminds us of the love, hope, and beauty she brought into our lives."

As she sang "Heaven," the lyrics flowed from her like an outpouring of profoundly painful and uplifting love. Each syllable echoed memories filled with laughter, moments of friendship shared on a college campus, whispered secrets in the dark, and late-night talks about dreams.

Oh, thinkin' about our younger years☐
There was only you and me,☐
We were young and wild and free.
Now, nothing can take you away from me.☐
We've been down that road before,☐
But that's over now
You keep me comin' back for more...

Her voice wavered as she battled back tears, but Leah found strength in remembering Kate's laughter—that joy intricately woven into their family's fabric. She willed herself to look up at the faces of the gathered friends and family, finding that bittersweet strength within those reflecting eyes.

As Leah sang, she felt Chris's presence beside her. His guitar provided gentle support and harmonized with her voice. His steady gaze helped ground her, reminding her they were sharing this moment. Behind every note was the reminder of the profound legacy Kate had left.

"We're in heaven..."

The last note lingered in the air, holding the church in a suspended moment of collective emotion. Leah's voice faded, but the feeling remained, reverberating through the hearts of everyone present. Tears streamed freely, washing away the grief that had settled like dust over the past few days.

When the music softened, and gentle applause broke the silence, Leah felt a rush of warmth and light—an embrace from every soul that had gathered to honor Kate. She glimpsed Louise's face, her expression a mixture of confusion and understanding, yet tinged with innocence. She felt Chris's hand on her back, providing the support she needed to step back to the safety of their unit.

As Grace Thompson stepped up to say a few words about Kate, Leah took a deep breath, still emotions swimming. "Kate was a brightness in all our lives," Grace spoke, her voice wavering but strong. "She gave every ounce of herself to her community—always willing to lend a hand, always ready with a complimentary word. We honor her today by carrying forward her spirit of love and kindness."

It was a gentle reminder of the legacy Kate had crafted—a legacy painted with the brushstrokes of laughter, joy, and fierce loyalty.

The service was wrapped in a warm cocoon of reminiscing, stories filled with light shared around the gathered community. As they moved to the garden afterward, Leah realized how these moments of vulnerability were the threads that wove their shared existence, connecting them with Kate even in her absence.

The garden gathering felt more like a celebration of life than a mourning of death. The soft rustle of leaves in the breeze mingled with the laughter and heartfelt conversations as stories flowed freely from those gathered. It felt like the air captured Kate's fierce spirit, wrapping it around every person present.

"Remember that time Kate tried to bake cookies for us and ended up just creating a gooey mess all over the kitchen?" one of her friends shared, drawing laughter from everyone present.

"That was hardly what anyone would call 'cookies,'" Leah laughed, envisioning the flour-dusted chaos they'd left behind and the celebration they had created from nothing but accidental disaster.

As stories like these continued to emerge, laughter mingled with tears, and Leah felt the warmth of the community enveloping her. Kate's essence lingered everywhere—in the smiles, shared anecdotes, and love that flowed freely from everyone her light had touched.

"Her warmth and spirit will always live on through us," Leah whispered to Chris, who stood close by, holding her to him as they shared silent comfort amid the festivities.

As the sun dipped low in the sky, casting a golden light over the gathering, Leah paused to take in the moment—the people, the laughter, the stories whispered amidst clinking glasses. This celebration was a tapestry of life that found its hues in joy and sorrow.

The evening deepened, and with each shared story and clink of glasses, they honored Kate's incredible spirit—her laughter echoing through those who loved her, bridging the gap between grief and gratitude. Leah stood amidst the gathering, both heavy with sorrow and buoyed by the love surrounding her.

As dusk settled in, the garden twinkled with fairy lights strung along the trees, creating a magical ambiance that felt Kate-like. Conversations morphed from moments of shared grief to laughter as more stories unfolded, each anecdote adding richness to Kate's collective memory.

"Do you remember her epic Halloween costume?" one of the community members recalled, eliciting chuckles. "She went as a giant pumpkin and tripped over her feet but insisted on finishing the trick-or-treating block! Her enthusiasm was unbeatable."

"Of course! She spent the next week discussing overthrowing the scary decorations—it was like she was on a mission!" Leah added, recalling the determined fire in Kate's eyes during that silly, naughty period.

Chris leaned closer, brushing a strand of hair behind Leah's ear. "She was the queen of turning every event into an adventure," he said, his voice carrying the tenderness that had become second nature to them both. "That's what made her so special."

Louise, meanwhile, was busy examining the flowers, picking petals, and dancing in her little world of imagination. The sight of her, innocent and unfettered by the day's weight, tugged at Leah's heart. In these moments, Kate's presence felt strongest, and she silently thanked her for the legacy left behind.

The sun dipped below the horizon, and as lanterns glowed warmly amidst the darkening garden, Leah reminded herself to keep Kate's spirit alive in Louise's laughter—through stories, music, and the simple joys they reclaimed from their shared lives.

Part Two: Letters of Light

The first letter appeared where Kate said it would be–tucked inside Louise's favorite book, a treasured collection of bedtime stories. The anticipation buzzed in the air as Leah lifted the pastel envelope, distinctly marked in Kate's curl of handwriting: "For After–Read First." Her heart raced, a mixture of joy and sorrow flooding her senses.

Leah's hands trembled as she opened the envelope, her breath catching as Louise cuddled against her, warmth radiating from her little body. Chris sat nearby, his reassuring presence anchoring her to the moment. The world outside faded as she honed in on the paper, the familiar scent of Kate's perfume still lingering on it, intertwining with the smell of the book—aged paper, a hint of lavender, a bit of magic.

"My dearest ones," Kate's words flowed from the page, vibrant as Leah could almost hear her voice, full of life. "If you're reading this, the angels finally won our argument about my earthly schedule. But don't think for a minute that means I'm done being part of your lives."

Louise traced the writing with tiny fingers, marveled at the unique loops and swirls.

"Auntie Kate's letters?" she asked, her wide eyes sparkling with curiosity.

"Yes, baby," Leah replied, her voice wavering as she continued reading through tears that gathered like morning dew.

"I've hidden letters everywhere–some for now, some for later, some for moments you don't even know you'll need yet. Consider it a treasure hunt from your favorite aunt. And Leah? Consider it my way of keeping my promise to always be there for you both."

The words enveloped Leah as she read, wrapping her in Kate's essence. She could almost picture her best friend, animated and mischievous, her sparkling eyes flickering with delight as she devised such a grand plan. The tactile nature of the letter was like holding onto a piece of Kate herself.

The letter explained how Kate had meticulously marked each envelope with dates or occasions, placing them in places imbued with significance—some with Grace at the church, others with Susan—a network of love spread across the lives they cherished. Leah wiped a tear from her cheek, smiling despite the ache in her heart; Kate's careful thoughts shone through each word.

The letter concluded, "Your job is to keep living beautifully, loving completely, and finding joy in small moments and big adventures. I'll be watching, cheering you on, and probably making inappropriate comments from my cloud. All my love, always and forever, Kate."

Chris's voice broke the silence, warm and soothing against Leah's trembling form. "She thought of everything," he said as he wrapped his arms around them. Louise, wise and compassionate even at her tender age, patted her mother's cheeks with tender concern, her tiny fingers brushing away the tears.

The treasure hunt began the next day, a glorious expedition bridging heartache and healing. In the art therapy room, they discovered an envelope marked "For Louise's First Day of School." Louise's excited giggle echoed against the walls as they peeled it open. Inside, Kate had written an encouraging note infused with warmth and wisdom that felt like an embrace.

At the church, Grace presented a collection of letters for future birthdays and holidays — a treasure trove that brought fresh tears yet laughter, each letter a glimmer of Kate's love shining forth. Leah felt like a child again in a world where magic still existed, the air thick with memories, each written word sparking joy among the familiar.

"How did she know?" Leah wondered aloud as she found an envelope marked "For Your Wedding Day" tucked into her old photo album. The pages were adorned with memories from her past, and this envelope felt like it had its heartbeat, pulsing with intentions Kate had crafted with care.

"Because she knew you," Chris answered, his voice steady and confident. "She knew your heart, future, and love would win." His eyes gleamed with affection as he glanced between Leah and Louise, wrapping them in the warmth of his love while reminding Leah of Kate's foresight and wisdom.

The most profound discoveries awaited in Kate's childhood room, a sacred space where time stood still. Susan had preserved everything exactly as it had been, rendering the nostalgia practically palpable. Leah's heart raced as they rifled through childhood treasures—the old toys, the photographs—and amongst them, letters slipped into yearbooks, hidden in jewelry boxes, tucked away in pages of old diaries.

"She spent months on this," Susan said, her voice tinged with reverence and loss as she watched Leah and Louise uncover each new treasure. "It gave her peace, knowing she'd still be part of your lives." Her eyes reflected a blend of admiration and heartache, and her words hung like a tender whisper.

One particular envelope marked drastically Leah–When You Find Your Strength contained a minor key within crisp paper folds. Leah's fingers clutched it, her heart pounding in her chest as she opened the accompanying letter, anticipation coursing through her veins. Inside awaited not just a key, but a promise—a way for Leah to unlock a safe deposit box and a piece of her best friend's love that would endure beyond their shared earthly moments.

As Leah uncovered the contents of the safe deposit box, it felt like treading into sacred ground. The documents ensured Louise's future, meticulously arranged by Kate, each piece imbued with a sisterly ardor that engulfed Leah. Letters marked with eloquent descriptions awaited, each intended for moments yet to come—"When You Think You Can't Go On," "When You Need Your Best Friend," and "When Chris Finally Proposes." They were like guiding stars across the unknown terrain of Leah's life, illuminating even the darkest corners.

"Oh, Kate," Leah whispered, emotion shuddering through her. She could almost hear her best friend's laughter, that unmistakable sound that could light up any room. It mingled with her sorrow, forming a bittersweet harmony. She felt tethered to Kate in a way she hadn't thought possible, an invisible thread binding their hearts, transcending even death.

Her fingers turned the journal pages at the bottom of the box, filled with Kate's thoughts and prayers throughout her illness. Each handwritten word encased her friend's spirit, a testament to resilience laced with vulnerability. The first page captured Leah's attention with a message so raw it resonated deep within her.

"I'm not writing this to make you sad," it began. "I'm writing it to show you how much joy you brought to my last days. How watching you with Chris and Louise gave me peace about leaving..." Leah's heart splintered with the weight of Kate's bittersweet honesty, her friend's love bathed in each line.

"How knowing you'll all have each other makes everything bearable." Leah closed her eyes, allowing the words to wash over her like cool rain on a hot summer's day.

Kate's voice seemed to echo in Leah's mind—encouraging, teasing, and loving. She pictured her friend standing beside her, a playful smile on her lips, coaxing Leah to embrace life. The gravity of the situation was palpable, and Leah felt solid and vulnerable as she read about the myriad of moments Kate had envisioned for her. Wisdom there, rooted in love, propelled Leah to cherish every heartbeat.

The last letter waited patiently in the church garden, where their stories had blossomed. Leah strolled there with Chris and Louise, the scent of blooming roses enveloping them, their petals glistening like jewels in the fading sunlight. It felt like magic, where they'd shared countless memories—the laughter of children, the solemnity of vows, the endless moments woven into the fabric of time.

As the sun dipped lower, painting the sky in strokes of gold and crimson, Leah found the letter buried amongst the petals, fluttering in the gentle breeze. It was wrapped in the familiar craft paper, a sight that sent waves of nostalgia crashing over her. She unfolded it, her heart racing with each word she read.

"My dearest Leah, By now, you've found most of my letters, my final attempts to be part of your ongoing story. But this one is different. This one is to say thank you."

Leah's breath caught in her throat. Gratitude poured from the ink, wrapping around her like a warm hug. "Thank you for being the sister I always wanted and loving me through everything. Thank you for giving me Louise to spoil and Chris to trust with your heart. For showing me what real strength looks like."

The words struck Leah with profound resonance, each line a thread weaving together their shared past, stitched with moments of laughter and tears alike. She could feel Chris's reassuring hand on her shoulder, lending her the strength she often sought in times of uncertainty.

"I'm not good at goodbyes—you know this about me. So instead, I'll say this: Live wildly. Love completely. Laugh often. Tell Louise stories about her crazy aunt who loved her before birth. Let Chris take care of you both the way you deserve."

Leah swallowed hard, choking back tears as awe and sadness intertwined within her heart. She imagined Kate crafting these words, pouring her heart into each line with palpable affection and passionate intent. The richness of Kate's personality flowed freely through the letter, vibrant and unyielding.

"And sometimes, when the sun hits the roses just right in this garden, or when Louise laughs exactly like you used to, or when life feels too heavy to bear alone—look for me in those moments. I'll be there, probably making inappropriate jokes and rolling my eyes at how long Chris's taking to propose."

Leah chuckled despite herself as the image of Kate rolling her eyes at Chris's indecision danced in her mind. It was a familiar scene they had all shared at some point—Kate's playful spirit imprinted in every laugh and memory.

"You are loved. You are strong. You are everything I always knew you could be," Leah read the final lines, the words reverberating in the garden's stillness. The sun had now set, casting long shadows mingling with dusk, yet Leah felt warm—an embrace that transcended time.

"Until we meet again (hopefully not too soon—I mean it, be careful!), Your best friend, always and forever, Kate."

Leah held the letter close to her heart, feeling its comforting weight against her chest as she looked up at the deepening sky, dotted with stars that twinkled like diamonds in a velvet expanse.

"Thank you," she whispered into the evening air, her voice quivering. "For everything." Each word felt like a prayer, a connection to a love that would never fade.

Beside her, Chris urged Louise to join them on the garden bench. The sight of their daughter's carefree laughter intertwining with the night's beauty reminded them that life continued, even in the shadow of loss. Louise twirled happily, her little feet barely touching the ground, and her laughter rang out like music—a melody that felt both joyful and achingly nostalgic.

"Mommy, can we tell a story about Auntie Kate?" she chirped, innocent eyes filled with curiosity and love.

Leah exchanged a knowing glance with Chris, a silent conversation of gratitude and longing. "Of course, baby. Auntie Kate would love to hear stories."

As Louise settled in her lap, Leah felt a mix of emotions surge—joy, sadness, and, most importantly, love. This was her reality now—a new chapter in which Kate's absence lingered like a whisper, yet her presence resonated in every memory and every letter.

"Once upon a time," Leah began, her voice steady, "there was a crazy, fun aunt named Kate who loved to make people laugh." She glanced at Chris, who smiled encouragingly, reminded her of the warmth Kate had instilled in their lives.

"She would take all of us on the most ridiculous adventures. Do you remember how she took us on that road trip to the beach, and we got lost but ended up having a picnic by that beautiful lake?"

Louise's eyes widened. "Yes! And Auntie Kate made us sandwiches with peanut butter and jelly, and we saw that big dog that rolled in the mud!"

"Exactly!" Leah laughed. "Auntie Kate laughed so hard when we tried to shower him off with water, only to get soaked ourselves!" The story flowed easily, memories spilling like sunbeams through the cracks of grief, illuminating the corners where joy lived.

As Leah spoke, she could almost see Kate sitting there with them, her infectious laughter mingling with Louise's delight. Each word felt like a revival, a resurrection of the spirit that Kate had given upon them, reminding them that even in the tension of loss, there was also life—fierce and beautiful.

"Before bed, she would tell us stories about her adventures— like when she tried to ride a bicycle down a hill and ended up in a bush!" Louise giggled uncontrollably, and Leah felt her heart swell.

"That's right! And do you know what she told me after that?" Leah continued, her voice softening. "She said that everyone falls sometimes, but what matters is how we get back up and keep trying. Auntie Kate was the best at getting back up, wasn't she?"

"Yes! She would laugh and try again," Louise giggled, and Leah felt the warmth of memories flood her heart.

The garden seemed to breathe with them, the soft petals whispering secrets, the stars twinkling more brightly as if in applause of the love being shared. Chris leaned closer, wrapping his arms around both Leah and Louise, a protective cocoon that felt like it could bridge any chasms that opened beneath them.

At that moment, Leah knew they were more than just grieving; they were celebrating Kate. They were living out the essence of her letters—the laughter, the love, the acceptance of each moment, both painful and beautiful.

"Louise, do you promise always to remember Auntie Kate?" Leah asked.

"Yes! I will tell everyone about her! And I will draw pictures for her," Louise replied resolutely, clenching her tiny fist in determination, and Leah's heart soared.

"And we will make sure her story lives on," Chris added, his voice assuring, affirmed their silent pact as guardians of Kate's legacy. "Every time we see the sun touch the roses just right or hear your laughter echo through the halls, we'll keep Auntie Kate alive in our hearts, reminding us of her love and strength," he said, caressing Louise's cheek as he spoke.

Leah felt an overwhelming sense of gratitude wash over her, mingling with the ache of missing Kate. "We will," she echoed, holding her daughter closer and inhaling the sweet scent of her hair, a blend of innocence and comfort. "We will carry her everywhere, like our shiny treasure."

The night deepened around them, the air fragrant with roses, and for a moment, it felt like everything was precisely as it needed to be. Leah looked up to the sky, where constellations glimmered like tiny promises, and she whispered a silent thank-you to Kate, wishing she could embrace her one last time.

Louise pointed excitedly at the sky. "Look! That star is winking! It's Auntie Kate saying hi!"

A smile broke across Leah's face—a radiant smile that lit up the shadows in her heart. "You're right, baby!" she said, her voice full of warmth and delight. "That's exactly what she'd do! She'd be up there winking and cheering us on."

Chris chuckled at their exchange, his eyes speaking of love and support. He took a moment to hold Leah's gaze, the kind of look that conveyed everything without the need for words. They were in this together, through every shadow and every light.

"Let's remember to celebrate her life, not just mourn her absence," Chris suggested, his voice carrying the gravity of their situation and the hope of what was to come. "Let's plan those adventures she would want us to take. We can create new memories while keeping her spirit alive."

"Yes, I like that." Leah replied, feeling a renewed sense of purpose. "We can take Louise to the beach this summer and tell stories about Auntie Kate as we splash in the waves. We can help her build sandcastles like Kate did with us."

"And we'll take plenty of silly pictures!" Louise chimed, her eyes alight with enthusiasm. "Auntie Kate would love that!"

"Yes, she would!" Leah laughed, feeling an overwhelming sense of warmth enveloping her. They were all together in that moment—past, present, and future intertwined, forming a tapestry of love that would never fray.

The sun had set on the horizon; the sky deepening into a rich indigo. As the first stars shimmered overhead, Leah realized that just as those stars would always shine, so too would Kate's love illuminate their lives, even in her absence.

They spent the following few moments sharing stories under the vast sky, Louise's laughter ringing out like delightful chimes, Chris's tender words connecting their hearts as they reminisced about the cherished moments with Kate.

"Mommy, what was Auntie Kate's favorite color?" Louise asked, her innocent curiosity prompting Leah to reflect.

"Purple," Leah answered, her voice soft as she conjured the memory. "I remember how she always wore that beautiful purple scarf that made her look like a queen."

"Let's paint something purple for her," Louise suggested, her tiny voice filled with hope. "Something wonderful to send to the stars."

"Let's do it," Chris agreed, his eyes sparkling with approval. "A beautiful painting. Maybe we can even decorate the garden with purple flowers in her memory in the spring."

Leah nodded, feeling an overwhelming sense of purpose as she envisioned their garden blossoming with purple—a vibrant tribute to the love that had filled their lives.

As the stars shone brighter and the moon cast its gentle glow upon them, Leah felt Kate's spirit embrace them, an ethereal bond that would never sever. She was a part of them, embedded in their hearts, whispering through the rustling leaves and singing in the wind.

With a heart full of bittersweet memories and dreams for tomorrow, Leah held Louise tight, Chris beside her, offering his unwavering love. They were a family, stitched together by love, connected through laughter and adventure, even in the face of loss.

"I love you both," Leah whispered, her heart swelling with affection.

"We love you too, Mommy!" Louise replied, her eyes gleaming with innocence.

As Leah peered into the depths of the night, she understood that in the chapters yet to come, Kate would always be their guiding star, reminding them to live wildly, love completely, and embrace each moment together.

In that garden, where love had flourished, and memories intermingled with the fragrant blooms, Leah knew they could boldly face the future, for Kate would always be a part of their story, cheering them on from the stars above.

As the night wore on, they lingered in the garden, immersing themselves in the warmth of each other's presence. This was a testament to resilience against the tides of grief, a sacred bond of love that transcended the limits of time. The warm glow from the moon cast shadows that danced among the roses, whispering secrets only they could hear. Leah embraced the stillness, her heart feeling a rare blend of comfort and hope.

"Should we make a wish on a star for Auntie Kate?" Louise suggested, her voice bright with anticipation.

"I think she would love that," Leah said, her heart swelling. They had always shared a tradition of wishing on stars, and tonight felt like the perfect moment to honor that simple yet profound connection.

"On the count of three, okay?" Chris said, leaning in closer, his warmth enveloping them both.

"Okay!" Louise bounced on her little feet, her excitement nearly palpable.

"One... Two... Three!" they called out together, arms outstretched toward the sky.

Leah closed her eyes tightly, imagining Kate's smiling face, her laughter, the texture of her hugs, and everything that made her the vibrant person she would always be in their lives. She wished for strength, joy, and the continuous presence of Kate's love in every moment they would share as a family.

Louise grinned widely as they opened their eyes, her cheeks rosy from excitement. "What did you wish for?" she asked, her curiosity wide-eyed.

"I wished for us to have the courage to embrace every adventure, knowing Auntie Kate was there with us," Leah replied, feeling a surge of warmth coursing through her. "What about you, mommy?"

"I wished to remember all the moments that made us smile with her," Leah continued, "So that we can fill our lives with joy just like she would have wanted."

Chris nodded, pride clear in his eyes. "Let's make it our mission to keep her legacy alive. Each letter she left is a piece of her heart. We'll cherish them and share them with Louise as she grows."

"Yes!" Louise exclaimed, clapping her hands. "I want to read all of them and draw pictures of Auntie Kate!"

A serene silence settled around them, a cocoon woven from love and shared memories glistening in the moonlight. As they sat together, Leah's heart brimmed with hope.

Time seemed to stretch, wrapping itself around the trio, coaxing them to savor the moment. They shared stories of silly misadventures and heartfelt conversations, recalling Kate's best moments—the time she tried to bake a cake but ended up creating an accidental volcano, the way she would burst into song when no one was watching, and the talks that would stretch into the early hours of the morning.

"Mommy, can we make a scrapbook of Auntie Kate?" Louise proposed, her little fingers gesturing animatedly. "We can put in our favorites—letters and pictures!"

"What a brilliant idea!" Leah exclaimed, excitement bubbling up in her chest. "We can gather all the letters and photos and even write our own stories to keep her memory close."

Chris grinned at them both, an expression of admiration swirling in his gaze. "And we can take turns adding to it over the years. It'll be something Louise can share with her kids someday."

Leah felt a swell of joy in knowing they were building something tangible that would live on beyond them, just like Kate's spirit.

The evening continued to unfold, with the three of them caught in a gentle rhythm, laughter punctuated by stories, memories intertwining with future dreams. As they reminisced, Leah felt the warmth of hope igniting within her—an understanding that life, although shadowed by loss, could still be filled with abundant joy, love, and connection.

As the night deepened and Louise yawned, Chris suggested it was time to head inside. "Let's tuck our little adventurer into bed."

Louise protested. "Just one more story, pleeeaaaase?" Her wide eyes shimmered with mischief.

Knowing they couldn't resist that pleading gaze, Leah relented with a smile. "How about one more story, but it has to be about Auntie Kate?"

"Yay!" Louise squealed, bouncing as she beamed with delight.

They headed back inside. The cozy house was welcoming them with comforting familiarity. As Leah settled Louise into bed, Chris gathered some of the freshly discovered letters from the day, placing them on the nightstand.

"Here's one that's just for you," Chris said, pulling out an envelope marked "For Louise's Laugh."

Louise's eyes widened in surprise. "For me?" she asked, clutching the letter excitedly.

"Yes, it was hidden for a reason—just like all the others," Leah explained, her heart swelling with love as she tucked the blankets around Louise.

"Will she make me laugh?" Louise asked expectantly.

"Kate always does," Leah said with a chuckle as she softly kissed Louise's forehead. "Just wait and see."

With her tiny hands clutching the letter, Louise's eyelids drooped, excitement mingling with sleepiness. "Tell me what it says, Mommy!" she urged, her voice faint but filled with enthusiasm.

Leah exchanged a knowing glance with Chris, who positioned himself on the edge of the bed, ready to be the second storyteller. "Alright, let's read it together," Leah suggested, her heart light with joy at the thought of sharing this moment.

Leah opened the envelope, the edges still crisp, as if Kate had just penned it moments before. Inside, a neatly folded piece of paper awaited them.

"To my sweet Louise," Leah began, adjusting her voice to reflect Kate's warmth and cheerfulness. "I hope this letter finds you giggling!'"

Louise's eyes widened in delight, her drowsiness forgotten.

'You are the giggliest little girl I know, and that's saying something since your mommy always knows how to find a laugh," Leah continued, sensing the humor in Kate's words, picturing her friend's grin as she wrote them.

'Whenever you find something funny—whether it's a joke or a silly face your mom makes—never hesitate to let that giggle out. Your laughter is like sunshine, and the world needs more of it!"

Leah's voice softened, a slight tremor touching her words as she imagined how much love and thought Kate had poured into this treasure.

'One time at the grocery store, I accidentally bumped into a display of cereal boxes and went tumbling down like a clumsy giraffe! The whole aisle burst into laughter, and I laughed so hard I almost forgot my name. So remember, my sweet Louise, never be afraid to fall over, literally or figuratively. Always own your laughter. You have a gift!"

As Leah read on, Kate's playful anecdotes painted vivid images—each filled with love, laughter, and the same energy they had known in life. She recalled how they both had a knack for turning mundane moments into comedic sketches, finding joy in the chaos of everyday life.

'And when life gets a little too serious, find a way to add a bit of silliness. Keep your laughter alive because it's the best challenge you'll ever face. Love, your partner in giggles, Auntie Kate."

When Leah finished reading, she glanced at Louise, her heart fluttering at the sight of her daughter's face light up with joy.

"That was so funny! The cereal thing!" Louise giggled, throwing her head back as she clutched her blanket. "Can we do that, Mommy? Can we make silly faces like Auntie Kate and fall over?"

Leah laughed heartily, imagining the scene. "Yes, we'll make it a tradition, just like Auntie Kate would want—silly faces for the rainy days and laughter for the sunny days."

Chris chuckled, leaning forward with an encouraging grin. "And we can catch it all on camera to show her how much fun we're having."

"Yes! I want to be just like Auntie Kate!" Louise declared with determination, her eyes gleaming with inspiration. "I want to make everyone laugh!"

As the night grew quieter, the moment's sweetness wrapped around them like a warm embrace. Leah felt grateful for the light that Kate had ignited in their lives, which would continue to guide them even in her absence.

"Okay, sweetheart," Leah said, snuggling into the sheets beside Louise. "But it's time to close those little eyes now and dream of all our adventures ahead of us with your Auntie Kate."

Louise's smile remained as she settled deeper into her pillow. "Goodnight, Mommy. Goodnight, Daddy. I love you!"

"Goodnight, little giggler," Chris responded, kissing her forehead. "We love you."

"Goodnight, my darling Louise. Remember, Auntie Kate will always be with us in our hearts," Leah whispered, pressing her lips against Louise's forehead, feeling a sense of peace settle over her.

As they exited the room, Chris paused at the door, glancing back at their daughter, whose slow breaths signified she was already embracing dreams of laughter and joy.

"Do you think she knows how much Auntie Kate would have adored her?" Chris asked, his voice laced with affection.

"I do," Leah replied, her heart swelling. "In her way, I think Kate lives on through Louise—the laughter, the joy, even the silliness. She'll carry that legacy forward."

With a gentle nod, Chris took Leah's hand, and together, they strolled down the hallway. The warmth of that night's memories braided tightly into their hearts as they went to the living room, where the familiar comfort of home enveloped them. The air was thick with the essence of shared moments, mingled with the scent of blooming roses wafting in from the garden as if Kate was reminding them of her eternal presence.

As Leah settled onto the couch, Chris joined her, pulling her close. They sighed in unison, feeling the day's exhaustion catch up with them, yet buoyed by the joyous remembrance they had shared.

"Do you think we'll ever stop hurting?" Leah mused, her voice a whisper tinged with vulnerability.

Chris looked at her, his expression thoughtful. "I don't think the hurt will ever go away. But with each story and each memory we create, it becomes a little easier. We learn to carry her with us instead of remembering the absence."

Leah nodded, resting her head against Chris's shoulder, comforted by his strength. The two of them were resilient; they had weathered so much together and would continue to face whatever came their way.

"Kate would want us to laugh through the hard times," Leah said, a trace of a smile emerging on her lips. "To find joy even amid sorrow. She would want us to cherish every moment."

"Exactly," Chris said, his voice a soft murmur against the background of the night. "And we will—for her, for ourselves, and for Louise. The adventure is just beginning, and she'll be with us."

Leah felt warmth radiate from his words, the idea of carrying Kate's spirit into their future like a shining beacon, guiding them with laughter and love. She closed her eyes for a moment, envisioning all the new memories they would create, the adventures that awaited them, and how they would weave Kate's legacy into the fabric of their lives.

As the moonlight filtered through the windows, casting a serene glow across the room, Leah felt a profound sense of peace settle over her. She realized it wasn't just about surviving loss but thriving in the face of it, carrying forward the love that would always be a part of them.

In that quiet moment, Leah knew that as long as they held onto Kate's memory, they would never truly lose her. She would remain an indelible part of their story, a gentle reminder that love is a binding force capable of transcending the limits of time and space.

"Here's to Auntie Kate," Leah whispered, raising an imaginary glass in the air, a playful gesture infused with sincerity.

"To Auntie Kate," Chris echoed, a smile breaking through even the heaviness of the evening.

CHAPTER 20

Family Shadows

The evening fell around the Johnson household, the golden light of the setting sun spilling over the garden like a blessing. Kate's end had come, akin to a sunset fading into twilight, and in the days that followed, Leah found herself in a nurturing rhythm—one that needed to be shared, woven together with both sorrow and joy.

With Chris by her side, the warmth of their shared love helped her navigate the depths of grief. They had all gathered in this home, surrounded by remnants of laughter, stories, and vibrant memories. Each corner whispered tales of Kate—their overflowing hearts working to keep her spirit alive.

"Chris, can you help me rearrange these flowers?" Mary Johnson's warm voice broke through Leah's thoughts. She looked over to see Mary gesturing with her hands, guiding the arrangements she had curated over the years. The garden represented seasons of growth, a metaphorical representation of love nurtured through hard work.

"Of course," Chris replied, stepping over to join her with a smile. The comfort of simplicity settled in as they worked together. Leah watched as Chris placed the flowers with care, his touch gentle as he adjusted the petals, bringing the blossoms into harmony.

"Your dad's doing a great job adjusting," Leah said, looking over at Tom, who was engrossed in conversations with other attendees in the kitchen. The smell of baked goods wafted through the air, mingling with the scent of fresh garden herbs that clung to Mary's apron.

"Yes, particularly with you and Louise around," Chris responded, glancing back with a thoughtful expression. "He sees how vibrant our little family is—different from his expectations. It's nice to see him blooming, too."

"Exactly," Leah replied. "Who knew a few flowers could turn everything around?"

"From a distance, it was shocking," Chris said, a hint of humor in his tone, "but once you learn to see through the thorns, you find opportunities in places you hadn't anticipated."

They shared a laugh as they continued to arrange the flowers, feeling the weight of grief lift, replaced by the simplicity of love threaded through every touch. The bell-like chime of laughter filled the air, echoing through the garden, glimmering like the stars, soon to grace the night sky.

During these quiet moments, Leah felt the essence of Kate the strongest. In the laughter shared amongst friends, the stories of childhood adventures, and the way Louise danced among the flowers—each movement embodying the joy Kate had cultivated in their lives.

Then, as if summoned by their thoughts, Louise emerged from inside with her favorite blanket dragging behind her, endearingly chaotic yet full of purpose. "Mama! Can we sing Auntie Kate's garden song now?" She clambered onto Chris's lap with enthusiasm.

"Of course, sweetheart!" Leah laughed, unable to resist the infectious joy radiating from her daughter. "We'll sing it together!"

"Yeah! The flower song," Louise cheered, her small hands waving excitedly.

Chris picked up his guitar, fingers nimble as they moved over the strings, eliciting a gentle, familiar melody stretching into the atmosphere surrounding them. With Louise nestled against him, her tiny body vibrating with anticipation, he strummed the notes filling the garden with laughter.

"Flowers grow from the softest dirt," Chris sang, his voice resonating warmly as he started the song. "Each one special, each one loved, just like little girls in the sun..."

The moment enveloped Leah, blending the music and laughter as Chris continued leading them through the simple lyrics, allowing Louise to join in with her precious voice. Each note was a tribute to Kate, each chorus a celebration of love, and as the words flowed over them, it was as if Kate lingered in the air, dancing with them as they sang.

In that context, Leah felt the ache of grief transform into a warmth that embraced her, carrying with it vibrations of hope. This was the legacy Kate had wanted them to create—a family that sang, laughed, and lived with a fullness that refused to be dimmed by sorrow.

As they finished the song, Leah's heart swelled with a mix of emotions—her daughter's laughter cascading like waves against rocks, Chris's steady smile illuminating the fabric of their lives. This was a moment etched in time, one they would one day look back on and remember how love had carried them through the most challenging days.

"More singing!" Louise demanded, her eyes sparkling with delight, insisted on yet another round of music, blissfully unaware of the profound depth of the moments unfolding around her.

"That's the spirit!" Chris laughed, adjusting Louise on his lap. "Let's keep celebrating Auntie Kate with another song, shall we?"

"Let's sing about rainbows!" Louise exclaimed, her enthusiasm infectious as she bounced up and down with glee. "And flowers! They can dance, too!"

"Rainbows it is!" Chris grinned, adjusting the guitar to play a more upbeat tune. "Alright, everyone, follow Louise's lead! Let's celebrate all the surrounding beauty!"

With newfound energy, Chris strummed a lively melody while Louise led them in exaggerated imitations of dancing rainbows and fluttering flowers. Her movements were wild and free, her tiny arms flailing to express joy in her unfiltered way, and Leah couldn't help but laugh, feeling the heaviness within her lift.

"Look, Mama! I'm a rainbow!" Louise shouted amid giggles, her energy spilling over into the space between them, illuminating the garden like a burst of sunlight.

"You're the brightest rainbow I've ever seen!" Leah exclaimed, her heart swelling with pride as she watched her daughter twirl, her little feet dancing over the grass. The laughter that bubbled up felt cleansing, washing away the melancholy that had lingered since Kate's passing.

"Don't forget the flowers!" Chris chimed in, his playful tone imitating a gardener, making gestures as if he were planting seeds on the rich earth. "What do flowers do when it rains?"

"Dance!" Louise shouted, leaping into the air with delight, her face aglow with joy.

As the three weaved laughter and music together, Leah felt gratitude. This was Kate's legacy, living vibrantly through the simplicity of precious moments—music, laughter, and the unbreakable bond they forged in love.

They wrapped up their impromptu concert, finally collapsing onto the grass in giggles as Louise fell into a pile of joy. Chris caught his breath, wiping a bead of sweat from his brow while Leah beamed at him, her heart whole knowing that amidst the sadness, here was life—loud, messy, and beautifully natural.

"Alright, little flower," Leah said, picking Louise back up and settling her onto her lap. "What do you want to do next? We could pick some more flowers for the kitchen table or begin our next masterpiece!"

"I want to do the rainbow again!" Louise exclaimed, her eyes wide with excitement. "Like Auntie Kate's garden!"

"That sounds perfect," Chris replied, laughter still twinkling in his eyes. "Let's do both! I'll bring more paint, and we can create a masterpiece dedicated to Auntie Kate, right?"

"Yes!" Louise clapped her hands, bouncing with renewed energy. "It will be the best rainbow ever!"

Back in the house, Leah retrieved the art supplies, a collection of brightly colored paints, glitter, and brushes, while Chris prepared the workspace. As they transitioned from the garden to the indoor activities, Leah felt the thrill of creativity bubbling over, enveloping them in life's rich colors.

Louise's tiny fingers moved with glee as they painted, applying bold strokes to the canvas with abandon. Chris joined in, guiding her lovingly while Leah captured the essence of the moment—the sounds of giggles, the shimmering sparkles as they flicked glitter into their creation, the splashes of color intermingled like their relationships.

"Careful with that glitter!" Leah teased, pulling Louise's hands away from the excessive sprinkling of sparkles. Yet her laughter echoed, knowing that the chaotic beauty of it all made these moments memorable.

"I'm making it special for Auntie Kate!" Louise insisted, undeterred by the scattered glitter already dusting the table, mixing in with paint-covered fingers and smiles.

Kate had always adored vibrant colors, the laughter of children, and the beauty of art that shone through every moment.

The atmosphere in the room filled with her spirit reminds us of how Kate would have encouraged their creativity, guiding them to see the world through a lens of joy.

Huddled together, they meticulously crafted the masterpiece—a rainbow adorned with flowers, set amidst the glowing sunlight streaming through the window. Each brushstroke was a proclamation of love, each color a reminder of the joy Kate had cultivated in their lives.

As they painted, laughter echoed through the house, a harmonious symphony of happiness marking the shift from sorrow to celebration, from loss to love. And through it all, Leah felt the gentle presence of her best friend guiding them, her spirit lingering as an everlasting testament to enduring friendship.

Later, as they completed the painting and Louise flopped down, exhausted from her artistic endeavors, Chris looked over at Leah. "This feels right, doesn't it?" he asked, genuine affection coloring his voice. "This is how we keep moving forward—by celebrating the love given to us."

Leah nodded, her heart brimming with emotion. "Yes," she affirmed, tears blurring her vision, "by holding Kate close in our hearts, living each day to the fullest, and demonstrating our love in countless ways."

They gathered their art supplies, Louise stumbling around with playful exhaustion, her tiny body still buzzing from the creative rush. The room felt warm, with memories being created anew and laughter lingering in the air like the last notes of a cherished song.

"Can we hang our masterpiece in the kitchen?" Louise asked, her voice sleepily determined as she wiped her paint-covered hands on her shirt, a proud grin plastered across her face.

"Of course! It belongs where we can see it every day, just like we keep Kate's memory alive," Leah said, her heart swelling with pride for her daughter's creativity and innocence. As she gathered the finished painting, holding it in front of her, the colors still gleamed with the brilliant vibrance of love and laughter.

They brought the painting into the kitchen, the inviting aroma of the day's earlier baking still wafting through the air. Leah had always envisioned a home filled with warmth and love, and this masterpiece would add a spark of life to the cozy space.

With Chris supporting the painting, Leah found a perfect spot above the dining table, a place that would welcome all their family and friends. "This golden light coming through the window will make it shine," she mused, stepping back and admired their handiwork once it was in place.

"It looks amazing," Chris agreed, wrapping an arm around her waist and kissing her temple. "It encapsulates all the love we've shared and will continue to share."

A comfortable silence settled over them as they stood together, creating a nest of warmth and reassurance. This silence spoke volumes—the understanding that they were building something beautiful and lasting even amid loss.

Louise, never one for lingering stillness, bounced back into view, eyes sparkling with unspent energy. "Can we go to the park?" she urged, tugging at Chris's sleeve.

"The park?" Chris raised an eyebrow, feigning contemplation. "Hmm... I think I can be persuaded. How about we make it a picnic? We'll bring some of those cookies Mary made and our favorite blanket!"

Louise clapped her hands together with glee, her enthusiasm contagious. "Yes! Cookies! And my rainbow napkin!" Her little legs danced eagerly in anticipation.

As they prepared to leave, Leah felt a flicker of excitement—an adventure waiting to unfold, a chance to embrace the sweetness of life after all the sorrow. They gathered everything they needed: an oversized picnic blanket, a basket filled with cookies and fruit, and Louise's favorite toys.

The sun blazed in the afternoon sky, and the air was crisp as they made their way to the park. Leah felt the tension on her shoulders dissipate, swept away by the wind that caressed her face.

When they arrived, the park buzzed with life—children's laughter echoed all around, and the sound of squeaky swings blended harmoniously with the rustling leaves. Louise ran ahead, her excitement radiating as she pointed toward the playground.

"Look! The swings! I want to swing!" She raced off, her giggles trailing behind her as she hurried toward a set of swings, Chris and Leah exchanging smiles as they took in her delight.

Once they settled on a spot with an unobstructed view of the playground, Chris helped Leah lay out the blanket, the fabric fluttering in the breeze like a flag of hope. They arranged the food in the middle, and soon, the three of them laughed and shared stories about all things about Kate, reminding them that joy nestled in shadows could still bloom brightly.

"Do you remember when we camped in the backyard and convinced ourselves there were monsters in the bushes?" Leah asked, her laughter bubbling as they watched Louise swing high into the air, her shouts of pure joy ringing in the clear sky.

"Kate swore she could fight them off with marshmallows," Chris replied, chuckling at the memory. "That was the best camping trip! We told ghost stories until dawn, mostly fueled by too many snacks."

"Oh, and remember Kate's epic ghost costume!" Leah added, wiping tears of laughter from her eyes. "She scared the neighbors half to death! Her idea of spooky was a little ridiculous."

"Ridiculous, yes," Chris said, his eyes crinkling with mirth. "But I have to admit, she made being scared an adventure. It's incredible how she could turn the simplest ideas into something fun and memorable."

Their laughter filled the park, weaving it into their encapsulated moment of joy. Chris caught Louise as she came bouncing back, her cheeks flushed with glee. "More cookies!" she squealed, pulling Chris's hand and leading him toward the blanket.

As they shared the cookies, Leah felt a sense of fullness wash over her—a moment where grief and joy, laughter and tears intertwined seamlessly—each bite of the delicious treats communicated love, hugs, and the warmth of memories shared. With every cookie they savored, the lingering taste of Kate's love infused with their delightful snack—the sweetness and embodiment of the joy she had brought in their lives.

As they sat together under the sprawling branches of an old oak tree, Louise's energy surged like the happy sunlight filtering through the leaves, illuminating her smile. "Can we make more art later?" she asked, her eyes glowing with the possibility.

"Definitely!" Leah agreed, her heart dancing at the thought of another art session full of laughter. "We can make an even bigger rainbow to hang in the living room."

Chris leaned back on the blanket, cradling Louise's delighted chatter. "And we'll throw in some musical notes this time," he said, a playful grin on his face as he ruffled Louise's hair. "Each note represents one of your favorite memories with Auntie Kate."

"Yes! The music party!" Louise beamed, her imagination whisking them away to another adventure.

The afternoon floated on like a soft breeze, each moment filled with laughter and connection. Leah leaned into Chris's side, an easy intimacy nesting between them as they watched their daughter play. Her joyful spirit radiated a warmth that felt like a balm for their hearts.

With the sun's warmth soaking into her skin, Leah felt some of her worries melting away, replaced by vibrant memories of love and laughter. A realization dawned on her—while she could never replace Kate, she could undoubtedly carry her spirit forward in their daily lives and Louise's future, ensuring her legacy continued to thrive.

As the shadows lengthened and the sun began its descent, painting the sky in hues of orange and pink, Leah suggested they gather for one last swing session before the evening call of home.

"Let's swing, Lou!" she called, her voice light with excitement.

Louise took off running toward the swings, her laughter mingling with the fading light. Chris stood and joined Leah, offering a hand as they followed their daughter. He squeezed her hand, an unspoken promise that they were navigating this life together.

After a few joyful minutes of swinging, Louise squealed, "Higher! Higher!" as if she could soar into the sky where Auntie Kate watched over them. Leah cheered alongside her, enjoying the moment's playful vitality and simple pleasure.

As the sun dipped below the horizon, painting the world in twilight, Leah finally turned to Chris. "You know, today was something special," she said, still feeling the echoes of joy in their hearts. "With the garden, the letters, our little picnic, it feels like Kate is still with us, guiding us to embrace the love we still have."

Chris nodded, his eyes thoughtful and warm, reflecting the fading light of day. "She's always going to be with us, Leah. We'll carry her in every song, every letter, every moment we celebrate together as a family."

With that, they collected their things, Louise leading the way back to the car—a small, determined girl ready to take on whatever adventure awaited. Leah felt a renewed sense of purpose swirling inside her; together, they sculpted a future filled with love, laughter, and memories that would bridge the gap between the past and the present.

As they drove home, the world outside twinkled with stars, each a reminder of Kate's enduring presence. She might have transitioned from this earthly realm, but her spirit would continue illuminating their paths, encouraging them to live, even amid the shadows.

When they arrived home, Leah glanced at the cozy living room, sweetly decorated with reflections of their lives—colorful drawings from Louise, remnants of their baking adventures, and the spirit of family that had blossomed in the absence of loss.

"Okay, my little artist! Time for your bath!" Leah announced, her voice light-hearted as she swept Louise into her arms.

"No bath! More music!" Louise protested, her little hands waving dramatically as they entered the house.

"How about we make some music while you get your bath ready?" Chris proposed, already retreating to retrieve his guitar once more. "We could sing that silly song we made up about Auntie Kate last week."

"Yes, the one about the dancing flowers!" Louise beamed, her earlier protests forgotten as excitement danced across her features.

With the guitar in hand, Chris struck a chord and began stringing the lively tune, instantly captivating Louise's attention. Leah couldn't help but smile, captivated by her daughter twirling in delight, her hair flying, and laughter echoing through the household.

As Chris played, Leah swayed to the music, every note a reminder of the love that enveloped them. She closed her eyes and surrendered to the moment, feeling Kate's presence in every chord—the warmth, the laughter, the joy that transcended loss.

As they danced together in the fading light of day, Leah promised herself and Kate—to carry forward the love they had built together, to embrace every moment, and to ensure that Louise grew up knowing the richness of that connection.

"Dancing flowers!" Louise exclaimed mid-twirl, her voice a delightful mix of imagination and innocence. "Sing louder, Daddy!"

"Alright, alright, let's turn it up!" Chris laughed, increasing the song's tempo, and gave a playful nod to their daughter's enthusiasm. The rhythm resonated through the house, vibrant and alive. Leah felt a surge of joy, realizing how contagious their happiness was and how it breathed life into the walls that had felt so heavy just days ago.

As they spun, twirled, and laughed together, Leah couldn't help but think about the legacy they were creating—one built on love, joy, and the memories they shared. The garden outside, filled with the last blooms of fall, stood as a testament to the beauty of the life they were reconstructing, even in the face of loss.

"Lou, what do you think Auntie Kate would say about all this?" Leah asked, holding her arms wide open as they finished another spin.

"Happy!" Louise declared, her face alight as she planted her feet and swayed to the rhythm. "She loves when we sing and dance!"

"Yes, exactly!" Leah affirmed, her heart swelling with pride as she swooped Louise into her arms and held her close. "Kate would love it. She'd be right here dancing with us."

As Chris continued to play, Leah's thoughts drifted to the letters Kate had hidden away. Each one was a treasure, a reminder of moments they could hold on to, a way to ensure that Kate remained a star in Louise's sky.

"Don't forget the glitter!" Leah called out. "I have some from the art day that we can sprinkle on the songs."

"Right! Glitter magic!" Louise exclaimed, clapping her hands together with excitement. She was enveloped in the joyous energy of the moment.

"Okay, you two, let's make this dance party sparkle!" Chris chuckled, his eyes glinting as he adjusted his playing tempo, fueling the atmosphere with a fun, infectious energy.

With that, they launched into a mini celebration of sound and color—Louise directing the glitter with her tiny hands as they applied it to various surfaces, adding a layer of magic to the music that flowed around them. Laughter mixed with melodies, each moment infused with the warmth of memory and hope.

Time lost its grip as they danced in a world of their making, swirling between notes, paint, and laughter, allowing the tranquility of the evening to wash over them. The living room became a canvas for their vibrant expression, representing everything Kate had inspired in them.

Finally, as the music faded into the background and Louise begged for one more round, Leah felt the moment's weight settle in. She looked at Chris and saw more than love and companionship—she saw an unwavering partnership willing to tackle whatever lay ahead.

Once Louise was tucked into bed, her tiny body drifting off into dreams with a smile still on her lips, Leah turned to Chris. "Tonight was incredible. I didn't know I could feel so much joy after everything we've been through."

Chris wrapped an arm around her, drawing her close. "This is what Kate wanted for us—to continue living fiercely and joyfully, to hold on to the love that binds us together. She wouldn't want us wallowing in sorrow but celebrating the life she lived and the love she shared."

As Leah nestled against him, feeling safe and loved, the weight of loss still lingered, yet it was softened by the love that enveloped them. She understood that while grief and joy could coexist, it was their choice to move forward together that would make the difference.

CHAPTER 21

Sacred Ground

The morning mist still clung to the cemetery gardens as Leah and Louise visited Kate's grave weekly. The air was crisp, imbued with the distinct scent of earth and fallen leaves, a reminder that fall was deepening. As they walked hand in hand, Leah felt a familiar mix of sadness and warmth in her chest. Louise clutched her usual bouquet—wildflowers picked from Mary's garden, vibrant marigolds mingling with the delicate white of Queen Anne's lace—their colors vibrant against the gray backdrop of the dreary morning.

"Careful steps," Leah reminded as Louise navigated the stone path, her little feet skipping. "Remember what we told Auntie Kate about being graceful?"

"Like a dancer," Louise nodded thoughtfully, though her toddler skips betrayed her excitement. "But Auntie Kate says dancing is better than walking, anyway."

Leah chuckled at that, the lightness that filled their conversation temporarily pushing grief aside. The air felt alive with Louise's innocent charm—her laughter always serving as a reminder of brighter days and untapped joy. When they reached Kate's stone, it stood beautifully in the early light, a simple yet elegant tribute reflecting the spirit of a complicated life.

"Mama, what color flowers should I put?" Louise asked, kneeling to arrange her offering with practiced care, chattering about her week as if Kate were sitting beside them.

"They can be any color your heart wishes, sweet girl," Leah encouraged, placing her hand on Louise's back. "What do you think Auntie Kate would like?"

"Pink!" Louise declared, her tiny finger pointing at the blossoms as she nested them into the earth. "Like in the garden!"

"Just as lovely as her favorite roses," Leah replied, noticing how the sunlight warmed the surface of the headstone—shining light on Kate's name, echoing reminders of happiness and love intertwined with loss.

A bittersweet ache filled Leah as she thought of their last moments, but that connection enveloped her heart. "You're creating beauty, Lou," she said, appreciating the moment as Louise finished arranging the flowers, patting at the stone.

"And Daddy's being silly," Louise concluded, her voice laced with mock outrage, "says he has a big surprise but won't even tell me!"

Leah's chest twisted with laughter and longing at her daughter's excitement. Something in her heart fluttered at the mention of Chris's recent mysterious behavior. The thought of him planning something kind stirred both curiosity and joy within her.

"I think Auntie Kate knows all about it," Louise declared with toddler certainty. "She knows everything now that she's with angels."

"She always knew everything," Leah agreed quietly, resting her fingers on the smooth stone, feeling as if she could somehow connect with Kate through the gentle touch.

They spent their customary hour at the grave, Louise performing her latest songs while Leah whispered updates about life—the joys, the heartaches, the ongoing legacy of love that Kate had ensured would thrive. The vibrant morning sun burned away the lingering mist, wrapping the peaceful garden in golden light as other visitors arrived.

"Time to go, sweet girl," Leah said, gathering Louise and ensuring the flowers were secure. "Daddy's waiting at church."

"Can we come back later?" Louise asked as they walked hand in hand toward the car, her innocent excitement bubbling over. "I forgot to tell Auntie Kate about the butterflies in Gamma's garden."

"We'll see," Leah smiled down at her daughter. In her heart, she knew they would indeed return before the day was done.

The rest of the day passed in a blur of normalcy tinged with anticipation. Chris was unusually quiet during choir practice, his smile betraying the secrets he held within. Even Louise seemed to be hiding something from Leah, her giggles muffled by her hands as Chris's whispers tickled her ear, a playful secret Leah couldn't understand.

As evening approached, Mary appeared to "borrow" Louise for some urgent grandmother business involving cookies and new dress-up clothes. Chris kissed Leah, promising to pick her up in an hour, the lingering warmth of his touch igniting butterflies in her stomach.

"What are you planning?" she called after him, a playful note in her voice, but his only response was a wave and a wink that left her heart skipping.

When Chris returned, the sun was setting, painting the sky in shades of promise—hues of pink and orange blending into the twilight. He looked handsome in more formal clothes than usual, though his guitar case was slung over his shoulder as always.

"Trust me?" he asked, offering his hand, his gaze filled with a playful earnestness that made Leah's heart race.

"Always," she answered, her sincerity unwavering, a vow that held years of devotion.

As they drove toward the cemetery, Leah felt anticipation coil within her. The atmosphere in the car was charged with expectation, each moment an unspoken promise of something significant about to unfold. Chris hummed softly, a melody that Leah recognized as one of Kate's favorites. His rich voice blended with the rhythmic sound of the tires against the asphalt.

When they arrived at the cemetery, it was transformed from the misty, somber place they had known. Soft lights twinkled amid the trees, casting a gentle glow that welcomed them in. A path of rose petals led toward Kate's grave, where candles flickered in glass holders, creating a serene sanctuary—all meticulously arranged, reflecting their love.

Leah's breath caught in her throat as she entered the scene. "Oh," she breathed, awe and clarity washing over her. "Chris, this is beautiful."

Louise stood near the entrance, wearing her new dress adorned with delicate, sparkling sequins. Her eyes sparkled with innocence against the backdrop of emotion. Mary stood at a distance with her phone, capturing the moment as if she, too, wanted to preserve the poignancy of the occasion.

"Surprise, Mama!" Louise declared, her excitement palpable. "We made it pretty for Auntie Kate!"

With tears in her eyes, Leah felt grateful as Chris led her to stand before Kate's headstone. "I had to do it here," he said, his voice brimming with emotion. "As Kate correctly stated, love stories ought to embrace imperfection, genuine beauty, and unvarnished truthfulness."

As the moment unfolded, Leah could hardly breathe, her heart racing as she watched Chris step back and kneel, pulling out a small velvet box. "This is for you, Leah," he said, holding it up, his voice steady despite the moment's gravity. "It's time."

Eyes wide with exhilaration, Louise presented her father's guitar as if it were an offering, clearly part of the carefully orchestrated surprise that made Leah's heart swell. "Play Auntie Kate's song!" she urged, bouncing on her toes as if anticipating something grand.

As the tension melted away, Chris opened the box to reveal a ring nestled inside—a delicate band adorned with intricate musical notes around a modest diamond that captured the light. It was simple yet significant, just like their love—a reflection of their path together.

"Leah Miller," Chris's firm voice rang out. "Will you marry me? Will you build a lifetime of music, love, and perfectly imperfect moments with me?"

"Yes!" Leah exclaimed, her heart racing as tears streamed down her cheeks, brimming with joy and disbelief. "Yes! A thousand times, yes!"

As Chris slipped the ring onto her finger, it was a perfect fit, destined to be there. They embraced tightly, feeling the weight of the moment wrap around them.

"Yay! More surprises!" Louise cheered, clapping her hands in delight. Her joyful laughter echoed through the sacred space.

"Mommy and Daddy are getting married!" Chris said, lifting Louise into the air and spinning her around as she squealed with laughter, filling the air with joy.

As they pulled away, Leah turned to touch Kate's grave, feeling a rush of emotion swell within her. "Thank you for everything," she whispered, gratitude pouring out. Thank you for guiding us to this moment and always believing in us.

The candles flickered, casting a warm glow on the surroundings, while the stars began to appear in the darkening sky—twinkling like promises made anew.

The celebration continued in the church garden, where their families awaited. The atmosphere was charged with love and excitement. People shared in their joy, happy tears mingling with laughter as Chris and Leah embraced those moments together—learning to carry Kate's memory forward amidst their new beginnings.

"Louise had a hand in this surprise!" Chris announced as they joined the gathering, making the little girl beam with pride. "She was my co-conspirator all along."

"Like Auntie Kate said, surprises are better with teamwork!" Louise declared, her energy infectious, carrying the joy of the moment within her.

With that, Leah felt the fabric of love surrounding their new family solidifying further. The bittersweet undertone of Kate's absence lingered, but it was countered by the vibrant energy of connection and support they had forged together.

As night enveloped them and the stars blazed brightly overhead, Leah reflected in awe at how they had come together—the intertwined histories, the shared laughter, and the promises of love that stretched beyond the confines of time.

Finally, as conversations melded into laughter and endless stories were shared under the starlit sky, Leah realized they were not just celebrating a proposal but embracing the beautiful, messy truth of life itself. Each shared story, each smile exchanged, was a thread weaving them closer together, stitching their hearts into a tapestry rich with affection and understanding.

As the evening wore on, the warmth of the gathering wrapped around Leah, Chris, and Louise. The Johnsons and Millers mingled seamlessly, the boundaries of past grievances softening in the light of love and shared memories.

"Let's toast!" Tom Johnson announced, a glass of sparkling cider lifted high. "To the love that binds us and to new beginnings!"

Glasses clinked in joyous unison as laughter echoed throughout the garden. "To love!" the voices echoed, a resounding affirmation reverberating through their hearts.

Leah glanced at Chris, who looked undeniably handsome and confident as he laughed with Tom. His eyes sparkled with warmth and light, reflecting a deep love that had grown since they first met. Leah felt a rush of gratitude wash over her. She knew that beneath their shared history lay an unbreakable bond that had proven its strength through laughter, tears, and the promise of tomorrow.

As the conversation drifted toward shared memories, stories of Kate's charm and personality flowed like honey, sweet and rich. "Remember the Halloween costume she wore?" one of their friends began, prompting a wave of laughter. "That pumpkin costume was the best—she could barely walk, but insisted on going trick-or-treating."

"I thought I'd never get the orange paint off her face!" another chimed in, the joy infectious as they recalled the humorous disaster.

"She had the best spirit," Leah said, joining in, her laughter pouring from her heart. "Whenever things got tough, she always made it an adventure."

"Exactly," Chris added, his gaze warm as it met Leah's. "That's the legacy we'll carry forward—embracing the beauty in every moment and keeping Kate's spirit alive through love and laughter."

Louise, ever the center of attention, danced around their legs, her tiny giggles pulling everyone's focus. "Let's keep celebrating!" she exclaimed, spinning delightfully in her dress, unaware of how she embodied Kate's joy.

As the night deepened, Mary Johnson stepped up to Leah, her expression softening as she watched the little girl. "You know, Kate would have loved to see all this," she said, embracing Leah tightly. "You both bring so much light into this world."

Leah felt the warmth of the embrace, which infused her spirit with the existence of family and community. "Thank you, Mary," she murmured. "For everything you've done, for being here for us."

"Kate would expect nothing less," Mary replied, a glimmer of pride in her eyes. "She left us a legacy to continue, and I have no doubt you and Chris will make it truly special."

As the night approached its final act, the laughter faded to lingering conversations, and ready hearts were filled with anticipation for the future. They shared stories around the flickering fire pit, planning family gatherings and projects to celebrate Kate's life.

However, Leah recognized the need for the day to end. She took a moment to step back, looking at the vibrant scene—the stars sparkling above, the faces lit with love and laughter, and the flowers still standing proud, kissed by the gentle fall air.

"I think it's time to head home," she said, feeling the weight of fatigue settle in, but her heart remained buoyant with joy.

Chris nodded, his gaze falling to Louise, who was now becoming a little tired despite her excitement. "Ready, little flower?" he asked, lifting her into his arms as she snuggled against his chest.

"Sleepy," Louise murmured, her eyelids growing heavy. "But happy."

"Me too, kiddo," Leah replied, her heart swelling with love as they made their way to the car. Their little family was whole and thriving, filled with the promise of tomorrow, with memories to be created and shared.

As they drove home, Leah watched the stars twinkle in the night sky, feeling Kate's spirit lingering among them, guiding their path. It was in the laughter, the warmth of Chris's hand holding hers, and the soft breaths of Louise as she rested peacefully in the back seat.

Arriving home, the outside chill wrapped around them, yet within, their home radiated warmth. The kitchen beckoned with the remnants of the night's joy—the plates from the gathered feast were still visible in the glow of the warm lights above.

"Let's clean up together," Leah suggested, turning towards Chris with a smile, her heart brightening at the idea. "Then we can cuddle up and watch a movie before bed."

"Sounds perfect," Chris replied, his expression soft as he took her hand, pulling her closer.

Working together in the kitchen, Leah and Chris buzzed with energy. They chatted easily about their day and cracked jokes as they cleared away the remnants of the gathering. The kitchen's warmth felt inviting, a sanctuary filled with memories made of laughter and love.

"It looks like we have enough leftovers to feed a small army," Chris mused as he stacked plates in the sink. The scent of baked goods was still wafting through the air, mingling with Louise's wildflowers from earlier.

"Definitely," Leah chuckled, pouring water to rinse the last few serving bowls. "But somehow, I don't think we'll have a hard time finishing them. Louise is still energetic; she could eat her weight in cookies."

Chris laughed, his heart full, as he watched Leah work. Her movements were efficient but infused gracefully as she navigated the kitchen. He appreciated the nurturing spirit she brought into their lives, transforming everyday tasks into delightful rituals that bound them together.

Once the dishes were clean and everything tidied up, Leah wiped her hands on a dish towel and turned to Chris, leaning against the counter, a soft smile playing on his lips. "What should we watch?" she asked, a hint of mischief in her tone.

"How about a classic? Something that both harkens back to childhood and feels timeless," he suggested, leaning closer, his deep brown eyes sparkling with mischief. "Like a musical— maybe Les Misérables?"

Leah raised an eyebrow in playful disbelief. "A musical? You know I need something light after the day we've had."

"Alright, how about a comedy then?" Chris grinned. "One of those classic romantic comedies—something with happiness at its core."

"Perfect," Leah agreed, letting out a soft laugh. "Let's go with the happiest one you can find."

After some deliberation, Leah settled on an old favorite—Crazy Rich Asians—a film bursting with humor, love, and stunning visuals. As they arranged themselves comfortably on the couch, Chris grabbed a few blankets and wrapped them around them snugly.

"Ready for a cozy movie night?" he asked, pulling her close.

"Absolutely," Leah said, feeling a comforting warmth envelop her as she snuggled against him, easing into their evening.

The movie flickered to life, the opening scenes transporting them into a vibrant world of family, culture, and love. As the colorful images danced across the screen, Leah felt a sense of joy—a release from the emotional tension of the earlier days.

Chris's arm draped around her shoulder, and Leah let herself relax, feeling the gentle vibration of his laughter resonate against her. Their fingers intertwined under the blankets, Leah found solace in the simple touch, each moment a reminder of how far they had both come.

The characters' whimsical antics provided humorous relief, and every laugh shared pulled Leah a little closer to Chris, their hearts syncing with each quip and charming moment. The world outside faded away; everything felt possible in their cocoon of warmth, laughter, and love.

About halfway through the film, as the characters navigated their challenges, Chris paused the movie, turning to look at Leah. "Can we talk about the ring for a moment?" His voice was serious yet warm, and Leah's heart skipped, a conflicting mix of nervousness and excitement flooding her senses.

"Of course," she replied, her pulse quickening as she braced for the conversation. She recalled the afternoon he had presented her with the ring, Chris kneeling amidst blooming roses, the love shared in that moment palpable.

"I want to make sure I follow through on everything," he began, his gaze steady. "We're building this family with Kate's love as our foundation, but I want us to focus on our journey together too."

"What do you mean?" Leah asked, intrigue coloring her voice.

"I mean," Chris said, taking a deep breath as he regarded her with sincerity. "I want you to feel secure in this relationship. I want Louise to feel safe as well. I know Kate would point out how vital those things are, especially for our daughter."

"I feel that security already, Chris," Leah assured, her heart fluttering at his words. "You've shown me what it's like to love and be loved. Together, we'll build something beautiful that honors Kate and the families we've created."

Chris's expression brightened with understanding. "I trust you and want us to remain honest about where we are. When we face challenges, I want us to confront them together for ourselves and Louise."

Leah felt the warmth of his resolve wrap around her. The strength of his commitment settled deep within her. "I promise," she said, her voice steady and sincere.

She could see the relief wash over Chris's face, as if her assurances had lifted an unseen burden from his shoulders. He took a moment. Their eyes locked, the connection between them palpable and rich with unspoken promises.

"Then let's make it official," Chris said, a playful smile emerging, his tone lightening as he shifted back into the playful bond they shared.

"What's a wedding without a little chaos? And who knows, we might end up with a beautiful disaster."

Leah couldn't help but laugh, feeling lighter than she had in days. "You mean like the cookies Kate tried to bake for us?"

Chris chuckled, the tension of the moment dissipating. "Exactly! Or like that time at the church fundraiser when we were setting up the refreshments. You remember? We both reached for the same serving bowl and nearly sent the entire punch fountain cascading."

"Wait—was that your fault or mine?" Leah teased, raising an eyebrow, remembering how they'd barely saved the crystal bowl, their hands brushing as they steadied it together.

"It was a joint effort!" he protested, holding up his hands in mock surrender before pulling her closer again, utterly at ease. "And you know what? I wouldn't change a thing."

"Me neither," Leah agreed, warmth flooding her heart as they sunk back into uninhibited laughter, comfort filling the surrounding air.

As they resumed watching the film, Leah felt the weight of the past few weeks ease, allowing her to enjoy the moment. She leaned into Chris's embrace, letting the laughter and scenes on the screen draw her in, each laugh shared grounding her further in the present.

When the credits rolled, Leah felt the movie's enchanting realm linger in her heart, provoking visions of love, family, and the vibrant life ahead. The house was quiet except for the gentle hum of the heating system and Louise's soft breathing from upstairs.

"Can we celebrate?" she suggested, her voice hushed with excitement. "Just us, here in the quiet. This moment feels too special to let it pass without marking it somehow."

"What did you have in mind?" Chris asked, his voice equally soft as he pulled her closer to the couch.

Leah turned to face him, touched by how the dim light caught the warmth in his eyes. "Let's just... be here. Together. Maybe you could play something? Something quiet, just for us?"

Chris smiled, reaching for his guitar that was never far away. "I know just the thing," he said, beginning to strum softly - so softly it wouldn't carry upstairs to disturb Louise's dreams. The melody was gentle, reminiscent of the song he'd played at Kate's memorial, but transformed into something new - something that spoke of hope and future and love rekindled.

As the music filled the space between them, Leah felt tears prick at her eyes. "Kate would have loved this," she whispered. "She always said music was the best way to celebrate life."

Chris set his guitar aside, drawing her into his arms. "She knew what really mattered," he agreed. "Family. Love. The quiet moments that change everything."

They sat together in comfortable silence, listening to the peaceful sounds of their sleeping home - the occasional creak of settling wood, the distant whisper of wind in the trees outside, the steady rhythm of their synchronized breathing.

"I love you," Leah said, the words carrying all the weight of choice and chance that had brought them to this moment. "Sometimes I think my heart knew it before I did - like it was just waiting for you to walk into our lives."

Chris's fingers traced gentle patterns on her arm as he held her. "You and Louise... you're my miracle," he murmured. "The answer to prayers I didn't even know I was making."

The night deepened around them, stars visible through the window like distant windows through which Kate might be watching. Their love felt both profound and every day - extraordinary in its ordinary perfection. No grand gestures needed, just the quiet certainty of hearts that had found their home in each other.

Tomorrow would bring its own adventures - wedding plans to make, family to tell, a future to build together. But for now, in this peaceful moment between what was and what would be, they could simply be. Two hearts finding harbor in each other, while upstairs their daughter slept soundly, her dreams perhaps touched by the gentle music of love that filled her home.

As midnight approached, they finally stirred from their comfortable embrace. "We should get some sleep," Chris said, pressing a kiss to Leah's temple. "Tomorrow's going to be a big day."

"Every day feels big now," Leah replied. Her smile was clear in her voice. "Every day feels like a gift."

They moved quietly through their nighttime routine, careful not to disturb Louise's peaceful slumber. The house settled around them like a warm embrace, holding the precious family they'd become - a family built on choice and love and the everyday miracle of hearts finding their way home.

Laying her head against Chris's shoulder in bed, Leah whispered, "Thank you for being my rock."

"Always," he replied, pulling her closer, the evening's warmth enveloping them as they drifted into peaceful sleep.

As dreams carried Leah into the depths of her mind, she could almost hear Kate's laughter mingling with the music, still resonating through their lives, like a butterfly dancing high in the sky, spreading joy and love wherever it went.

CHAPTER 22

When Garden Blooms Again

The email from John sat in Leah's inbox for three days before she opened it. His words were careful, measured—like everything about him—asking if they could meet for coffee. His signature line read "John Miller, Senior Vice President, Wellington & Associates," the corporate shield he'd chosen after selling Miller Financial, after deciding that building another empire from scratch held less appeal than quietly excelling in someone else's.

The café he suggested was neutral ground, neither his new corporate domain nor her artistic space. Leah arrived early, watching through the window as her father approached. He seemed different somehow, less the towering figure of her childhood and more a man learning to carry his power differently. His suit was still impeccable—some habits never changed—but there was a subtle softness to his bearing that she didn't remember from before.

"You look good," he said as he sat down, though his eyes caught on the shadows beneath hers—evidence of sleepless nights and grief's lasting imprint.

"Thanks." Leah wrapped her hands around her coffee cup, seeking warmth. "You look... different."

"Wellington's is different," he acknowledged, a slight smile touching his lips. "Less pressure when you're not the name on the door. Though old habits die hard—I still find myself working late some nights."

The admission hung between them, a gentle reminder of how work had always been his refuge, his armor. But there was something new in his tone now—awareness, perhaps even regret.

"I heard they made you Senior VP last month," Leah said, remembering Grace's brief mention of their father's career shift. "That's quite a jump for someone who joined only a few years ago."

"Numbers don't lie," he replied, then winced slightly at his own corporate response. "Sorry. I'm trying to... well, I'm trying to be more than just the bottom line these days." He paused, setting down his coffee cup. "Which reminds me—I saw Chris's post with Louise at her music class. The one where she's reaching for that tambourine?" His voice softened. "She has your smile, Leah. The real one."

Leah felt warmth bloom in her chest at the unexpected observation. "You follow Chris on social media?"

"I do my research," John admitted, a hint of his old methodical self showed through. "When you told me about the engagement... well, I wanted to know more about the man who makes my daughter so happy." He cleared his throat. "I haven't met him properly yet, but anyone who can bring that light back to your eyes—the one I thought died with Kate—he must be pretty special."

"He is," Leah whispered, touched by her father's effort to understand, to connect. "Dad, about the engagement—"

"I'm happy for you," he interrupted, reaching across the table to squeeze her hand briefly. "Truly happy. The way he is with Louise, how he supports your art therapy work... You've found a good man, Leah. A really good man."

The warmth of his approval settled between them, softening edges that had been sharp for so long. Something flickered across John's face then—a shadow of remembrance, as if happiness and loss were two notes striking at once. He withdrew his hand slowly, fingers curling around his coffee cup as if anchoring himself to the present moment. When he looked up again, his eyes carried a weight that hadn't been there seconds before.

"Leah, I... I've also been wanting to tell you how sorry I am. About Kate," John added, his voice carried the rough edges of long-held grief. The mention of her name still felt like a physical touch, both comfort and pain intertwined. Leah's hands tightened around her cup.

"I went to the service," John continued softly. "Stayed in the back. I didn't want to intrude, but... I needed to be there. For her. For you."

"You were there?" Leah looked up, surprised. "I didn't see—"

"She was extraordinary, you know." His voice carried a weight of genuine admiration. "Even as a teenager, when you'd both be studying in my home office. I'd watch her organize your notes, break down complex problems into manageable pieces. She made you laugh even during finals week." He smiled faintly at the memory. "She taught me things about you that I should have seen for myself."

Tears pressed against Leah's eyes. "She did?"

"She wasn't afraid to tell me when I was being too hard on you. Remember that art school application? I was so focused on med school programs, but Kate... she marched into my office with your portfolio." John's voice roughened. "Told me I was missing who you really were. She was right, of course."

Leah wiped at her eyes, remembering Kate's fierce loyalty, her unwavering support. "She always fought for the people she loved."

"Until the very end," John agreed quietly. "I saw her once, at the hospital. I was there for a board meeting, and she was in the garden with Louise." His voice caught. "Even then, weak as she was, she was teaching Louise about colors and shapes. Making art from her hospital bed."

The memory hung between them, delicate as blown glass, before John cleared his throat. "I should have been there more. For both of you. There's so much I should have done differently..."

"Dad," Leah set down her cup, the gentle clink sharp in the space between them. "What really happened? That night when Mom left... when everything fell apart?"

John's hands tightened around his coffee, knuckles whitening. For a moment, Leah thought he would deflect, as he always had, retreat behind his wall of corporate propriety. But something had changed in him—perhaps the absence of his CEO armor, or simply the weight of carrying secrets for so long.

"There was a client," he began, his voice dropping. "The Castillo Group. They seemed legitimate at first—import-export business, growing portfolio. But during an audit, I found..." He glanced around, old habits dying hard. "Their books didn't add up. The money flows, the profit margins... it was cartel money."

Leah felt the blood drain from her face. "What?"

"I couldn't just report it immediately. They had... connections. Information about our family. About you kids." His voice cracked slightly. "So I worked with the authorities, quietly. Those late nights your mother suspected were affairs? I was meeting with Detective Rodriguez, building a case."

"Oh, God." Leah pressed a hand to her mouth, memories realigning themselves like puzzle pieces, finally finding their proper places. "Mom thought..."

"I let her think it," John admitted, his voice heavy with old pain. "It was safer that way. If she left believing I was unfaithful, they wouldn't... they wouldn't see her as a threat."

"You could have told us," Leah's voice shook with anger and understanding, a complex emotion she hadn't known existed until this moment. "We could have helped, supported you..."

"And put you all at risk?" John shook his head. "I watched their operation destroy families, Leah. The thought of you, or Grace, or Brian..." He straightened his tie, a gesture so familiar it made her heart ache. "I made my choice. I lost my marriage, my family's trust, but you were safe. That's what mattered."

"And now?" Leah asked, though she could see the answer in the new lines around his eyes, the slight tremor in his usually steady hands.

"The case is closed. The Castillo Group is finished. I sold the firm." He met her eyes directly. "I'm just... trying to find my way back. To you. To being a grandfather, if you'll let me."

Leah felt tears spill onto her cheeks, hot and unexpected. "You sacrificed everything to protect us, and we..." She thought of the years of anger, of distance, of assumptions that had created valleys between them.

"I made my choices," John said quietly. "Right or wrong, I lived with them. But now..." He pulled out his wallet, removing a small photo. "I took this from one of Chris's social media photos and printed it."

The picture showed Louise beaming at the camera, dark curls wild, Chris's hands steadying her as she reached for a tambourine. It was worn at the edges—handled often, Leah realized, by a father trying to bridge the gap to his family one precious photograph at a time.

"She has your smile," John said softly. "The real one, not the one you learned to wear at corporate functions."

Something broke in Leah then—a wall she hadn't known she'd built. "Oh, Dad," she whispered, reaching across the table to take his hand. His fingers trembled slightly in hers, and she remembered suddenly how he used to hold her hand crossing streets when she was small, his grip firm and sure, protecting her from unseen dangers.

They sat there, father and daughter, their coffee growing cold between them, as the afternoon light shifted and softened. Outside, life continued its steady rhythm, but inside this moment, something was healing—slowly, tenderly, like a long-broken bone finally setting right.

When Leah left the café that day, her heart felt simultaneously lighter and heavier—lighter with understanding, heavier with the weight of truth. She walked to her car thinking about transformation, about how her father had stepped back from empire-building to focus on rebuilding what mattered most.

The healing begun that afternoon was tentative, like spring's first tendrils breaking through winter soil. In the weeks that followed, John's texts came more frequently—small offerings of connection, each one a tiny bridge across the chasm years of silence had carved between them. Pictures of ties he was considering ("Louise says I need more musical ones like Chris's"), questions about her art therapy programs, gentle inquiries about weekend plans.

Then came another email, this one carrying an unexpected weight in its simplicity: "I'm planning to move. Smaller place, closer to the city. The house feels too big now, and I could use some help sorting through things, if you're willing. No pressure."

Leah read it twice, recognizing the careful casualness for what it was—her father's awkward attempt at creating space for them to simply be together. It was such a John Miller way to reach out; she thought with a mix of exasperation and fondness, structuring even emotional reconnection around a practical task.

"It's strange," she said to Chris that evening, as Louise arranged her stuffed animals for their nightly concert. "He's never asked for help before. With anything."

Chris smiled, tuning his guitar for Louise's bedtime song. "Your dad's trying. In his own very organized way."

So on a crisp morning, weeks after their café conversation, Leah stood in her father's home office, surrounded by boxes labeled with his precise handwriting. The room still carried echoes of her childhood—the heavy desk where she'd watched him work late into the night, the window where she'd pressed her forehead on rainy days, waiting for his attention.

"Most of this is headed for storage," John said, his usual corporate confidence wavering slightly as he surveyed the room. "But there are some old files that need sorting first. Things from before the sale of Miller Financial."

Leah nodded, noting how he lingered near the doorway, as if uncertain of his place in this careful new dance they were attempting. "Where should we start?"

"Maybe those boxes by the window?" He gestured to a stack marked 'Archives - 1990s.' "I kept meaning to go through them after the sale, but..."

"But it was easier not to?" Leah supplied, understanding how the weight of the past could make even simple tasks feel monumental.

They worked in companionable silence for a while, the rustle of papers and occasional murmur of "keep" or "shred" creating their own quiet rhythm. Leah studied her father when he wasn't looking—the new lines around his eyes, the way his shoulders seemed less rigid than she remembered, as if retirement from Miller Financial had allowed him to set down some invisible burden.

The morning light shifted, painting patterns on the carpet through the window blinds, when Leah's hands closed around a folder that made her pause. The label read "Johnson & Sons Auto Supply," the ink faded but still clear against the manila paper. Something about it tugged at her memory—Chris mentioning his family's business once, a story of loss wrapped in his father's quiet dignity.

She opened the folder, and the universe seemed to hold its breath. In that moment, surrounded by the physical artifacts of her father's past, Leah had no way of knowing that she stood on the precipice of a discovery that would test their newly rebuilt understanding in ways neither of them could have expected.

The past was about to collide with her present, and the echoes would reshape everything she thought she knew about family, forgiveness, and the complex legacy of choices made long ago.

"Johnson & Sons Auto Supply," she read aloud, something tugging at her memory. Chris had mentioned his family's business once, how they'd lost it when he was young. "Dad? What's this?"

The change in John's expression was subtle, but immediate. He set down the papers he had been holding, and for the first time in Leah's memory, her father looked uncertain.

"That's ancient history," he said. "Part of the Baldwin Motors acquisition from twenty years ago."

Something in his tone—an unspoken barrier that hinted at more—pulled Leah deeper into the documents. Yellowed with age, the pages bore dates from two decades ago and were filled with legal language about assets and liabilities. Yet, a signature at the bottom made her heart stutter.

"Thomas Johnson," she whispered, the name hitting her with new significance. Chris's father–the man who now tended the church garden, who always had a kind word and a cookie for Louise, who wore his hardships with such quiet dignity. "Dad, was this Chris's family's business?"

The silence in the office stretched, heavy with implications. John finally turned from his computer, his brow furrowing under the weight of past decisions.

"It was a different time," he began cautiously, each word distinct in the quiet room. "Baldwin Motors was our biggest client, and they wanted to merge their supply chain. Johnson & Sons was in the way."

"In the way?" Leah's voice edged with disbelief as she delved deeper into the pages. "According to this, they'd been Baldwin's suppliers for three generations. They had contracts, agreements..."

John seemed to shrink under her unwavering gaze, his veneer of businesslike detachment crumbling. "They had handshake deals and outdated practices," he replied, though his voice lacked conviction. "The market was changing. Baldwin needed modern suppliers—computerized inventory and streamlined operations. Johnson & Sons was obsolete."

The word 'obsolete' hung between them like an accusation. Leah thought about Chris's modest childhood home, the pride he took in remembering his summer jobs at the shop, the way his father still carried himself with such grace despite everything.

Leah's hands trembled as she kept reading, each document revealing another piece of the puzzle. Memories of Chris's casual comments took on a new meaning–why they had moved to a smaller house when he was six, why his mother took in sewing work, why his father had worked multiple jobs to keep Chris in music lessons.

"What did you do?" But she could see it in the papers–legal maneuvers, contract terminations, a systematic dismantling of a family's legacy. Her father's signature appeared on page after page, each one another nail in the coffin of Johnson & Sons.

"I did my job." John's defensiveness rang hollow. "I protected our client's interests, modernized their supply chain, increased their profitability. That's business, Leah. It's not personal."

"Not personal?" She picked up the bankruptcy filing, her throat tight. "This was Chris's family's livelihood. Their legacy. Their..." She thought of Mary Johnson's mismatched teacups, how she had apologized for not having a proper set the first time Leah visited.

Now she understood–they had probably sold the good China years ago.

"Does Chris know?" she asked quietly, though the answer was already forming. Chris had mentioned once how proud his father had been of the business, how it had been in their family for generations, but he had never explained why it ended.

"I doubt it," John sighed, looking older. "He would have been just a kid then. Tom Johnson... he handled it with dignity. Never made it public, never fought back. Just accepted it."

"Like he had a choice?" The bitterness in Leah's voice surprised even her. "Against your legal team, your corporate resources?"

"Leah—"

"I have to go." She gathered the papers with shaking hands. "I need to think."

The drive to their place was a blur, every mile bringing new realizations. All those stories he had told about his childhood–moving houses framed as a "fresh start," his father's multiple jobs explained as "staying busy," the proud way they never discussed their struggles...

Chris opened the door with his usual warm smile, still wearing his choir director's collar. The smile faded quickly when he saw her face.

"What's wrong? Is it Louise?"

"No, she's fine," Leah managed, clutching the manila folder like a lifeline. "I found something. At Dad's office. You need to see this."

They settled on his worn couch–the one his mother had reupholstered herself, Leah now realized, probably because they couldn't afford new furniture. Her throat tightened at all these little details she'd never truly understood before.

"These are about your family's business," she said, hands trembling as she opened the folder. "About what happened to it."

Chris went very still beside her as he began reading. The only sound in the apartment was the gentle ticking of the clock his grandfather had salvaged from the old shop–another piece of history that now carried extra weight.

"I remember that summer," he said finally, his voice controlled but vulnerable. "Dad coming home early one day, Mom crying in the kitchen. I was six. They said we needed a change, a new start. The smell of motor oil and leather cleaner, how it clung to Dad's clothes even after three washes. The way the fluorescent lights buzzed overhead while I did homework in the back office, surrounded by invoices and parts catalogs." His fingers traced the edge of the folder. "The shop bell had this particular ring—bright, hopeful. Like it was announcing good news every time."

Memory seemed to catch him then, his eyes distant. "There was this wall of photographs behind the counter—customers with their cars, three generations of satisfied clients. Mr. Davidson with his '57 Chevy, restored piece by piece. The Martinez family's delivery van that Dad kept running through two decades of grocery routes." His voice caught. "All gone now. Just...gone."

"I'm so sorry," Leah whispered, reaching for his hand. "If I had known—"

"It wasn't you," Chris interrupted, gripping her fingers tightly. "You were just a kid, too." He stared at the documents, recognition dawning. "It explains so much. Why Dad worked three jobs to keep me in music lessons. Why Mom took in sewing for my college applications. They never wanted me to feel the loss."

"They protected you," Leah said, her heart aching at the quiet heroism of it all.

"Like my dad always said—what matters isn't what happens to you, but how you handle it." Chris looked at her, concern replacing his own shock. "Leah... what does this mean for us?"

"For us?" Leah echoed, realizing Chris was worried about their relationship. "Chris, this doesn't change how I feel about you."

"But your father..." he gestured at the papers between them. "My family's business, everything my parents lost... Leah, he's Louise's grandfather. Your dad. The man who just started being part of our lives again."

"And your parents are the most gracious, loving people I know," Leah said. "They've welcomed me, loved Louise, never once mentioned..." She paused, a thought striking her. "Do you think they knew? All this time?"

Chris ran a hand through his hair, a gesture that reminded her painfully of his father. "Mom always changed the subject when I asked about the old business. Dad would just say, 'some things are better left in the past.'" He looked at the papers again. "I guess now I know why."

"We have to tell them we know," Leah whispered. "They deserve that much."

"And your father?"

"He'll have to face it, too. All of it. The past, the present..." Leah squeezed his hand. "Our future."

Chris was quiet for a long moment, studying their intertwined fingers. "You know what's strange? All those years struggling, working extra jobs, moving to a smaller house... they never seemed bitter. Dad still went to church every Sunday, Mom still baked cookies for everyone, they still gave what little they had to others."

"Because they understood what really matters," Leah realized. "They chose love over bitterness. Just like they're doing now, with us."

"With us," Chris repeated. He turned to face her. "Leah, are you sure about this? About us? Knowing what my family lost because of yours?"

Leah reached up to cup Chris's face, making him look at her. "The only thing I'm more sure about is Louise. Your parents taught you how to love unconditionally, how to choose grace over grudges. That's who you are, Chris. That's who I fell in love with."

His eyes searched hers. "And when Louise finds out someday? About her grandfather?"

"Then we'll tell her the truth. About mistakes and forgiveness, about how love is stronger than pride or profit." Leah's voice grew stronger. "About how her grandparents on both sides chose to heal rather than hate."

"We don't know that yet," Chris reminded her. "We haven't told them we know."

"Then let's tell them. Together." Leah straightened her shoulders. "Your parents first. They deserve to know we found out, and..." she hesitated, "I need to apologize."

"For what?"

"For my father's actions. For what your family lost."

Chris shook his head. "You were a child, Leah. You didn't—" "I know. But they're going to be my family, too. They already are, in all the ways that matter. They deserve to hear it."

He studied her for a long moment, then nodded. "Okay. Together." He glanced at his watch. "Mom always has Sunday dinner ready by five. We could..."

"Now?" Leah's heart jumped. "Unless you need more time?"

Leah thought about the weight of secrets, about how they grew heavier with time. "No. Let's do it now. While we have the courage."

Chris stood, pulling her up with him. "You know what Dad always says? 'The truth isn't always comfortable, but it's always right.'"

"Your dad is wise," Leah managed a small smile.

"He is." Chris gathered the papers. "That's why I know, whatever happens next, they'll handle it with grace."

The drive to the Johnson home felt longer than usual. The manila folder sat between them like a ticking clock, and Leah noticed Chris's hands were tight on the steering wheel.

"They'll be in the garden," he said. "Dad always tends his roses before Sunday dinner."

Sure enough, Tom Johnson was kneeling among his prized roses when they pulled up, Mary beside him with her pruning shears. They looked up at the sound of the car, their welcoming smiles faltering at Chris and Leah's serious expressions.

"You're early for dinner," Mary said, brushing dirt from her gardening apron.

"We need to talk to you both. About something we found."

Tom stood slowly, and Leah saw the knowing look that passed between him and Mary. They had been expecting this, she realized. All these years, they had known this day might come.

Inside, the house was warm with the smell of pot roast–Mary's Sunday specialty. The familiar mismatched teacups came out, the good ones they had kept, Leah now understood. They settled in the living room, where family photos told the story of survival through tough times.

Chris placed the folder on the coffee table. "Dad... Mom... we found these at John Miller's office."

Tom reached for the papers with weathered hands that had rebuilt a life from ruins. "So it's finally come out," he said, his fingers tracing the old Johnson & Sons logo. "We wondered when this day would come."

"You knew?" Chris's voice cracked. "All this time?"

"Of course we knew, sweetheart," Mary said. "Your father may not have fought it in court, but he knew exactly what was happening. The Miller firm's reputation... everyone knew."

"Why didn't you tell me?" Chris looked at his parents; the realization dawned in his eyes. "All those extra jobs, the moving, my college fund..."

"Because bitterness is a poison," Tom said, his voice carrying years of hard-won wisdom. "We chose to focus on what we could control–loving each other, working hard, keeping our dignity... And look what came of it," he gestured to Chris with quiet pride. "A son who makes beautiful music, teaches children to find their voice, loves purely despite history."

"But what they did—" Chris started, but Mary interrupted.

"What they did was business," she stated steadily, yet without hatred. "What we did was family. And now..." her gaze softened as she looked at Leah, "God has seen fit to bring healing through love. Who are we to question His methods?"

Leah felt tears spill down her cheeks. "I'm so sorry," she whispered. "What my father did—"

"Was not your doing," Tom cut in kindly. "You were a child, Leah. And now you're the woman who makes our son happy, who's given us a granddaughter to cherish. That's what matters."

"But how can you just..." Chris struggled with the words. "How can you accept it so easily?"

Mary reached for her son's hand. "Who says it was easy? We had our dark nights, our moments of anger. But we chose, every day, to let love win. And now look–our son found the love of his life. We have a beautiful granddaughter, and even John Miller is learning to be a better man through Louise."

"I still need to tell him," Leah said. "About us. About everything."

"Then we'll tell him together," Chris replied, taking her hand. "All of us. It's time for truth."

Tom nodded slowly. "Perhaps it is. The church garden, maybe? Neutral ground, and a place where God's grace seems closer somehow."

"Tomorrow?" Leah suggested. "After morning service?"

"Tomorrow," Mary agreed, then stood with purpose. "But tonight, we eat. As a family. Because that's what we are now, regardless of the past."

Sunday morning dawned clear and crisp. Leah dressed Louise in her favorite dress–the one Mary had made her–while Chris made breakfast, his movements in their kitchen as natural as his music.

Leah caught Chris's eye across the kitchen. He'd worn his father's old tie today–the only piece of Johnson & Sons merchandise they'd kept, its faded logo barely visible. The significance wasn't lost on either of them.

"Mom called," Chris said. "Dad's been up since dawn, tending the garden. Says he always finds God's wisdom clearer among the roses."

"And my dad?" Leah asked, adjusting Louise's ribbon.

"Already at church. Grace saw him in his office, going through old photos."

The drive to church felt surreal. Louise sang happily in her car seat, oblivious to the tension. They arrived to find both sets of parents already there. Mary was arranging flowers at the altar, her movements precise and peaceful. Tom worked in his garden, his weathered hands steady among the roses. And John... John stood alone in the church office, staring at the old photographs.

"That's from the business opening," he said without turning as Leah entered. "Your grandfather took it. Thomas Johnson and my father, shaking hands over the first contract." He finally faced her. "I found it this morning."

"Dad..."

"You're wearing Tom's tie," he said to Chris, who'd followed Leah in. "I remember when they ordered those. Special occasion items, for client meetings."

"It was all Dad kept," Chris replied quietly. "Said some things are worth remembering, even when they're gone."

John touched the photograph one last time, then straightened his shoulders. "Mary invited me to meet in the garden. I assume..." he glanced between them, "this isn't just about old business records anymore, is it?"

"No," Leah said. "It's about the past, yes, but also about the future. Our future."

From outside, they could hear Louise's delighted laughter, the sound carrying through the morning air like bells.

"She's wearing the dress Mary made," John observed. "I noticed... I've noticed a lot of things lately. How natural they are with her. How much she loves them."

"They're going to be her grandparents too, Dad," Leah said, observing his face.

Through the window, they could see Tom and Mary in the garden, heads bent together near the roses. Twenty years of dignity and grace embodied in their simple presence.

"They knew," John blurted. "All this time, watching me with Louise, helping with the children's choir... they knew exactly who I was."

"They chose love," Leah said. "Every single time, they chose love."

The church garden held the crisp clarity of morning light when they gathered—the Millers and the Johnsons, three generations bound by choices made decades ago. Louise's laughter carried from the playground where they all watched her explore the flower beds, the child's joy a counterpoint to the weight settling around the adults.

Tom straightened as they approached, his weathered hands steady on his gardening tools. Mary stepped closer to him, their unity visible in the simple movement.

"Mr. Miller," Tom's voice carried decades of earned wisdom. "It's been a while."

"Tom," John's corporate confidence wavered. "Mary. I understand we need to talk."

"Yes," Mary said, gesturing to the garden benches they'd arranged in a circle. "Shall we sit?"

The morning sun filtered through the trees, casting dappled shadows across their small gathering. From the playground, Louise's voice carried clearly: "Look! My roses are growing!"

John flinched at the word 'my,' at this evidence of how the Johnsons had already embedded themselves in his granddaughter's life. His fingers drummed against his knee—an old tell from boardroom negotiations.

"I destroyed your family's legacy," he said abruptly, the words seeming to burst from him. "Everything you'd built—"

"You destroyed a business," Tom corrected, his tone firm but not unkind. "Our legacy?" He looked at Chris, something profound passing between father and son. "Our legacy is sitting right here. A son who creates music instead of margins. Who found love despite history."

"Dad..." Chris started, but Tom raised a hand.

"We're not here to re-litigate old decisions, John," he continued. "That little girl over there," he nodded toward Louise, "she deserves better than inherited grudges."

Mary leaned forward, her practical nature asserting itself. "The question is simple, John. Are you ready to face the past so we can build something new?"

John watched Louise for a long moment, her dark curls bouncing as she played. "I have a photo," he said finally, his voice rough. "In my office. Leah at that age, playing in this same garden. I missed so much, focused on deals like..." He gestured helplessly at Tom. "And now I have a second chance, only to find out..."

"That life is more complicated than balance sheets?" Tom suggested. His hands, calloused from years of manual labor after losing the business, rested steadily on his knees. "That sometimes what looks like an ending becomes something else entirely?"

"I don't deserve—" John began, but Mary cut him off.

"This isn't about deserving," she said simply. "It's about choosing. Every day, we choose how to carry our history. The question is, John Miller, what will you choose now?"

Louise ran over, her dress grass-stained from play. "Grandpa!" She reached for John, then turned to Tom. "Grandpa Tom, look! The roses you showed me—they're bigger!"

The simple way she claimed them both—no distinction, no hierarchy—seemed to strike them all silent. John lifted her onto his lap, his movements careful, almost reverent.

"Tom," he said finally, looking at the man who had rebuilt his life from the ashes of Miller Financial's decisions, "if you're willing... I'd like to learn about roses. About patience and growth and..." he glanced at Louise, then at Leah and Chris, "about building something that lasts."

Tom's smile was subtle, but genuine. "The garden's always open, John."

Later, as families gathered for Sunday dinner, the afternoon light painted shadows of possibility across their joined tables. Some traditions, like Mary's cookies and Tom's roses, were worth keeping. Others, like old grievances and corporate armor, could finally be set aside.

In the end, it was Louise who bridge their worlds completely, her small hands reaching for both grandfathers with equal trust. She couldn't know the weight of history that touch dissolved, but perhaps that was the point—love, in its purest form, knew nothing of balance sheets and boardrooms. It simply grew where it was planted, thorns and all.

Later that evening, after Louise was asleep and their families had departed, Chris and Leah stood in the garden again. The setting sun painted the roses in shades of gold and promise.

"Did you ever imagine," Leah asked, "when you first taught me about harmony, that this is where we'd end up?"

Chris pulled her close, humming the first notes of their song. "Maybe not the exact path," he smiled, "but the destination? Finding unexpected grace, building something beautiful from broken pieces? That's what my parents taught me. That's what we'll teach Louise."

Above them, the first stars appeared, witnesses to healing begun and love renewed. In the distance, church bells chimed the hour–the same bells that would ring for their wedding, for Louise's milestones, for all the moments yet to come.

"Together," Leah whispered, fitting herself against Chris's side.

"Together," he agreed, his voice carrying the music of certainty. "In perfect harmony."

CHAPTER 23

Truth and Trust

T he church community center glowed with celebration, strings of lights casting warm shadows across familiar faces and joyful spirits that converged to honor Leah and Chris's engagement. The soft hum of chatter intertwined with laughter, wrapping them all in a blanket of shared happiness. Louise twirled in her flower girl dress, the fabric swishing around her like petals caught in a gentle breeze, while Chris strummed his guitar, providing a musical backdrop that held the gathering together.

"Look at her go!" Claire smiled, her eyes sparkling fondly as she watched her granddaughter spin. "She's got your grace," she added, glancing at Leah, who felt a pang of nostalgia, remembering her childhood dances.

"And Chris's musical timing," Leah finished, chuckled as she observed Chris guiding the children, his warm patience overflowing as he gently encouraged them to join in the music's rhythm.

Leah could feel the glittering happiness around her, mingling sweetly with the steady buzz of excitement that filled the air. She touched her engagement ring, still new enough to bring a smile each time the small diamond caught the light. It was a simple piece, understated yet full of meaning—a legacy of love held in a design that felt entirely right.

"Yay!" With a joyful squeal, Louise spun again, her sheer excitement palpable as she basked in the moment's thrill. "Daddy's playing my music!"

Chris looked down at his daughter with a warmth that made Leah's heart swell. "And how is my little conductor doing today?" he asked, sweeping her into his arms with practiced ease, her giggles ringing like wind chimes.

Louise instantly directed him, waving her arms dramatically. "More dance! More song!"

The laughter surrounding them was buoyant, and Leah felt that familiar sense of community—the friends, the smiles, the support—all woven together in this precious moment. It reminded her of Kate's presence, how she had always sought to brighten their lives, filling them with love and laughter, regardless of the storms that may surround them.

It was easy to forget they were in a community center meant for mourning. After Kate's loss, the place once felt somber. It was alive with light, a garden of friendship blooming amid their shared grief.

"Speaking of bright," Leah said, her thoughts trailing back to earlier days, "we should have a surprise celebration each year for Auntie Kate. Do some baking and plant flowers to keep her spirit alive."

The conversation flowed fluidly, the planning taking root as their hearts opened to creating something meaningful in Kate's memory. Now captivated by the tunes, Louise began spinning again, her little dress flaring around her as she laughed and beamed joyfully.

"That's it! Keep dancing, my sweet girl!" Leah encouraged, her laughter spilling out as she leaned against Chris, grateful for their harmony.

As the festivities continued, they mingled with friends, each interaction infused with warmth and camaraderie. The light of the chandelier above twinkled like stars, casting intricate shadows that danced across the walls, embodying the memories they shared.

Soon, however, Leah felt a shift in the atmosphere as the doors opened with an unexpected gust of fall air. Ryan Matthews stood in the doorway, his figure silhouetted against the bright light from outside. He was dressed in an expensive suit, an awkward contrast to the warmth of the celebration. His appearance sent a ripple of tension through the room, and conversations faltered as people glanced toward him.

"Leah," Ryan called, his voice slicing through the comfortable buzz of laughter. "We need to talk. It's important."

Louise, ever the vigilant observer, paused her twirling and ran to Chris's side, instinctively seeking her father's safety. Leah felt a protective instinct surge within her as she stepped forward, her heart racing at the sudden tension in the air.

"There is nothing to discuss here," Chris interjected softly, his presence grounding Leah at that moment. A shield against the discomfort Ryan's entrance had invoked. This is family, and today is about celebration.

Ryan's expression went from regret to determination in an instant. "That's why I'm here," he asserted, each word dripping with poorly concealed motivation. "I have something important to discuss regarding Louise's future."

The palpable silence that enveloped the room held a mix of disbelief and concern. Claire moved closer to her daughter, protective instinct kicked in as they watched Ryan from a distance, ready to safeguard against misunderstandings.

Leah's heart raced. "My daughter's future is secure," she stated, grounding herself in the truth they had created together. "With her real family."

"Ah, but that's where you're wrong." Ryan unfolded an envelope from his expensive jacket with practiced ease. "I've been doing some research. About fathers' rights, about legal precedents…"

"Ryan," Leah began, her voice steady yet edged with the steel of conviction. "You signed those rights away. Remember? Right after you decided you didn't want to have any part of all of this. The paperwork is very clear."

The tension in the room coiled tighter. Chris stood protectively next to Leah, his body slightly angled, a shield for both her and Louise, who were now holding onto his leg with wide, vigilant eyes.

"Paperwork can be challenged!" Ryan shot back, his voice rising above the hum of gasps and whispers around them. "And I'm here to remind you I'm not going away quietly. This is about my daughter as much as the truth."

"Is that a threat?" Chris's voice remained calm. A quiet strength radiated from him as he stared Ryan down, the protective father in him rising to the surface.

"Daddy!" Louise piped up, her innocent voice slicing through the tension. "No talking! You make sad happen!"

The simple wisdom in her declaration hung in the air, lightening the thick atmosphere. For a fleeting moment, Leah felt hope bloom in Louise's innocence—a reminder of love existing in pure forms, unclouded by ulterior motives.

Before Ryan could respond, the church's gentle, authoritative voice echoed through the space. Father Michael had entered the room, his presence ushering a sense of calm as he approached. "I think this discussion should happen elsewhere," he said, addressing Ryan directly. "Not during a celebration of love and family."

Ryan's bravado faltered as the priest's firm yet gentle demeanor took charge. "Fine," he huffed, straightening his jacket, his mask slipping. "But we need to talk, Leah. This isn't over." And with that, he turned and left, the tension of his departure lingering like a charged cloud.

"Thank you, Father," Leah breathed, relief washing over her as the church returned to its rightful spirit of love and celebration.

"I am always ready to support my flock," Father Michael replied, their eyes knowingly sharing, holding an unsaid understanding of the burdens carried.

"Are you okay?" Chris asked once Ryan was out of earshot, concern deepening in his voice. He tightened his grip on Leah's hand, grounding her once more.

"I'm okay," Leah replied, the adrenaline from the confrontation slowly fading. "It's just... I thought we'd put all of that behind us. I didn't expect him to show up today."

"I know," Chris said, his gaze steady. "But we'll handle it together, no matter what comes next. The important thing is right now—we are all here, we are celebrating."

They moved back to the gathering, a lightness slowly returned as laughter resumed to fill the space. Leah forced a bright smile, determined to reflect the moment's joy. Time passed, stories unfolded, cake was cut, and love blossomed amid the community surrounding them.

As evening dripped into twilight, Leah took a few moments to embrace the scene that unfolded before her. She caught glimpses of Claire laughing with the Johnsons, Mary smiling as she recounted joyful memories of Kate and other friends joining in, creating connections through shared love and loss.

When the evening wound down, Leah watched Louise dart around, playing tag with the children. Her laughter echoed through the air as warmth filled the garden.

"Do you think we honored Kate today?" Leah asked Chris, her heart still processing the course of events.

"Absolutely," he replied without hesitation. "We laughed for her, loved for her, and that's what she would have wanted—her spirit reminding us of all that truly matters."

Leah kissed him, feeling gratitude swell in her heart for everything they had together. As Louise returned, breathless from playing, she nestled against Chris, rubbing an eye as she tried to stay awake.

"Time for bed, my little flower," Leah said, and Chris stood, lifting Louise into his arms.

"Can we sing a song?" Louise asked sleepily, her little voice threading into the comfortable silence surrounding them.

"Of course," Chris responded, his heart full as he hummed a gentle melody that wrapped around them like a warm blanket as they made their way to the car.

Once they arrived home, Leah settled Louise into her sleeping space, lovingly tucking her daughter under soft blankets. In those simple moments, she felt the weight of love filling their home, echoing Kate's promise to always be with them.

As Leah slipped into the living room, she found Chris waiting for her, an affectionate smile gracing his lips as he brought her close. "You handled today like a champion," he praised, his fingers tenderly brushing a lock of hair behind her ear. "I know it wasn't easy, especially with Ryan showing up. You kept it together, for Louise's sake."

"Thank you," Leah said, feeling the warmth of his words wrap around her. "I just want to create a safe space for her—one where she feels loved and cherished, just like Kate would have wanted."

Chris nodded, his gaze serious but infused with an unwavering strength. "We will. We'll nurture that space and fill it with joy and laughter. You have me, Leah; I'm here, always."

As they stood silhouetted against the soft glow of the living room light, Leah felt a shimmer of hope rising within her—the culmination of love, family, and healing that would continue to grow, even in the shadows of loss. The challenges they faced only strengthened their bond.

"Do you want something to drink?" Leah asked, her worry fading as she focused on the present. "It might help us unwind after everything."

"Sure," Chris replied.

She watched Chris move about the kitchen; his brow furrowed in concentration as he prepared their drinks. It was in these small, mundane moments that Leah recognized the steadiness of their relationship. Its realness anchored her.

"Anything in particular you want?" he asked, tilting his head, shooting her a playful grin.

"Surprise me," Leah responded, her heart swelling with affection. "You always seem to pick the perfect one."

They settled into the cozy corner of the living room, Louise's soft breaths from her room serving as a soothing backdrop. As they curled up on the couch, Leah leaned onto Chris's shoulder, feeling the warmth of his body enveloping her.

"Do you think we'll tell her about Ryan someday?" Leah asked quietly, her voice barely above a whisper, lost in the moment's comfort yet wary of future conversations.

Chris sighed, thoughtfully. "Only when she's old enough to understand. We must protect her from anything that could dim her light."

"Yes," Leah agreed, the words coming from a place of deep love and understanding. "I want Louise to grow up knowing that her family is here for her—with real love, real connections, and without the ghosts of the past."

Silence settled between them, profound and unbroken. Comfort wrapped around them, a haven against the world outside. Leah's mind drifted to the memories they would forge together—every rainy day inside, every summer picnic, every winter night spent cozying up with books. She wanted the sweetness of those moments to overshadow any bitterness left from the past.

Leah rested against Chris, feeling her body's tension dissipating. There was a grounding certainty in shared silence, where words weren't needed to convey the depth of their feelings.

Chris broke the tranquil quiet. "Let's make a promise," he suggested, his voice firm yet filled with warmth. "In honor of Kate, we'll dedicate time every month to create memories together—days where we remember her and celebrate the love that surrounds us."

"That sounds wonderful," Leah replied, her heart fluttering. "We can rotate activities—one-month art and music, another month baking or storytelling. We can keep her memory alive in everything we do."

"Exactly!" Chris beamed; his enthusiasm was infectious. "We'll build a family culture that honors her spirit. We'll create a legacy for Louise filled with love and laughter."

Their plans took shape, woven together amidst laughter and shared dreams. In the night's glow, Leah felt a sense of peace settle in—a promise made not just in words but in actions, a roadmap marked by love's radiant light guiding them forward.

With their glasses empty, Chris glanced at the clock, concern lining his features. "It's getting late. We should get some rest—tomorrow is another busy day of remembering and creating."

Leah nodded, but a flicker of excitement surged within her.

"You know, I'd like to stay up just a bit longer," she said, a hint of mischief sparkling in her eyes. "There's something special about the quiet of the night—a spark of inspiration waiting to be seized."

Chris looked at her thoughtfully, understanding the creativity bubbling within her. "Alright, I'm in. But let's keep it light. How about sharing some of our favorite memories of Kate?"

As the night deepened around them, so did the stories they told in hushed tones, their laughter mixing with nostalgia. Leah leaned back against the couch, Chris's arm draped comfortably around her, creating an intimate bubble where the outside world faded.

"I remember when we first went to that little art fair together," Leah began, her mind conjuring the vivid memory of a sunny day filled with color and laughter. "Kate insisted we try that pottery wheel. I was terrible at it, clay flying everywhere—"

"What a mess!" Chris interjected, laughing. "I remember you went home covered in it; hair all stuck together!"

"Yes!" Leah chuckled, her face lighting up at the thought. "And Kate tried to help me out, but all she did was laugh until she cried. We spent the rest of the day creating ridiculous shapes instead of actual pottery."

Chris shook his head in amusement. "That sounds like a classic Kate memory. She always saw the fun in every situation. How you two turned a seemingly disastrous outing into one filled with laughter speaks volumes about her spirit."

Leah smiled, the warmth of the memories serving as a balm against the edge of grief still lingering in her heart. "She taught me to see life differently—to embrace the chaos and find joy in every moment."

In the quiet that followed, Chris's fingers absently brushed through Leah's hair, a soothing act that felt intimate and natural. "I miss those carefree times, but I'm glad we can keep her spirit alive," he said, his tone serious but kind. "She would want us to remember the happy moments."

"For sure," Leah replied, a profound appreciation for Kate's enduring impact flooding her heart. "And I want Louise to grow up hearing those stories—about how her auntie made life colorful, even in the face of challenges."

"Speaking of colorful, do you remember that time Kate painted the entire kitchen in neon colors for a party?" Chris asked, laughter shining in his eyes. "How she nearly painted the refrigerator a wild shade of green?"

Leah laughed, the sound bouncing around the cozy room. "She convinced us it was art! We all thought we would get kicked out of the apartment, but somehow, the landlord didn't seem to mind as long as we paid our rent on time."

"Classic Kate! Unapologetically herself," Chris responded, a touch of admiration creeping into his voice. Leah could hear his heart swell with fondness for everything that encapsulated Kate, a shared love connecting them still.

They continued their evening of storytelling, recalling moments filled with laughter and warmth, weaving a fabric of love that honored Kate's memory. Each story was a thread binding the past to the present, fortifying their commitment to carry on the spirit of love she embodied.

As the conversation turned soft, Leah felt the weight of exhaustion settle into her bones. The embrace of night wrapped its gentle arms around the house, lulling them into the comfort of familiarity. She leaned against Chris, feeling the steady rhythm of his heartbeat sync with her own, a serene melody in the quiet.

"Let's get some rest," Chris suggested gently, his voice was low and soothing as he brushed his lips against her forehead. "Tomorrow will be a new day, and I want you to feel refreshed."

Leah nodded, agreed, as the protective cocoon of his embrace pulled her deeper into its warmth. She stood, pulling Chris up, and they moved toward their bedroom. The tiredness tugged at her limbs.

Once they settled in, the cool sheets wrapping around them and the soft glow of the bedside lamp illuminating their faces, Leah felt a swell of contentment. Chris glanced at her, reading her thoughts in the gentle curve of her smile.

"Hey," he said, his tone soft as he pulled her close, "I want you to know that no matter what happens, we're in this together. We've got a lifetime of moments to create, and I'm proud to be alongside you."

Tears prickled in Leah's eyes. Not from sadness, but from a profound love and connection. "I feel that too, Chris. You've changed my life in ways I never thought possible. The way you love me and Louise... means everything to me."

"Then let's keep that love alive, not just for us but for Louise too," he murmured, brushing a thumb across her cheek.

With the conversations about the past still echoing through her mind, Leah leaned into Chris, her heart swelling as he wrapped his arms around her. A delightful anticipation was in the air—a flicker of something more profound than love pulling them closer together.

"Do you want to..." Chris hesitated.

"What?" Leah asked, her cheeks flushing with nervous excitement.

He paused, his gaze locked with hers, and she could see a spark of desire flickering behind those deep brown eyes. "Do you want to make love?" he asked, his voice low and filled with tenderness.

Leah felt the warmth flood her cheeks as she met his gaze, her heart racing at the moment's weight. Anticipation blossomed within her, mingled with the bittersweet memories of the day and the echoes of Kate's spirit surrounding them. "Yes," she replied. "I want that..."

There was something electric in the air as Chris moved closer, his fingers brushing against Leah's hair, the touch gentle yet filled with intention. The world around them faded into the background as they sank into the cocoon of their shared intimacy. Every moment felt heightened, alive with the promise of connection, love, and the essence of who they were together.

It was as if time held its breath, suspended in this space, filled with longing and warmth. Chris leaned in slowly, capturing Leah's lips in a soft kiss that ignited a spark deep within her. The kiss deepened, both tender and passionate, their shared breaths mingling as they explored the familiar terrain of each other's hearts.

"Leah..." Chris whispered against her lips, his voice thick with emotion. "Being with you feels like coming home."

Leah threaded her fingers through his hair, feeling the gentle pull of connection surge between them. Her heart raced as she pulled him closer, wrapping her arms tightly around him. "You are home to me, always," she confessed, breathlessly. "With you, I feel safe enough to express my true self without fear of judgment."

Chris, emboldened by her words, deepened the kiss, the warmth of her skin against his sending shivers down his spine, their lips fitting together seamlessly. Leah felt the heat radiating between them, every spark igniting her senses as they connected on every level—emotionally, spiritually, and physically.

As the world around them faded, leaving only the two of them, time seemed to dissolve into a timeless, intimate dance; they could feel the music resonating in their bones, a silent symphony. Chris's hands explored the contours of her back, sending ripples of warmth through her. Every brush of his fingers sparked electricity beneath her skin, awakening every nerve, every instinct.

Leah pulled back to catch her breath, her heart pounding wildly. "Chris, I want this to be special... I want to honor Kate's memory and the love we share."

His eyes flickered with understanding, a deep emotion shining brightly as he cupped her face. "We will honor Kate's love, Leah. We'll carry her spirit with us in everything we do, ensuring we remember every moment of joy she brought into our lives."

Reassured, Leah leaned into him again, capturing his mouth with hers. Their kiss deepened once more than passion surged. She could feel his heart racing in sync with hers, a steady drumbeat echoing through their shared connection.

Chris's kisses grew more fervent, igniting a fire within her as he lifted her effortlessly, cradling her against him. She felt weightless, as if they were rising above their world and soaring into the sky. They shed layers of worry and grief with each kiss and caress, allowing desire to eclipse everything else.

As they moved together toward the bed, Leah felt the cool sheets against her skin, contrasting with the warmth of Chris's body beside hers. The world beyond their bedroom faded away, leaving only the two in this sacred space, where love flowed freely, and memories thrived.

With careful movements, Chris cradled her face in his hands, his voice a soft murmur. "You're so beautiful, Leah. You always have been."

Leah felt a rush of heat at his words, and she responded with a kiss of her own, pouring all of her love and longing into that one gesture. Their bodies intertwined, the rhythm of their hearts syncing—a perfect harmony that felt reassuring and exhilarating.

Leah became lost in Chris in that intimate cocoon; every touch ignited a desire that surged through her veins. The air was thick with the scent of warmth and intimacy, embers of connection weaving around them as if they were the only two souls in the universe.

"Tell me what you want," Chris whispered, his breath warm against her ear.

"I want to feel all of you," she breathed back, the vulnerability in her voice urged him closer, deeper. "I want us to lose ourselves in each other."

With that invitation, the world fell away entirely. Chris's mouth roamed the curve of her neck, trailing soft kisses that ignited her senses into flames. Leah tilted her head back, relishing in the sensations coursing through her as he worshipped her with each brush of his lips.

Every curve and line of her body felt alive under his touch, each moment charged with an electricity that enveloped them in warmth. She could feel the connection growing more profound with every kiss, whispered word, and the soft caress of Chris's hands against her skin.

"Leah," he murmured, his voice thick and low as he caressed her arms. "You have no idea how long I've wanted this—with you, completely."

"I want you too, Chris," she replied, the urgency and longing rolling off her tongue. "I want to share everything—my heart, soul, love—for you and Kate."

Their eyes met, and in that moment, Leah saw deeper into Chris—not just the man she loved but the father he had become, the partner he had always been, the protector who embraced her with an assurance that only grew stronger in adversity. The world around them melted into nothingness as their connection deepened, echoing the love that had blossomed between them even before sadness threatened to overshadow their lives.

With a gentle, deliberate movement, Chris captured her waist, lifting her closer as they leaned into one another. Their breaths mingled with a heady mix of sweetness and desire. Each kiss grew more passionate and urgent, igniting flames that danced between them.

Leah's fingers tangled in Chris's soft hair, pulling him closer as she surrendered to the intoxicating sensations swirling within. The warmth of his body pressed against hers was familiar yet new—a thrilling reminder they were weathering life's storms together and now navigating the joyous intimacy that awaited them.

"I want to remember this forever," Chris murmured against her mouth, his eyes dark with desire and yearning. "Every moment, every whisper, every laugh."

"Yes," Leah breathed, feeling the truth of his words flutter within her. The weight of profound love mingled with a gentle sadness that was both a reminder of loss and a celebration of life. She craved this connection, the unity that enveloped them, grounding her against the tides of grief that ebbed and flowed in her mind.

As they lost themselves in the experience, time seemed to stretch, each moment unfurling like blossoms on a spring morning. The world outside their sanctuary faded, replaced by the warmth of whispered promises. Leah could feel every brush of Chris's hand, each kiss igniting sparks that reverberated deep within her soul.

Their bodies moved together fluidly, a dance of desire that transcended the boundaries of grief, loss, and uncertainty. The air was thick with intimacy, with every caress igniting a fire that coursed through them, filling the space with love that felt almost tangible.

"Let me show you how much you mean to me," Chris whispered, his voice husky as he guided Leah's hands to explore his chest. He felt the steady beat of his heart thumping in synchronization with her own.

Leah felt exhilarated. Every kiss and touch brought them closer to the realization that they were no longer mere individuals—they were a united force, a family tethered by love, each moment intertwined in an intricate tapestry of existence. A wave of passion enveloped them, carrying them away from the past and into shared dreams.

As Chris's hands drifted lower, exploring the contours of her waist, Leah felt her body respond eagerly, igniting with warmth and anticipation. It felt right—so beautifully right—and she reveled in the sensation of exploring each other anew.

In the flickering candlelight that danced around them, Leah caught sight of the ring Chris had given her—the simple yet elegant design catching glimmers of light, much like their love. She brushed her fingers against it, feeling the fresh history they were crafting together.

"Together, Leah," Chris murmured as they surrendered to the moment, his hands cradling her face as if she were the most precious treasure in the world. "Let's create something unforgettable."

As they embraced each other, their breaths became one, a symphony of desire and love—a beautiful melody that crescendoed in harmony. Each caress became a promise; each kiss an anchor, and each whisper a testament to their love—a love that would carry them through any storm.

The world disappeared as Leah and Chris danced, their bodies close, the music swirling around them, their passion igniting a warmth that banished everything else.

They lost track of time, surrendering to the experience entirely and letting love wash over them in waves. The moments felt suspended, drenched in intimacy and wild joy as Leah felt each shiver, sigh, and heartbeat pulsing in their intertwined bodies.

As the night deepened, they explored not just the physical realm but the emotional tapestry they were weaving—the bonds of love, trust, and shared dreams that flourished amid the complexity of their lives.

As fatigue settled in, they found themselves wrapped in each other, their bodies still tingling from the intimacy they had shared. Chris's warm breath brushed against Leah's hair, grounding her as they basked in the afterglow of their connection. The world outside their bedroom faded away, leaving only the soft rustle of sheets and the ambient sounds of the night—a comforting whisper that signaled the security of their love.

Leah nestled deeper into Chris's embrace, feeling his heart steady against her ear. The rhythmic beating was a soothing reminder they were in this together. She closed her eyes, allowing herself to drift, surrounded by a sanctuary built on love and trust.

"Do you think we'll ever stop being surprised by how much we love each other?" she murmured, her voice nearly a whisper as she traced circles on his chest with her fingertips.

"Never," Chris replied, a sleepy yet earnest tone lacing his words. "Every day, we discover more layers than what that love can be. Just like tonight. Each moment brings something new."

Leah smiled at his response, marveled how even simple conversations held the power to deepen their connection. "You're right. I thought I knew love, but you showed me an entirely different depth—a kind that feels like a warm embrace on the coldest days."

"That's what we're meant to do for each other," Chris said, tilting his head gently to capture her gaze. The sincerity in his eyes radiated a fierce warmth, enveloping her in a sense of safety and belonging. "We lift each other, make each other better. That's what Kate always wanted for us."

A moment of silence hung between them, filled with understanding and gratitude for the love they held and those they cherished. Leah felt Kate's spirit echoing in the stillness, like a gentle whisper reminding them of the bond they forged together through all the challenges they faced.

"Do you think she's proud of us?" Leah asked, a hint of vulnerability creeping into her voice.

"I know she is," Chris said, drawing her closer as they nestled deeper into the comfort of the bed. "She wanted nothing more than to see us happy, building a life together."

As Leah reflected on Kate's unwavering spirit, she remembered how her best friend had always uplifted them. Kate had built a resilient and profound foundation of love, and Leah felt more connected to that legacy in this moment of intimacy. "More than anything, I want Louise to remember Auntie Kate for the joy she brought into our lives."

"She will," Chris assured, the depth of sincerity in his tone fueling her heart. "With each story we tell and each memory we create, Kate's essence will echo through our family. And the more we talk about her, the more we bring her into our journey."

The night air was cool against their skin as Leah pulled the blankets tighter around them, a sanctuary of warmth amidst the chill. She felt wrapped in the cocoon of their love, the simple beauty of companionship filling her with a profound sense of belonging.

Chris shifted, tracing gentle patterns on her arms. "What do you think Kate would say if she were here right now?"

Leah chuckled, her mind conjuring Kate's familiar voice filled with mischief and light. "Probably something like 'It's about time you two figured it out!'"

"Definitely," Chris laughed, his eyes lighting up with affection. "But I think she'd also remind us to enjoy the ride. Life is too short not to savor every delicious moment."

"Exactly!" Leah exclaimed, a warmth blooming in her chest as she contemplated their journey together. "To dream big and love fiercely, like she did."

As the conversation faded into a comfortable silence, Leah felt the warmth of Chris's presence wrapped around her, a soft blanket of safety. She closed her eyes, giving in to the fatigue that draped over her like a comforting shawl, drifting into a deep sleep filled with thoughts of Kate, love, laughter, and the unforgettable adventures ahead.

CHAPTER 24

Healing Bridges

T he Johnson's garden was alive with late summer blooms as friends and family gathered to help plan the wedding.

"Grandpa John!" Louise shouted, her voice bursting with excitement. "Come see! The tomatoes need counting!"

John Miller, appearing somewhat out of place in his casual clothes, hesitated as he glanced skeptically at the garden soil beneath his designer loafers. He had spent decades maneuvering in corporate boardrooms and had yet to adapt to this more modest existence. And yet, when he spotted Louise's eager face, his reservations melted away.

"Coming, sweetheart," he called, moving to avoid stepping on delicate blooms. "Though I'm not sure tomatoes need such precise inventory..."

"Everything needs counting!" Louise declared, as if her assertion was the ultimate truth. "Daddy says that's how we know if the garden's happy."

Chris, who was helping Tom repair a trellis nearby, glanced at Leah. They had both been watching this transformation unfold—John shifting from corporate precision to garden wisdom, finding joy in a three-year-old's unshakeable certainty.

"Seven red ones!" Louise exclaimed proudly after counting. "And... lots of green ones. Grandpa John, help with big numbers?"

John knelt beside her, designer clothes meeting garden soil with surprising ease. "Let's see... twelve green tomatoes. So nineteen total!" His voice carried a genuine tone of eagerness now, unearthing the joy of the moment, feeling the connection to his granddaughter bloom.

"Good math," Tom called from the trellis, constructing it with practical need. "Those business skills come in handy in the garden, too."

A flicker of surprise crossed John's face at the compliment, giving him a reflection on the worth beyond numbers and profit margins. "I suppose they do," he admitted, his voice gaining warmth. "I must admit, I never thought I'd apply them to vegetable inventory."

"Life has surprising ways of teaching us what matters," Mary said, emerging from the kitchen with pitchers of lemonade and trays of cookies that filled the air with sweetness.

"Like grandchildren teaching us new forms of counting," she added, her eyes bright as she watched Louise proudly recount her findings.

Louise beamed, her tomato arithmetic forgotten as she helped Mary serve drinks. The innocence of the moment washed over John, softening barriers he had held so tightly—the rigid walls constructed over decades of professional life seemed to crumble like dried leaves fluttering away in the wind.

"You know," Tom said as they all settled onto garden chairs and overturned planters, "I once thought success was measured in profit margins. Until we lost the business."

The truth floated in the air like a gentle leaf, and John's expression displayed a glimmer of empathy as he listened to Tom's experience.

"The best thing that could have happened, looking back," Tom continued, his voice laced with wisdom drawn from perseverance. "It taught us to measure wealth differently. In moments like this—a family gathering, garden growing, love multiplying."

"Like tomatoes!" Louise pronounced, making everyone laugh and easing the weight of the moment.

Claire, who had been quietly observing, joined in. "I'm learning that too. After the divorce... after everything... I thought losing our social position was the worst thing. Now I realize..."

"Real position is about love," Mary injected, offering more cookies. "About choice and growth and finding beauty in unexpected places."

John watched Louise as she helped Chris and Tom, the child's unyielding energy guiding them through tasks with her innocent wisdom. The sight was a poignant display of family dynamics that sparked hope for new beginnings amidst the shadows of the past.

"She's so happy here," he remarked quietly, observing how Louise carried the enthusiasm and wonder of youth as she engaged in her tasks. "So... herself."

"She's loved here," Leah said, sensing the shift in her father's perspective as he looked at her. "For exactly who she is."

The words pulled at John, revealing layers of vulnerability beneath his well-crafted exterior. "Like you are," he said, steadying his gaze on Leah. "Loved for yourself."

Leah felt the gravity of that realization pull her closer to her father, the recognition of their shared humanity bridging the gap that had often felt insurmountable. "Yes," she whispered, allowing the warmth of his words to wrap around her. "I've learned that my worth isn't measured by societal expectations, but by the love we share as a family."

As Louise continued to tend to the tomatoes and share her playful wisdom, Leah saw John watching her with newfound appreciation. He understood that true wealth comes not from social stature or corporate success, but from the bonds they created—the connections that grew from love and choice.

"Every day we spend together, whether in the garden or joyful chaos, reminds me of what truly matters," John said, the dawn of understanding breaking in his voice. "I've realized I've been measuring success with the wrong criteria."

As if sensing their serious tone, Louise turned from her actions, her tiny brow furrowed in contemplation. "Grandpa John, what do we do if the tomatoes are sad?" she asked, her innocence shining through.

"Then we give them love, Louise," John said, kneeling to her level, his heart swelling with affection for this little girl who had shifted his perspective. "We tend to them—water them, make sure they get enough sunlight. Just like how we love each other."

The wisdom in his words caught Leah off guard, her heart fluttering at the realization of how much this moment had shifted their family dynamics. Love, she recognized, was not just about the grand gestures; it was found in the tender exchanges, the vulnerability sighed over the soil, and the shared laughter.

Tom laughed, his voice warm. "You see, John? It all comes back to love, always. That's what keeps our garden vibrant."

Their conversations flowed seamlessly, moving from gardening to childhood memories, each story another thread binding the family closer together. John found a surprising comfort in being among people who embraced him without judgment and encouraged him to step back from the corporate mindset he had known for so long.

As the day turned to dusk, the air cooled, and the first stars twinkled in the sky; Leah took a moment to pause and breathe in the evening's beauty. The garden was alive with color and light, the evening blooms releasing their fragrance into the air, a combined effect that mirrored the connections forming around her.

Still high on excitement and sugar from the cookies, Louise prompted Chris to play songs. Leaning against a nearby tree, he adjusted his guitar and began stringing a lively tune, prompting Louise to jump and dance under the fading light.

During the next few moments, the garden filled with music, laughter, and the soft sounds of children playing. Leah couldn't help but smile, watching her daughter twirl under the stars, the garden serving as a backdrop to a joyful dance that seemed to transcend reality. She felt Kate's spirit mingling with the guitar sounds, her presence in their daughter's laughter, and the love radiating among them all.

As Chris transitioned to a softer melody, the atmosphere became more intimate. Leah felt her energy settle, and she walked over to Chris, joining him under the twinkling stars. He smiled as she slipped her hand into his, softly squeezing it. The warmth between them felt alive and potent, a reminder of the love they had cultivated together.

"Hey," Chris said, his voice low. "I know today was emotional, and tomorrow could be hard, too. But remember, we've built something special—it carries all the love Kate gave us."

"I know," Leah replied, leaning her head against his shoulder. "Today felt like a step forward. I don't want to keep living in the shadow of loss."

Chris nodded, kissing the top of her head. "That's exactly what we will do. We'll keep her spirit alive through every moment. We'll share stories, laugh, love, and ensure Louise knows how magical she was."

As the night thickened around them, stars blinked like eternal witnesses to their promises. Amidst the gatherings and conversations around them, Leah felt a deep commitment to honoring Kate's legacy and solidifying the connections forged through love and understanding.

Later that night, in the quiet of their bedroom, Leah felt Chris's warmth beside her as they discussed Kate's letters and their hopes for the future. His presence was steady and reassuring, a reminder of the life they were building together.

"I love you," Chris whispered, drawing her close. Their kiss deepened, tender yet passionate, as moonlight filtered through the window. In these precious moments, they found solace in each other's arms, their connection strengthened by shared memories and dreams of tomorrow.

Afterward, as they lay together in the gentle darkness, Leah traced her fingers along Chris's arm. "Why does everything feel so perfect right now?" she asked.

"Because we are," Chris replied, his voice warm. "We're building something real, something rooted in truth and love."

Leah felt a sense of promise threading through her dreams as she drifted into slumber—a swirling tapestry of laughter, love, and Kate's spirit. In the quiet embrace of night, Leah could almost hear

Kate's laughter, like fairy dust sprinkled upon their lives, filling them with magic and light.

The following day dawned with the chirping of birds and soft morning light filtering through the curtains. Leah opened her eyes, stretching with a sense of renewed purpose. She could sense Chris beside her, still asleep, his presence a rock of stability as she gathered her thoughts.

Once dressed and ready, Leah ventured into the kitchen to prepare breakfast. The aroma of freshly brewed coffee filled the air, mingling delightfully with the morning scent. Louise was still tucked away in her room, lost in sleep, which Leah took as a moment to savor the peace before the day unfolded.

As she moved around the kitchen, Leah thought about Kate's legacy. The letters had become constant in her mind, like breadcrumbs guiding her toward a love-filled future. She felt the relentless urge to embrace each one as an opportunity to delve into pieces of Kate's spirit that would forever be intertwined with their lives.

Once breakfast was prepared, Leah heard the soft patter of tiny feet approaching. Louise appeared in the doorway, her hair tousled and eyes still half-closed, but the moment she caught sight of Leah and the breakfast spread, her face lit up with excitement.

"Mama! You made pancakes?" she exclaimed, bounding into the kitchen as if her sleepy moments had vanished with the enticing smell of warm syrup.

"Sure did!" Leah replied cheerfully, setting a plate down for her daughter. "Your favorite—chocolate chip pancakes, just how you like them."

"Yummy!" Louise climbed up onto her chair, her compact frame bouncing with enthusiasm as she settled in to reveal her morning energy. "Can we put sprinkles on it, too?"

Before Leah could respond, a familiar voice drifted in behind her. "Of course we can! Rainbows are necessary for any meal." Chris appeared in the kitchen, his smiled brightening the morning even further.

"Daddy!" Louise shouted, reaching out for him to assist her. "Join me! We get to make pancakes together!"

Chris jumped into the kitchen rhythm effortlessly, grabbing a bowl and pouring colorful sprinkles onto Louise's plate. "Just like Auntie Kate would want, right? Fun and vibrant!"

Leah felt a rush of happiness as she watched them, their easy banter bringing light into the room. The simple joys resonated—this was the life Kate had cherished and celebrated, and now they were doing the same in her honor.

As laughter filled the kitchen, Leah couldn't shake the sense of gratitude that resonated strongly within her. These moments, intertwined with memories of Kate, reminded her that life was more robust than grief—it was about love, laughter, and nurturing the relationships that mattered most.

After breakfast, they all tidied up together, packing the remnants away while Louise hummed a tune, her voice a sweet melody that poured from her spirit. Chris watched her with a soft smile, the kind that held a multitude of promises for the future.

"Are you ready to dive into some of those letters today?" Chris asked Leah, referencing the treasure trove they had yet to explore.

"Definitely!" Leah replied, her heart fluttering with anticipation at the thought of uncovering more pieces of Kate's wisdom. "Louise can help us crack the treasure hunt code!"

"Yay!" Louise cheered, her face lighting up at the idea of being an adventurer in their family story. "Operation Treasure Hunt! I'm ready!"

They gathered in the living room afterward; the sunlight pouring in through the windows, creating a warm, inviting space. Leah set up a cozy corner, laying out the letters, each one waiting to share its secrets. The excitement was palpable as they expected the adventure that lay ahead.

Chris picked up the first letter, marked for "When You Need to Know About Love." He opened it, the familiarity of Kate's handwriting instantly filling the room with warmth. "Let's see what Auntie Kate wants to share with us today," he said, his tone filled with reverence.

Leah watched as Chris read, his voice steady and clear, weaving Kate's words into a growing narrative that felt like a balm for their hearts.

"Dear Leah and Louise," he read, slowly and deliberately, as if absorbing each word. "If you're reading this, it means I'm already doing a better job at being an angel than I ever managed here on earth..."

With each word, Leah felt memories flood back, and images of Kate sprang to life—her laughter, the way she lit up every room she entered, and the love she channeled into every relationship she nurtured. As Chris continued reading through the letter, the teachings of love unfolded like a flower blooming in the sunlight.

"So why is love so essential?" Chris continued reading. "Because it is what gives us strength in the hardest times. It is about being there for each other, about compassion, kindness, and understanding. Life is often messy, but love makes everything worthwhile. Cherish it; hold on to it tightly."

As Chris's voice tapered off, Leah felt warmth blossom in her chest. "She would always remind us," Leah said, her heart swelling with affection. "Through music, through letters, through her constant encouragement."

"Yes. And we get to carry that message forward." Chris smiled, placing the letter back down. "This is what she wanted for us—to celebrate love and to see its beauty wherever we go."

Sensing the moment's significance, Louise said, "Auntie Kate says love is magic. It always makes us happy!"

"Yes, it does!" Leah said, her eyes shining as she looked at Chris and Louise, feeling warmth enveloping them. "And remember, love can heal anything, even sadness."

With each letter they uncovered and each note she read; Leah felt Kate's presence growing stronger. The connection reaffirmed that love is an enduring force transcending time and space.

The excitement around the letters grew as they continued to explore Kate's treasure trove of memories and insights. Each letter unveiled stories of love, hope, and lessons learned, all infused with Kate's unmistakable humor and spirit. Leah felt as if Kate were with them, encouraging them to embrace every moment and celebrate life with the same enthusiasm she had.

Louise bounced in her seat as Chris flipped through the envelopes. "What's next?" she asked eagerly, her eyes sparkling with anticipation.

Chris chuckled, pulling another letter from the pile. "This one's labeled 'For Louise—When You Think You Can't Go On.' Let's see what Auntie Kate wants to share with you, sweet girl."

With that, he read aloud, his voice warm and inviting as he shared Kate's wisdom with Louise, who was snuggled against Leah's side, clutching a small stuffed animal like her treasure.

"Dear Louise," Chris began, his eyes flickering with emotion as he read, "If you're reading this, it means you've encountered a bump in your path. Maybe something doesn't go your way, or a friend hurts your feelings. Remember this: feeling sad or frustrated is okay, but don't let those feelings block your sunshine."

Louise listened intently; her attention captured by the words as Chris continued. "Find the fun in every day, the magic in the little things—the way the flowers bloom, how the sun always rises after the storm, and the laughter that fills your heart when you dance."

"That sounds like Auntie Kate," Louise beamed, her spirit lifting with every word. "She loved dancing!"

"She sure did," Leah agreed, feeling a warm rush of affection for the incredible woman who had cared for them. "And she'd want you to find your dance, to let happiness be a part of your every day."

Chris finished the letter, his gaze softening as he spoke to Louise directly. "Whenever you feel sad or lost, remember Auntie Kate's magic is still guiding you through."

Louise nodded; her little brow furrowed in concentration. "I can see her!" she said with surprising certainty. "When the butterflies come, that's Auntie Kate. She's the best butterfly in the whole sky!"

Leah felt a profound warmth swell in her heart. Louise's belief was a testament to the love and spirit Kate had instilled in them, proving that even in their absence, a connection could transcend through pure love. "Yes, baby," she whispered, pulling her daughter into a tight hug. "Auntie Kate will always be around us, especially when you see those butterflies."

They moved on to the following letter, Chris opening it. "This one's for you, Leah. It's titled 'For When You Need Your Best Friend.'"

Leah's heart skipped a beat as he read. "Dear Leah, if you're reading this, I can only imagine the whirlwind of life's chaos swirling around you. I want you to remember that you have always been your kind of magic. Your resilience, creativity, and how you elevate everyone around you make you truly special."

Tears stung Leah's eyes, but she couldn't suppress the soft smile on her lips. "She always knew what I needed to hear."

Chris's voice continued, steady and bright. "When you face the storms, please remember that leaning on others is okay. You don't have to shoulder everything alone. Your family loves you deeply—let them help you carry the load."

Leah closed her eyes, feeling the truth of those words echo powerfully, a healing balm against her heart's deepest scars. "I've been trying so hard to be strong for everyone," she whispered, squeezing Chris's hand.

"Don't be afraid to lean on us," Chris reassured, his grip firm. "You're not alone in this. We're a team."

"Exactly!" Louise declared, raising her little hand. "We're all family! Team family!"

They shared a laugh; the lightness of Louise's spirit reminded them of the beauty of their bond; the way love intertwined their lives made everything more vibrant.

Chris moved on to the following letter, the title catching his eye. "This one is marked 'For Your Wedding Day.'"

"I can't believe she thought of everything," Leah said, a mixture of admiration and disbelief swirling in her heart. "How could she have known?"

"She just did," Chris replied softly, his eyes glinting as he opened the letter. "She always seemed to have a sixth sense for moments that mattered."

As he read through the heartfelt suggestions and playful anecdotes, Leah felt transported into a world where Kate's laughter echoed around them, her spirit infusing every word with life. There were bits about choosing flowers, deciding on a playlist filled with songs that represented their journey, and even chickening out on the idea of wearing matching outfits—remarkable details that brought tears and laughter to Leah in equal measure.

'And don't forget the dance floor," Chris read aloud, his voice filled with emotion as he continued. 'You'll need space to spin, twirl, and celebrate the love you've found. Dance like nobody's watching and remember that Auntie Kate will be right there with you, probably rolling her eyes at how long it takes Chris to choose the right song."

Leah giggled through her tears, remembering Kate's teasing way and the many times she would have gone to great lengths to ensure the fun was maximized at any gathering.

"Exactly," Chris said, his gaze holding Leah's as he finished the letter. "Let's keep that spirit alive—every moment we share, every laugh we have, is a celebration of her memory."

As they wrapped up the treasure hunt for the day, gathering letters from warm, sunlit corners, Chris and Leah returned to a steadiness that filled the air—like a melody finding its rhythm again.

CHAPTER 25

Shadows Before the Storm

T he cream-colored envelope sat unopened on Leah's kitchen counter, its law firm letterhead a stark contrast to the soft morning light filtering through Kate's old lace curtains. The corporate precision of the typing—"Wallace & Associates, Attorneys at Law"—carried none of the messiness of real relationships, none of the early-morning chaos of Louise's half-eaten breakfast or Chris's coffee-stained sheet music spread across the table.

When Leah opened it, the letter's language betrayed its author's fundamental disconnect:

Dear Ms. Miller,□

This correspondence serves as formal notice that our client, Mr. Ryan Matthews, despite his prior voluntary relinquishment of parental rights, intends to petition the court regarding minor child Louise Danielle Miller on the grounds of financial stability and the child's best interests.□

Mr. Matthews is prepared to present comprehensive evidence regarding his capacity to provide enhanced opportunities for Louise's well-being and future development.

Your counsel is directed to contact our office within 21 days to begin discussions. Failure to respond within this timeframe will result in the immediate filing of court proceedings.

Be advised that any attempts to relocate with the minor child or impede this process will be met with swift legal action.

Regards,□
James P. Wallace III, Esq.□
Senior Partner
Wallace & Associates, LLP.

The brevity of the letter belies its weight - each carefully chosen word carrying the gravity of a father's desperate reach across the chasm of his own making. The clinical language serves as armor, protecting the raw desperation beneath its polished surface. In its shortened form, the letter becomes less a legal document and more a harbinger, its crisp folds containing the first tremors of a storm that would soon break over all their lives.

The legal precision of the words made Leah's throat tighten. This was how Ryan had always approached emotional complexity, like an engineering problem that required the right sequence of commands and procedures to resolve. She remembered him using similar methodical language years ago, explained why he couldn't "compromise his career trajectory" for an unplanned pregnancy, how his "professional development timeline" precluded any deviation for family obligations.

Now, years later, here was the same calculated approach, weaponized through expensive letterhead and legal muscle. But beneath the threatening phrases and formal declarations, she heard something else—the desperate grasp of a man who'd watched his meticulously engineered life lose its perfect calibration. A man who'd seen his relationship with Jessica dissolve despite following all his careful protocols, who'd witnessed Kate's illness, defied every attempt at logical analysis and control. Someone realizing that his blueprints for success felt meaningless when there was no one to witness his achievements, no legacy beyond corporate accolades and patent applications.

Leah stared at the letter, her coffee growing cold beside her. The happiness she'd found with Chris these past months felt like a delicate bubble, and now Ryan was threatening to burst it. In two days, she would walk down the aisle to marry the man who had helped her believe in love again. Everything was perfect—too perfect, perhaps. That thought made her chest tighten.

"All good things come to an end," she whispered to herself, then immediately felt guilty for the pessimism. Chris had taught her to hope again, to believe in second chances. But this... this was different.

The sound of Chris humming in the shower upstairs made her heart ache. He'd been so excited about the rehearsal dinner tonight, wanting everything to be perfect for their families to blend. How could she tell him about this now? More importantly, should she involve him in a battle that wasn't his to fight?

"Morning, beautiful," Chris's voice startled her, and she quickly slipped the letter into her pocket. He wrapped his arms around her from behind, still warm from the shower. "Ready for tonight?"

"Yeah," she managed, though her voice sounded distant even to her own ears. "Just nervous about everything coming together."

Chris turned her to face him, concern flickering in his eyes. "Hey, what's really going on? You've been a little off."

"It's nothing," she lied, hating herself for it. "Just wedding jitters, I guess."

"Leah..." Chris started, but Louise's cheerful voice interrupted them as she bounded into the kitchen, clutching one of Kate's old letters.

Throughout the day, Leah moved through wedding preparations like a ghost, her mind constantly returning to Ryan's letter. Chris noticed, of course. He always noticed.

"Talk to me," he pleaded during a quiet moment while they arranged flowers. "Whatever it is, we can handle it together."

Leah forced a smile. "After the rehearsal dinner, okay? Let's just get through tonight."

Late afternoon sunlight streamed through the kitchen windows as Leah arranged appetizer platters. Chris leaned against the counter, watching her with concerned eyes.

"You've barely said two words all day," he said. "Something's clearly bothering you."

Leah kept her focus on the food, afraid her eyes might betray her. "I promise we'll talk about it after the rehearsal dinner."

"Why not now?" Chris moved closer, gently touching her arm. "We have time before everyone arrives."

"Chris, please," Leah's voice wavered. "Can we just focus on tonight? I promise it's nothing that can't wait a few more hours."

"You're scaring me a little here," Chris admitted, running a hand through his hair. "Is it about the wedding? About us?"

Leah immediately turned to face him, placing her hands on his chest. "No! God, no. I want to marry you more than anything. Please don't doubt that."

Some tension left Chris's shoulders, but concern still lined his face. "Then what is it?"

"After dinner," Leah repeated, though she softened it with a small smile. "I promise we'll talk about everything then. Right now, let's focus on making this evening special."

Chris studied her face for a long moment before he sighed. "I don't like it, but okay. After dinner."

Trying to lighten the mood, he wrapped his arms around her waist. "You know what I am excited about? You will finally get to meet everyone, especially Tyler."

"Your older brother, right?" Leah welcomed the change of subject. "The one in Seattle?"

"Yeah," Chris's face lit up. "He's almost ten years older than me, so he was already off to college when I was still in elementary school. We didn't get much time together growing up, but he's always been my hero, you know? The way he carved his own path, started his own business."

"You never really talk about him," Leah observed, relaxing into Chris's embrace.

"Because he's been so far away, I guess. But he's actually a lot like you – determined, independent, always putting family first. He'll love you." Chris paused, then added with a grin, "Though probably not as much as I do."

Leah stretched up to kiss him softly, pushing away thoughts of Ryan's letter. For now, she would focus on this moment, on the joy of bringing their families together. The storm could wait a few more hours.

"We should finish setting up," she said, reluctantly pulling away. "Your aunt Terry is probably already on her way, ready to critique my flower arrangements."

Chris laughed, though his eyes still held a hint of worry. "Just remember, my parents adore you. And that's what really matters."

Leah nodded, turning back to the appetizers. As Chris moved to check on Louise upstairs, she touched her pocket where the letter sat like a weight. Soon, she told herself. Soon she would tell him everything, and they would face it together. But first, they had a celebration to host.

The late afternoon sun painted golden streaks across the Johnson's backyard as the first guests began arriving for the rehearsal dinner.

Chris squeezed Leah's hand reassuringly as his grandparents' car pulled into the driveway.

"Grandma Emma and Grandpa Billy are going to love you," he whispered, his eyes bright with excitement. "They've been the heart of this family since before I was born."

Emma Henderson, still elegant in her eighties, emerged from the car with Billy's steady support. Her face lit up at the sight of her grandson. "Chris!" she called out, opening her arms wide.

Chris rushed forward to embrace them both, then turned to Leah with pride. "Grandma, Grandpa, this is Leah, and that little butterfly running through the garden is Louise."

Emma's warm hands clasped around Leah's. "My dear, we've heard such wonderful things about you both. Welcome to our family."

Billy's weathered face creased with a gentle smile. "Anyone who brings that kind of joy to our grandson's eyes is already family in our books."

Before Leah could respond, another car arrived, bringing the O'Donnell's—Terry, Randy, and their three children. Kourtney, the eldest, practically bounded out of the car, her pregnant belly not slowing her enthusiasm.

"Chris!" she squealed, rushing to hug her favorite cousin. Her husband Michael, Chris's best friend in high school, followed with an affable grin.

"Finally getting to meet the woman who tamed our Chris," Michael teased, extending his hand to Leah. Kourtney embraced Leah warmly. "I've been dying to meet you! Chris says Louise is around the same age as our Tommy - they'll have to have playdates."

The garden continued to be filling with guests as Leah spotted her parents' car pulling up. Despite her nerves, warmth spread through her chest seeing them arrive together. It had taken years, but John and Claire Miller had been in the same room without tension crackling between them.

"There's my girl," Claire called out, hurrying forward to embrace Leah. She looked elegant in a deep blue dress, her silver hair swept into a soft updo. John followed more slowly, but his smile was genuine as he hugged Leah.

"The place looks beautiful, sweetheart," he said, glancing around the garden. "Kate would have loved all these flowers."

Chris joined them, shaking John's hand warmly. "Mr. and Mrs. Miller, thank you for coming. Louise has been asking for her Grandpa John all afternoon - she wants to show you the tomatoes she's been growing."

"Well then, I better not keep my gardening partner waiting," John chuckled, heading toward where Louise played near the vegetable beds.

Her sister, Grace, arrived next with her husband David, their twin boys racing ahead to join Louise. "Sorry we're late," she called out, breathless. "Our flight got a bit delayed."

Brian and his wife Christine weren't far behind, bearing a massive arrangement of sunflowers. "From that little flower shop you love," Brian explained, kissing Leah's cheek. "Christine insisted we needed the biggest bouquet they had."

"Because nothing less would do for my favorite future sister-in-law," Christine winked. Her warm personality had been a perfect match for Brian's quiet strength since they'd met three years ago.

As everyone settled in, Leah felt a pang at how small her side of the gathering was compared to Chris's extensive family network. But watching her loved ones interact with Chris's family warmed her heart. Her father was deep in conversation with Billy Henderson about their shared love of gardening. Grace's twins had found instant friends in Terry's younger kids, their laughter echoing across the yard. Even Claire was chatting animatedly with Emma about wedding details.

Christine had quickly found common ground with Kourtney. They are both teachers. They shared stories about their elementary school classrooms. "You should see what my third graders came up with for their science fair," Christine laughed, while Kourtney nodded in understanding.

"Oh, that's nothing," Kourtney replied, resting a hand on her pregnant belly. "Try explaining Shakespeare to eighth graders while dealing with morning sickness!" Brian stood nearby, contentedly listening to their animated discussion about the joys and challenges of teaching.

Leah welcomed the lighthearted conversation, grateful for the distraction from her own troubled thoughts. She'd been on edge all evening, knowing she'd eventually have to face Chris's family. Still, nothing had prepared her for...

"Ms. Miller?" a voice called, and Leah turned to find Chris's brother Tyler approaching. His casual tone carried an edge that made her skin prickle. "Got a minute?"

"Of course," Leah replied, though her stomach clenched.

Tyler guided them to a quiet corner, his practiced smile never quite reaching his eyes. "You know, it's funny," he began, swirling his drink deliberately. "Chris has always been so open with us about everything, but with you... he's been surprisingly quiet, secretive almost."

Leah's fingers tightened around her glass. "Has he?"

"Mm-hmm." Tyler took a calculated sip of his drink. "Been hearing some interesting talk around town lately. Apparently, Ryan Matthews is moving back - leaving quite the position at Tesla, from what I understand. Setting up his own contracting business here." His eyes flickered to her face with practiced casualness. "You wouldn't happen to have heard anything about that, would you? Has he reached out at all?"

The deliberate innocence in his tone made Leah's chest tighten. She fought to keep her expression neutral.

"Little Louise just turned three, right?" Tyler continued, his eyes studying her face. "Chris mentioned you two have been dating for over a year now. Our parents are incredibly supportive, always have been. Sometimes, they can be way too supportive. You know, they just want their sons to be happy." He paused, taking another sip of his drink. "But you know how parents are - they always worry."

Leah felt the room spin. The memories she'd carefully locked away threatened to surface. "I should..." she gestured vaguely, her throat closing.

"Of course," Tyler said smoothly, stepping back. "We'll have plenty of time to get to know each other. Mom and Dad will welcome you with open arms - they're just that kind of people. But..." he let the word hang in the air.

"Excuse me," Leah managed, turning quickly. She barely made it to the empty hallway before pressing her palm against the wall, struggling to steady her breathing. The implications in Tyler's words echoed in her head: He knew something about her past with Ryan, about Louise, about everything she'd tried to leave behind.

And Ryan was coming back.

She heard footsteps approaching and quickly straightened, wiping her dampened palms on her dress just as Chris rounded the corner.

"Everything okay?" he asked, concern etched on his face.

Behind him, Tyler appeared, offering that same practiced smile. "Just getting to know my future sister-in-law," he said smoothly, but his eyes held both a warning and a promise of more conversations to come.

The catering staff began setting out appetizers as Chris clinked his glass for attention. "Before we start the official rehearsal, I want to thank everyone for being here tonight. Family means everything to us - both the ones we're born with and the ones we choose."

His eyes found Leah's across the crowd, and she felt strength in his steady gaze. Brian squeezed her hand supportively as Chris continued.

"Some of you may not know this, but it was actually Kate who orchestrated our first meeting." A soft murmur rippled through the gathering. "Kate and Leah had been best friends since grade school - practically inseparable. But I didn't meet Kate until she started volunteering at our church outreach program. And in typical Kate fashion, she immediately decided she needed to play matchmaker."

Chris's smile widened as he recalled the memory. "After working with me for a few weeks, Kate got this determined look in her eyes - the one we all knew meant she was plotting something good. She convinced me to attend the upcoming church social, while separately persuading her best friend Leah that she absolutely needed to be there too."

He glanced at Leah, his expression softening. "What Kate didn't tell me was how completely unprepared I'd be for that first moment I saw Leah. There she was, helping Louise arrange cookies on the refreshment table, and I just stood there, holding my coffee cup, completely mesmerized. Kate found me later and just said, 'I told you she was special.'"

Mary dabbed at her eyes with a napkin as Chris raised his glass. "Kate had known Leah most of her life, knew exactly the kind of person she was, and somehow knew she'd be perfect for me too. So this toast is to family - past, present, and future. To Kate, who knew our hearts before we did, and whose love continues to bless us. And to love that grows stronger through every season."

"To family," the group echoed, though Leah noticed Terry and Tyler's response was notably subdued.

As everyone moved toward the dinner tables, Claire pulled Leah aside. "You okay, honey? I noticed some whispers earlier."

"I'm fine, Mom," Leah assured her, though her voice wavered. "It's just... there's some complications with Ryan that we need to handle."

Claire's face tightened with concern, but before she could respond, Chris's voice called out: "Leah! Come help me rescue Louise - she's trying to convince Grandpa John to let her serve the appetizers!"

Grateful for the interruption, Leah squeezed her mother's hand and moved to join her daughter and future husband. The evening stretched ahead, a mix of joy and tension, love and uncertainty, all woven together like the fairy lights twinkling overhead.

Later that night, after guests departed and Louise slept soundly upstairs, Leah showed Chris the letter. Her hands trembled as she pulled the crumpled paper from her drawer, where she'd hidden it like a ticking bomb.

"We'll face this together," Chris assured her, though concern creased his brow as his eyes scanned Ryan's threats about custody arrangements and legal rights. "Ryan won't tear apart what we've built."

"Your family already thinks I'm complicated enough," Leah whispered, Tyler's earlier probing questions still burning in her mind. "This will only confirm their fears. The timing of everything... Louise's age... Ryan's return." Her voice caught. "They'll think I've been hiding things."

"Hey," Chris tilted her chin up, his touch gentle but firm. "You and Louise are my family now too. Nothing changes that. Not Ryan, not anyone's opinions." But Leah could see the shadow of worry in his eyes, the same fear she'd been carrying since Ryan's letter arrived.

They settled onto the porch swing, the night air heavy with jasmine. Above them, Louise's nightlight cast a soft glow through her bedroom window—a reminder of everything at stake. Chris pulled out one of Kate's letters—this one marked "For When You Need Courage." The envelope was worn at the edges, testament to how many times they'd sought Kate's wisdom in moments of doubt.

"Dear ones," he read softly, his voice steady despite the tension in his shoulders. "Life rarely follows our careful plans. But true love multiplies through every challenge, growing stronger in the storms..."

As Kate's words washed over them, Leah felt her resolve strengthen, even as her mind raced with all the what-ifs. What if Ryan demanded DNA tests and demanded shared custody? What if Tyler's subtle threats today were just the beginning?

The path ahead held uncertainty—Ryan's custody claims looming like storm clouds, family tensions crackling like electricity in the air, wedding preparations now shadowed by the weight of unspoken truths. Louise's future hung in the balance, and Leah couldn't shake the image of her daughter's trusting smile, unaware of the brewing battle for her life.

Yet listening to Chris read Kate's letter, feeling Louise's presence in the quiet house above them, Leah knew their love could withstand the gathering storm. She thought of how Kate had faced her own battles with grace and courage, leaving behind these paper lifelines for moments exactly like this.

"I will not let him win," Leah whispered fiercely, surprising herself with the steel in her voice. Chris's hand tightened around hers in silent support.

The days to come would bring their own trials—lawyers to consult, family to face, truths to confront. But tonight, wrapped in the peace of their garden sanctuary, surrounded by reminders of Kate's enduring wisdom, they could simply be. Two hearts finding harbor in each other, ready to protect the precious family they'd built, even as thunder rumbled on the horizon.

Leah closed her eyes, breathing in the jasmine-scented air, trying to memorize this moment of calm before the storm. Whatever Ryan had planned, whatever judgments Chris's family might make, she would fight. For Louise. For Chris. For the family they'd become, learning to love again in the wake of loss.

Kate's words echoed in her mind: "True love multiplies through every challenge." They would need that truth in the days ahead, as they faced the gathering darkness together.

"He mentioned Tesla today," Leah said, breaking the silence. "Tyler did. About Ryan's success there." She leaned back, crossing her arms around her body. "It wasn't random conversation, Chris. He was fishing, trying to gauge my reaction."

Chris shifted on the swing, the chains creaking softly. "Tyler's always been protective of our family. Maybe too protective sometimes."

"He knows something." Leah's voice quivered. "The way he brought up Louise's age, asking about Ryan... I could see it in his eyes." She stood up abruptly, pacing the length of the porch. "What if Ryan's already reached out to your family? What if—"

A soft thud from upstairs interrupted her spiral. Louise's familiar footsteps padded across the floor above them.

"Mommy?" came the sleepy call.

"I'll go," Chris said, standing. But Leah shook her head.

"No, I need to." She needed to see her daughter, a reminder of what she was fighting for.

Louise was sitting up in bed, her dark-brown curls mussed from sleep, clutching her favorite stuffed elephant. "Bad dream," she mumbled as Leah sat on the edge of her bed.

"Want to tell me about it?" Leah smoothed back Louise's hair.

"The thunder was chasing me," Louise said, burrowing into her mother's side. "But Daddy wasn't there to make the funny thunder voices."

Leah's heart clenched. Chris had started that tradition during their first summer thunderstorm together, making goofy voices for each rumble until Louise's fears turned to giggles. It was such a small thing, but it represented everything she feared losing.

"Chris is right downstairs, sweet pea. Want him to come up?"

Louise nodded, already half-asleep again. Moments later, Chris appeared in the doorway, his presence filling the room with a sense of security that made Leah's eyes burn with tears.

"Thunder monster bothering you again?" he asked, crouching beside the bed.

"Mmhmm," Louise mumbled.

"Well, we can't have that." He settled on the edge of the bed, his voice dropping to that special storytelling tone that always soothed Louise. "Remember the story about the brave little star?"

Louise nodded drowsily, snuggling deeper into her blankets as Chris began the familiar tale. "Once there was a tiny star who lived in the darkest corner of the sky. While all the other stars stayed in their bright clusters, this little star wandered alone, exploring the shadows..."

Leah watched from the doorway as he continued the story—one he'd created during their first month together, when Louise was struggling with nightmares. It was a simple tale about finding light in darkness, about being brave enough to shine alone. Now, watching her daughter's eyes grow heavy as Chris's gentle voice filled the room, Leah felt the weight of everything pressing down on her. This moment, this precious family they'd built—it was worth fighting for. But the cost... the inevitable pain and chaos that would come with Ryan's return...

Back on the porch, Chris pulled her close. "I saw your face up there," he said. "Stop thinking about what we might lose. Focus on what we have right now."

"Kate would know what to do," Leah whispered against his chest.

"Kate knew what we'd face," Chris replied, reaching for another letter from the box. This one was marked simply: "For When The Past Returns."

Leah's breath caught. "How did she—"

"Because she was Kate," Chris said simply, breaking the seal. "She saw everything, understood everything. Even the things we couldn't say."

As he unfolded the letter, a photograph slipped out—Kate holding newborn Louise in the hospital, her smile radiant. On the back, in Kate's flowing script: "Love makes a family. Everything else is just details."

Chris's voice wavered as he read:

My dearest ones,

If you're reading this, the past has come knocking, demanding answers to questions we thought were safely buried. I know the fear you're feeling—the way it sits like ice in your stomach, making you question everything you've built.

But listen carefully: The truth of a family isn't in its beginnings, but in its daily choosing. In the bandaged knees and breakfast giggles, to changing soiled diapers and weathering sickness, in the thousand small moments that weave hearts together until they can't be untangled.

Leah, my sweet friend, you've always carried more guilt than you deserve. The choices you made were born of love and protection. Hold on to that truth when doubts creep in. And Chris, your heart has always been your compass. Trust it now.□

Louise needs the love that surrounds her—all of it, in whatever form it takes. Sometimes life brings us more love than we planned for, and that's never a tragedy.

Leah wiped her eyes. "She knew. Somehow, she knew this would happen."

"There's more," Chris said, turning the page.

To the three of you: Don't let fear of what might steal the joy of what is. The path ahead may be messy and complicated, but the best families usually are. They're built on love and trust and forgiveness—not perfect circumstances.□

Remember what I told you both before I left: Love multiplies. It doesn't divide. There's room in Louise's heart for all the love that comes her way. Your job isn't to control that love, but to help her navigate it.□

Be brave, my darlings. Be honest. Be kind—especially to yourselves. And know that I'm watching over you all, probably rolling my eyes at how unnecessarily dramatic you're being about the whole thing.□

All my love,☐
Kate

P.S. Leah, check the blue box in my closet. I left something there.

The porch swing creaked as Leah shifted. "The blue box... I never opened it. Kate told me to wait."

Chris folded the letter. "Maybe it's time."

"Tomorrow," Leah said, her voice stronger now. She turned to face him, her eyes shining with renewed determination.

Chris squeezed her hand. "This time tomorrow, you'll be Mrs. Johnson. No letter, no threat, no ghost from the past can change that."

"I can't wait," Leah whispered, touching the engagement ring on her finger. "Louise is so excited to be the flower girl. She's been practicing her walk all week."

"And tomorrow night, we'll be a family in every way that matters – legally, officially." Chris pulled her closer. "Ryan's timing might be calculated, but he's too late. Nothing can stop us from becoming a family now."

"I love you," Leah said. "Thank you for choosing us, for choosing this complicated mess of a life with me and Louise."

"Every single day," Chris agreed, pressing a kiss to her temple. "And twice on Sundays. Tomorrow, in front of everyone we love, I'll make that choice official." He smiled. "Though between you and me, my heart made that choice the moment you both walked into my life."

Above them, Louise's nightlight continued its gentle vigil, a beacon in the gathering dark. Whatever storms Ryan's return might bring, they would face it together—as husband and wife, as a family bound by both law and love, just as Kate had known they would.

Tomorrow would bring its own trials. But tonight, wrapped in the peace of their garden sanctuary, surrounded by reminders of Kate's enduring wisdom, they could simply be. Two hearts finding harbor in each other, ready to protect the precious family they'd built.

CHAPTER 26

Full Circle

T he afternoon light filtered through the church's stained- glass windows, painting the bride's room in promising colors as Leah stood before the mirror. Her wedding dress - simple yet elegant - caught the light like captured joy, while Kate's blue ribbon, woven into her bouquet, provided the perfect "something blue." Outside, July pressed against the ancient stone walls, the weight of summer thick with promise and unspoken possibilities.

"Mama pretty!" Louise twirled in her flower girl dress, "Like a princess in Daddy's songs!"

Claire adjusted Leah's veil with trembling hands while Mary added the final touch - a rose from her garden, its petals echoing on the blush on the bride's cheeks.

"Kate would love this moment," Claire said, meeting Mary's eyes in the mirror. Both mothers shared a look of deep understanding that came from watching love grow through every season.

A knock at the door revealed Grace Thompson. Grace held the blue box with reverent care, its velvet surface catching the colored light like a piece of sky fallen to earth.

"Found in the church office this morning, right where she said it would be," she explained, her voice carrying that weight of fulfilling a friend's final wish.

Leah's hands trembled as she lifted the lid, revealing a delicate charm bracelet nestled in white silk—each charm carefully chosen, each a silvery testament to Kate's understanding of their shared hopes and deeper truths.

The butterfly charm caught the light first, its wings seeming to quiver with possibility, followed by the musical note and finally the heart, its intricate design speaking of love's ability to weave strength from delicate threads. Tears threatened as Leah traced each charm with gentle fingers, remembering countless conversations about dreams and futures, about the power of symbols to carry love beyond time's boundaries.

When Grace produced the envelope marked "For the moment before" in Kate's familiar script, the bracelet felt warm in Leah's palm, as if it had absorbed some essence of her friend's enduring presence. She opened the letter with care, each movement measured against the weight of what this moment meant, what Kate had wanted to share on this pivotal day.

Leah's hands shook as she opened it; she read:

My dearest Leah,☐

If you're reading this, you're about to marry the man who taught you that real love is better than perfect love. Good choice: I said, 'I told you so' from my cloud. Remember when we were kids, planning our dream weddings? You wanted everything perfect—the right flowers, the right music, the right timing. But standing here now (well, there for you, here for me), I hope you see that love isn't about perfection. It's about finding someone who makes the imperfect moments beautiful. □

Chris does that for you. How he loves Louise creates music from chaos and sees your heart - the real magic. That's the kind of love worth celebrating. And speaking of Louise, watch how the charms on her bracelet catch light as she practices her flower girl twirl. □

Each one carries its own story, its own promise. The butterfly, which she loves to trace with her small fingers when she's nervous, speaks to her wild spirit - that beautiful, untamable joy that's so much like your own. I chose it, remembering how she would flutter beneath your heart, turning rigid prenatal checkups into dance recitals. Even then, she was transforming life's strict measures into music of her own making. □

The musical note (which Chris will appreciate) marks how she's always found a rhythm in chaos. Remember those sleepless nights when only your humming would soothe her? How she turned your tears into lullabies, your fear into fierce love songs? That's pure Louise - finding melody where others see only noise. □

The heart charm carries more than just my love. Look closely at its design - see how the silver strands weave together, creating strength from delicate threads? That's your story, Leah. How you've taken life's scattered pieces and woven them into something beautiful. How you and Chris have built love from choice rather than chance. I'm with you today - in every rose that blooms, in every note of music, in every smile Louise shares. Look for me in the moments between moments, in the quiet joy of belonging, and in the love that surrounds you.□

Now, marry that wonderful man. Let Louise scatter her petals enthusiastically (we both know she's been practicing). Let your families share their joy. Let love win, as it always should.□

All my love, forever and always,□
Kate

Fresh tears threatened, but Louise was ready with the special handkerchief she'd guarded all morning.

"No crying, Mama," she instructed. "Auntie Kate says today is for happy dancing."

"Come here, sweet pea," she called to Louise, who twirled in her flower girl dress. Her dark curls caught light the same way the silver did - wild and beautiful, defying any attempt at control. "Let's put your special bracelet on."

Louise extended her wrist, watching the charms catch rainbow light from the stained glass. "Auntie Kate said they're magic," she whispered, touching each one with reverent fingers: butterfly for freedom, music note for joy, heart for love that reached beyond boundaries.

"The very best kind," Leah agreed, securing the clasp with hands that had steadied. Here was Kate's perfect balance of protection - beauty that brought joy, truth that brought strength, love that transformed delicate silver into unbreakable shields.

"Ready?" she called to Louise, who twirled in her flower girl dress, transformed by childhood magic into a fairy princess for the day.

Through the vestry window, Leah glimpsed an unfamiliar figure in an impeccable suit, speaking with Tyler before disappearing around the church's corner. The sight registered briefly, lost in the swirl of final preparations, like a shadow passing over sun-warmed stone. She turned back to the mirror, adjusting her veil, while Claire fussed with the train of her dress.

Tyler's phone buzzed once, the sound sharp against the church's ancient quiet. His eyes met Leah's in the mirror as he checked it, his usual corporate mask slipping to reveal something harder beneath. The moment hung in the dust-moted air before he tucked the phone away, his practiced smile returned as he excused himself to "check on some details."

Grace moved forward, her presence filling the space Tyler had vacated with warmth and fierce protection. Her hands were steady as she adjusted Leah's veil, positioning herself between the bride and the door through which Tyler had disappeared. The gesture spoke volumes - Grace had always understood more than she said, reading the margins of their story with careful attention.

The sanctuary filled with music like rising water, each note from Chris's students building upon the last until the composition he'd written seemed to breathe with its own life. Grace stood near the center aisle, her position offered clear sight lines to both the altar and the back of the church where the mysterious man had briefly

465

appeared. Her photographer's eye didn't miss how Tyler's attention kept sliding toward that now-empty space, like a compass finding true north.

The afternoon sun penetrated the ancient windows. It transformed ordinary air into something sacred - dust motes dancing like memories caught in amber, while Mary's roses released their perfume in tiny surrenders to the July heat. Even the atmosphere felt significant, holding its breath to witness what this day would bring.

Louise preceded them, scattering rose petals with artistic flair while humming along with the music - a perfect blend of her parents' gifts. Each petal settled on the worn wooden floors like a promise taking root, while the charm bracelet at her wrist caught the light and scattered it like stars.

John Miller squeezed his daughter's arm. "Kate would be so proud," he whispered, his voice carrying that familiar catch whenever he spoke her name. Leah leaned into his steadying presence, drawing strength from the simple truth of his words. Whatever shadows gathered at the edges of this day, this moment belonged to love - to the family she and Chris had built, to the choice they made every morning to face life together.

Through the stained glass, light fractured into prisms of ruby and sapphire, painting their path forward in colors that spoke of both passion and constancy. When she caught Tyler checking his phone, the movement brief but deliberate as a conductor's cue, Leah focused on Chris waiting at the altar - on how his eyes found hers through the kaleidoscope of colored light, holding her steady as she walked toward their future.

Perspiration beaded at his temple - whether from the summer heat or emotion, Leah couldn't tell. But she barely heard him, her eyes drawn to an unfamiliar figure slipping into the back of the church - a man in an expertly tailored suit who seemed immune to the day's warmth, his presence as sharp and cool as a shadow passing over sun-warmed stone. He exchanged a subtle nod with Tyler before taking his seat, the gesture quick but deliberate.

The wedding march continued, its notes swimming through the thick afternoon air. Leah couldn't shake the growing sense of watchfulness from the back of the church, that feeling of eyes tracking her progress like heat lightning on a summer horizon. Her steps faltered until John's steady presence guided her forward, his hand anchoring her to the present moment even as her thoughts threatened to scatter like the rose petals beneath her feet.

Chris waited at the altar, his face illuminated with pure love, and for a moment everything else faded away - the July heat, the whispered tensions, the weight of unspoken threats. But as they joined hands, his palm warm and steady against hers, Leah noticed his brother's expression behind him - Tyler's usual mask of polite interest had slipped, revealing something harder as he checked his phone once more. The gesture carried all the warning of distant thunder on a summer afternoon.

Their vows were simple but profound, spoken with voices that carried years of growing love, each word rising through the heavy air like a prayer:

"I choose you," Chris promised, his hands steady around Leah's. "Through every season, every song, every moment yet to come. I choose our family - the one we've built with love, trust, and daily choice."

"I choose you," Leah responded, tears making her voice shimmer like sunlight through rain. "Through every note, every color, every adventure ahead. I choose our love."

When Chris slipped the ring onto her finger, she caught movement at the back of the church - the mysterious latecomer was gone, leaving only an empty space and Tyler's knowing smile. His departure carried the weight of orchestrated timing - slipping away precisely as Chris and Leah joined hands, as if his absence itself was a message. The empty space he left behind pulsed with possibility, a void that seemed to grow larger with each passing moment, consuming the joy around it like a black hole drawing in light.

Later, when Louise skipped past that abandoned pew, her charm bracelet caught a glint of sunlight and for just a moment, the shadow of something - a business card perhaps, or a folded note - whispered against the aged wood before disappearing into a pocket of Tyler's pressed suit.

The rest of the ceremony passed in a blur of joy and sacred moments, but an undercurrent of unease rippled beneath the surface like a shadow passing under still water. As they turned to face their guests as husband and wife, Leah's eyes met Tyler's across the sanctuary. His expression was unreadable, but his slight nod carried the weight of unspoken challenges to come.

The final notes of the ceremony music lingered in the heavy summer air as Chris and Leah turned to face their guests. Afternoon light filtered through the stained-glass windows, casting kaleidoscope shadows across the wooden pews - beautiful, but somehow unsettling in their fractured brilliance. Like the day itself, Leah thought, everything familiar transformed into something more complex, more demanding of attention.

The recessional became a slow dance of forced smiles and careful steps. Each face they passed seemed to hold a different weight - Mary's tearful joy, Claire's fierce pride, Tyler's calculating assessment. The mysterious man's empty seat at the back of the church drew

Leah's eyes like a bruise on perfect skin, its vacancy somehow more threatening than his presence had been.

"You're trembling," Chris whispered as they paused in the church vestibule, waiting for the wedding party to assemble for photos. His thumb traced gentle circles on her palm, a gesture that usually calmed her racing thoughts.

"Just overwhelmed," Leah managed, though the word felt inadequate for the storm brewing beneath her bridal smile. Through the open church doors, she could see their reception tent gleaming white against the afternoon sky, paper lanterns swaying in the humid breeze like pendulums marking time until... until what? The question nestled in her chest like a held breath.

Louise darted between guests, her flower girl dress catching light and shadow as she moved, unaware of the undercurrents swirling around her. She paused near Tyler, who bent to whisper something in her ear that made her giggle. The sound, usually a balm to Leah's soul, now sent a chill down her spine.

"Ready for pictures?" The photographer's cheerful voice cut through Leah's mounting unease. She forced herself to focus on the familiar ritual - family groupings, wedding party poses, each flash of the camera freezing moments that should have been purely joyful. But with every shot, she scanned the backgrounds, searching for that familiar-yet-strange figure in the tailored suit, half-expecting him to materialize in the margins of their perfect day.

The July heat pressed against them as they moved through the church gardens, roses nodding heavily in the afternoon light. A perfect white butterfly danced among the blooms - the detail that would have seemed magical earlier, but now felt like a warning. Nature itself, holding its breath, waiting.

"Just a few more," the photographer called, but Leah caught Tyler checking his phone again, his expression shifting like light through leaves. Whatever message he'd received painted unfamiliar shadows across his features. He glanced up, meeting her eyes with a look that carried all the weight of approaching thunder.

The reception tent beckoned ahead, filled with music and laughter and all the trappings of celebration. But standing there in the garden, caught between ceremony and celebration, Leah felt the ground shifting beneath her feet. Everything was different now - legally, officially, irrevocably changed. She'd taken Chris's name, bound their lives together in front of witnesses. It should have felt like a shield against whatever storms had approached.

Instead, she counted the hours until the mysterious man's absence would transform into presence again, until Tyler's subtle warnings would crystalize into an explicit threat, until Ryan's legal letters would evolve into something more demanding. The weight of it all pressed against her wedding dress like humid air before rain. "Shall we?" Chris asked, offering his arm. His smile was steady, untouched by the shadows she felt gathering. She took his arm, drawing strength from his solid presence even as her mind raced ahead to unseen challenges.

They paused at the tent's entrance, that liminal space between one chapter and the next. Inside, their guests waited with raised glasses and bright expectations. Music spilled out into the garden, along with the scent of flowers and the murmur of cheerful voices. All the elements of a perfect celebration were in place.

The music - Chris's composition - began softly, building like a conversation between hearts that had learned each other's rhythms through countless shared moments. Each note carried echoes of their story: the first tentative meetings, Louise's growing trust, the way love had crept up on them both until it became as natural as breathing. As they moved together, the rest of the world seemed to blur into gentle watercolors, leaving only this: his hand steady at her waist, her fingers curled against his shoulder, their hearts finding the same rhythm.

"I love you," Chris whispered, the words carrying all the weight of choice and chance that had brought them here. "You and Louise - you're my home now."

Leah drew back to meet his eyes, finding in their depths all the certainty she'd ever needed. "I love you," she breathed, her voice trembling with the truth that transforms ordinary moments into poetry. "Sometimes I think my heart knew it before I did - like it was just waiting for you to walk into our lives." Her fingers tightened on his shoulder, anchoring them both in this perfect moment. "You're our miracle, Chris. The answer to prayers I didn't even know I was making."

He pulled her closer. His touch was gentle but sure, as if even their shadows couldn't be allowed space between them. Their gathered loved ones around them faded into soft focus - Mary dabbing at her eyes while Tom held her close, Claire and John sharing a look of profound understanding, Grace watching Louise with fierce protectiveness.

The fairy lights overhead scattered stars across Chris's face as he leaned down to press his forehead to hers. "I choose you," he murmured, echoing their vows with quiet fervor. "Every day, every moment, I choose this family we've built."

Even Tyler's presence at the edge of the dance floor, his phone appearing briefly like a conductor's baton, couldn't diminish the pure joy radiating between them. Whatever tomorrow might bring, tonight they were wrapped in the certainty of their choice - knowing that love, real and imperfect and chosen daily, was stronger than any force that might try to shake it.

"I love you," Chris said, his voice carrying all the weight of choice and chance that had brought them here. "Whatever comes next, we face it together."

Leah leaned into him, drawing strength from his steadiness even as her mind raced ahead to unseen challenges. The garden lights painted their shadows long across the grass - two figures merged into one, while somewhere in the darkness beyond, other shadows gathered, waiting to test the bonds they'd forged this day.

The reception flowed like a river finding its course through ancient stones, each moment carrying its own current of joy and complexity. Mary had transformed the garden tent into a bower of soft lights and sweeping fabrics, while Tom's well-curated playlist wove through conversations like golden thread through tapestry.

Grace moved through the celebration with practiced ease, her teacher's instinct for observation serving a deeper purpose now. She'd positioned herself near the cake table, offering the perfect vantage point to watch Tyler's careful movements through the crowd while keeping Louise's joyful dancing in clear view.

When Tyler's phone appeared again, Grace smoothly intercepted his path toward Louise, her casual redirection appearing effortless - a question about family traditions, a reminder about upcoming toasts. Her positioning was deliberate but natural, maintaining the celebration's delicate balance while allowing joy its full measure.

Louise darted between family groups, her charm bracelet singing with each movement - a tiny orchestra marking her path through love's geography. She paused longest with John, her grandfather's steady presence drawing her like a compass finding the true north. His weathered hands, so sure in their garden work, now cradled her stories of fairy wings and butterfly dreams with equal reverence.

"She has your imagination," Claire murmured to Leah, mother's pride warming her voice. "But there's something else there too - the way she sees patterns in everything, builds little worlds from scattered pieces."

The observation shimmered with unspoken awareness. Across the tent, Tyler stood in conversation with his wife, his corporate posture softened by wedding champagne, but his eyes still tracking Louise's movement with calculated interest. Each charm on her bracelet caught the light differently as she moved: butterfly taking flight, musical note holding melody.

Chris appeared at Leah's side, his hand finding the small of her back with practiced certainty. The touch carried all the weight of choice - of love that grew through daily tending rather than strategic planning. "Mom's about to start the toasts," he said. "Ready to face Terry's novel-length speech about family tradition?"

His gentle humor diffused the moment's growing tension, transforming a corporate observation into family celebration. Louise spun back toward them, her flower girl dress transformed by motion into wings of joy. The charm bracelet chimed - nature's wind bells marking time's passage.

"Daddy!" she called, all childhood's trust wrapped in one word. "Tell the thunder story again!"

Chris swept her up, his laugh carrying none of the weight that had shadowed Tyler's earlier questions about parentage and process. This was love's simplest mathematics: a child's need plus a heart's answer equaling family.

The afternoon light began its slow surrender to evening, painting the reception tent's white fabric in watercolor washes of amber and rose. The band transitioned to slower songs as shadows lengthened across the garden. Grace exchanged a knowing look with Claire before moving to intercept Tyler, who had been working his way toward Louise with that same corporate precision that had marked his earlier interactions. Her casual redirection appeared effortless - a question about the music, a reminder about family traditions - but her positioning was deliberate, a quiet guardian maintaining the celebration's delicate balance.

Through the tent's gauzy walls, the garden beckoned with deepening gold light and the promise of quiet moments between the day's orchestrated joy. Chris caught Leah's eye across the crowd, and something in his gaze drew her toward the rose-lined paths where their story had first bloomed.

In a quiet corner of the garden, just beyond the reception tent's glow, Leah found Chris watching Louise dance with John. Each movement of Louise's charm bracelet scattered light like captured wishes, while the roses Kate had planted years ago held their secrets in velvet folds.

"She's been practicing that twirl all week," Leah said, threading her fingers through Chris's. The simple contact grounded her, even as her mind circled back to Tyler's earlier words about family assets and managed expectations. How could anyone try to quantify this? The way Louise's laugh transformed the garden air into something sacred, how her dark curls caught light with that familiar wave that both claimed and released her.

Chris turned to her, and the love in his eyes made her breath catch - not just for its intensity, but for its complete lack of calculation. Here was the difference that Tyler couldn't grasp, that Ryan had never understood: love that grew wild and true, defying spreadsheets and strategy meetings. "Perfect is right here," Chris said, drawing her closer. "You, me, Louise - this family we've built. Sometimes I wonder if Kate knew, even then, exactly what my heart was missing."

Leah reached up to trace the line of his jaw, marveled at how this man had transformed her understanding of love. Not just romantic love, but the kind that built families from choice rather than chance, which saw beauty in imperfect moments and strength in vulnerability. "She knew," she whispered, rising on her toes to brush her lips against his. "She always saw the truth of hearts." Her fingers found the place where his pulse beat steady and strong, its rhythm a counterpoint to the distant music. "I love you, Chris Johnson. Not just for loving me, but for loving her so completely. For making room in your heart for all our complicated pieces."

His kiss was gentle but fierce with promise, speaking of choices made and battles yet to face. When they parted, Leah rested her head against his chest, listening to the heart that had chosen them both. Above them, evening gathered like a mother drawing blankets over tired children, while closer to earth, Louise's laughter carried across the garden like wind chimes in summer air - delicate music that somehow held more power than any corporate strategy or legal document ever could.

The night settled around them like a benediction, fairy lights overhead blooming like stars being born. Louise had long since drifted to sleep in Chris's arms. Her small body curved against his chest with that instinctive trust that no document could codify, no strategy could manufacture. Her charm bracelet caught the fading light in fragments - each silver charm marking a chapter in their family's story: the heart from Kate carrying whispered promises, the musical note commemorating her first piano lesson with Chris, the butterfly transforming engineering precision into childhood magic.

Leah watched them together, her heart so full it ached. This was what Ryan had missed in his pursuit of measurable outcomes and efficiency metrics - the countless small moments that transformed strangers into family. The quiet miracle of earned embraces and thunder-scared tears, of skinned knees and sunrise laughter. How could anyone quantify the way Louise's fingers curled around Chris's collar in sleep, or how his hummed lullabies had become her shield against darkness?

Chris's free hand found hers in the gathering shadows, their fingers intertwining with practiced ease. Above them, stars emerged like distant windows through which Kate might be watching. While closer to earth, the garden held summer's warmth in its roses - each bloom a testament to patient tending, to love that grew stronger through every season.

Through the vestry window earlier, Leah had glimpsed an unfamiliar figure in an impeccable suit, his presence sharp as a paper cut against the day's soft joy. Now, in this quiet moment between what was and what would be, she felt the weight of approaching storms. Tyler's corporate calculations, Ryan's engineered precision, all circling their garden sanctuary like wolves testing fences.

The night air carried the scent of Kate's roses and the weight of approaching change. Tomorrow would bring what it would:

honeymoon joy tinged knowing that forces had been set in motion, this day - forces that would test every bond, every choice, every truth they thought they knew. Tyler's casual words about family assets and managed relationships hung in the air like storm clouds gathering strength.

But for now, wrapped in the peace of their garden sanctuary, surrounded by reminders of Kate's enduring wisdom, they could simply be. Two hearts finding harbor in each other, their love a force as wild and unstoppable as nature itself. The butterfly charm caught one last glint of starlight - its silver wings holding both beauty and warning, like the precious, precarious future stretching before them.

The thunder, when it came, would find them ready. Ready to protect what they'd built, ready to fight for this family forged in choice rather than chance. Ready to prove that love, real and imperfect and chosen daily, was stronger than any force that sought to contain or control it.

Grace's earlier words echoed against the stone walls of their sanctuary: "Some gardens grow stronger for the storms they weather." Looking at Chris and Louise, at this precious family they'd built, Leah knew the truth of it. Whatever approached on tomorrow's horizon would find them rooted deep in love's wild soil, hearts entwined like vines that grew stronger through every season.

END OF BOOK ONE

www.ingramcontent.com/pod-product-compliance
Lightning Source LLC
Chambersburg PA
CBHW020001120726
47903CB00004B/1091